'TIS THE SEASON,
and Silhouette Books is proud to present
two unforgettable stories in one volume
from two extraordinary authors,
where deeply held wishes come true
at Christmastime for two special women....

*Every woman wishes for that first, perfect kiss
from the man she's destined to marry.*

Read about the kiss that changed everything in
CHRISTMAS MASQUERADE
by Debbie Macomber

*"...Macomber has a gift for evoking the emotions
that are at the heart of the
genre's popularity."*
—*Publishers Weekly*

*Every woman wishes, just once,
to know the protection and devotion of a
dashing bodyguard.*

Read about the man who would go to any lengths
to keep his woman safe in
SNOWBOUND
by Lisa Jackson

*"Lisa Jackson is a real treat. She writes the kind of
books I like to read."*
—*National bestselling author Kat Martin*

DEBBIE MACOMBER

always enjoyed telling stories—first to her baby-sitting clients and then to her own four children. As a full-time wife and mother and an avid romance reader, she dreamed of one day sharing her stories with a wider audience. In the autumn of 1982 she sold her first book, and that was only the beginning. Debbie has been making regular appearances on the *USA Today* bestseller list—not surprising, considering that there are over forty million copies of her books in print worldwide!

LISA JACKSON

is a national bestselling author who has been writing romances for over fifteen years. With over forty Silhouette novels to her credit, she divides her time between writing on the computer, researching her next novel, keeping in touch with her college-age sons and playing tennis. Many of the fictitious small towns in her books resemble Molalla, Oregon, a small logging community where she and her sister, Silhouette author Natalie Bishop, grew up.

DEBBIE MACOMBER

LISA JACKSON

'TIS THE
Season

Silhouette Books

Published by Silhouette Books
America's Publisher of Contemporary Romance

SILHOUETTE BOOKS

ISBN 0-373-48395-3

by Request

'TIS THE SEASON

Copyright © 1999 by Harlequin Books S.A.

The publisher acknowledges the copyright holders
of the individual works as follows:

CHRISTMAS MASQUERADE
Copyright © 1985 by Debbie Macomber

SNOWBOUND
Copyright © 1987 by Lisa Jackson

Visit us at www.romance.net

Printed in U.S.A.

CONTENTS

Dearest Reader,

Merry Christmas! Anyone who's followed my writing career knows how much I love Christmas. What I enjoy most is having my family all together. This last year my parents arrived on Christmas Eve just as the snow started to fall. My sons, who are both in their twenties, hurried outside to build snow forts and snowmen. Soon the girls and the grandkids were involved. While Mom and I baked pies and reviewed the Christmas Eve menu, my dad napped and my husband assembled toys for the grandkids. I think it was a perfect Christmas Eve as everyone bundled up and headed for church, singing carols along the way.

I've written a number of books that involve the holidays, but *Christmas Masquerade* was one of the first. The tender, magical story of Jo Marie and Andrew holds a special place in my heart, and my wish as you pick up this book is that you, too, will experience the love, joy and peace of the holiday season. And may it snow on Christmas Eve at your house, too!

Warmest wishes for the holiday season,

Debbie Macomber

CHRISTMAS MASQUERADE
by Debbie Macomber

For Tara
A woman of grace, charm and sensitivity
Thank you

Prologue

The blast of a jazz saxophone that pierced the night was immediately followed by the jubilant sounds of a dixieland band. A shrieking whistle reverberated through the confusion. Singing, dancing, hooting and laughter surrounded Jo Marie Early as she painstakingly made her way down Tulane Avenue. Attracted by the parade, she'd arrived just in time to watch the flambeaux carriers light a golden arc of bouncing flames from one side of the street to the other. Now she was trapped in the milling mass of humanity when she had every intention of going in the opposite direction. The heavy Mardi Gras crowds hampered her progress to a slow crawl. The observation of the "Fat Tuesday" had commenced two weeks earlier with a series of parades and festive balls. Tonight the celebrating culminated in a frenzy of singing, lively dancing and masqueraders who roamed the brilliant streets.

New Orleans went crazy at this time of year, throwing a city-wide party that attracted a million guests. After twenty-three years, Jo Marie thought she would be accustomed to the maniacal behavior in the city she loved. But how could she criticize when she was a participant herself? Tonight, if she ever made it out of this crowd, she was attending a private party dressed as Florence Nightingale. Not her most original costume idea, but the best she could do on such short notice. Just this morning she'd been in a snowstorm in Minnesota and had arrived back this afternoon to hear the news that her roommate, Kelly Beaumont, was in the hospital for a tonsillectomy. Concerned, Joe Marie had quickly donned one of Kelly's nurse's uniforms so she could go directly to the party after visiting Kelly in the hospital.

With a sigh of abject frustration, Jo Marie realized she was being pushed in the direction opposite the hospital.

"Please, let me through," she called, struggling against the swift current of the merrymaking crowd.

"Which way?" a gravelly, male voice asked in her ear. "Do you want to go this way?" He pointed away from the crowd.

"Yes...please."

The voice turned out to be one of three young men who cleared a path for Jo Marie and helped her onto a side street.

Laughing, she turned to find all three were dressed as cavaliers of old. They bowed in gentlemanly fashion, tucking their arms at their waists and sweeping their plumed hats before them.

"The Three Musketeers at your disposal, fair lady."

"Your rescue is most welcome, kind sirs," Jo Marie shouted to be heard above the sound of the boisterous celebration.

"Your destination?"

Rather than try to be heard, Jo Marie pointed toward the hospital.

"Then allow us to escort you," the second offered gallantly.

Jo Marie wasn't sure she should trust three young men wearing red tights. But after all, it was Mardi Gras and the tale was sure to cause Kelly to smile. And that was something her roommate hadn't been doing much of lately.

The three young men formed a protective circle around Jo Marie and led the way down a less crowded side street, weaving in and out of the throng when necessary.

Glancing above to the cast iron balcony railing that marked the outer limits of the French Quarter, Jo Marie realized her heroes were heading for the heart of the partying, apparently more interested in capturing her for themselves than in delivering her to the hospital. "We're headed the wrong way," she shouted.

"This is a short cut," the tallest of the trio explained humorously. "We know of several people this way in need of nursing."

Unwilling to be trapped in their game, Jo Marie broke away from her gallant cavaliers and walked as quickly as her starched white uniform would allow. Dark tendrils of her hair escaped the carefully coiled chignon and framed her small face. Her fingers pushed them aside, uncaring for the moment.

Heavy footsteps behind her assured Jo Marie that the Three Musketeers weren't giving up on her so easily. Increasing her pace, she ran across the street and was within a half block of the hospital parking lot when she collided full speed into a solid object.

Stunned, it took Jo Marie a minute to recover and recognize that whatever she'd hit was warm and lean. Jo Marie raised startled brown eyes to meet the intense gray eyes of the most striking man she had ever seen. His hands reached for her shoulder to steady her.

"Are you hurt?" he asked in a deep voice that was low and resonant, oddly sensuous.

Jo Marie shook her head. "Are you?" There was some quality so mesmerizing about this man that she couldn't move her eyes. Although she was self-consciously staring, Jo Marie was powerless to break eye contact. He wasn't tall—under six feet so that she had only to tip her head back slightly to meet his look. Nor dark. His hair was brown, but a shade no deeper than her own soft chestnut curls. And he wasn't handsome. Not in the urbane sense. Although his look and his clothes spoke of wealth and breeding, Jo Marie knew intuitively that this man worked, played and loved hard. His brow was creased in what looked like a permanent frown and his mouth was a fraction too full.

Not tall, not dark, not handsome, but the embodiment of every fantasy Jo Marie had ever dreamed.

Neither of them moved for a long, drawn-out moment. Jo Marie felt as if she'd turned to stone. All those silly, schoolgirl dreams she'd shelved in the back of her mind as products of a whimsical imagination stood before her. He was the swashbuckling pirate to her captured maiden, Rhett Butler to her Scarlett O'Hara, Heathcliff to her Catherine....

"Are you hurt?" He broke into her thoughts. Eyes as gray as a winter sea narrowed with concern.

"No." She assured him with a shake of her head and forced her attention over her shoulder. Her three gallant heroes had discovered another female attraction and had directed their attention elsewhere, no longer interested in following her.

His hands continued to hold her shoulder. "You're a nurse?" he asked softly.

"Florence Nightingale," she corrected with a soft smile.

His finger was under her chin. Lifting her eyes, she saw his softly quizzical gaze. "Have we met?"

"No." It was on the tip of her tongue to tell him that yes they had met once, a long time ago in her romantic daydreams. But he'd probably laugh. Who wouldn't? Jo Marie wasn't a star-struck teenager, but a woman who had long since abandoned the practice of reading fairy tales.

His eyes were intent as they roamed her face, memorizing every detail, seeking something he couldn't define. He seemed as caught up in this moment as she.

"You remind me of a painting I once saw," he said, then blinked, apparently surprised that he'd spoken out loud.

"No one's ever done my portrait," Jo Marie murmured, frozen into immobility by the breathless bewilderment that lingered between them.

His eyes skidded past her briefly to rest on the fun-seeking Musketeers. "You were running from them?"

The spellbinding moment continued.

"Yes."

"Then I rescued you."

Jo Marie confirmed his statement as a large group of merrymakers crossed the street toward them. But she barely noticed. What captured her attention was the way in which this dream man was studying her.

"Every hero deserves a reward," he said.

Jo Marie watched him with uncertainty. "What do you mean?"

"This." The bright light of the streetlamp dimmed as he lowered his head, blocking out the golden rays. His warm mouth settled over hers, holding her prisoner, kissing her with a hunger as deep as the sea.

In the dark recesses of her mind, Jo Marie realized she should pull away. A man she didn't know was kissing her deeply, passionately. And the sensations he aroused were far beyond anything she'd ever felt. A dream that had become reality.

Singing voices surrounded her and before she could recognize the source the kiss was abruptly broken.

The Three Musketeers and a long line of others were doing a gay rendition of the rumba. Before she could protest, before she was even aware of what was happening, Jo Marie was grabbed from behind by the waist and forced to join in the rambunctious song and dance.

Her dark eyes sought the dream man only to discover that he was frantically searching the crowd for her, pushing people aside. Desperately, Jo Marie fought to break free, but couldn't. She called out, but to no avail, her voice drowned out by the song of the others. The long line of singing pranksters turned the corner, forcing Jo Marie to go with them. Her last sight of the dream man was of him pushing his way through the crowd to find her, but by then it was too late. She, too, had lost him.

Chapter One

"**Y**ou've got that look in your eye again," pixie-faced Kelly Beaumont complained. "I swear every time you pick me up at the hospital something strange comes over you."

Jo Marie forced a smile, but her soft mouth trembled with the effort. "You're imagining things."

Kelly's narrowed look denied that, but she said nothing.

If Jo Marie had felt like being honest, she would have recognized the truth of what her friend was saying. Every visit to the hospital produced a deluge of memories. In the months that had passed, she was certain that the meeting with the dream man had blossomed and grown out of proportion in her memory. Every word, every action had been relived a thousand times until her mind had memorized the smallest detail, down to the musky, spicy scent of him. Jo Marie had never told anyone about that night of the Mardi

Gras. A couple of times she'd wanted to confide in Kelly, but the words wouldn't come. Late in the evenings after she'd prepared for bed, it was the dream man's face that drifted into her consciousness as she fell asleep. Jo Marie couldn't understand why this man who had invaded her life so briefly would have such an overwhelming effect. And yet those few minutes had lingered all these months. Maybe in every woman's life there was a man who was meant to fulfill her dreams. And, in that brief five-minute interlude during Mardi Gras, Jo Marie had found hers.

"...Thanksgiving's tomorrow and Christmas is just around the corner." Kelly interrupted Jo Marie's thoughts. The blaring horn of an irritated motorist caused them both to grimace. Whenever possible, they preferred taking the bus, but both wanted an early start on the holiday weekend.

"Where has the year gone?" Jo Marie commented absently. She was paying close attention to the heavy traffic as she merged with the late evening flow that led Interstate 10 through the downtown district. The freeway would deliver them to the two-bedroom apartment they shared.

"I saw Mark today," Kelly said casually.

Something about the way Kelly spoke caused Jo Marie to turn her head. "Oh." It wasn't unnatural that her brother, a resident doctor at Tulane, would run into Kelly. After all, they both worked in the same hospital. "Did World War Three break out?" Jo Marie had never known any two people who could find more things to argue about. After three years, she'd given up trying to figure out why Mark and Kelly couldn't get along. Saying that they rubbed each other the wrong way seemed too trite an explanation. Antagonistic behavior wasn't characteristic of either of them. Kelly was a dedicated nurse and Mark a struggling resident doctor. But when the two were together, the lightning arced between them like a turbulent electrical storm. At one time Jo Marie had thought Kelly and Mark might be interested in each other. But after months of constant bickering she was forced to believe that the only thing between them was her overactive imagination.

"What did Mark have to say?"

Pointedly, Kelly turned her head away and stared out the window. "Oh, the usual."

The low, forced cheerfulness in her roommate's voice didn't fool Jo Marie. Where Kelly was concerned, Mark was merciless. He didn't mean to be cruel or insulting, but he loved to tease Kelly about her family's wealth. Not that money or position was that important to Kelly. "You mean he was kidding you about playing at being a nurse again." That was Mark's favorite crack.

One delicate shoulder jerked in response. "Sometimes I think he must hate me," she whispered, pretending a keen interest in the view outside the car window.

The soft catch in Kelly's voice brought Jo Marie's attention from the freeway to her friend. "Don't mind Mark. He doesn't mean anything by it. He loves to tease. You should hear some of the things he says about my job—you'd think a travel agent did nothing but hand out brochures for the tropics."

Kelly's abrupt nod was unconvincing.

Mentally, Jo Marie decided to have a talk with her

big brother. He shouldn't tease Kelly as if she were his sister. Kelly didn't know how to react to it. As the youngest daughter of a large southern candy manufacturer, Kelly had been sheltered and pampered most of her life. Her only brother was years older and apparently the age difference didn't allow for many sibling conflicts. With four brothers, Jo Marie was no stranger to family squabbles and could stand her own against any one of them.

The apartment was a welcome sight after the twenty-minute freeway drive. Jo Marie and Kelly thought of it as their port in the storm. The two-floor apartment buidling resembled the historic mansion from *Gone With the Wind*. It maintained the flavor of the Old South without the problem of constant repairs typical of many older buildings.

The minute they were in the door, Kelly headed for her room. "If you don't mind I think I'll pack."

"Sure. Go ahead." Carelessly, Jo Marie kicked off her low-heeled shoes. Slouching on the love seat, she leaned her head back and closed her eyes. The strain of the hectic rush hour traffic and the tension of a busy day ebbed away with every relaxing breath.

The sound of running bathwater didn't surprise Jo Marie. Kelly wanted to get an early start. Her family lived in an ultramodern home along Lakeshore Drive. The house bordered Lake Pontchartrain. Jo Marie had been inside the Beaumont home only once. That had been enough for her to realize just how good the candy business was.

Jo Marie was sure that Charles Beaumont may have disapproved of his only daughter moving into an apartment with a "nobody" like her, but once he'd learned that she was the great-great granddaughter of Jubal Anderson Early, a Confederate Army colonel, he'd sanctioned the move. Sometime during the Civil War, Colonel Early had been instrumental in saving the life of a young Beaumont. Hence, a-hundred-and-some-odd years later, Early was a name to respect.

Humming Christmas music softly to herself, Jo Marie wandered into the kitchen and pulled the orange juice from the refrigerator shelf.

"Want a glass?" She held up the pitcher to Kelly who stepped from the bathroom, dressed in a short terry-cloth robe, with a thick towel securing her bouncy blond curls. One look at her friend and Jo Marie set the ceramic container on the kitchen counter.

"You've been crying." They'd lived together for three years, and apart from one sad, sentimental movie, Jo Marie had never seen Kelly cry.

"No, something's in my eye," she said and sniffled.

"Then why's your nose so red?"

"Maybe I'm catching a cold." She offered the weak explanation and turned sharply toward her room.

Jo Marie's smooth brow narrowed. This was Mark's doing. She was convinced he was the cause of Kelly's uncharacteristic display of emotion.

Something rang untrue about the whole situation between Kelly and Mark. Kelly wasn't a soft, southern belle who fainted at the least provocation. That was another teasing comment Mark enjoyed hurling at her. Kelly was a lady, but no shrinking violet. Jo Marie had witnessed Kelly in action, fighting for her patients and several political causes. The girl didn't back down often. After Thanksgiving, Jo Marie would help Kelly fine-tune a few witty comebacks. As Mark's sister, Jo Marie was well acquainted with her brother's weak spots. The only way to fight fire was with fire she mused humorously. Together, Jo Marie and Kelly would teach Mark a lesson.

"You want me to fix something to eat before you head for your parents?" Jo Marie shouted from the kitchen. She was standing in front of the cupboard, scanning its meager contents. "How does soup and a sandwich sound?"

"Boring," Kelly returned. "I'm not really hungry."

"Eight hours of back-breaking work on the surgical ward and you're not interested in food? Are you having problems with your tonsils again?"

"I had them out, remember?"

Slowly, Jo Marie straightened. Yes, she remembered. All too well. It had been outside the hospital that she'd literally run into the dream man. Unbidden thoughts of him crowded her mind and forcefully she shook her head to free herself of his image.

Jo Marie had fixed herself dinner and was sitting in front of the television watching the evening news by the time Kelly reappeared.

"I'm leaving now."

"Okay." Jo Marie didn't take her eyes off the television. "Have a happy Thanksgiving; don't eat too much turkey and trimmings."

"Don't throw any wild parties while I'm away." That was a small joke between them. Jo Marie rarely dated these days. Not since—Mardi Gras. Kelly couldn't understand this change in her friend and affectionately teased Jo Marie about her sudden lack of an interesting social life.

"Oh, Kelly, before I forget—" Jo Marie gave her a wicked smile "—bring back some pralines, would you? After all, it's the holidays, so we can splurge."

At any other time Kelly would rant that she'd grown up with candy all her life and detested the sugary sweet concoction. Pralines were Jo Marie's weakness, but the candy would rot before Kelly would eat any of it.

"Sure, I'll be happy to," she agreed lifelessly and was gone before Jo Marie realized her friend had slipped away. Returning her attention to the news, Jo Marie was more determined than ever to have a talk with her brother.

The doorbell chimed at seven. Jo Marie was spreading a bright red polish on her toenails. She grumbled under her breath and screwed on the top of the bottle. But before she could answer the door, her brother strolled into the apartment and flopped down on the sofa that sat at right angles to the matching love seat.

"Come in and make yourself at home," Jo Marie commented dryly.

"I don't suppose you've got anything to eat around here." Dark brown eyes glanced expectantly into the kitchen. All five of the Early children shared the same dusty, dark eyes.

"This isn't a restaurant, you know."

"I know. By the way, where's money bags?"

"Who?" Confused, Jo Marie glanced up from her toes.

"Kelly."

Jo Marie didn't like the reference to Kelly's family wealth, but decided now wasn't the time to comment. Her brother worked long hours and had been out of sorts lately. "She's left for her parents' home already."

A soft snicker followed Jo Marie's announcement.

"Damn it, Mark, I wish you'd lay off Kelly. She's not used to being teased. It really bothers her."

"I'm only joking," Mark defended himself. "Kell knows that."

"I don't think she does. She was crying tonight and I'm sure it's your fault."

"Kelly crying?" He straightened and leaned forward, linking his hands. "But I was only kidding."

"That's the problem. You can't seem to let up on her. You're always putting her down one way or another."

Mark reached for a magazine, but not before Jo Marie saw that his mouth was pinched and hard. "She asks for it."

Rolling her eyes, Jo Marie continued adding the fire-engine-red color to her toes. It wouldn't do any good for her to argue with Mark. Kelly and Mark had to come to an agreement on their own. But that didn't mean Jo Marie couldn't hand Kelly ammunition now and again. Her brother had his vulnerable points, and Jo Marie would just make certain Kelly was aware of them. Then she could sit back and watch the sparks fly.

Busy with her polish, Jo Marie didn't notice for several minutes how quiet her brother had become. When she lifted her gaze to him, she saw that he had a pained, troubled look. His brow was furrowed in thought.

"I lost a child today," he announced tightly. "I couldn't understand it either. Not medically, I don't mean that. Anything can happen. She'd been brought in last week with a ruptured appendix. We knew from the beginning it was going to be touch and go." He paused and breathed in sharply. "But you know, deep down inside I believed she'd make it. She was their only daughter. The apple of her parents' eye. If all the love in that mother's heart couldn't hold back death's hand, then what good is medical science? What good am I?"

Mark had raised these questions before and Jo Marie had no answers. "I don't know," she admitted solemnly and reached out to touch his hand in reassurance. Mark didn't want to hear the pat answers. He couldn't see that now. Not when he felt like he'd failed this little girl and her parents in some obscure way. At times like these, she'd look at her brother who was a strong, committed doctor and see the doubt in his eyes. She had no answers. Sometimes she wasn't even sure she completely understood his questions.

After wiping his hand across his tired face, Mark stood. "I'm on duty tomorrow morning so I probably won't be at the folks' place until late afternoon. Tell Mom I'll try to make it on time. If I can't, the least you can do is to be sure and save a plate for me."

Knowing Mark, he was likely to go without eating until tomorrow if left to his own devices. "Let me fix you something now," Jo Marie offered. From his unnatural pallor, Jo Marie surmised that Mark couldn't even remember when he'd eaten his last decent meal, coffee and a doughnut on the run excluded.

He glanced at his watch. "I haven't got time. Thanks anyway." Before she could object, he was at the door.

Why had he come? Jo Marie wondered absently. He'd done a lot of that lately—stopping in for a few minutes without notice. And it wasn't as if her apartment were close to the hospital. Mark had to go out of his way to visit her. With a bemused shrug, she followed him to the front door and watched as he sped away in that run-down old car he was so fond of driving. As he left, Jo Marie mentally questioned if her instincts had been on target all along and Kelly and Mark did hold some deep affection for each other. Mark hadn't come tonight for any specific reason. His first question had been about Kelly. Only later had he mentioned losing the child.

"Jo Marie," her mother called from the kitchen. "Would you mind mashing the potatoes?"

The large family kitchen was bustling with activity. The long white counter top was filled with serving bowls ready to be placed on the linen-covered dining room table. Sweet potato and pecan pies were cooling on the smaller kitchen table and the aroma of spice and turkey filled the house.

"Smells mighty good in here," Franklin Early proclaimed, sniffing appreciatively as he strolled into the kitchen and placed a loving arm around his wife's waist.

"Scat," Jo Marie's mother cried with a dismissive wave of her hand. "I won't have you in here sticking your fingers in the pies and blaming it on the boys. Dinner will be ready in ten minutes.''

Mark arrived, red faced and slightly breathless. He kissed his mother on the cheek and when she wasn't looking, popped a sweet pickle into his mouth. ''I hope I'm not too late.''

''I'd say you had perfect timing,'' Jo Marie teased and handed him the electric mixer. ''Here, mash these potatoes while I finish setting the table.''

''No way, little sister.'' His mouth was twisted mockingly as he gave her back the appliance. ''I'll set the table. No one wants lumpy potatoes.''

The three younger boys, all in their teens, sat in front of the television watching a football game. The Early family enjoyed sports, especially football. Jo Marie's mother had despaired long ago that her only daughter would ever grow up properly. Instead of playing with dolls, her toys had been cowboy boots and little green army men. Touch football was as much a part of her life as ballet was for some girls.

With Mark out of the kitchen, Jo Marie's mother turned to her. ''Have you been feeling all right lately?''

''Me?'' The question caught her off guard. ''I'm feeling fine. Why shouldn't I be?''

Ruth Early lifted one shoulder in a delicate shrug. ''You've had a look in your eye lately.'' She turned and leaned her hip against the counter, her head tilted at a thoughtful angle. ''The last time I saw that look was in your Aunt Bessie's eye before she was married. Tell me, Jo Marie, are you in love?''

Jo Marie hesitated, not knowing how to explain her feelings for a man she had met so briefly. He was more illusion than reality. Her own private fantasy. Those few moments with the dream man were beyond explaining, even to her own mother.

"No," she answered finally, making busy work by placing the serving spoons in the bowls.

"Is he married? Is that it? Save yourself a lot of grief, Jo Marie, and stay away from him if he is. You understand?"

"Yes," she murmured, her eyes avoiding her mother's. For all she knew he could well be married.

Not until late that night did Jo Marie let herself into her apartment. The day had been full. After the huge family dinner, they'd played cards until Mark trapped Jo Marie into playing a game of touch football for old times' sake. Jo Marie agreed and proved that she hadn't lost her "touch."

The apartment looked large and empty. Kelly stayed with her parents over any major holidays. Kelly's family seemed to feel that Kelly still belonged at home and always would, no matter what her age. Although Kelly was twenty-four, the apartment she shared with Jo Marie was more for convenience sake than any need to separate herself from her family.

With her mother's words echoing in her ear, Jo Marie sauntered into her bedroom and dressed for bed. Friday was a work day for her as it was for both Mark and Kelly. The downtown area of New Orleans would be hectic with Christmas shoppers hoping to pick up their gifts from the multitude of sales.

As a travel agent, Jo Marie didn't have many walk-in customers to deal with, but her phone rang continuously. Several people wanted to book holiday vacations, but there was little available that she could offer. The most popular vacation spots had been booked months in advance. Several times her information was accepted with an irritated grumble as if she were to blame. By the time she stepped off the bus outside her apartment, Jo Marie wasn't in any mood for company.

No sooner had the thought formed than she caught sight of her brother. He was parked in the lot outside the apartment building. Hungry and probably looking for a hot meal, she guessed. He knew that their mother had sent a good portion of the turkey and stuffing home with Jo Marie so Mark's appearance wasn't any real surprise.

"Hi," she said and knocked on his car window. The faraway look in his eyes convinced her that after all these years Mark had finally learned to sleep with his eyes open. He was so engrossed in his thoughts that Jo Marie was forced to tap on his window a second time.

"Paging Dr. Early," she mimicked in a high-pitched hospital voice. "Paging Dr. Mark Early."

Mark turned and stared at her blankly. "Oh, hi." He sat up and climbed out of the car.

"I suppose you want something to eat." Her greeting wasn't the least bit cordial, but she was tired and irritable.

The edge of Mark's mouth curled into a sheepish grin. "If it isn't too much trouble."

"No," she offered him an apologetic smile. "It's just been a rough day and my feet hurt."

"My sister sits in an office all day, files her nails, reads books and then complains that her feet hurt."

Jo Marie was too weary to rise to the bait. "Not

even your acid tongue is going to get a rise out of me tonight."

"I know something that will," Mark returned smugly.

"Ha." From force of habit, Jo Marie kicked off her shoes and strolled into the kitchen.

"Wanna bet?"

"I'm not a betting person, especially after playing cards with you yesterday, but if you care to impress me, fire away." Crossing her arms, she leaned against the refrigerator door and waited.

"Kelly's engaged."

Jo Marie slowly shook her head in disbelief. "I didn't think you'd stoop to fabrications."

That familiar angry, hurt look stole into Mark's eyes. "It's true, I heard it from the horse's own mouth."

Lightly shaking her head from side to side to clear her thoughts, Jo Marie still came up with a blank. "But who?" Kelly wasn't going out with anyone seriously.

"Some cousin. Rich, no doubt," Mark said and straddled a kitchen chair. "She's got a diamond as big as a baseball. Must be hard for her to work with a rock that size weighing down her hand."

"A cousin?" New Orleans was full of Beaumonts, but none that Kelly had mentioned in particular. "I can't believe it," Jo Marie gasped. "She'd have said something to me."

"From what I understand, she tried to phone last night, but we were still at the folks' house. Just as well," Mark mumbled under his breath. "I'm not about to toast this engagement. First she plays at being nurse and now she wants to play at being a wife."

Mark's bitterness didn't register past the jolt of surprise that Jo Marie felt. "Kelly engaged," she repeated.

"You don't need to keep saying it," Mark snapped.

"Saying what?" A jubilant Kelly walked in the front door.

"Never mind," Mark said and slowly stood. "It's time for me to be going, I'll talk to you later."

"What about dinner?"

"There's someone I'd like you both to meet," Kelly announced.

Ignoring her, Mark turned to Jo Marie. "I've suddenly lost my appetite."

"Jo Marie, I'd like to introduce you to my fiancé, Andrew Beaumont."

Jo Marie's gaze swung from the frustrated look on her brother's face to an intense pair of gray eyes. There was only one man on earth with eyes the shade of a winter sea. The dream man.

Chapter Two

Stunned into speechlessness, Jo Marie struggled to maintain her composure. She took in a deep breath to calm her frantic heartbeat and forced a look of pleasant surprise. Andrew Beaumont apparently didn't even remember her. Jo Marie couldn't see so much as a flicker of recognition in the depth of his eyes. In the last nine months it was unlikely that he had given her more than a passing thought, if she'd been worthy of even that. And yet, she vividly remembered every detail of him, down to the crisp dark hair, the broad, muscular shoulders and faint twist of his mouth.

With an effort that was just short of superhuman, Jo Marie smiled. "Congratulations, you two. But what a surprise."

Kelly hurried across the room and hugged her tightly. "It was to us, too. Look." She held out her hand for Jo Marie to admire the flashing diamond. Mark hadn't been exaggerating. The flawless gem mounted in an antique setting was the largest Jo Marie had ever seen.

"What did I tell you," Mark whispered in her ear.

Confused, Kelly glanced from sister to brother. "Drew and I are celebrating tonight. We'd love it if you came. Both of you."

"No," Jo Marie and Mark declared in unison.

"I'm bushed," Jo Marie begged off.

"...and tired," Mark finished lamely.

For the first time, Andrew spoke. "We insist." The deep, resonant voice was exactly as Jo Marie remembered. But tonight there was something faintly arrogant in the way he spoke that dared Jo Marie and Mark to put up an argument.

Brother and sister exchanged questioning glances, neither willing to be drawn into the celebration. Each for their own reasons, Jo Marie mused.

"Well—" Mark cleared his throat, clearly ill at ease with the formidable fiancé "—perhaps another time."

"You're Jo Marie's brother?" Andrew asked with a mocking note.

"How'd you know?"

Kelly stuck her arm through Andrew's. "Family resemblance, silly. No one can look at the two of you and not know you're related."

"I can't say the same thing about you two. I thought it was against the law to marry a cousin." Mark didn't bother to disguise his contempt.

"We're distant cousins," Kelly explained brightly. Her eyes looked adoringly into Andrew's and Jo Marie felt her stomach tighten. Jealousy. This sickening feeling in the pit of her stomach was the green-eyed monster. Jo Marie had only experienced brief tastes of the emotion; now it filled her mouth until she thought she would choke on it.

"I...had a horribly busy day." Jo Marie sought frantically for an excuse to stay home.

"And I'd have to go home and change," Mark added, looking down over his pale gray cords and sport shirt.

"No, you wouldn't," Kelly contradicted with a provocative smile. "We're going to K-Paul's."

"Sure, and wait in line half the night." A muscle twitched in Mark's jaw.

K-Paul's was a renowned restaurant that was ranked sixth in the world. Famous, but not elegant. The small establishment served creole cooking at its best.

"No," Kelly supplied, and the dip in her voice revealed how much she wanted to share this night with her friends. "Andrew's a friend of Paul's."

Mark looked at Jo Marie and rolled his eyes. "I should have known," he muttered sarcastically.

"What time did you say we'd be there, darling?"

Jo Marie closed her eyes to the sharp flash of pain at the affectionate term Kelly used so freely. These jealous sensations were crazy. She had no right to feel this way. This man...Andrew Beaumont, was a blown-up figment of her imagination. The brief moments they shared should have been forgotten long ago. Kelly was her friend. Her best friend. And Kelly deserved every happiness.

With a determined jut to her chin, Jo Marie flashed her roommate a warm smile. "Mark and I would be honored to join you tonight."

"We would?" Mark didn't sound pleased. Irritation rounded his dark eyes and he flashed Jo Marie a look that openly contradicted her agreement. Jo Marie wanted to tell him that he owed Kelly this much for all the teasing he'd given her. In addition, her look pleaded with him to understand how much she needed his support tonight. Saying as much was impossible, but she hoped her eyes conveyed the message.

Jo Marie turned slightly so that she faced the tall figure standing only a few inches from her. "It's generous of you to include us," she murmured, but discovered that she was incapable of meeting Andrew's penetrating gaze.

"Give us a minute to freshen up and we'll be on our way," Kelly's effervescent enthusiasm filled the room. "Come on, Jo Marie."

The two men remained in the compact living room. Jo Marie glanced back to note that Mark looked like a jaguar trapped in an iron cage. When he wasn't pacing, he stood restlessly shifting his weight repeatedly from one foot to the other. His look was weary and there was an uncharacteristic tightness to his mouth that narrowed his eyes.

"What do you think," Kelly whispered, and gave a long sigh. "Isn't he fantastic? I think I'm the luckiest girl in the world. Of course, we'll have to wait until after the holidays to make our announcement official. But isn't Drew wonderful?"

Jo Marie forced a noncommittal nod. The raw disappointment left an aching void in her heart. Andrew should have been hers. "He's wonderful." The words came out sounding more like a tortured whisper than a compliment.

Kelly paused, lowering the brush. "Jo, are you all right? You sound like you're going to cry."

"Maybe I am." Tears burned for release, but not for the reason Kelly assumed. "It's not every day I lose my best friend."

"But you're not losing me."

Jo Marie's fingers curved around the cold bathroom sink. "But you are planning to get married?"

"Oh yes, we'll make an official announcement in January, but we haven't set a definite date for the wedding."

That surprised Jo Marie. Andrew didn't look like the kind of man who would encourage a long engagement. She would have thought that once he'd made a decision, he'd move on it. But then, she didn't know Andrew Beaumont. Not really.

A glance in the mirror confirmed that her cheeks were pale, her dark eyes haunted with a wounded, perplexed look. A quick application of blush added color to her bloodless face, but there was little she could do to disguise the troubled look in her eyes. She could only pray that no one would notice.

"Ready?" Kelly stood just outside the open door.

Jo Marie's returning smile was frail as she mentally braced herself for the coming ordeal. She paused long enough to dab perfume to the pulse points at the hollow of her neck and at her wrists.

"I, for one, am starved," Kelly announced as they returned to the living room. "And from what I remember of K-Paul's, eating is an experience we won't forget."

Jo Marie was confident that every part of this evening would be indelibly marked in her memory, but not for the reasons Kelly assumed.

Andrew's deep blue Mercedes was parked beside Mark's old clunker. The differences between the two men were as obvious as the vehicles they drove.

Clearly ill at ease, Mark stood on the sidewalk in front of his car. "Why don't Jo Marie and I follow you?"

"Nonsense," Kelly returned, "there's plenty of room in Drew's car for everyone. You know what the traffic is like. We could get separated. I wouldn't want that to happen."

Mark's twisted mouth said that he would have given a weeks' pay to suddenly disappear. Jo Marie studied her brother carefully from her position in the back seat. His displeasure at being included in this evening's celebration was confusing. There was far more than reluctance in his attitude. He might not get along with Kelly, but she would have thought that Mark would wish Kelly every happiness. But he didn't. Not by the stiff, unnatural behavior she'd witnessed from him tonight.

Mark's attitude didn't change any at the restaurant. Paul, the robust chef, came out from the kitchen and greeted the party himself.

After they'd ordered, the small party sat facing one another in stony silence. Kelly made a couple of attempts to start up the conversation, but her efforts were to no avail. The two men eyed each other, looking as if they were ready to do battle at the slightest provocation.

Several times while they ate their succulent Shrimp Remoulade, Jo Marie found her gaze drawn to Andrew. In many ways he was exactly as she remembered. In others, he was completely different. His voice was low pitched and had a faint drawl. And he wasn't a talker. His expression was sober almost to the point of being somber, which was unusual for a man celebrating his engagement. Another word that her mind tossed out was disillusioned. Andrew Beaumont looked as though he was disenchanted with life. From everything she'd learned he was wealthy and successful. He owned a land development firm. Delta Development, Inc. had been in the Beaumont family for three generations. According to Kelly, the firm had expanded extensively under Andrew's direction.

But if Jo Marie was paying attention to Andrew, he was nothing more than polite to her. He didn't acknowledge her with anything more than an occasional look. And since she hadn't directed any questions to him, he hadn't spoken either. At least not to her.

Paul's special touch for creole cooking made the meal memorable. And although her thoughts were troubled and her heart perplexed, when the waitress took Jo Marie's plate away she had done justice to the meal. Even Mark, who had sat uncommunicative and sullen through most of the dinner, had left little on his plate.

After K-Paul's, Kelly insisted they visit the French Quarter. The others were not as enthusiastic. After an hour of walking around and sampling some of the best jazz sounds New Orleans had to offer, they returned to the apartment.

"I'll make the coffee," Kelly proposed as they climbed from the luxury car.

Mark made a show of glancing at his watch. "I think I'll skip the chicory," he remarked in a flippant tone. "Tomorrow's a busy day."

"Come on, Mark—" Kelly pouted prettily "—don't be a spoil sport."

Mark's face darkened with a scowl. "If you insist."

"It isn't every day I celebrate my engagement. And, Mark, have you noticed that we haven't fought once all night? That must be some kind of a record."

A poor facsimile of a smile lifted one corner of his mouth. "It must be," he agreed wryly. He lagged behind as they climbed the stairs to the second-story apartment.

Jo Marie knew her brother well enough to know he'd have the coffee and leave as soon as it was polite to do so.

They sat in stilted silence, drinking their coffee.

"Do you two work together?" Andrew directed his question to Jo Marie.

Flustered she raised her palm to her breast. "Me?"

"Yes. Did you and Kelly meet at Tulane Hospital?"

"No, I'm a travel agent. Mark's the one in the family with the brains." She heard the breathlessness in her voice and hoped that he hadn't.

"Don't put yourself down," Kelly objected. "You're no dummy. Did you know that Jo Marie is actively involved in saving our wetlands? She volunteers her time as an office worker for the Land For The Future organization."

"That doesn't require intelligence, only time," Jo

Marie murmured self-consciously and congratulated herself for keeping her voice even.

For the first time that evening, Andrew directed his attention to her and smiled. The effect it had on Jo Marie's pulse was devastating. To disguise her reaction, she raised the delicate china cup to her lips and took a tentative sip of the steaming coffee.

"And all these years I thought the LFTF was for little old ladies."

"No." Jo Marie was able to manage only the one word.

"At one time Jo Marie wanted to be a biologist," Kelly supplied.

Andrew arched two thick brows. "What stopped you?"

"Me," Mark cut in defensively. "The schooling she required was extensive and our parents couldn't afford to pay for us both to attend university at the same time. Jo Marie decided to drop out."

"That's not altogether true." Mark was making her sound noble and self-sacrificing. "It wasn't like that. If I'd wanted to continue my schooling there were lots of ways I could have done so."

"And you didn't?" Again Andrew's attention was focused on her.

She moistened her dry lips before continuing. "No. I plan to go back to school someday. Until then I'm staying active in the causes that mean the most to me and to the future of New Orleans."

"Jo Marie's our neighborhood scientist," Kelly added proudly. "She has a science club for children every other Saturday morning. I swear she's a natural with those kids. She's always taking them on hikes and planning field trips for them.''

"You must like children.'' Again Andrew's gaze slid to Jo Marie.

"Yes,'' she answered self-consciously and lowered her eyes. She was grateful when the topic of conversation drifted to other subjects. When she chanced a look at Andrew, she discovered that his gaze centered on her lips. It took a great deal of restraint not to moisten them. And even more to force the memory of his kiss from her mind.

Once again, Mark made a show of looking at his watch and standing. "The evening's been—'' he faltered looking for an adequate description ''—interesting. Nice meeting you, Beaumont. Best wishes to you and Florence Nightingale.''

The sip of coffee stuck in Jo Marie's throat, causing a moment of intense pain until her muscles relaxed enough to allow her to swallow. Grateful that no one had noticed, Jo Marie set her cup aside and walked with her brother to the front door. "I'll talk to you later,'' she said in farewell.

Mark wiped a hand across his eyes. He looked more tired than Jo Marie could remember seeing him in a long time. "I've been dying to ask you all night. Isn't Kelly's rich friend the one who filled in the swampland for that housing development you fought so hard against?''

"And lost.'' Jo Marie groaned inwardly. She had been a staunch supporter of the environmentalists and had helped gather signatures against the project. But to no avail. "Then he's also the one who bought out Rose's,'' she murmured thoughtfully as a feeling of dread washed over her. Rose's Hotel was in the French Quarter and was one of the landmarks of Louisiana. In addition to being a part of New Orleans' history, the hotel was used to house transients. It was true that Rose's was badly in need of repairs, but Jo Marie hated to see the wonderful old building destroyed in the name of progress. If annihilating the breeding habitat of a hundred different species of birds hadn't troubled Andrew Beaumont, then she doubted that an old hotel in ill-repair would matter to him either.

Rubbing her temple to relieve an unexpected and throbbing headache, Jo Marie nodded. "I remember Kelly saying something about a cousin being responsible for Rose's. But I hadn't put the two together."

"He has," Mark countered disdainfully. "And come up with megabucks. Our little Kelly has reeled in quite a catch, if you like the cold, heartless sort."

Jo Marie's mind immediately rejected that thought. Andrew Beaumont may be the man responsible for several controversial land acquisitions, but he wasn't heartless. Five minutes with him at the Mardi Gras had proven otherwise.

Mark's amused chuckle carried into the living room. "You've got that battle look in your eye. What are you thinking?"

"Nothing," she returned absently. But already her mind was racing furiously. "I'll talk to you tomorrow."

"I'll give you a call," Mark promised and was gone.

When Jo Marie returned to the living room, she

found Kelly and Andrew chatting companionably. They paused and glanced at her as she rejoined them.

"You've known each other for a long time, haven't you?" Jo Marie lifted the half-full china cup, making an excuse to linger. She sat on the arm of the love seat, unable to decide if she should stay and speak her mind or repress her tongue.

"We've known each other since childhood." Kelly answered for the pair.

"And Andrew is the distant cousin you said had bought Rose's."

Kelly's sigh was uncomfortable. "I was hoping you wouldn't put two and two together."

"To be honest, I didn't. Mark figured it out."

A frustrated look tightened Kelly's once happy features.

"Will someone kindly tell me what you two are talking about?" Andrew asked.

"Rose's," they chimed in unison.

"Rose's," he repeated slowly and a frown appeared between his gray eyes.

Apparently Andrew Beaumont had so much land one small hotel didn't matter.

"The hotel."

The unexpected sharpness in his voice caused Jo Marie to square her shoulders. "It may seem like a little thing to you."

"Not for what that piece of land cost me," he countered in a hard voice.

"I don't think Drew likes to mix business with pleasure," Kelly warned, but Jo Marie disregarded the well-intended advice.

"But the men living in Rose's will have nowhere to go."

"They're bums."

A sadness filled her at the insensitive way he referred to these men. "Rose's had housed homeless men for twenty years. These men need someplace where they can get a hot meal and can sleep."

"It's a prime location for luxury condominiums," he said cynically.

"But what about the transients? What will become of them?"

"That, Miss Early, is no concern of mine."

Unbelievably Jo Marie felt tears burn behind her eyes. She blinked them back. Andrew Beaumont wasn't the dream man she'd fantasized over all these months. He was cold and cynical. The only love he had in his life was profit. A sadness settled over her with a weight she thought would be crippling.

"I feel very sorry for you, Mr. Beaumont," she said smoothly, belying her turbulent emotions. "You may be very rich, but there's no man poorer than one who has no tolerance for the weakness of others."

Kelly gasped softly and groaned. "I knew this was going to happen."

"Are you always so opinionated, Miss Early?" There was no disguising the icy tones.

"No, but there are times when things are so wrong that I can't remain silent." She turned to Kelly. "I apologize if I've ruined your evening. If you'll excuse me now, I think I'll go to bed. Good night, Mr. Beaumont. May you and Kelly have many years of happiness together." The words nearly stuck in her throat but she managed to get them out before walking from the room.

"If this offends you in any way I won't do it." Jo Marie studied her roommate carefully. The demonstration in front of Rose's had been planned weeks ago. Jo Marie's wooden picket sign felt heavy in her hand. For the first time in her life, her convictions conflicted with her feelings. She didn't want to march against Andrew. It didn't matter what he'd done, but she couldn't stand by and see those poor men turned into the streets, either. Not in the name of progress. Not when progress was at the cost of the less fortunate and the fate of a once lovely hotel.

"This picket line was arranged long before you met Drew."

"That hasn't got anything to do with this. Drew is important to you. I wouldn't want to do something that will place your relationship with him in jeopardy."

"It won't."

Kelly sounded far more confident than Jo Marie felt.

"In fact," she continued, "I doubt that Drew even knows anything about the demonstration. Those things usually do nothing to sway his decision. In fact, I'd say they do more harm than good as far as he's concerned."

Jo Marie had figured that much out herself, but she couldn't stand by doing nothing. Rose's was scheduled to be shut down the following week...a short month before Christmas. Jo Marie didn't know how anyone could be so heartless. The hotel was to be torn down a week later and new construction was scheduled to begin right after the first of the year.

Kelly paused at the front door while Jo Marie picked up her picket sign and tossed the long strap of her purse over her shoulder.

"You do understand why I can't join you?" she asked hesitatingly.

"Of course," Jo Marie said and exhaled softly. She'd never expected Kelly to participate. This fight couldn't include her friend without causing bitter feelings.

"Be careful." Her arms wrapped around her waist to chase away a chill, Kelly walked down to the parking lot with Jo Marie.

"Don't worry. This is a peaceful demonstration. The only wounds I intend to get are from carrying this sign. It's heavy."

Cocking her head sideways, Kelly read the sign for the tenth time. Save Rose's Hotel. A Piece Of New Orleans History. Kelly chuckled and slowly shook her head. "I should get a picture of you. Drew would get a real kick out of that."

The offer of a picture was a subtle reminder that Drew wouldn't so much as see the sign. He probably wasn't even aware of the protest rally.

Friends of Rose's and several others from the Land For The Future headquarters were gathered outside the hotel when Jo Marie arrived. Several people who knew Jo Marie raised their hands in welcome.

"Have the television and radio stations been notified?" the organizer asked a tall man Jo Marie didn't recognize.

"I notified them, but most weren't all that interested. I doubt that we'll be given air time."

A feeling of gloom settled over the group. An unexpected cloudburst did little to brighten their mood. Jo Marie hadn't brought her umbrella and was drenched in minutes. A chill caused her teeth to chatter and no matter how hard she tried, she couldn't stop shivering. Uncaring, the rain fell indiscriminately over the small group of protesters.

"You little fool," Mark said when he found her an hour later. "Are you crazy, walking around wet and cold like that?" His voice was a mixture of exasperation and pride.

"I'm making a statement," Jo Marie argued.

"You're right. You're telling the world what a fool you are. Don't you have any better sense than this?"

Jo Marie ignored him, placing one foot in front of the other as she circled the sidewalk in front of Rose's Hotel.

"Do you think Beaumont cares?"

Jo Marie refused to be drawn into his argument. "Instead of arguing with me, why don't you go inside and see what's holding up the coffee?"

"You're going to need more than a hot drink to prevent you from getting pneumonia. Listen to reason for once in your life."

"No!" Emphatically Jo Marie stamped her foot. "This is too important."

"And your health isn't?"

"Not now." The protest group had dwindled down to less than ten. "I'll be all right." She shifted the sign from one shoulder to the other and flexed her stiff fingers. Her back ached from the burden of her message. And with every step the rain water in her shoes squished noisily. "I'm sure we'll be finished in another hour."

"If you aren't, I'm carting you off myself," Mark shouted angrily and returned to his car. He shook his finger at her in warning as he drove past.

True to his word, Mark returned an hour later and followed her back to the apartment.

Jo Marie could hardly drive she was shivering so violently. Her long chestnut hair fell in limp tendrils over her face. Rivulets of cold water ran down her neck and she bit into her bottom lip at the pain caused by gripping the steering wheel. Carrying the sign had formed painful blisters in the palms of her hands. This was one protest rally she wouldn't soon forget.

Mark seemed to blame Andrew Beaumont for the fact that she was cold, wet and miserable. But it wasn't Andrew's fault that it had rained. Not a single forecaster had predicted it would. She'd lived in New Orleans long enough to know she should carry an umbrella with her. Mark was looking for an excuse to dislike Andrew. Any excuse. In her heart, Jo Marie couldn't. No matter what he'd done, there was something deep within her that wouldn't allow any bitterness inside. In some ways she was disillusioned and hurt that her dream man wasn't all she'd thought. But that was as deep as her resentments went.

"Little fool," Mark repeated tenderly as he helped her out of the car. "Let's get you upstairs and into a hot bath."

"As long as I don't have to listen to you lecture all night," she said, her teeth chattering as she climbed the stairs to the second-story apartment. Although she was thoroughly miserable, there was a spark of humor in her eyes as she opened the door and stepped inside the apartment.

"Jo Marie," Kelly cried in alarm. "Good grief, what happened?"

A light laugh couldn't disguise her shivering. "Haven't you looked out the window lately? It's raining cats and dogs."

"This is your fault, Beaumont," Mark accused harshly and Jo Marie sucked in a surprised breath. In her misery, she hadn't noticed Andrew, who was casually sitting on the love seat.

He rose to a standing position and glared at Mark as if her brother were a mad man. "Explain yourself," he demanded curtly.

Kelly intervened, crossing the room and placing a hand on Andrew's arm. "Jo Marie was marching in that rally I was telling you about."

"In front of Rose's Hotel," Mark added, his fists tightly clenched at his side. He looked as if he wanted to get physical. Consciously, Jo Marie moved closer to her brother's side. Fist fighting was so unlike Mark. He was a healer, not a boxer. One look told Jo Marie that in a physical exchange, Mark would lose.

Andrew's mouth twisted scornfully. "You, my dear Miss Early, are a fool."

Jo Marie dipped her head mockingly. "And you, Mr. Beaumont, are heartless."

"But rich," Mark intervened. "And money goes a long way in making a man attractive. Isn't that right, Kelly?"

Kelly went visibly pale, her blue eyes filling with

tears. "That's not true," she cried, her words jerky as she struggled for control.

"You will apologize for that remark, Early." Andrew's low voice held a threat that was undeniable.

Mark knotted and unknotted his fists. "I won't apologize for the truth. If you want to step outside, maybe you'd like to make something of it."

"Mark!" Both Jo Marie and Kelly gasped in shocked disbelief.

Jo Marie moved first. "Get out of here before you cause trouble." Roughly she opened the door and shoved him outside.

"You heard what I said," Mark growled on his way out the door.

"I've never seen Mark behave like that," Jo Marie murmured, her eyes lowered to the carpet where a small pool of water had formed. "I can only apologize." She paused and inhaled deeply. "And, Kelly, I'm sure you know he didn't mean what he said to you. He's upset because of the rally." Her voice was deep with emotion as she excused herself and headed for the bathroom.

A hot bath went a long way toward making her more comfortable. Mercifully, Andrew was gone by the time she had finished. She didn't feel up to another confrontation with him.

"Call on line three."

Automatically Jo Marie punched in the button and reached for her phone. "Jo Marie Early, may I help you?"

"You won."

"Mark?" He seldom phoned her at work.

"Did you hear me?" he asked excitedly.

"What did I win?" she asked humoring him.

"Beaumont."

Jo Marie's hand tightened around the receiver. "What do you mean?"

"It just came over the radio. Delta Development, Inc. is donating Rose's Hotel to the city," Mark announced with a short laugh. "Can you believe it?"

"Yes," Jo Marie closed her eyes to the onrush of emotion. Her dream man hadn't let her down. "I can believe it."

Chapter Three

"But you must come," Kelly insisted, sitting across from Jo Marie. "It'll be miserable without you."

"Kell, I don't know." Jo Marie looked up from the magazine she was reading and nibbled on her lower lip.

"It's just a Christmas party with a bunch of stuffy people I don't know. You know how uncomfortable I am meeting new people. I hate parties."

"Then why attend?"

"Drew says we must. I'm sure he doesn't enjoy the party scene any more than I do, but he's got to go or offend a lot of business acquaintances."

"But I wasn't included in the invitation," Jo Marie argued. She'd always liked people and usually did well at social functions.

"Of course you were included. Both you and Mark," Kelly insisted. "Drew saw to that."

Thoughtfully, Jo Marie considered her roommate's request. As much as she objected, she really would like to go, if for no more reason than to thank Andrew for his generosity regarding Rose's. Although she'd seen him briefly a couple of times since, the opportunity hadn't presented itself to express her appreciation. The party was one way she could do that. New Orleans was famous for its festive balls and holiday parties. Without Kelly's invitation, Jo Marie doubted that there would ever be the chance for her to attend such an elaborate affair.

"All right," she conceded, "but I doubt that Mark will come." Mark and Andrew hadn't spoken since the last confrontation in the girls' living room. The air had hung heavy between them then and Jo Marie doubted that Andrew's decision regarding Rose's Hotel would change her brother's attitude.

"Leave Mark to me," Kelly said confidently. "Just promise me that you'll be there."

"I'll need a dress." Mentally Jo Marie scanned the contents of her closet and came up with zero. Nothing she owned would be suitable for such an elaborate affair.

"Don't worry, you can borrow something of mine," Kelly offered with a generosity that was innate to her personality.

Jo Marie nearly choked on her laughter. "I'm three inches taller than you." And several pounds heavier, but she preferred not to mention that. Only once before had Jo Marie worn Kelly's clothes. The night she'd met Andrew.

Kelly giggled and the bubbly sound was pleasant to the ears. "I heard miniskirts were coming back into style."

"Perhaps, but I doubt that the fashion will arrive in time for Christmas. Don't worry about me, I'll go out this afternoon and pick up some material for a dress."

"But will you have enough time between now and the party to sew it?" Kelly's blue eyes rounded with doubt.

"I'll make time." Jo Marie was an excellent seamstress. She had her mother to thank for that. Ruth Early had insisted that her only daughter learn to sew. Jo Marie had balked in the beginning. Her interests were anything but domestic. But now, as she had been several times in the past, she was grateful for the skill.

She found a pattern of a three-quarter-length dress with a matching jacket. The simplicity of the design made the outfit all the more appealing. Jo Marie could dress it either up or down, depending on the occasion. The silky, midnight blue material she purchased was perfect for the holiday, and Jo Marie knew that shade to be one of her better colors.

When she returned to the apartment, Kelly was gone. A note propped on the kitchen table explained that she wouldn't be back until dinner time.

After washing, drying, and carefully pressing the material, Jo Marie laid it out on the table for cutting. Intent on her task, she had pulled her hair away from her face and had tied it at the base of her neck with a rubber band. Straight pins were pressed between her lips when the doorbell chimed. The neighborhood children often stopped in for a visit. Usually Jo Marie welcomed their company, but she was busy now and interruptions could result in an irreparable mistake. She toyed with the idea of not answering.

The impatient buzz told her that her company was irritated at being kept waiting.

"Damn, damn, damn," she grumbled beneath her breath as she made her way across the room. Extracting the straight pins from her mouth, she stuck them in the small cushion she wore around her wrist.

"Andrew!" Secretly she thanked God the pins were out of her mouth or she would have swallowed them in her surprise.

"Is Kelly here?"

"No, but come in." Her heart was racing madly as he walked into the room. Nervous fingers tugged the rubber band from her chestnut hair in a futile attempt to look more presentable. She shook her hair free, then wished she'd kept it neatly in place. For days Jo Marie would have welcomed the opportunity to thank Andrew, but she discovered as she followed him into the living room that her tongue was tied and her mouth felt gritty and dry. "I'm glad you're here...I wanted to thank you for your decision about Rose's...the hotel."

He interrupted her curtly. "My dear Miss Early, don't be misled. My decision wasn't—"

Her hand stopped him. "I know," she said softly. He didn't need to tell her his reasoning. She was already aware it wasn't because of the rally or anything that she'd done or said. "I just wanted to thank you for whatever may have been your reason."

Their eyes met and held from across the room. Countless moments passed in which neither spoke. The air was electric between them and the urge to reach out and touch Andrew was almost overwhelming. The same breathlessness that had attacked her the night of the Mardi Gras returned. Andrew had to remember, he had to. Yet he gave no indication that he did.

Jo Marie broke eye contact first, lowering her gaze to the wool carpet. "I'm not sure where Kelly is, but she said she'd be back by dinner time." Her hand shook as she handed him the note off the kitchen counter.

"Kelly mentioned the party?"

Jo Marie nodded.

"You'll come?"

She nodded her head in agreement. "If I finish sewing this dress in time." She spoke so he wouldn't think she'd suddenly lost the ability to talk. Never had she been more aware of a man. Her heart was hammering at his nearness. He was so close all she had to do was reach out and touch him. But insurmountable barriers stood between them. At last, after all these months she was alone with her dream man. So many times a similar scene had played in her mind. But Andrew didn't remember her. The realization produced an indescribable ache in her heart. What had been the most profound moment in her life had been nothing to him.

"Would you like to sit down?" she offered, remembering her manners. "There's coffee on if you'd like a cup."

He shook his head. "No, thanks." He ran his hand along the top of the blue cloth that was stretched across the kitchen table. His eyes narrowed and he looked as if his thoughts were a thousand miles away.

"Why don't you buy a dress?"

A smile trembled at the edge of her mouth. To a

man who had always had money, buying something as simple as a dress would seem the most logical solution.

"I sew most of my own things," she explained softly, rather than enlightening him with a lecture on economics.

"Did you make this?" His fingers touched the short sleeve of her cotton blouse and brushed against the sensitive skin of her upper arm.

Immediately a warmth spread where his fingers had come into contact with her flesh. Jo Marie's pale cheeks instantly flushed with a crimson flood of color. "Yes," she admitted hoarsely, hating the way her body, her voice, everything about her, was affected by this man.

"You do beautiful work."

She kept her eyes lowered and drew in a steadying breath. "Thank you."

"Next weekend I'll be having a Christmas party at my home for the employees of my company. I would be honored if both you and your brother attended."

Already her heart was racing with excitement; she'd love to visit his home. But seeing where he lived was only an excuse. She'd do anything to see more of him. "I can't speak for Mark," she answered after several moments, feeling guilty for her thoughts.

"But you'll come?"

"I'd be happy to. Thank you." Her only concern was that no one from Delta Development would recognize her as the same woman who was active in the protest against the housing development and in saving Rose's Hotel.

"Good," he said gruffly.

The curve of her mouth softened into a smile. "I'll tell Kelly that you were by. Would you like her to phone you?"

"No, I'll be seeing her later. Goodbye, Jo Marie."

She walked with him to the door, holding onto the knob longer than necessary. "Goodbye, Andrew," she murmured.

Jo Marie leaned against the door and covered her face with both hands. She shouldn't be feeling this eager excitement, this breathless bewilderment, this softness inside at the mere thought of him. Andrew Beaumont was her roommate's fiancé. She had to remember that. But somehow, Jo Marie recognized that her conscience could repeat the information all day, but it would have little effect on her restless heart.

The sewing machine was set up at the table when Kelly walked into the apartment a couple of hours later.

"I'm back," Kelly murmured happily as she hung her sweater in the closet.

"Where'd you go?"

"To see a friend."

Jo Marie thought she detected a note of hesitancy in her roommate's voice and glanced up momentarily from her task. She paused herself, then said, "Andrew was by."

A look of surprise worked its way across Kelly's pixie face. "Really? Did he say what he wanted?"

"Not really. He didn't leave a message." Jo Marie strove for nonchalance, but her fingers shook slightly and she hoped that her friend didn't notice the telltale mannerism.

"You like Drew, don't you?"

For some reason, Jo Marie's mind had always referred to him as Andrew. "Yes." She continued with the mechanics of sewing, but she could feel Kelly's eyes roam over her face as she studied her. Immediately a guilty flush reddened her cheeks. Somehow, some way, Kelly had detected how strongly Jo Marie felt about Andrew.

"I'm glad," Kelly said at last. "I'd like it if you two would fall in..." She hesitated before concluding with, "Never mind."

The two words were repeated in her mind like the dwindling sounds of an echo off canyon walls.

The following afternoon, Jo Marie arrived home from work and took a crisp apple from the bottom shelf of the refrigerator. She wanted a snack before pulling out her sewing machine again. Kelly was working late and had phoned her at the office so Jo Marie wouldn't worry. Holding the apple between her teeth, she lugged the heavy sewing machine out of the bedroom. No sooner had she set the case on top of the table than the doorbell chimed.

Releasing a frustrated sigh, she swallowed the bite of apple.

"Sign here, please." A clipboard was shoved under her nose.

"I beg your pardon," Jo Marie asked.

"I'm making a delivery, lady. Sign here."

"Oh." Maybe Kelly had ordered something without telling her. Quickly, she penned her name along the bottom line.

"Wait here," was the next abrupt instruction.

Shrugging her shoulder, Jo Marie leaned against the door jamb as the brusque man returned to the brown truck parked below and brought up two large boxes.

"Merry Christmas, Miss Early," he said with a sheepish grin as he handed her the delivery.

"Thank you." The silver box was the trademark of New Orleans' most expensive boutique. Gilded lettering wrote out the name of the proprietor, Madame Renaux Marceau, across the top. Funny, Jo Marie couldn't recall Kelly saying she'd bought something there. But with the party coming, Kelly had apparently opted for the expensive boutique.

Dutifully Jo Marie carried the boxes into Kelly's room and set them on the bed. As she did so the shipping order attached to the smaller box, caught her eye. The statement was addressed to her, not Kelly.

Inhaling a jagged breath, Jo Marie searched the order blank to find out who would be sending her anything. Her parents could never have afforded something from Madame Renaux Marceau.

The air was sucked from her lungs as Jo Marie discovered Andrew Beaumont's name. She fumbled with the lids, peeled back sheer paper and gasped at the beauty of what lay before her. The full-length blue dress was the same midnight shade as the one she was sewing. But this gown was unlike anything Jo Marie had ever seen. A picture of Christmas, a picture of elegance. She held it up and felt tears prickle the back of her eyes. The bodice was layered with intricate rows of tiny pearls that formed a V at the waist. The gown was breathtakingly beautiful. Never had Jo Marie thought to own anything so perfect or so lovely. The second box contained a matching cape with an ornate display of tiny pearls.

Very carefully, Jo Marie folded the dress and cape and placed them back into the boxes. An ache inside her heart erupted into a broken sob. She wasn't a charity case. Did Andrew assume that because she sewed her own clothes that what she was making for the party would be unpresentable?

The telephone book revealed the information she needed. Following her instincts, Jo Marie grabbed a sweater and rushed out the door. She didn't stop until she pulled up in front of the large brick building with the gold plaque in the front that announced that this was the headquarters for Delta Development, Inc.

A listing of offices in the foyer told her where Andrew's was located. Jo Marie rode the elevator to the third floor. Most of the building was deserted, only a few employees remained. Those that did gave her curious stares, but no one questioned her presence.

The office door that had Andrew's name lettered on it was closed, but that didn't dissuade Jo Marie. His receptionist was placing the cover over her typewriter when Jo Marie barged inside.

"I'd like to see Mr. Beaumont," she demanded in a breathless voice.

The gray-haired receptionist glanced at the boxes under Jo Marie's arms and shook her head. "I'm sorry, but the office is closed for the day."

Jo Marie caught the subtle difference. "I didn't ask about the office. I said I wanted to see Mr. Beaumont." Her voice rose with her frustration.

A connecting door between two rooms opened. "Is there a problem, Mrs. Stewart?"

"I was just telling..."

"Jo Marie." Andrew's voice was an odd mixture

of surprise and gruffness, yet gentle. His narrowed look centered on the boxes clasped under each arm. "Is there a problem?"

"As a matter of fact there is," she said, fighting to disguise the anger that was building within her to volcanic proportions.

Andrew stepped aside to admit her into his office.

"Will you be needing me further?" Jo Marie heard his secretary ask.

"No, thank you, Mrs. Stewart. I'll see you in the morning."

No sooner had Andrew stepped in the door than Jo Marie whirled on him. The silver boxes from the boutique sat squarely in the middle of Andrew's huge oak desk.

"I think you should understand something right now, Mr. Beaumont," she began heatedly, not bothering to hold back her annoyance. "I am not Cinderella and you most definitely are not my fairy godfather."

"Would I be amiss to guess that my gift displeases you?"

Jo Marie wanted to scream at him for being so calm. She cut her long nails into her palms in an effort to disguise her irritation. "If I am an embarrassment to you wearing a dress I've sewn myself, then I'll simply not attend your precious party."

He looked shocked.

"And furthermore, I am no one's poor relation."

An angry frown deepened three lines across his wide forehead. "What makes you suggest such stupidity?"

"I may be many things, but stupid isn't one of them."

"A lot of things?" He stood behind his desk and leaned forward, pressing his weight on his palms. "You mean like opinionated, headstrong, and impatient."

"Yes," she cried and shot her index finger into the air. "But not stupid."

The tight grip Andrew held on his temper was visible by the way his mouth was pinched until the grooves stood out tense and white. "Maybe not stupid, but incredibly inane."

Her mouth was trembling and Jo Marie knew that if she didn't get away soon, she'd cry. "Let's not argue over definitions. Stated simply, the gesture of buying me a presentable dress was not appreciated. Not in the least."

"I gathered that much, Miss Early. Now if you'll excuse me, I have a dinner engagement."

"Gladly." She pivoted and stormed across the floor ready to jerk open the office door. To her dismay, the door stuck and wouldn't open, ruining her haughty exit.

"Allow me," Andrew offered bitterly.

The damn door! It would have to ruin her proud retreat.

By the time she was in the parking lot, most of her anger had dissipated. Second thoughts crowded her mind on the drive back to the apartment. She could have at least been more gracious about it. Second thoughts quickly evolved into constant recriminations so that by the time she walked through the doorway of the apartment, Jo Marie was thoroughly miserable.

"Hi." Kelly was mixing raw hamburger for meat-loaf with her hands. "Did the dress arrive?"

Kelly knew! "Dress?"

"Yes. Andrew and I went shopping for you yesterday afternoon and found the most incredibly lovely party dress. It was perfect for you."

Involuntarily, Jo Marie stiffened. "What made you think I needed a dress?"

Kelly's smile was filled with humor. "You were sewing one, weren't you? Drew said that you were really attending this function as a favor to me. And since this is such a busy time of year he didn't want you spending your nights slaving over a sewing machine."

"Oh." A sickening feeling attacked the pit of her stomach.

"Drew can be the most thoughtful person," Kelly commented as she continued to blend the ground meat. Her attention was more on her task than on Jo Marie. "You can understand why it's so easy to love him."

A strangled sound made its way past the tightness in Jo Marie's throat.

"I'm surprised the dress hasn't arrived. Drew gave specific instructions that it was to be delivered today in case any alterations were needed."

"It did come," Jo Marie announced, more miserable than she could ever remember being.

"It did?" Excitement elevated Kelly's voice. "Why didn't you say something? Isn't it the most beautiful dress you've ever seen? You're going to be gorgeous." Kelly's enthusiasm waned as she turned around. "Jo, what's wrong? You look like you're ready to burst into tears."

"That's...that's because I am," she managed and covering her face with her hands, she sat on the edge of the sofa and wept.

Kelly's soft laugh only made everything seem worse. "I expected gratitude," Kelly said with a sigh and handed Jo Marie a tissue. "But certainly not tears. You don't cry that often."

Noisily Jo Marie blew her nose. "I...I thought I was an embarrassment...to you two...that...you didn't want me...at the party...because I didn't have...the proper clothes...and..."

"You thought what?" Kelly interrupted, a shocked, hurt look crowding her face. "I can't believe you'd even think anything so crazy."

"That's not all. I...." She swallowed. "I took the dress to...Andrew's office and practically...threw it in his face."

"Oh, Jo Marie." Kelly lowered herself onto the sofa beside her friend. "How could you?"

"I don't know. Maybe it sounds ridiculous, but I really believed that you and Andrew would be ashamed to be seen with me in an outfit I'd made myself."

"How could you come up with something so dumb? Especially since I've always complimented you on the things you've sewn."

Miserably, Jo Marie bowed her head. "I know."

"You've really done it, but good, my friend. I can just imagine Drew's reaction to your visit." At the thought Kelly's face grew tight. "Now what are you going to do?"

"Nothing. From this moment on I'll be conveniently tucked in my room when he comes for you..."

"What about the party?" Kelly's blue eyes were rounded with childlike fright and Jo Marie could only speculate whether it was feigned or real. "It's only two days away."

"I can't go, certainly you can understand that."

"But you've got to come," Kelly returned adamantly. "Mark said he'd go if you were there and I need you both. Everything will be ruined if you back out now."

"Mark's coming?" Jo Marie had a difficult time believing her brother would agree to this party idea. She'd have thought Mark would do anything to avoid another confrontation with Andrew.

"Yes. And it wasn't easy to get him to agree."

"I can imagine," Jo Marie returned dryly.

"Jo Marie, please. Your being there means so much to me. More than you'll ever know. Do this one thing and I promise I won't ask another thing of you as long as I live."

Kelly was serious. Something about this party was terribly important to her. Jo Marie couldn't understand what. In order to attend the party she would need to apologize to Andrew. If it had been her choice she would have waited a week or two before approaching him, giving him the necessary time to cool off. As it was, she'd be forced to do it before the party while tempers continued to run hot. Damn! She should have waited until Kelly was home tonight before jumping to conclusions about the dress. Any half-wit would have known her roommate was involved.

"Well?" Kelly regarded her hopefully.

"I'll go, but first I've got to talk to Andrew and explain."

Kelly released a rush of air, obviously relieved. "Take my advice, don't explain a thing. Just tell him you're sorry."

Jo Marie brushed her dark curls from her forehead. She was in no position to argue. Kelly obviously knew Andrew far better than she. The realization produced a rush of painful regrets. "I'll go to his office first thing tomorrow morning," she said with far more conviction in her voice than what she was feeling.

"You won't regret it," Kelly breathed and squeezed Jo Marie's numb fingers. "I promise you won't."

If that was the case, Jo Marie wanted to know why she regretted it already.

To say that she slept restlessly would be an understatement. By morning, dark shadows had formed under her eyes that even cosmetics couldn't completely disguise. The silky blue dress was finished and hanging from a hook on her cloest door. Compared to the lovely creation Andrew had purchased, her simple gown looked drab. Plain. Unsophisticated. Swallowing her pride had always left a bitter aftertaste, and she didn't expect it to be any different today.

"Good luck," Kelly murmured her condolences to Jo Marie on her way out the door.

"Thanks, I'll need that and more." The knot in her stomach grew tighter every minute. Jo Marie didn't know what she was going to say or even where to begin.

Mrs. Stewart, the gray-haired guardian, was at her station when Jo Marie stepped inside Andrew's office.

"Good morning."

The secretary was too well trained to reveal any surprise.

"Would it be possible to talk to Mr. Beaumont for a few minutes?"

"Do you have an appointment?" The older woman flipped through the calendar pages.

"No," Jo Marie tightened her fists. "I'm afraid I don't."

"Mr. Beaumont will be out of the office until this afternoon."

"Oh." Discouragement nearly defeated her. "Could I make an appointment to see him then?"

The paragon of virtue studied the appointment calendar. "I'm afraid not. Mr. Beaumont has meetings scheduled all week. But if you'd like, I could give him a message."

"Yes, please," she returned and scribbled out a note that said she needed to talk to him as soon as it was convenient. Handing the note back to Mrs. Stewart, Jo Marie offered the woman a feeble smile. "Thank you."

"I'll see to it that Mr. Beaumont gets your message," the efficient woman promised.

Jo Marie didn't doubt that the woman would. What she did question was whether Andrew would respond.

By the time Jo Marie readied for bed that evening, she realized that he wouldn't. Now she'd be faced with attending the party with the tension between them so thick it would resemble an English fog.

Mark was the first one to arrive the following evening. Dressed in a pin-stripe suit and a silk tie he looked exceptionally handsome. And Jo Marie didn't mind telling him so.

"Wow." She took a step in retreat and studied him thoughtfully. "Wow," she repeated.

"I could say the same thing. You look terrific."

Self-consciously, Jo Marie smoothed out an imaginary wrinkle from the skirt of her dress. "You're sure?"

"Of course, I am. And I like your hair like that."

Automatically a hand investigated the rhinestone combs that held the bouncy curls away from her face and gave an air of sophistication to her appearance.

"When will money bags be out?" Mark's gaze drifted toward Kelly's bedroom as he took a seat.

"Any minute."

Mark stuck a finger in the collar of his shirt and ran it around his neck. "I can't believe I agreed to this fiasco."

Jo Marie couldn't believe it either. "Why did you?"

Her brother's shrug was filled with self-derision. "I don't know. It seemed to mean so much to Kelly. And to be honest, I guess I owe it to her for all the times I've teased her."

"How do you feel about Beaumont?"

Mark's eyes narrowed fractionally. "I'm trying not to feel anything."

The door opened and Kelly appeared in a red frothy creation that reminded Jo Marie of Christmas and Santa and happy elves. She had seen the dress, but on Kelly the full-length gown came to life. With a lissome grace Jo Marie envied, Kelly sauntered into the room. Mark couldn't take his eyes off her as he slowly rose to a standing position.

"Kelly." He seemed to have difficulty speaking. "You...you're lovely."

Kelly's delighted laughter was filled with pleasure. "Don't sound so shocked. You've just never seen me dressed up is all."

For a fleeting moment Jo Marie wondered if Mark had ever really seen her roommate.

The doorbell chimed and three pairs of eyes glared at the front door accusingly. Jo Marie felt her stomach tighten with nervous apprehension. For two days she'd dreaded this moment. Andrew Beaumont had arrived.

Kelly broke away from the small group and answered the door. Jo Marie watched her brother's eyes narrow as Kelly stood on her tiptoes and lightly brushed her lips across Andrew's cheek. The involuntary reaction stirred a multitude of questions in Jo Marie about Mark's attitude toward Kelly. And her own toward Andrew.

When her gaze drifted from her brother, Jo Marie discovered that Andrew had centered his attention on her.

"You look exceedingly lovely, Miss Early."

"Thank you. I'm afraid the dress I should have worn was mistakenly returned." She prayed he understood her message.

"Let's have a drink before we leave," Kelly suggested. She'd been in the kitchen earlier mixing a concoction of coconut milk, rum, pineapple and several spices.

The cool drink helped relieve some of the tightness

in Jo Marie's throat. She sat beside her brother, across from Andrew. The silence in the room was interrupted only by Kelly, who seemed oblivious to the terrible tension. She chattered all the way out to the car.

Again Mark and Jo Marie were relegated to the back seat of Andrew's plush sedan. Jo Marie knew that Mark hated this, but he submitted to the suggestion without comment. Only the stiff way he held himself revealed his discontent. The party was being given by an associate of Andrew's, a builder. The minute Jo Marie heard the name of the firm she recognized it as the one that had worked on the wetlands project.

Mark cast Jo Marie a curious glance and she shook her head indicating that she wouldn't say a word. In some ways, Jo Marie felt that she was fraternizing with the enemy.

Introductions were made and a flurry of names and faces blurred themselves in her mind. Jo Marie recognized several prominent people, and spoke to a few. Mark stayed close by her side and she knew without asking that this whole party scene made him uncomfortable.

In spite of being so adamant about needing her, Kelly was now nowhere to be seen. A half hour later, Jo Marie noticed that Kelly was sitting in a chair against the wall, looking hopelessly lost. She watched amazed as Mark delivered a glass of punch to her and claimed the chair beside her roommate. Kelly brightened immediately and soon the two were smiling and chatting.

Scanning the crowded room, Jo Marie noticed that Andrew was busy talking to a group of men. The room suddenly felt stuffy. An open glass door that led to a balcony invited her outside and into the cool evening air.

Standing with her gloved hands against the railing, Jo Marie glanced up at the starlit heavens. The night was clear and the black sky was adorned with a thousand glittering stars.

"I received a message that you wanted to speak to me." The husky male voice spoke from behind her.

Jo Marie's heart leaped to her throat and she struggled not to reveal her discomfort. "Yes," she said with a relaxing breath.

Andrew joined her at the wrought-iron railing. His nearness was so overwhelming that Jo Marie closed her eyes to the powerful attraction. Her long fingers tightened their grip.

"I owe you an apology. I sincerely regret jumping to conclusions about the dress. You were only being kind."

An eternity passed before Andrew spoke. "Were you afraid I was going to demand a reward, Florence Nightingale?"

Chapter Four

Jo Marie's heart went still as she turned to Andrew with wide, astonished eyes. "You do remember." They'd spent a single, golden moment together so many months ago. Not once since Kelly had introduced Andrew as her fiancé had he given her the slightest inkling that he remembered.

"Did you imagine I could forget?" he asked quietly.

Tightly squeezing her eyes shut, Jo Marie turned back to the railing, her fingers gripping the wrought iron with a strength she didn't know she possessed.

"I came back every day for a month," he continued in a deep, troubled voice. "I thought you were a nurse."

The color ebbed from Jo Marie's face, leaving her pale. She'd looked for him, too. In all the months since the Mardi Gras she'd never stopped looking. Every time she'd left her apartment, she had silently searched through a sea of faces. Although she'd never known his name, she had included him in her thoughts every day since their meeting. He was her dream man, the stranger who had shared those enchanted moments of magic with her.

"It was Mardi Gras," she explained in a quavering voice. "I'd borrowed Kelly's uniform for a party."

Andrew stood beside her and his wintry eyes narrowed. "I should have recognized you then," he said with faint self-derision.

"Recognized me?" Jo Marie didn't understand. In the short time before they were separated, Andrew had said she reminded him of a painting he'd once seen.

"I should have known you from your picture in the newspaper. You were the girl who so strongly protested the housing development for the wetlands."

"I...I didn't know it was your company. I had no idea." A stray tendril of soft chestnut hair fell forward as she bowed her head. "But I can't apologize for demonstrating against something which I believe is very wrong."

"To thine own self be true, Jo Marie Early." He spoke without malice and when their eyes met, she discovered to her amazement that he was smiling.

Jo Marie responded with a smile of her own. "And you were there that night because of Kelly."

"I'd just left her."

"And I was on my way in." Another few minutes and they could have passed each other in the hospital corridor without ever knowing. In some ways Jo Marie wished they had. If she hadn't met Andrew that night, then she could have shared in her friend's joy at the coming marriage. As it was now, Jo Marie was forced to fight back emotions she had no right to feel. Andrew belonged to Kelly and the diamond ring on her finger declared as much.

"And...and now you've found Kelly," she stammered, backing away. "I want to wish you both a life filled with much happiness." Afraid of what her expressive eyes would reveal, Jo Marie lowered her lashes which were dark against her pale cheek. "I should be going inside."

"Jo Marie."

He said her name so softly that for a moment she wasn't sure he'd spoken. "Yes?"

Andrew arched both brows and lightly shook his head. His finger lightly touched her smooth cheek, following the line of her delicate jaw. Briefly his gaze darkened as if this was torture in the purest sense. "Nothing. Enjoy yourself tonight." With that he turned back to the railing.

Jo Marie entered the huge reception room and mingled with those attending the lavish affair. Not once did she allow herself to look over her shoulder toward the balcony. Toward Andrew, her dream man, because he wasn't hers, would never be hers. Her mouth ached with the effort to appear happy. By the time she made it to the punch bowl her smile felt brittle and was decidedly forced. All these months she'd hoped to find the dream man because her heart couldn't forget him. And now that she had, nothing had ever been more difficult. If she didn't learn to curb the strong sensual pull she felt toward him, she could ruin his and Kelly's happiness.

Soft Christmas music filled the room as Jo Marie

found a plush velvet chair against the wall and sat down, a friendly observer to the party around her. Forcing herself to relax, her toe tapped lightly against the floor with an innate rhythm. Christmas was her favorite time of year—no, she amended, Mardi Gras was. Her smile became less forced.

"You look like you're having the time of your life," Mark announced casually as he took the seat beside her.

"It is a nice party."

"So you enjoy observing the life-style of the rich and famous." The sarcastic edge to Mark's voice was less sharp than normal.

Taking a sip of punch, Jo Marie nodded. "Who wouldn't?"

"To be honest I'm surprised at how friendly everyone's been," Mark commented sheepishly. "Obviously no one suspects that you and I are two of the less privileged."

"Mark," she admonished sharply. "That's a rotten thing to say."

Her brother had the good grace to look ashamed. "To be truthful, Kelly introduced me to several of her friends and I must admit I couldn't find anything to dislike about them."

"Surprise, surprise." Jo Marie hummed the Christmas music softly to herself. "I suppose the next thing I know, you'll be playing golf with Kelly's father."

Mark snorted derisively. "Hardly."

"What have you got against the Beaumonts anyway? Kelly's a wonderful girl."

"Kelly's the exception," Mark argued and stiffened.

"But you just finished telling me that you liked several of her friends that you were introduced to tonight."

"Yes. Well, that was on short acquaintance."

Standing, Jo Marie set her empty punch glass aside. "I think you've got a problem, brother dearest."

A dark look crowded Mark's face, and his brow was furrowed with a curious frown. "You're right, I do." With an agitated movement he stood and made his way across the room.

Jo Marie mingled, talking with a few women who were planning a charity benefit after the first of the year. When they asked her opinion on an important point, Jo Marie was both surprised and pleased. Although she spent a good portion of the next hour with these older ladies, she drifted away as they moved toward the heart of the party. If Andrew had recognized her as the girl involved in the protest against the wetlands development, others might too. And she didn't want to do anything that would cause him and Kelly embarrassment.

Kelly, with her blue eyes sparkling like sapphires, rushed up to Jo Marie. "Here you are!" she exclaimed. "Drew and I have been looking for you."

"Is it time to leave?" Jo Marie was more than ready, uncomfortably aware that she could be recognized at any moment.

"No...no, we just wanted to be certain some handsome young man didn't cart you away."

"Me?" Jo Marie's soft laugh was filled with incredulity. Few men would pay much attention to her, especially since she'd gone out of her way to remain unobtrusively in the background.

"It's more of a possibility than you realize," Andrew spoke from behind her, his voice a gentle rasp against her ear. "You're very beautiful tonight."

"Don't blush, Jo Marie," Kelly teased. "You really are lovely and if you'd given anyone half a chance, they'd have told you so."

Mark joined them and murmured something to Kelly. As he did so, Andrew turned his head toward Jo Marie and spoke so that the other two couldn't hear him. "Only Florence Nightingale could be more beautiful."

A tingling sensation raced down Jo Marie's spine and she turned so their eyes could meet, surprised that he would say something like that to her with Kelly present. Silently, she pleaded with him not to make this any more difficult for her. Those enchanted moments they had shared were long past and best forgotten for both their sakes.

Jo Marie woke to the buzz of the alarm early the next morning. She sat on the side of the bed and raised her arms high above her head and yawned. The day promised to be a busy one. She was scheduled to work in the office that Saturday morning and then catch a bus to LFTF headquarters on the other side of the French Quarter. She was hoping to talk to Jim Rowden, the director and manager of the conservationists' group. Jim had asked for additional volunteers during the Christmas season. And after thoughtful consideration, Jo Marie decided to accept the challenge. Christmas was such a busy time of year that many of the other volunteers wanted time off.

The events of the previous night filled her mind.

Lowering her arms, Jo Marie beat back the unexpected rush of sadness that threatened to overcome her. Andrew hadn't understood any of the things she'd tried to tell him last night. Several times she found him watching her, his look brooding and thoughtful as if she'd displeased him. No matter where she went during the course of the evening, when she looked up she found Andrew studying her. Once their eyes had met and held and everyone between them had seemed to disappear. The music had faded and it was as if only the two of them existed in the party-filled crowd. Jo Marie had lowered her gaze first, frightened and angry with them both.

Andrew and Mark had been sullen on the drive home. Mark had left the apartment almost immediately and Jo Marie had fled to the privacy of her room, unwilling to witness Andrew kissing Kelly good-night. She couldn't have borne it.

Now, in the light of the new day, she discovered that her feelings for Andrew were growing stronger. She wanted to banish him to a special area of her life, long past. But he wouldn't allow that. It had been in his eyes last night as he studied her. Those moments at the Mardi Gras were not to be forgotten by either of them.

At least when she was at the office, she didn't have to think about Andrew or Kelly or Mark. The phone buzzed continually. And because they were short-staffed on the weekends, Jo Marie hardly had time to think about anything but airline fares, bus routes and train schedules the entire morning.

She replaced the telephone receiver after talking with the Costa Lines about booking a spring Caribbean cruise for a retired couple. Her head was bowed as she filled out the necessary forms. Jo Marie didn't hear Paula Shriver, the only other girl in the office on Saturday, move to her desk.

"Mr. Beaumont's been waiting to talk to you," Paula announced. "Lucky you," she added under her breath as Andrew took the seat beside Jo Marie's desk.

"Hello, Jo Marie."

"Andrew." Her hand clenched the ballpoint pen she was holding. "What can I do for you?"

He crossed his legs and draped an arm over the back of the chair giving the picture of a man completely at ease. "I was hoping you could give me some suggestions for an ideal honeymoon."

"Of course. What did you have in mind?" Inwardly she wanted to shout at him not to do this to her, but she forced herself to smile and look attentive. "What would you suggest?"

She lowered her gaze. "Kelly's mentioned Hawaii several times. I know that's the only place she'd enjoy visiting."

He dismissed her suggestion with a short shake of his head. "I've been there several times. I was hoping for something less touristy."

"Maybe a cruise then. There are several excellent lines operating in the Caribbean, the Mediterranean or perhaps the inside passage to Alaska along the Canadian west coast."

"No." Again he shook his head. "Where would *you* choose to go on a honeymoon?"

Jo Marie ignored his question, not wanting to answer him. "I have several brochures I can give you that could spark an idea. I'm confident that any one of these places would thrill Kelly." As she pulled out her bottom desk drawer, Jo Marie was acutely conscious of Andrew studying her. She'd tried to come across with a strict business attitude, but her defenses were crumbling.

Reluctantly, he accepted the brochures she gave him. "You didn't answer my question. Shall I ask it again?"

Slowly, Jo Marie shook her head. "I'm not sure I'd want to go anywhere," she explained simply. "Not on my honeymoon. Not when the most beautiful city in the world is at my doorstep. I'd want to spend that time alone with my husband. We could travel later." Briefly their eyes met and held for a long, breathless moment. "But I'm not Kelly, and she's the one you should consider while planning this trip."

Paula stood and turned the sign in the glass door, indicating that the office was no longer open. Andrew's gaze followed her movements. "You're closing."

Jo Marie's nod was filled with relief. She was uncomfortable with Andrew. Being this close to him was a test of her friendship to Kelly. And at this moment, Kelly was losing...they both were. "Yes. We're only open during the morning on Saturdays."

He stood and placed the pamphlets on the corner of her desk. "Then let's continue our discussion over lunch."

"Oh, no, really that isn't necessary. We'll be finished in a few minutes and Paula doesn't mind waiting."

"But I have several ideas I want to discuss with you and it could well be an hour or so."

"Perhaps you could return another day."

"Now is the more convenient time for me," he countered smoothly.

Everything within Jo Marie wanted to refuse. Surely he realized how difficult this was for her. He was well aware of her feelings and was deliberately ignoring them.

"Is it so difficult to accept anything from me, Jo Marie?" he asked softly. "Even lunch?"

"All right," she agreed ungraciously, angry with him and angrier with herself. "But only an hour. I've got things to do."

A half smile turned up one corner of his mouth. "As you wish," he said as he escorted her to his Mercedes.

Jo Marie was stiff and uncommunicative as Andrew drove through the thick traffic. He parked on a narrow street outside the French Quarter and came around to her side of the car to open the door for her.

"I have reservations at Chez Lorraine's."

"Chez Lorraine's?" Jo Marie's surprised gaze flew to him. The elegant French restaurant was one of New Orlean's most famous. The food was rumored to be exquisite, and expensive. Jo Marie had always dreamed of dining there, but never had.

"Is it as good as everyone says?" she asked, unable to disguise the excitement in her voice.

"You'll have to judge for yourself," he answered, smiling down on her.

Once inside, they were seated almost immediately and handed huge oblong menus featuring a wide variety of French cuisine. Not having sampled several of the more traditional French dishes, Jo Marie toyed with the idea of ordering the calf's sweetbread.

"What would you like?" Andrew prompted after several minutes.

"I don't know. It all sounds so good." Closing the menu she set it aside and lightly shook her head. "I think you may regret having brought me here when I'm so hungry." She'd skipped breakfast, and discovered now that she was famished.

Andrew didn't look up from his menu. "Where you're concerned, there's very little I regret." As if he'd made a casual comment about the weather, he continued. "Have you decided?"

"Yes...yes," she managed, fighting down the dizzying effect of his words. "I think I'll try the salmon, but I don't think I should try the French pronunciation."

"Don't worry, I'll order for you."

As if by intuition, the waiter reappeared when they were ready to place their order. "The lady would like *les mouilles à la crème de saumon fumé*, and I'll have the *le canard de rouen braise*."

With a nod of approval the red-jacketed waiter departed.

Self-consciously, Jo Marie smoothed out the linen napkin on her lap. "I'm impressed," she murmured, studying the old world French provincial decor of the room. "It's everything I thought it would be."

The meal was fabulous. After a few awkward moments Jo Marie was amazed that she could talk as freely to Andrew. She discovered he was a good listener and she enjoyed telling him about her family.

"So you were the only girl."

"It had its advantages. I play a mean game of touch football."

"I hope you'll play with me someday. I've always enjoyed a rousing game of touch football."

The fork was raised halfway to her mouth and Jo Marie paused, her heart beating double time. "I...I only play with my brothers."

Andrew chuckled. "Speaking of your family, I find it difficult to tell that you and Mark are related. Oh, I can see the family resemblance, but Mark's a serious young man. Does he ever laugh?"

Not lately, Jo Marie mused, but she didn't admit as much. "He works hard, long hours. Mark's come a long way through medical school." She hated making excuses for her brother. "He doesn't mean to be rude."

Andrew accepted the apology with a wry grin. "The chip on his shoulder's as big as a California redwood. What's he got against wealth and position?"

"I don't know," she answered honestly. "He teases Kelly unmercifully about her family. I think Kelly's money makes him feel insecure. There's no reason for it; Kelly's never done anything to give him that attitude. I never have understood it."

Pushing her clean plate aside, Jo Marie couldn't recall when she'd enjoyed a meal more—except the dinner they'd shared at K-Paul's the night Kelly and Andrew had announced their engagement. Some of the contentment faded from her eyes. Numbly, she folded her hands in her lap. Being here with Andrew, sharing this meal, laughing and talking with him wasn't right. Kelly should be the one sitting across the table from him. Jo Marie had no right to enjoy his company this way. Not when he was engaged to her best friend. Pointedly, she glanced at her watch.

"What's wrong?"

"Nothing." She shook her head slightly, avoiding his eyes, knowing his look had the ability to penetrate her soul.

"Would you care for some dessert?"

Placing her hand on her stomach, she declined with a smile. "I couldn't," she declared, but her gaze fell with regret on the large table display of delicate French pastries.

The waiter reappeared and a flurry of French flew over her head. Like everything else Andrew did, his French was flawless.

Almost immediately the waiter returned with a plate covered with samples of several desserts which he set in front of Jo Marie.

"Andrew," she objected, sighing his name, "I'll get fat."

"I saw you eyeing those goodies. Indulge. You deserve it."

"But I don't. I can't possibly eat all that."

"You can afford to put on a few pounds." His voice deepened as his gaze skimmed her lithe form.

"Are you suggesting I'm skinny?"

"My, my," he said, slowly shaking his head from side to side. "You do like to argue. Here, give me the plate. I'll be the one to indulge."

"Not on your life," she countered laughingly, and dipped her fork into the thin slice of chocolate cheesecake. After sampling three of the scrumptious desserts, Jo Marie pushed her plate aside. "Thank you, Andrew," she murmured as her fingers toyed with the starched, linen napkin. "I enjoyed the meal and...and the company, but we can't do this again." Her eyes were riveted to the tabletop.

"Jo Marie—"

"No. Let me finish," she interrupted on a rushed breath. "It...it would be so easy...to hurt Kelly and I won't do that. I can't. Please, don't make this so difficult for me." With every word her voice grew weaker and shakier. It shouldn't be this hard, her heart cried, but it was. Every womanly instinct was reaching out to him until she wanted to cry with it.

"Indulge me, Jo Marie," he said tenderly. "It's my birthday and there's no one else I'd rather share it with."

No one else...his words reverberated through her mind. They were on treacherous ground and Jo Marie felt herself sinking fast.

"Happy birthday," she whispered.

"Thank you."

They stood and Andrew cupped her elbow, leading her to the street.

"Would you like me to drop you off at the apartment?" Andrew asked several minutes later as they walked toward his parked car.

"No. I'm on my way to the LFTF headquarters." She stuck both hands deep within her sweater pockets.

"Land For The Future?"

She nodded. "They need extra volunteers during the Christmas season."

His wide brow knitted with a deep frown. "As I

recall, that building is in a bad part of town. Is it safe for you to—"

"Perfectly safe." She took a step in retreat. "Thank you again for lunch. I hope you have a wonderful birthday," she called just before turning and hurrying along the narrow sidewalk.

Jo Marie's pace was brisk as she kept one eye on the darkening sky. Angry gray thunderclouds were rolling in and a cloud burst was imminent. Everything looked as if it was against her. With the sky the color of Andrew's eyes, it seemed as though he was watching her every move. Fleetingly she wondered if she'd ever escape him...and worse, if she'd ever want to.

The LFTF headquarters were near the docks. Andrew's apprehensions were well founded. This was a high crime area. Jo Marie planned her arrival and departure times in daylight.

"Can I help you?" The stocky man with crisp ebony hair spoke from behind the desk. There was a speculative arch to his bushy brows as he regarded her.

"Hello." She extended her hand. "I'm Jo Marie Early. You're Jim Rowden, aren't you?" Jim had recently arrived from the Boston area and was taking over the manager's position of the nonprofit organization.

Jim stepped around the large oak desk. "Yes, I remember now. You marched in the demonstration, didn't you?"

"Yes, I was there."

"One of the few who stuck it out in the rain, as I recall."

"My brother insisted that it wasn't out of any sense of purpose, but from a pure streak of stubbornness." Laughter riddled her voice. "I'm back because you mentioned needing extra volunteers this month."

"Do you type?"

"Reasonably well. I'm a travel agent."

"Don't worry I won't give you a time test."

Jo Marie laughed. "I appreciate that more than you know."

The majority of the afternoon was spent typing personal replies to letters the group had received after the demonstration in front of Rose's. In addition, the group had been spurred on by their success, and was planning other campaigns for future projects. At four-thirty, Jo Marie slipped the cover over the typewriter and placed the letters on Jim's desk for his signature.

"If you could come three times a week," Jim asked, "it would be greatly appreciated."

She left forty minutes later feeling assured that she was doing the right thing by offering her time. Lending a hand at Christmas seemed such a small thing to do. Admittedly, her motives weren't pure. If she could keep herself occupied, she wouldn't have to deal with her feelings for Andrew.

A lot of her major Christmas shopping was completed, but on her way to the bus stop, Jo Marie stopped in at a used-book store. Although she fought it all afternoon, her thoughts had been continually on Andrew. Today was his special day and she desperately wanted to give him something that would relay her feelings. Her heart was filled with gratitude. Without him, she may never have known that sometimes dreams can come true and that fairy tales aren't always for the young.

She found the book she was seeking. A large leather-bound volume of the history of New Orleans. Few cities had a more romantic background. Included in the book were hundreds of rare photographs of the city's architecture, courtyards, patios, ironwork and cemeteries. He'd love the book as much as she. Jo Marie had come by for weeks, paying a little bit each pay day. Not only was this book rare, but extremely expensive. Because the proprietor knew Jo Marie, he had made special arrangements for her to have this volume. But Jo Marie couldn't think of anything else Andrew would cherish more. She wrote out a check for the balance and realized that she would probably be short on cash by the end of the month, but that seemed a small sacrifice.

Clenching the book to her breast, Jo Marie hurried home. She had not right to be giving Andrew gifts, but this was more for her sake than his. It was her thank you for all that he'd given her.

The torrential downpour assaulted the pavement just as Jo Marie stepped off the bus. Breathlessly, while holding the paper-wrapped leather volume to her stomach, she ran to the apartment and inserted her key into the dead bolt. Once again she had barely escaped a thorough drenching.

Hanging her Irish knit cardigan in the hall closet, Jo Marie kicked off her shoes and slid her feet into fuzzy, worn slippers.

Kelly should arrive any minute and Jo Marie rehearsed what she was going to say to Kelly. She had to have some kind of explanation to be giving her friend's fiancé a birthday present. Her thoughts came back empty as she paced the floor, wringing her hands. It was important that Kelly understand, but finding a plausible reason without revealing herself was difficult. Jo Marie didn't want any ill feelings between them.

When her roommate hadn't returned from the hospital by six, Jo Marie made herself a light meal and turned on the evening news. Kelly usually phoned if she was going to be late. Not having heard from her friend caused Jo Marie to wonder. Maybe Andrew had picked her up after work and had taken her out to dinner. It was, after all, his birthday; celebrating with his fiancé would only be natural. Unbidden, a surge of resentment rose within her and caused a lump of painful hoarseness to tighten her throat. Mentally she gave herself a hard shake. *Stop it,* her mind shouted. *You have no right to feel these things. Andrew belongs to Kelly, not you.*

A mixture of pain and confusion moved across her smooth brow when the doorbell chimed. It was probably Mark, but for the first time in recent memory, Jo Marie wasn't up to a sparring match with her older brother. Tonight she wanted to be left to her own thoughts.

But it wasn't Mark.

"Andrew." Quickly she lowered her gaze, praying he couldn't read her startled expression.

"Is Kelly ready?" he asked as he stepped inside the entryway. "We're having dinner with my mother."

"She isn't home from work yet. If you'd like I could call the hospital and see what's holding her up.'' So they were going out tonight. Jo Marie successfully managed to rein in her feelings of jealousy, having dealt with them earlier.

''No need, I'm early. If you don't mind, I'll just wait.''

''Please, sit down.'' Self-consciously she gestured toward the love seat. ''I'm sure Kelly will be here any minute.''

Impeccably dressed in a charcoal-gray suit that emphasized the width of his muscular shoulders, Andrew took a seat.

With her hands linked in front of her, Jo Marie fought for control of her hammering heart. ''Would you like a cup of coffee?''

''Please.''

Relieved to be out of the living room, Jo Marie hurried into the kitchen and brought down a cup and saucer. Spending part of the afternoon with Andrew was difficult enough. But being alone in the apartment with him was impossible. The tension between them was unbearable as it was. But to be separated by only a thin wall was much worse. She yearned to touch him. To hold him in her arms. To feel again, just this once, his mouth over hers. She had to know if what had happened all those months ago was real.

''Jo Marie,'' Andrew spoke softly from behind her.

Her pounding heart leaped to her throat. Had he read her thoughts and come to her? Her fingers dug unmercifully into the kitchen counter top. Nothing would induce her to turn around.

''What's this?'' he questioned softly.

A glance over her shoulder revealed Andrew holding the book she'd purchased earlier. Her hand shook as she poured the coffee. "It's a book about the early history of New Orleans. I found it in a used-book store and..." Her voice wobbled as badly as her hand.

"There was a card on top of it that was addressed to me."

Jo Marie set the glass coffeepot down. "Yes...I knew you'd love it and I wanted you to have it as a birthday present." She stopped just before admitting that she wanted him to remember her. "I also heard on the news tonight that...that Rose's Hotel is undergoing some expensive and badly needed repairs, thanks to you." Slowly she turned, keeping her hands behind her. "I realize there isn't anything that I could ever buy for you that you couldn't purchase a hundred times over. But I thought this book might be the one thing I could give you...." She let her voice fade in midsentence.

A slow faint smile touched his mouth as he opened the card and read her inscription. "To Andrew, in appreciation for everything." Respectfully he opened the book, then laid it aside. "Everything, Jo Marie?"

"For your generosity toward the hotel, and your thoughtfulness in giving me the party dress and..."

"The Mardi Gras?" He inched his way toward her.

Jo Marie could feel the color seep up her neck and tinge her cheeks. "Yes, that too." She wouldn't deny how speical those few moments had been to her. Nor could she deny the hunger in his hard gaze as he concentrated on her lips. Amazed, Jo Marie watched as Andrew's gray eyes darkened to the shade of a stormy Arctic sea.

No pretense existed between them now, only a shared hunger that could no longer be repressed. A surge of intense longing seared through her so that when Andrew drew her into his embrace she gave a small cry and went willingly.

"Haven't you ever wondered if what we shared that night was real?" he breathed the question into her hair.

"Yes, a thousand times since, I've wondered." She gloried in the feel of his muscular body pressing against the length of hers. Freely her hands roamed his back. His index finger under her chin lifted her face and her heart soared at the look in his eyes.

"Jo Marie," he whispered achingly and his thumb leisurely caressed the full curve of her mouth.

Her soft lips trembled in anticipation. Slowly, deliberately, Andrew lowered his head as his mouth sought hers. Her eyelids drifted closed and her arms reached up and clung to him. The kiss was one of hunger and demand as his mouth feasted on hers.

The feel of him, the touch, the taste of his lips filled her senses until Jo Marie felt his muscles strain as he brought her to him, riveting her soft form to him so tightly that she could no longer breathe. Not that she cared.

Gradually the kiss mellowed and the intensity eased until he buried his face in the gentle slope of her neck. "It was real," he whispered huskily. "Oh, my sweet Florence Nightingale, it was even better than I remembered."

"I was afraid it would be." Tears burned her eyes and she gave a sad little laugh. Life was filled with ironies and finding Andrew now was the most painful.

Tenderly he reached up and wiped the moisture from her face. "I shouldn't have let this happen."

"It wasn't your fault." Jo Marie felt she had to accept part of the blame. She'd wanted him to kiss her so badly. "I...I won't let it happen again." If one of them had to be strong, then it would be her. After years of friendship with Kelly she owed her roommate her loyalty.

Reluctantly they broke apart, but his hands rested on either side of her neck as though he couldn't bear to let her go completely. "Thank you for the book," he said in a raw voice. "I'll treasure it always."

The sound of the front door opening caused Jo Marie's eyes to widen with a rush of guilt. Kelly would take one look at her and realize what had happened. Hot color blazed in her cheeks.

"Jo Marie!" Kelly's eager voice vibrated through the apartment.

Andrew stepped out of the kitchen, granting Jo Marie precious seconds to compose herself.

"Oh, heavens, you're here already, Drew. I'm sorry I'm so late. But I've got so much to tell you."

With her hand covering her mouth to smother the sound of her tears, Jo Marie leaned against the kitchen counter, suddenly needing its support.

Chapter Five

"Are you all right?" Andrew stepped back into the kitchen and brushed his hand over his temples. He resembled a man driven to the end of his endurance, standing with one foot in heaven and the other in hell. His fingers were clenched at his side as if he couldn't decide if he should haul her back into his arms or leave her alone. But the tortured look in his eyes told Jo Marie how difficult it was not to hold and reassure her.

"I'm fine." Her voice was eggshell fragile. "Just leave. Please. I don't want Kelly to see me." Not like this, with tears streaming down her pale cheeks and her eyes full of confusion. Once glance at Jo Marie and the astute Kelly would know exactly what had happened.

"I'll get her out of here as soon as she changes clothes," Andrew whispered urgently, his stormy gray eyes pleading with hers. "I didn't mean for this to happen."

"I know." With an agitated brush of her hand she dismissed him. "Please, just go."

"I'll talk to you tomorrow."

"No." Dark emotion flickered across her face. She didn't want to see him. Everything about today had been wrong. She should have avoided Andrew, feeling as she did. But in some ways, Jo Marie realized that the kiss had been inevitable. Those brief magical moments at the Mardi Gras demanded an exploration of the sensation they'd shared. Both had hoped to dismiss that February night as whimsy—a result of the craziness of the season. Instead, they had discovered how real it had been. From now on, Jo Marie vowed, she would shun Andrew. Her only defense was to avoid him completely.

"I'm sorry to keep you waiting." Kelly's happy voice drifted in from the other room. "Do I look okay?"

"You're lovely as always."

Jo Marie hoped that Kelly wouldn't catch the detached note in Andrew's gruff voice.

"You'll never guess who I spent the last hour talking to."

"Perhaps you could tell me on the way to mother's?" Andrew responded dryly.

"Drew." Some of the enthusiasm drained from Kelly's happy voice. "Are you feeling ill? You're quite pale."

"I'm fine."

"Maybe we should cancel this dinner. Really, I wouldn't mind."

"There's no reason to disappoint my mother."

"Drew?" Kelly seemed hesitant.

"Are you ready?" His firm voice brooked no disagreement.

"But I wanted to talk to Jo Marie."

"You can call her after dinner," Andrew responded shortly, his voice fading as they moved toward the entryway.

The door clicked a minute later and Jo Marie's fingers loosened their death grip against the counter. Weakly, she wiped a hand over her face and eyes. Andrew and Kelly were engaged to be married. Tonight was his birthday and he was taking Kelly to dine with his family. And Jo Marie had been stealing a kiss from him in the kitchen. Self-reproach grew in her breast with every breath until she wanted to scream and lash out with it.

Maybe she could have justified her actions if Kelly hadn't been so excited and happy. Her roommate had come into the apartment bursting with enthusiasm for life, eager to see and talk to Andrew.

The evening seemed interminable and Jo Marie had a terrible time falling asleep, tossing and turning long past the time Kelly returned. Finally at the darkest part of the night, she flipped on the beside lamp and threw aside the blankets. Pouring herself a glass of milk, Jo Marie leaned against the kitchen counter and drank it with small sips, her thoughts deep and dark. She couldn't ask Kelly to forgive her for what had happened without hurting her roommate and perhaps ruining their friendship. The only person there was to confront and condemn was herself.

Once she returned to bed, Jo Marie lay on her back,

her head clasped in her hands. Moon shadows fluttered against the bare walls like the flickering scenes of a silent movie.

Unhappy beyond words, Jo Marie avoided her roommate, kept busy and occupied her time with other friends. But she was never at peace and always conscious that her thoughts never strayed from Kelly and Andrew. The episode with Andrew wouldn't happen again. She had to be strong.

Jo Marie didn't see her roommate until the following Monday morning. They met in the kitchen where Jo Marie was pouring herself a small glass of grapefruit juice.

"Morning." Jo Marie's stiff smile was only slightly forced.

"Howdy, stranger. I've missed you the past couple of days."

Jo Marie's hand tightened around the juice glass as she silently prayed Kelly wouldn't ask her about Saturday night. Her roommate must have known Jo Marie was in the apartment, otherwise Andrew wouldn't have been inside.

"I've missed you," Kelly continued. "It seems we hardly have time to talk anymore. And now that you're going to be doing volunteer work for the foundation, we'll have even less time together. You're spreading yourself too thin."

"There's always something going on this time of year." A chill seemed to settle around the area of Jo Marie's heart and she avoided her friend's look.

"I know, that's why I'm looking forward to this weekend and the party for Drew's company. By the way, he suggested that both of us stay the night on Saturday.''

"Spend the night?" Jo Marie repeated like a recording and inhaled a shaky breath. That was the last thing she wanted.

"It makes sense, don't you think? We can lay awake until dawn the way we used to and talk all night." A distant look came over Kelly as she buttered the hot toast and poured herself a cup of coffee. "Drew's going to have enough to worry about without dragging us back and forth. From what I understand, he goes all out for his company's Christmas party."

Hoping to hide her discomfort, Jo Marie rinsed out her glass and deposited it in the dishwasher, but a gnawing sensation attacked the pit of her stomach. Although she'd promised Kelly she would attend the lavish affair, she had to find a way of excusing herself without arousing suspicion. "I've been thinking about Andrew's party and honestly feel I shouldn't go—"

"Don't say it. You're going!" Kelly interrupted hastily. "There's no way I'd go without you. You're my best friend, Jo Marie Early, and as such I want you with me. Besides, you know how I hate these things.''

"But as Drew's wife you'll be expected to attend a lot of these functions. I won't always be around."

A secret smile stole over her friend's pert face. "I know, that's why it's so important that you're there now."

"You didn't seem to need me Friday night."

Round blue eyes flashed Jo Marie a look of disbelief. "Are you crazy? I would have been embarrassingly uncomfortable without you."

It seemed to Jo Marie that Mark had spent nearly as much time with Kelly as she had. In fact, her brother had spent most of the evening with Kelly at his side. It was Mark whom Kelly really wanted, not her. But convincing her roommate of that was a different matter. Jo Marie doubted that Kelly had even admitted as much to herself.

"I'll think about going," Jo Marie promised. "But I can't honestly see that my being there or not would do any good."

"You've got to come," Kelly muttered, looking around unhappily. "I'd be miserable meeting and talking to all those people on my own." Silently, Kelly's bottomless blue eyes pleaded with Jo Marie. "I promise never to ask anything from you again. Say you'll come. Oh, please, Jo Marie, do this one last thing for me."

An awkward silence stretched between them and a feeling of dread settled over Jo Marie. Kelly seemed so genuinely distraught that it wasn't in Jo Marie's heart to refuse her. As Kelly had pointedly reminded her, she was Kelly's best friend. "All right, all right," she agreed reluctantly. "But I don't like it."

"You won't be sorry, I promise." A mischievous gleam lightened Kelly's features.

Jo Marie mumbled disdainfully under her breath as she moved out of the kitchen. Pausing at the closet, she took her trusted cardigan from the hanger. "Say, Kell, don't forget this is the week I'm flying to Mazatlán." Jo Marie was scheduled to take a familiarization tour of the Mexican resort town. She'd be flying with ten other travel agents from the city and staying at the Riviera Del Sol's expense. The luxury hotel was sponsoring the group in hopes of having the agents book their facilities for their clients. Jo Marie usually took the "fam" tours only once or twice a year. This one had been planned months before and she mused that it couldn't have come at a better time. Escaping from Andrew and Kelly was just the thing she needed. By the time she returned, she prayed, her life could be back to normal.

"This is the week?" Kelly stuck her head around the kitchen doorway. "Already?"

"You can still drive me to the airport, can't you?"

"Sure," Kelly answered absently. "But if I can't, Drew will."

Jo Marie's heart throbbed painfully. "No," she returned forcefully.

"He doesn't mind."

But I do, Jo Marie's heart cried as she fumbled with the buttons of her sweater. If Kelly wasn't home when it came time to leave for the airport, she would either call Mark or take a cab.

"I'm sure Drew wouldn't mind," Kelly repeated.

"I'll be late tonight," she answered, ignoring her friend's offer. She couldn't understand why Kelly would want her to spend time with Andrew. But so many things didn't make sense lately. Without a backward glance, Jo Marie went out the front door.

Joining several others at the bus stop outside the apartment building en route to the office, Jo Marie fought down feelings of guilt. She'd honestly thought she could get out of attending the party with Kelly. But there was little to be done, short of offending her friend. These constant recriminations regarding Kelly and Andrew were disrupting her neatly ordered life, and Jo Marie hated it.

Two of the other girls were in the office by the time Jo Marie arrived.

"There's a message for you," Paula announced. "I think it was the same guy who stopped in Saturday morning. You know, I'm beginning to think you've been holding out on me. Where'd you ever meet a hunk like that?"

"He's engaged," she quipped, seeking a light tone.

"He is?" Paula rolled her office chair over to Jo Marie's desk and handed her the pink slip. "You could have fooled me. He looked on the prowl, if you want my opinion. In fact, he was eyeing you like a starving man looking at a cream puff."

"Paula!" Jo Marie tried to toss off her co-worker's observation with a forced laugh. "He's engaged to my roommate."

Paula lifted one shoulder in a half shrug and scooted the chair back to her desk. "If you say so." But both her tone and her look were disbelieving.

Jo Marie read the message, which listed Andrew's office number and asked that she call him at her earliest convenience. Crumbling up the pink slip, she tossed it in the green metal wastebasket beside her desk. She might be attending this party, but it was under duress. And as far as Andrew was concerned, she had every intention of avoiding him.

Rather than rush back to the apartment after work, Jo Marie had dinner in a small café near her office. From there she walked to the Land For The Future headquarters.

She was embarrassingly early when she arrived outside of the office door. The foundation's headquarters were on the second floor of an older brick building in a bad part of town. Jo Marie decided to arrive earlier than she'd planned rather than kill time by walking around outside. From the time she'd left the travel agency, she'd wandered around with little else to do. Her greatest fear was that Andrew would be waiting for her at the apartment. She hadn't returned his call and he'd want to know why.

Jim Rowden, the office manager and spokesman, was busy on the telephone when Jo Marie arrived. Quietly she slipped into the chair at the desk opposite him and glanced over the letters and other notices that needed to be typed. As she pulled the cover from the top of the typewriter, Jo Marie noticed a shadowy movement from the other side of the milky white glass inset of the office door.

She stood to investigate and found a dark-haired man with a worn felt hat that fit loosely on top of his head. His clothes were ragged and the faint odor of cheap wine permeated the air. He was curling up in the doorway of an office nearest theirs.

His eyes met hers briefly and he tugged his thin sweater around his shoulders. "Are you going to throw me out of here?" The words were issued in subtle challenge.

Jo Marie teetered with indecision. If she did tell him to leave he'd either spend the night shivering in the cold or find another open building. On the other hand if she were to give him money, she was confident it wouldn't be a bed he'd spend it on.

"Well?" he challenged again.

"I won't say anything," she answered finally. "Just go down to the end of the hall so no one else will find you."

He gave her a look of mild surprise, stood and gathered his coat before turning and ambling down the long hall in an uneven gait. Jo Marie waited until he was curled up in another doorway. It was difficult to see that he was there without looking for him. A soft smile of satisfaction stole across her face as she closed the door and returned to her desk.

Jim replaced the receiver and smiled a welcome at Jo Marie. "How'd you like to attend a lecture with me tonight?"

"I'd like it fine," she agreed eagerly.

Jim's lecture was to a group of concerned city businessmen. He relayed the facts about the dangers of thoughtless and haphazard land development. He presented his case in a simple, straightforward fashion without emotionalism or sensationalism. In addition, he confidently answered their questions, defining the difference between building for the future and preserving a link with the past. Jo Marie was impressed and from the looks on the faces of his audience, the businessmen had been equally affected.

"I'll walk you to the bus stop," Jim told her hours later after they'd returned from the meeting. "I don't like the idea of you waiting at the bus stop alone. I'll go with you."

Jo Marie hadn't been that thrilled with the prospect herself. "Thanks, I'd appreciate that."

Jim's hand cupped her elbow as they leisurely strolled down the narrow street, chatting as they went. Jim's voice was drawling and smooth and Jo Marie

mused that she could listen to him all night. The
lamplight illuminated little in the descending fog and
would have created an eerie feeling if Jim hadn't been
at her side. But walking with him, she barely noticed
the weather and instead found herself laughing at his
subtle humor.

"How'd you ever get into this business?" she queried. Jim Rowden was an intelligent, warm human
being who would be a success in any field he chose
to pursue. He could be making twice and three times
the money in the business world that he collected
from the foundation.

At first introduction, Jim wasn't the kind of man
who would bowl women over with his striking good
looks or his suave manners. But he was a rare, dedicated man of conscience. Jo Marie had never known
anyone like him and admired him greatly.

"I'm fairly new with the foundation," he admitted,
"and it certainly wasn't what I'd been expecting to
do with my life, especially since I struggled through
college for a degree in biology. Afterward I went to
work for the state, but this job gives me the opportunity to work first hand with saving some of the—
well, you heard my speech."

"Yes, I did, and it was wonderful."

"You're good for my ego, Jo Marie. I hope you'll
stick around."

Jo Marie's eyes glanced up the street, wondering
how long they'd have to wait for a bus. She didn't
want their discussion to end. As she did, a flash of
midnight blue captured her attention and her heart
dropped to her knees as the Mercedes pulled to a stop
alongside the curb in front of them.

Andrew practically leaped from the driver's side. "Just what do you think you're doing?" The harsh anger in his voice shocked her.

"I beg your pardon?" Jim answered on Jo Marie's behalf, taking a step forward.

Andrew ignored Jim, his eyes cold and piercing as he glanced over her. "I've spent the good part of an hour looking for you."

"Why?" Jo Marie demanded, tilting her chin in an act of defiance. "What business is it of yours where I am or who I'm with?"

"I'm making it my business."

"Is there a problem here, Jo Marie?" Jim questioned as he stepped forward.

"None whatsoever," she responded dryly and crossed her arms in front of her.

"Kelly's worried sick," Andrew hissed. "Now I suggest you get in the car and let me take you home before...." He let the rest of what he was saying die. He paused for several tense moments and exhaled a sharp breath. "I apologize, I had no right to come at you like that." He closed the car door and moved around the front of the Mercedes. "I'm Andrew Beaumont," he introduced himself and extended his hand to Jim.

"From Delta Development?" Jim's eyes widened appreciatively. "Jim Rowden. I've been wanting to meet you so that I could thank you personally for what you did for Rose's Hotel."

"I'm pleased I could help."

When Andrew decided to put on the charm it was like falling into a jar of pure honey, Jo Marie thought. She didn't know of a man, woman or child who couldn't be swayed by his beguiling showmanship. Having been under his spell in the past made it all the more recognizable now. But somehow, she realized, this was different. Andrew hadn't been acting the night of the Mardi Gras, she was convinced of that.

"Jo Marie was late coming home and luckily I remembered her saying something about volunteering for the foundation. Kelly asked that I come and get her. We were understandably worried about her taking the bus alone at this time of night."

"I'll admit I was a bit concerned myself," Jim returned, taking a step closer to Jo Marie. "That's why I'm here."

As Andrew opened the passenger's side of the car, Jo Marie turned her head to meet his gaze, her eyes fiery as she slid into the plush velvet seat.

"I'll see you Friday," she said to Jim.

"Enjoy Mexico," he responded and waved before turning and walking back toward the office building. A fine mist filled the evening air and Jim pulled up his collar as he hurried along the sidewalk.

Andrew didn't say a word as he turned the key in the ignition, checked the rearview mirror and pulled back onto the street.

"You didn't return my call." He stopped at a red light and the full force of his magnetic gray eyes was turned on her.

"No," she answered in a whisper, struggling not to reveal how easily he could affect her.

"Can't you see how important it is that we talk?"

"No." She wanted to shout the word. When their eyes met, Jo Marie was startled to find that only a few inches separated them. Andrew's look was centered on her mouth and with a determined effort she averted her gaze and stared out the side window. "I don't want to talk to you." Her fingers fumbled with the clasp of her purse in nervous agitation. "There's nothing more we can say." She hated the husky emotion-filled way her voice sounded.

"Jo Marie." He said her name so softly that she wasn't entirely sure he'd spoken.

She turned back to him, knowing she should pull away from the hypnotic darkness of his eyes, but doing so was impossible.

"You'll come to my party?"

She wanted to explain her decision to attend—she hadn't wanted to go—but one glance at Andrew said that he understood. Words were unnecessary.

"It's going to be difficult for us both for a while."

He seemed to imply things would grow easier with time. Jo Marie sincerely doubted that they ever would.

"You'll come?" he prompted softly.

Slowly she nodded. Jo Marie hadn't realized how tense she was until she exhaled and felt some of the coiled tightness leave her body. "Yes, I'll...be at the party." Her breathy stammer spoke volumes.

"And wear the dress I gave you?"

She ended up nodding again, her tongue unable to form words.

"I've dreamed of you walking into my arms wearing that dress," he added on a husky tremor, then shook his head as if he regretted having spoken.

Being alone with him in the close confines of the car was torture. Her once restless fingers lay limp in her lap. Jo Marie didn't know how she was going to avoid Andrew when Kelly seemed to be constantly throwing them together. But she must for her own peace of mind…she must.

All too quickly the brief respite of her trip to Mazatlán was over. Saturday arrived and Kelly and Jo Marie were brought to Andrew's home, which was a faithful reproduction of an antebellum mansion.

The dress he'd purchased was hanging in the closet of the bedroom she was to share with Kelly. Her friend threw herself across the canopy bed and exhaled on a happy sigh.

"Isn't this place something?"

Jo Marie didn't answer for a moment, her gaze falling on the dress that hung alone in the closet. "It's magnificent." There was little else that would describe this palace. The house was a three-story structure with huge white pillars and dark shutters. It faced the Mississippi River and had a huge garden in the back. Jo Marie learned that it was his mother who took an avid interest in the wide variety of flowers that grew in abundance there.

The rooms were large, their walls adorned with paintings and works of art. If Jo Marie was ever to doubt Andrew's wealth and position, his home would prove to be a constant reminder.

"Drew built it himself," Kelly explained with a proud lilt to her voice. "I don't mean he pounded in every nail, but he was here every day while it was being constructed. It took months."

"I can imagine." And no expense had been spared from the look of things.

"I suppose we should think about getting ready," Kelly continued. "I don't mind telling you that I've had a queasy stomach all day dreading this thing."

Kelly had! Jo Marie nearly laughed aloud. This party had haunted her all week. Even Mazatlán hadn't been far enough away to dispel the feeling of dread.

Jo Marie could hear the music drifting in from the reception hall by the time she had put on the finishing touches of her makeup. Kelly had already joined Andrew. A quick survey in the full-length mirror assured her that the beautiful gown was the most elegant thing she would ever own. The reflection that came back to her of a tall, regal woman was barely recognizable as herself. The dark crown of curls was styled on top of her head with a few stray tendrils curling about her ears. A lone strand of pearls graced her neck.

Self-consciously she moved from the room, closing the door. From the top of the winding stairway, she looked down on a milling crowd of arriving guests. Holding in her breath, she placed her gloved hand on the polished bannister, exhaled, and made her descent. Keeping her eyes on her feet for fear of tripping, Jo Marie was surprised when she glanced down to find Andrew waiting for her at the bottom of the staircase.

As he gave her his hand, their eyes met and held in a tender exchange. "You're beautiful."

The deep husky tone in his voice took her breath away and Jo Marie could do nothing more than smile in return.

Taking her hand, Andrew tucked it securely in the crook of his elbow and led her into the room where the other guests were mingling. Everyone was meeting for drinks in the huge living room and once the party was complete they would be moving up to the ballroom on the third floor. The evening was to culminate in a midnight buffet.

With Andrew holding her close by his side, Jo Marie had little option but to follow where he led. Moving from one end of the room to the other, he introduced her to so many people that her head swam trying to remember their names. Fortunately, Kelly and Andrew's engagement hadn't been officially announced and Jo Marie wasn't forced to make repeated explanations. Nonetheless, she was uncomfortable with the way he was linking the two of them together.

"Where's Kelly?" Jo Marie asked under her breath. "She should be the one with you. Not me."

"Kelly's with Mark on the other side of the room."

Jo Marie faltered in midstep and Andrew's hold tightened as he dropped his arm and slipped it around her slim waist. "With Mark?" She couldn't imagine her brother attending this party. Not feeling the way he did about Andrew.

Not until they were upstairs and the music was playing did Jo Marie have an opportunity to talk to her brother. He was sitting against the wall in a high-backed mahogany chair with a velvet cushion. Kelly was at his side. Jo Marie couldn't recall a time she'd seen her brother dress so formally or look more handsome. He'd had his hair trimmed and was clean shaven. She'd never dreamed she'd see Mark in a tuxedo.

"Hello, Mark."

Her brother looked up, guilt etched on his face. "Jo Marie." Briefly he exchanged looks with Kelly and stood, offering Jo Marie his seat.

"Thanks," she said as she sat and slipped the high-heeled sandals from her toes. "My feet could use a few moments' rest."

"You certainly haven't lacked for partners," Kelly observed happily. "You're a hit, Jo Marie. Even Mark was saying he couldn't believe you were his sister."

"I've never seen you look more attractive," Mark added. "But then I bet you didn't buy that dress out of petty cash either."

If there was a note of censure in her brother's voice, Jo Marie didn't hear it. "No." Absently her hand smoothed the silk skirt. "It was a gift from Andrew...and Kelly." Hastily she added her roommate's name. "I must admit though, I'm surprised to see you here."

"Andrew extended the invitation personally," Mark replied, holding his back ramrod stiff as he stared straight ahead.

Not understanding, Jo Marie glanced at her roommate. "Mark came for me," Kelly explained, her voice soft and vulnerable. "Because I...because I wanted him here."

"We're both here for you, Kelly," Jo Marie reminded her and punctuated her comment by arching her brows.

"I know, and I love you both for it."

"Would you care to dance?" Mark held out his hand to Kelly, taking her into his arms when they reached the boundary of the dance floor as if he never wanted to let her go.

Confused, Jo Marie watched their progress. Kelly was engaged to be married to Andrew, yet she was gazing into Mark's eyes as if he were her knight in shining armor who had come to slay dragons on her behalf. When she'd come upon them, they'd acted as if she had intruded on their very private party.

Jo Marie saw Andrew approach her, his brows lowered as if something had displeased him. His strides were quick and decisive as he wove his way through the throng of guests.

"I've been looking for you. In fact, I was beginning to wonder if I'd ever get a chance to dance with you." The pitch of his voice suggested that she'd been deliberately avoiding him. And she had.

Jo Marie couldn't bring herself to meet his gaze, afraid of what he could read in her eyes. All night she'd been pretending it was Andrew who was holding her and yet she'd known she wouldn't be satisfied until he did.

"I believe this dance is mine," he said, presenting her with his hand.

Peering up at him, a smile came and she paused to slip the strap of her high heel over her ankle before standing.

Once on the dance floor, his arms tightened around her waist, bringing her so close that there wasn't a hair's space between them. He held her securely as if challenging her to move. Jo Marie discovered that she couldn't. This inexplicable feeling was beyond argument. With her hands resting on his muscular shoulders, she leaned her head against his broad chest and sighed her contentment.

She spoke first. "It's a wonderful party."

"You're more comfortable now, aren't you?" His fingers moved up and down her back in a leisurely exercise, drugging her with his firm caress against her bare skin.

"What do you mean?" She wasn't sure she understood his question and slowly lifted her gaze.

"Last week, you stayed on the outskirts of the crowd afraid of joining in or being yourself."

"Last week I was terrified that someone would recognize me as the one who had once demonstrated against you. I didn't want to do anything that would embarrass you," she explained dryly. Her cheek was pressed against his starched shirt and she thrilled to the uneven thump of his heart.

"And this week?"

"Tonight anyone who looked at us would know that we've long since resolved our differences."

She sensed more than felt Andrew's soft touch. The moment was quickly becoming too intimate. Using her hands for leverage, Jo Marie straightened, creating a space between them. "Does it bother you to have my brother dance with Kelly?"

Andrew looked back at her blankly. "No. Should it?"

"She's your fiancée." To the best of Jo Marie's knowledge, Andrew hadn't said more than a few words to Kelly all evening.

A cloud of emotion darkened his face. "She's wearing my ring."

"And...and you care for her."

Andrew's hold tightened painfully around her waist. "Yes, I care for Kelly. We've always been close." His eyes darkened to the color of burnt silver. "Perhaps too close."

The applause was polite when the dance number finished.

Jo Marie couldn't escape fast enough. She made an excuse and headed for the powder room. Andrew wasn't pleased and it showed in the grim set of his mouth, but he didn't try to stop her. Things weren't right. Mark shouldn't be sitting like an avenging angel at Kelly's side and Andrew should at least show some sign of jealousy.

When she returned to the ballroom, Andrew was busy and Jo Marie decided to sort through her thoughts in the fresh night air. A curtained glass door that led to the balcony was open, and unnoticed she slipped silently into the dark. A flash of white captured her attention and Jo Marie realized she wasn't alone. Inadvertently, she had invaded the private world of two young lovers. With their arms wrapped around each other they were locked in a passionate embrace. Smiling softly to herself, she turned to escape as silently as she'd come. But something stopped her. A sickening knot tightened her stomach.

The couple so passionately embracing were Kelly and Mark.

Chapter Six

Jo Marie woke just as dawn broke over a cloudless horizon. Standing at the bedroom window, she pressed her palms against the sill and surveyed the beauty of the landscape before her. Turning, she glanced at Kelly's sleeping figure. Her hands fell limply to her side as her face darkened with uncertainty. Last night while they'd prepared for bed, Jo Marie had been determined to confront her friend with the kiss she'd unintentionally witnessed. But when they'd turned out the lights, Kelly had chatted happily about the success of the party and what a good time she'd had. And Jo Marie had lost her nerve. What Mark and Kelly did wasn't any of her business, she mused. In addition, she had no right to judge her brother and her friend when she and Andrew had done the same thing.

The memory of Andrew's kiss produce a breathlessness, and surrendering to the feeling, Jo Marie closed her eyes. The infinitely sweet touch of his mouth seemed to have branded her. Her fingers shook as she raised them to the gentle curve of her lips. Jo Marie doubted that she would ever feel the same overpowering rush of sensation at another man's touch. Andrew was special, her dream man. Whole lifetimes could pass and she'd never find anyone she'd love more. The powerful ache in her heart drove her to the closet where a change of clothes were hanging.

Dawn's light was creeping up the stairs, awaking a sleeping world, when Jo Marie softly clicked the bedroom door closed. Her overnight bag was clenched tightly in her hand. She hated to sneak out, but the thought of facing everyone over the breakfast table was more than she could bear. Andrew and Kelly needed to be alone. Time together was something they hadn't had much of lately. This morning would be the perfect opportunity for them to sit down and discuss their coming marriage. Jo Marie would only be an intruder.

Moving so softly that no one was likely to hear her, Jo Marie crept down the stairs to the wide entry hall. She was tiptoeing toward the front door when a voice behind her interrupted her quiet departure.

"What do you think you're doing?"

Releasing a tiny, startled cry, Jo Marie dropped the suitcase and held her hand to her breast.

"Andrew, you've frightened me to death."

"Just what are you up to?"

"I'm...I'm leaving."

"That's fairly easy to ascertain. What I want to

know is why." His angry gaze locked with hers, refusing to allow her to turn away.

"I thought you and Kelly should spend some time together and...and I wanted to be gone this morning before everyone woke." Regret crept into her voice. Maybe sneaking out like this wasn't such a fabulous idea, after all.

He stared at her in the dim light as if he could examine her soul with his penetrating gaze. When he spoke again, his tone was lighter. "And just how did you expect to get to town. Walk?"

"Exactly."

"But it's miles."

"All the more reason to get an early start," she reasoned.

Andrew studied her as though he couldn't believe what he was hearing. "Is running away so important that you would sneak out of here like a cat burglar and not tell anyone where you're headed?"

How quickly her plan had backfired. By trying to leave unobtrusively she'd only managed to offend Andrew when she had every reason to thank him. "I didn't mean to be rude, although I can see now that I have been. I suppose this makes me look like an ungrateful house guest."

His answer was to narrow his eyes fractionally.

"I want you to know I left a note that explained where I was going to both you and Kelly. It's on the nightstand."

"And what did you say?"

"That I enjoyed the party immensely and that I've never felt more beautiful in any dress."

A brief troubled look stole over Andrew's face.

"Once," he murmured absently. "Only onece have you been more lovely." There was an unexpectedly gentle quality to his voice.

Her eyelashes fluttered closed. Andrew was reminding her of that February night. He too hadn't been able to forget the Mardi Gras. After all this time, after everything that had transpired since, neither of them could forget. The spell was as potent today as it had been those many months ago.

"Is that coffee I smell?" The question sought an invitation to linger with Andrew. Her original intent had been to escape so that Kelly could have the opportunity to spend this time alone with him. Instead, Jo Marie was seeking it herself. To sit in the early light of dawn and savor a few solitary minutes alone with Andrew was too tempting to ignore.

"Come and I'll get you a cup." Andrew led her toward the back of the house and his den. The room held a faint scent of leather and tobacco that mingled with the aroma of musk and spice.

Three walls were lined with leather-bound books that reached from the floor to the ceiling. Two wing chairs were angled in front of a large fireplace.

"Go ahead and sit down. I'll be back in a moment with the coffee."

A contented smile brightened Jo Marie's eyes as she sat and noticed the leather volume she'd given him lying open on the ottoman. Apparently he'd been reading it when he heard the noise at the front of the house and had left to investigate.

Andrew returned and carefully handed her the steaming earthenware mug. His eyes followed her gaze which rested on the open book. "I've been reading it. This is a wonderful book. Where did you ever find something like this?''

''I've known about it for a long time, but there were only a few volumes available. I located this one about three months ago in a used-book store.''

''It's very special to me because of the woman who bought it for me.''

''No.'' Jo Marie's eyes widened as she lightly tossed her head from side to side. ''Don't let that be the reason. Appreciate the book for all the interesting details it gives of New Orleans' colorful past. Or admire the pictures of the city architects' skill. But don't treasure it because of me.''

Andrew looked for a moment as if he wanted to argue, but she spoke again.

''When you read this book ten, maybe twenty, years from now, I'll only be someone who briefly passed through your life. I imagine you'll have trouble remembering what I looked like.''

''You'll never be anyone who flits in and out of my life.''

He said it with such intensity that Jo Marie's fingers tightened around the thick handle of the mug. ''All right,'' she agreed with a shaky laugh. ''I'll admit I barged into your peaceful existence long before Kelly introduced us but—''

''But,'' Andrew interrupted on a short laugh, ''it seems we were destined to meet. Do you honestly believe that either of us will ever forget that night?'' A faint smile touched his eyes as he regarded her steadily.

Jo Marie knew that she never would. Andrew was her dream man. It had been far more than mere fate that had brought them together, something almost spiritual.

"No," she answered softly. "I'll never forget."

Regret moved across his features, creasing his wide brow and pinching his mouth. "Nor will I forget," he murmured in a husky voice that sounded very much like a vow.

The air between them was electric. For months she'd thought of Andrew as the dream man. But coming to know him these past weeks had proven that he wasn't an apparition, but real. Human, vulnerable, proud, intelligent, generous—and everything that she had ever hoped to find in a man. She lowered her gaze and studied the dark depths of the steaming coffee. Andrew might be everything she had ever wanted in a man, but Kelly wore his ring and her roommate's stake on him was far more tangible than her own romantic dreams.

Taking an exaggerated drink of her coffee, Jo Marie carefully set aside the rose-colored mug and stood. "I really should be leaving."

"Please stay," Andrew requested. "Just sit with me a few minutes longer. It's been in this room that I've sat and thought about you so often. I'd always hoped that someday you would join me here."

Jo Marie dipped her head, her heart singing with the beauty of his words. She'd fantasized about him too. Since their meeting, her mind had conjured up his image so often that it wouldn't hurt to steal a few more moments of innocent happiness. Kelly would have him for a lifetime. Jo Marie had only today.

"I'll stay," she agreed and her voice throbbed with the excited beat of her heart.

"And when the times comes, I'll drive you back to the city."

She nodded her acceptance and finished her coffee. "It's so peaceful in here. It feels like all I need to do is lean my head back, close my eyes and I'll be asleep."

"Go ahead," he urged in a whispered tone.

A smile touched her radiant features. She didn't want to fall asleep and miss these precious moments alone with him. "No." She shook her head. "Tell me about yourself. I want to know everything."

His returning smile was wry. "I'd hate to bore you."

"Bore me!" Her small laugh was incredulous. "There's no chance of that."

"All right, but lay back and close your eyes and let me start by telling you that I had a good childhood with parents who deeply loved each other."

As he requested, Jo Marie rested her head against the cushion and closed her eyes. "My parents are wonderful too."

"But being raised in an ideal family has its drawbacks," Andrew continued in a low, soothing voice. "When it came time for me to think about a wife and starting a family there was always a fear in the back of my mind that I would never find the happiness my parents shared. My father wasn't an easy man to love. And I won't be either."

In her mind, Jo Marie took exception to that, but she said nothing. The room was warm, and slipping off her shoes, she tucked her nylon-covered feet under her. Andrew continued speaking, his voice droning on as she tilted her head back.

"When I reached thirty without finding a wife, I became skeptical about the women I was meeting. There were some who never saw past the dollar signs and others who were interested only in themselves. I wanted a woman who could be soft and yielding, but one who wasn't afraid to fight for what she believes, even if it meant standing up against tough opposition. I wanted someone who would share my joys and divide my worries. A woman as beautiful on the inside as any outward beauty she may possess."

"Kelly's like that." The words nearly stuck in Jo Marie's throat. Kelly was everything Andrew was describing and more. As painful as it was to admit, Jo Marie understood why Andrew had asked her roommate to marry him. In addition to her fine personal qualities, Kelly had money of her own and Andrew need never think that she was marrying him for any financial gains.

"Yes, Kelly's like that." There was a doleful timbre to his voice that caused Jo Marie to open her eyes.

Fleetingly she wondered if Andrew had seen Mark and Kelly kissing on the terrace last night. If he had created the picture of a perfect woman in his mind, then finding Kelly in Mark's arms could destroy him. No matter how uncomfortable it became, Jo Marie realized she was going to have to confront Mark about his behavior. Having thoughtfully analyzed the situation, Jo Marie believed it would be far better for her to talk to her brother. She could speak more freely with him. It may be the hardest thing she'd ever do, but after listening to Andrew, Jo Marie realized that she must talk to Mark. The happiness of too many people was at stake.

Deciding to change the subject, Jo Marie shifted her position in the supple leather chair and looked to Andrew. "Kelly told me that you built the house yourself."

Grim amusement was carved in his features. "Yes, the work began on it this spring."

"Then you've only been living in it a few months?"

"Yes. The construction on the house kept me from going insane." He held her look, revealing nothing of his thoughts.

"Going insane?" Jo Marie didn't understand.

"You see, for a short time last February, only a matter of moments really, I felt my search for the right woman was over. And in those few, scant moments I thought I had met that special someone I could love for all time."

Jo Marie's heart was pounding so fast and loud that she wondered why it didn't burst right out of her chest. The thickening in her throat made swallowing painful. Each breath became labored as she turned her face away, unable to meet Andrew's gaze.

"But after those few minutes, I lost her," Andrew continued. "Ironically, I'd searched a lifetime for that special woman, and within a matter of minutes, she was gone. God knows I tried to find her again. For a month I went back to the spot where I'd last seen her and waited. When it seemed that all was lost I discovered I couldn't get the memory of her out of my mind. I even hired a detective to find her for me. For months he checked every hospital in the city, searching for her. But you see, at the time I thought she was a nurse."

Jo Marie felt moisture gathering in the corner of her eyes. Never had she believed that Andrew had looked for her to the extent that he hired someone.

"For a time I was convinced I was going insane. This woman, whose name I didn't even know, filled my every waking moment and haunted my sleep. Building the house was something I've always wanted to do. It helped fill the time until I could find her again. Every room was constructed with her in mind."

Andrew was explaining that he'd built the house for her. Jo Marie had thought she'd be uncomfortable in such a magnificent home. But she'd immediately felt the welcome in the walls. Little had she dreamed the reason why.

"Sometimes," Jo Marie began awkwardly, "people build things up in their minds and when they're confronted with reality they're inevitably disappointed." Andrew was making her out to be wearing angel's wings. So much time had passed that he no longer saw her as flesh and bone, but a wonderful fantasy his mind had created.

"Not this time," he countered smoothly.

"I wondered where I'd find the two of you." A sleepy-eyed Kelly stood poised in the doorway of the den. There wasn't any censure in her voice, only her usual morning brightness. "Isn't it a marvelous morning? The sun's up and there's a bright new day just waiting for us."

Self-consciously, Jo Marie unwound her feet from beneath her and reached for her shoes. "What time is it?"

"A quarter to eight." Andrew supplied the information.

Jo Marie was amazed to realize that she'd spent the better part of two hours talking to him. But it would be time she'd treasure all her life.

"If you have no objections," Kelly murmured and paused to take a wide yawn, "I thought I'd go to the hospital this morning. There's a special...patient I'd like to stop in and visit."

A patient or Mark, Jo Marie wanted to ask. Her brother had mentioned last night that he was going to be on duty in the morning. Jo Marie turned to Andrew, waiting for a reaction from him. Surely he would say or do something to stop her. Kelly was his fiancée and both of them seemed to be regarding their commitment to each other lightly.

"No problem." Andrew spoke at last. "In fact I thought I'd go into the city myself this morning. It is a beautiful day and there's no better way to spend a portion of it than in the most beautiful city in the world. You don't mind if I tag along with you, do you, Jo Marie?"

Half of her wanted to cry out in exaltation. If there was anything she wished to give of herself to Andrew it was her love of New Orleans. But at the same time she wanted to shake both Andrew and Kelly for the careless attitude they had toward their relationship.

"I'd like you to come." Jo Marie spoke finally, answering Andrew.

It didn't take Kelly more than a few moments to pack her things and be ready to leave. In her rush, she'd obviously missed the two sealed envelopes Jo Marie had left propped against the lamp on Kelly's nightstand. Or if she had discovered them, Kelly chose not to mention it. Not that it mattered, Jo Marie decided as Andrew started the car. But Kelly's actions revealed what a rush she was in to see Mark. If it was Mark that she was indeed seeing. Confused emotions flooded Jo Marie's face, pinching lines around her nose and mouth. She could feel Andrew's caressing gaze as they drove toward the hospital.

"Is something troubling you?" Andrew questioned after they'd dropped Kelly off in front of Tulane Hospital. Amid protests from Jo Marie, Kelly had assured them that she would find her own way home. Standing on the sidewalk, she'd given Jo Marie a happy wave, before turning and walking toward the double glass doors that led to the lobby of the hospital.

"I think Kelly's going to see Mark," Jo Marie ventured in a short, rueful voice.

"I think she is too."

Jo Marie sat up sharply. "And that doesn't bother you?"

"Should it?" Andrew gave her a bemused look.

"Yes," she said and nodded emphatically. She would never have believed that Andrew could be so blind. "Yes, it should make you furious."

He turned and smiled briefly. "But it doesn't. Now tell me where you'd like to eat breakfast. Brennan's?"

Jo Marie felt trapped in a labyrinth in which no route made sense and from which she could see no escape. She was thoroughly confused by the actions of the three people she loved.

"I don't understand any of this," she cried in frustration. "You should be livid that Kelly and Mark are together."

A furrow of absent concentration darkened Andrew's brow as he drove. Briefly he glanced in her direction. "The time will come when you do understand," he explained cryptically.

Rubbing the side of her neck in agitation, Jo Marie studied Andrew as he drove. His answer made no sense, but little about anyone's behavior this last month had made sense. She hadn't pictured herself as being obtuse, but obviously she was.

Breakfast at Brennan's was a treat known throughout the south. The restaurant was built in the classic Vieux Carre style complete with courtyard. Because they didn't have a reservation, they were put on a waiting list and told it would be another hour before there would be a table available. Andrew eyed Jo Marie, who nodded eagerly. For all she'd heard, the breakfast was worth the wait.

Taking her hand in his, they strolled down the quiet streets that comprised the French Quarter. Most of the stores were closed, the streets deserted.

"I was reading just this morning that the French established New Orleans in 1718. The Spanish took over the 3,000 French inhabitants in 1762, although there were so few Spaniards that barely anyone noticed until 1768. The French Quarter is like a city within a city."

Jo Marie smiled contentedly and looped her hand through his arm. "You mean to tell me that it takes a birthday present for you to know about your own fair city?"

Andrew chuckled and drew her closer by circling

his arm around her shoulders. "Are you always snobbish or is this act for my benefit?"

They strolled for what seemed far longer than a mere hour, visiting Jackson Square and feeding the pigeons. Strolling back, with Andrew at her side, Jo Marie felt she would never be closer to heaven. Never would she want for anything more than today, this minute, with this man. Jo Marie felt tears mist her dusty eyes. A tremulous smile touched her mouth. Andrew was here with her. Within a short time he would be married to Kelly and she must accept that, but for now, he was hers.

The meal was everything they'd been promised. Ham, soft breads fresh from the bakery, eggs and a fabulous chicory coffee. A couple of times Jo Marie found herself glancing at Andrew. His expression revealed little and she wondered if he regretted having decided to spend this time with her. She prayed that wasn't the case.

When they stood to leave, Andrew reached for her hand and smiled down on her with shining gray eyes.

Jo Marie's heart throbbed with love. The radiant light of her happiness shone through when Andrew's arm slipped naturally around her shoulder as if branding her with his seal of protection.

"I enjoy being with you," he said and she couldn't doubt the sincerity in his voice. "You're the kind of woman who would be as much at ease at a formal ball as you would fishing from the riverside with rolled-up jeans."

"I'm not Huck Finn," she teased.

"No," he smiled, joining in her game. "Just my

Florence Nightingale, the woman who has haunted me for the last nine months.''

Self-consciously, Jo Marie eased the strap of her leather purse over her shoulder. ''It's always been my belief that dreams have a way of fading, especially when faced with the bright light of the sun and reality.''

''Normally, I'd agree with you,'' Andrew responded thoughtfully, ''but not this time. There are moments so rare in one's life that recognizing what they are can sometimes be doubted. Of you, of that night, of us, I have no doubts.''

''None?'' Jo Marie barely recognized her own voice.

''None,'' he confirmed.

If that were so, then why did Kelly continue to wear his ring? How could he look at her with so much emotion and then ask another woman to share his life?

The ride to Jo Marie's apartment was accomplished in a companionable silence. Andrew pulled into the parking space and turned off the ignition. Jo Marie's gaze centered on the dashboard. Silently she'd hoped that he wouldn't come inside with her. The atmosphere when they were alone was volatile. And with everything that Andrew had told her this morning, Jo Marie doubted that she'd have the strength to stay out of his arms if he reached for her.

''I can see myself inside.'' Gallantly, she made an effort to avoid temptation.

''Nonsense,'' Andrew returned, and opening the car door, he removed her overnight case from the back seat.

Jo Marie opened her side and climbed out, not waiting for him to come around. A feeling of doom settled around her heart.

Her hand was steady as she inserted the key into the apartment lock, but that was the only thing that was. Her knees felt like rubber as the door swung open and she stepped inside the room, standing in the entryway. The drapes were pulled, blocking out the sunlight, making the apartment's surroundings all the more intimate.

"I have so much to thank you for," she began and nervously tugged a strand of dark hair behind her ear. "A simple thank you seems like so little." She hoped Andrew understood that she didn't want him to come any farther into the apartment.

The door clicked closed and her heart sank. "Where would you like me to put your suitcase?"

Determined not to make this situation any worse for them, Jo Marie didn't move. "Just leave it here."

A smoldering light of amused anger burned in his eyes as he set the suitcase down. "There's no help for this," he whispered as his hand slid slowly, almost unwillingly along the back of her waist. "Be angry with me later."

Any protests died the moment his mouth met hers in a demanding kiss. An immediate answering hunger seared through her veins, melting all resistance until she was molded against the solid wall of his chest. His caressing fingers explored the curve of her neck and shoulders and his mouth followed, blazing a trail that led back to her waiting lips.

Jo Marie rotated her head, giving him access to any part of her face that his hungry mouth desired. She offered no protest when his hands sought the fullness of her breast, then sighed with the way her body responded to the gentleness of his fingers. He kissed her expertly, his mobile mouth moving insistently over hers, teasing her with light, biting nips that made her yearn for more and more. Then he'd change his tactics and kiss her with a hungry demand. Lost in a mindless haze, she clung to him as the tears filled her eyes and ran unheeded down her cheeks. Everything she feared was happening. And worse, she was powerless to stop him. Her throat felt dry and scratchy and she uttered a soft sob in a effort to abate the flow of emotion.

Andrew went still. He cupped her face in his hands and examined her tear-streaked cheeks. His troubled expression swam in and out of her vision.

"Jo Marie," he whispered, his voice tortured. "Don't cry, darling, please don't cry." With an infinite tenderness he kissed away each tear and when he reached her trembling mouth, the taste of salt was on his lips. A series of long, drugging kisses only confused her more. It didn't seem possible she could want him so much and yet that it should be so wrong.

"Please." With every ounce of strength she possessed Jo Marie broke from his embrace. "I promised myself this wouldn't happen again," she whispered feeling miserable. Standing with her back to him, her hands cradled her waist to ward off a sudden chill.

Gently he pressed his hand to her shoulder and Jo Marie couldn't bring herself to brush it away. Even his touch had the power to disarm her.

"Jo Marie." His husky tone betrayed the depths of his turmoil. "Listen to me."

"No, what good would it do?" she asked on a quavering sob. "You're engaged to be married to my best friend. I can't help the way I feel about you. What I feel, what you feel, is wrong as long as Kelly's wearing your ring." With a determined effort she turned to face him, tears blurring her sad eyes. "It would be better if we didn't see each other again...at least until you're sure of what you want..or who you want."

Andrew jerked his hand through his hair. "You're right. I've got to get this mess straightened out."

"Promise me, Andrew, please promise me that you won't make an effort to see me until you know in your own mind what you want. I can't take much more of this." She wiped the moisture from her cheekbones with the tips of her fingers. "When I get up in the morning I want to look at myself in the mirror. I don't want to hate myself."

Andrew's mouth tightened with grim displeasure. He looked as if he wanted to argue. Tense moments passed before he slowly shook his head. "You deserve to be treated so much better than this. Someday, my love, you'll understand. Just trust me for now."

"I'm only asking one thing of you," she said unable to meet his gaze. "Don't touch me or make an effort to see me as long as Kelly's wearing your ring. It's not fair to any one of us." Her lashes fell to veil the hurt in her eyes. Andrew couldn't help but know that she was in love with him. She would have staked her life that her feelings were returned full measure. Fresh tears misted her eyes.

"I don't want to leave you like this."

"I'll be all right," she murmured miserably.

"There's nothing that I can do. Everything rests with you, Andrew. Everything."

Dejected, he nodded and added a promise. "I'll take care of it today."

Again Jo Marie wiped the wetness from her face and forced a smile, but the effort was almost more than she could bear.

The door clicked, indicating that Andrew had gone and Jo Marie released a long sigh of pent-up emotion. Her reflection in the bathroom mirror showed that her lips were parted and trembling from the hungry possession of his mouth. Her eyes had darkened from the strength of her physical response.

Andrew had asked that she trust him and she would, with all her heart. He loved her, she was sure of it. He wouldn't have hired a detective to find her or built a huge home with her in mind if he didn't feel something strong toward her. Nor could he have held her and kissed her the way he had today without loving and needing her.

While she unpacked the small overnight bag a sense of peace came over her. Andrew would explain everything to Kelly, and she needn't worry. Kelly's interests seemed to be centered more on Mark lately, and maybe...just maybe, she wouldn't be hurt or upset and would accept that neither Andrew nor Jo Marie had planned for this to happen.

Time hung heavily on her hands and Jo Marie toyed with the idea of visiting her parents. But her mother knew her so well that she'd take one look at Jo Marie and want to know what was bothering her daughter. And today Jo Marie wasn't up to explanations.

A flip of the radio dial and Christmas music drifted into the room, surrounding her with its message of peace and love. Humming the words softly to herself, Jo Marie felt infinitely better. Everything was going to be fine, she felt confident.

A thick Sunday paper held her attention for the better part of an hour, but at the slightest noise, Jo Marie's attention wandered from the printed page and she glanced up expecting Kelly. One look at her friend would be enough to tell Jo Marie everything she needed to know.

Setting the paper aside, Jo Marie felt her nerves tingle with expectancy. She felt weighted with a terrible guilt. Kelly obviously loved Andrew enough to agree to be his wife, but she showed all the signs of falling in love with Mark. Kelly wasn't the kind of girl who would purposely hurt or lead a man on. She was too sensitive for that. And to add to the complications were Andrew and Jo Marie who had discovered each other again just when they had given up all hope. Jo Marie loved Andrew, but she wouldn't find her own happiness at her friend's expense. But Andrew was going to ask for his ring back, Jo Marie was sure of it. He'd said he'd clear things up today.

The door opened and inhaling a calming breath, Jo Marie stood.

Kelly came into the apartment, her face lowered as her gaze avoided her friend's.

"Hi," Jo Marie ventured hesitantly.

Kelly's face was red and blotchy; tears glistened in her eyes.

"Is something wrong?" Her voice faltered slightly.

"Drew and I had a fight, that's all." Kelly raised

her hand to push back her hair and as she did so the engagement ring Andrew had given her sparkled in the sunlight.

Jo Marie felt the knot tighten in her stomach. Andrew had made his decision.

Chapter Seven

Somehow Jo Marie made it through the following
days. She didn't see Andrew and made excuses to
avoid Kelly. Her efforts consisted of trying to get
through each day. Once she left the office, she often
went to the LFTF headquarters, spending long hours
helping Jim. Their friendship had grown. Jim helped
her laugh when it would have been so easy to cry. A
couple of times they had coffee together and talked.
But Jim did most of the talking. This pain was so all-
consuming that Jo Marie felt like a newly fallen leaf
tossed at will by a fickle wind.

Jim asked her to accompany him on another speaking engagement which Jo Marie did willingly. The
talk was on a stretch of wetlands Jim wanted pre-
served and it had been well received. Silently, Jo Marie mocked herself for not being attracted to someone
as wonderful as Jim Rowden. He was everything a
woman could want. In addition, she was convinced

that he was interested in her. But it was Andrew who continued to fill her thoughts, Andrew who haunted her dreams, Andrew whose soft whisper she heard in the wind.

Lost in the meandering trail of her musing, Jo Marie didn't hear Jim's words as they sauntered into the empty office. Her blank look prompted him to repeat himself. "I thought it went rather well tonight, didn't you?" he asked, grinning boyishly. He brushed the hair from his forehead and pulled out the chair opposite hers.

"Yes," Jo Marie agreed with an absent shake of her head. "It did go well. You're a wonderful speaker." She could feel Jim's gaze watching her and in an effort to avoid any questions, she stood and reached for her purse. "I'd better think about getting home."

"Want some company while you walk to the bus stop?"

"I brought the car tonight." She almost wished she was taking the bus. Jim was a friendly face in a world that had taken on ragged, pain-filled edges.

Kelly had been somber and sullen all week. Half the time she looked as if she were ready to burst into tears at the slightest provocation. Until this last week, Jo Marie had always viewed her roommate as an emotionally strong woman, but recently Jo Marie wondered if she really knew Kelly. Although her friend didn't enjoy large parties, she'd never known Kelly to be intimidated by them. Lately, Kelly had been playing the role of a damsel in distress to the hilt.

Mark had stopped by the apartment only once and

he'd resembled a volcano about to explode. He'd left after fifteen minutes of pacing the living-room carpet when Kelly didn't show.

And Andrew—yes, Andrew—by heaven's grace she'd been able to avoid a confrontation with him. She'd seen him only once in the last five days and the look in his eyes had seared her heart. He desperately wanted to talk to her. The tormented message was clear in his eyes, but she'd gently shaken her head, indicating that she intended to hold him to his word.

"Something's bothering you, Jo Marie. Do you want to talk about it?" Dimples edged into Jim's round face. Funny how she'd never noticed them before tonight.

Sadness touched the depths of her eyes and she gently shook her head. "Thanks, but no. Not tonight."

"Venturing a guess, I'd say it had something to do with Mr. Delta Development."

"Oh?" Clenching her purse under her arm, Jo Marie feigned ignorance. "What makes you say that?"

Jim shook his head. "A number of things." He rose and tucked both hands in his pants pockets. "Let me walk you to your car. The least I can do is see that you get safely outside."

"The weather's been exceptionally cold lately, hasn't it?"

Jim's smile was inviting as he turned the lock in the office door. "Avoiding my questions, aren't you?"

"Yes." Jo Marie couldn't see any reason to lie.

"When you're ready to talk, I'll be happy to listen.'' Tucking the keys in his pocket, Jim reached for Jo Marie's hand, placing it at his elbow and patting it gently.

"Thanks, I'll remember that."

"Tell me something more about you," Jo Marie queried in a blatant effort to change the subject. Briefly Jim looked at her, his expression thoughtful.

They ventured onto the sidewalk. The full moon was out, its silver rays clearing a path in the night as they strolled toward her car.

"I'm afraid I'd bore you. Most everything you already know. I've only been with the foundation a month."

"LFTF needs people like you, dedicated, passionate, caring."

"I wasn't the one who gave permission for a transient to sleep in a doorway."

Jo Marie softly sucked in her breath. "How'd you know?"

"He came back the second night looking for a handout. The guy knew a soft touch when he saw one."

"What happened?"

Jim shrugged his shoulder and Jo Marie stopped walking in mid-stride. "You gave him some money!" she declared righteously. "And you call me a soft touch."

"As a matter of fact, I didn't. We both knew what he'd spend it on."

"So what did you do?"

"Took him to dinner."

A gentle smile stole across her features at the picture that must have made. Jim dressed impeccably in his business suit and the alcoholic in tattered, ragged clothes.

"It's sad to think about." Slowly, Jo Marie shook her head.

"I got in touch with a friend of mine from a mission. He came for him afterward so that he'll have a place to sleep at least. To witness, close at hand like that, a man wasting his life is far worse to me than..." he paused and held her gaze for a long moment, looking deep into her brown eyes. Then he smiled faintly and shook his head. "Sorry, I didn't mean to get so serious."

"You weren't," Jo Marie replied, taking the car keys from her purse. "I'll be back Monday and maybe we could have a cup of coffee."

The deep blue eyes brightened perceptively. "I'd like that and listen, maybe we could have dinner one night soon."

Jo Marie nodded, revealing that she'd enjoy that as well. Jim was her friend and she doubted that her feelings would ever go beyond that, but the way she felt lately, she needed someone to lift her from the doldrums of self-pity.

The drive home was accomplished in a matter of minutes. Standing otuside her apartment building, Jo Marie heaved a steadying breath. She dreaded walking into her own home—what a sad commentary on her life! Tonight, she promised herself, she'd make an effort to clear the air between herself and Kelly. Not knowing what Andrew had said to her roommate about his feelings for her, if anything, or the details of the argument, had put Jo Marie in a precarious position. The air between Jo Marie and her best friend was like the stillness before an electrical storm. The problem was that Jo Marie didn't know what to say to Kelly or how to go about making things right.

She made a quick survey of the cars in the parking lot to assure herself that Andrew wasn't inside. Relieved, she tucked her hands inside the pockets of her cardigan and hoped to give a nonchalant appearance when she walked through the front door.

Kelly glanced up from the book she was reading when Jo Marie walked inside. The red, puffy eyes were a testimony of tears, but Kelly didn't explain and Jo Marie didn't pry.

"I hope there's something left over from dinner," she began on a forced note of cheerfulness. "I'm starved."

"I didn't fix anything," Kelly explained in an ominously quiet voice. "In fact I think I'm coming down with something. I've got a terrible stomachache."

Jo Marie had to bite her lip to keep from shouting that she knew what was wrong with the both of them. Their lives were beginning to resemble a three-ring circus. Where once Jo Marie and Kelly had been best friends, now they rarely spoke.

"What I think I'll do is take a long, leisurely bath and go to bed."

Jo Marie nodded, thinking Kelly's sudden urge for a hot soak was just an excuse to leave the room and avoid the problems that faced them.

While Kelly ran her bathwater, Jo Marie searched through the fridge looking for something appetizing. Normally this was the time of the year that she had to watch her weight. This Christmas she'd probably end up losing a few pounds.

The radio was playing a series of spirited Christmas carols and Jo Marie started humming along. She took out bread and cheese slices from the fridge. The cupboard offered a can of tomato soup.

By the time Kelly came out of the bathroom, Jo Marie had set two places at the table and was pouring hot soup into deep bowls.

"Dinner is served," she called.

Kelly surveyed the table and gave her friend a weak, trembling smile. "I appreciate the effort, but I'm really not up to eating."

Exhaling a dejected sigh, Jo Marie turned to her friend. "How long are we going to continue pretending like this? We need to talk, Kell."

"Not tonight, please, not tonight."

The doorbell rang and a stricken look came over Kelly's pale features. "I don't want to see anyone," she announced and hurried into the bedroom, leaving Jo Marie to deal with whoever was calling.

Resentment burned in her dark eyes as Jo Marie crossed the room. If it was Andrew, she would simply explain that Kelly was ill and not invite him inside.

"Merry Christmas." A tired-looking Mark greeted Jo Marie sarcastically from the other side of the door.

"Hi." Jo Marie watched him carefully. Her brother looked terrible. Tiny lines etched about his eyes revealed lack of sleep. He looked as though he was suffering from both mental and physical exhaustion.

"Is Kelly around?" He walked into the living room, sat on the sofa and leaned forward, roughly rubbing his hands across his face as if that would keep him awake.

"No, she's gone to bed. I don't think she's feeling well."

Briefly, Mark stared at the closed bedroom door and as he did, his shoulder hunched in a gesture of defeat.

"How about something to eat? You look like you haven't had a decent meal in days."

"I haven't." He moved lackadaisically to the kitchen and pulled out a chair.

Lifting the steaming bowls of soup from the counter, Jo Marie brought them to the table and sat opposite her brother.

As Mark took the soup spoon, his tired eyes held a distant, unhappy look. Kelly's eyes had revealed the same light of despair. "We had an argument," he murmured.

"You and Kell?"

"I said some terrible things to her." He braced his elbow against the table and pinched the bridge of his nose. "I don't know what made me do it. The whole time I was shouting at her I felt as if it was some stranger doing this. I know it sounds crazy but it was almost as if I were standing outside myself watching, and hating myself for what I was doing."

"Was the fight over something important?"

Defensively, Mark straightened. "Yeah, but that's between Kelly and me." He attacked the toasted cheese sandwich with a vengeance.

"You're in love with Kelly, aren't you?" Jo Marie had yet to touch her meal, more concerned about what was happening between her brother and her best friend than about her soup and sandwich.

Mark hesitated thoughtfully and a faint grimness

closed off his expression. "In love with Kelly? I am?"

"You obviously care for her."

"I care for my cat, too," he returned coldly and his expression hardened. "She's got what she wants—money. Just look at who she's marrying. It isn't enough that she's wealthy in her own right. No, she sets her sights on J. Paul Getty."

Jo Marie's chin trembled in a supreme effort not to reveal her reaction to his words. "You know Kelly better than that." Averting her gaze, Jo Marie struggled to hold back the emotion that tightly constricted her throat.

"Does either one of us really know Kelly?" Mark's voice was taut as a hunter's bow. Cyncism drove deep grooved lines around his nose and mouth. "Did she tell you that she and Drew have set their wedding date?" Mark's voice dipped with contempt.

A pain seared all the way through Jo Marie's soul. "No, she didn't say." With her gaze lowered, she struggled to keep her hands from shaking.

"Apparently they're going to make it official after the first of the year. They're planning on a spring wedding."

"How...nice." Jo Marie nearly choked on the words.

"Well, all I can say is that those two deserve each other." He tossed the melted cheese sandwich back on the plate and stood. "I guess I'm not very hungry, after all."

Jo Marie rose with him and glanced at the table. Neither one of them had done more than shred their sandwiches and stir their soup. "Neither am I," she said, and swallowed at the tightness gripping her throat.

Standing in the living room, Mark stared for a second time at the closed bedroom door.

"I'll tell Kelly you were by." For a second it seemed that Mark hadn't heard.

"No," he murmured after a long moment. "Maybe it's best to leave things as they are. Good night, sis, thanks for dinner." Resembling a man carrying the weight of the world on his shoulders, Mark left.

Leaning against the front door, Jo Marie released a bitter, pain-filled sigh and turned the dead bolt. Tears burned for release. So Andrew and Kelly were going to make a public announcement of their engagement after Christmas. It shouldn't shock her. Kelly had told her from the beginning that they were. The wedding plans were already in the making. Wiping the salty dampness from her cheek, Jo Marie bit into the tender skin inside her cheek to hold back a sob.

"There's a call for you on line one," Paula called to Jo Marie from her desk.

"Thanks." With an efficiency born of years of experience, Jo Marie punched in the telephone tab and lifted the receiver to her ear. "This is Jo Marie Early, may I help you?"

"Jo Marie, this is Jim. I hope you don't mind me calling you at work."

"No problem."

"Good. Listen, you, ah, mentioned something the other night about us having coffee together and I said something about having dinner."

If she hadn't known any better, Jo Marie would have guessed that Jim was uneasy. He was a gentle man with enough sensitivity to campaign for the future. His hesitancy surprised her now. "I remember."

"How would you feel about this Wednesday?" he continued. "We could make a night of it."

Jo Marie didn't need to think it over. "I'd like that very much." After Mark's revelation, she'd realized the best thing to do was to put the past and Andrew behind her and build a new life for herself.

"Good." Jim sounded pleased. "We can go Wednesday night...or would you prefer Friday?"

"Wednesday's fine." Jo Marie doubted that she could ever feel again the deep, passionate attraction she'd experienced with Andrew, but Jim's appeal wasn't built on fantasy.

"I'll see you then. Goodbye, Jo Marie."

"Goodbye Jim, and thanks."

The mental uplifting of their short conversation was enough to see Jo Marie through a hectic afternoon. An airline lost her customer's reservations and the tickets didn't arrive in time. In addition the phone rang repeatedly.

By the time she walked into the apartment, her feet hurt and there was a nagging ache in the small of her back.

"I thought I heard you." Kelly sauntered into the kitchen and stood in the doorway dressed in a robe and slippers.

"How are you feeling?"

She lifted one shoulder in a weak shrug. "Better."

"You stayed home?" Kelly had still been in bed

when Jo Marie left for work. Apparently her friend had phoned in sick.

"Yeah." She moved into the living room and sat on the sofa.

"Mark was by last night." Jo Marie mentioned the fact casually, waiting for a response from her roommate. Kelly didn't give her one. "He said that the two of you had a big fight," she continued.

"That's all we do anymore—argue."

"I don't know what he said to you, but he felt bad about it afterward."

A sad glimmer touched Kelly's eyes and her mouth formed a brittle line that Jo Marie supposed was meant to be a smile. "I know he didn't mean it. He's exhausted. I swear he's trying to work himself to death."

Now that her friend mentioned it, Jo Marie realized that she hadn't seen much of her brother lately. It used to be that he had an excuse to show up two or three times a week. Except for last night, he had been to the apartment only twice since Thanksgiving.

"I don't think he's eaten a decent meal in days," Kelly continued. "He's such a good doctor, Jo Marie, because he cares so much about his patients. Even the ones he knows he's going to lose. I'm a nurse, I've seen the way the other doctors close themselves off from any emotional involvement. But Mark's there, always giving." Her voice shook uncontrollably and she paused to bite into her lip until she regained her composure. "I wanted to talk to him the other night, and do you know where I found him? In pediatrics holding a little boy who's suffering with terminal cancer. He was rocking this child, holding him in his arms and telling him the pain wouldn't last too much longer. From the hallway, I heard Mark talk about heaven and how there wouldn't be any pain for him there. Mark's a wonderful man and wonderful doctor.''

And he loves you so much it's tearing him apart, Jo Marie added silently.

''Yesterday he was frustrated and angry and he took it out on me. I'm not going to lie and say it didn't hurt. For a time I was devastated, but I'm over that now.''

''But you didn't go to work today.'' They both knew why she'd chosen to stay home.

''No, I felt Mark and I needed a day away from each other.''

''That's probably a good idea.'' There was so much she wanted to say to Kelly, but everything sounded so inadequate. At least they were talking, which was a major improvement over the previous five days.

The teakettle whistled sharply and Jo Marie returned to the kitchen bringing them both back a steaming cup of hot coffee.

''Thanks.'' Kelly's eyes brightened.

''Would you like me to talk to Mark?'' Jo Marie's offer was sincere, but she wasn't exactly sure what she'd say. And in some ways it could make matters worse.

''No. We'll sort this out on our own.''

The doorbell chimed and the two exchanged glances. ''I'm not expecting anyone,'' Kelly murmured and glanced down self-consciously at her attire. ''In fact I'd rather not be seen, so if you don't mind I'll vanish inside my room.''

The last person Jo Marie expected to find on the other side of the door was Andrew. The welcome died in her eyes as their gazes met and clashed. Jo Marie quickly lowered hers. Her throat went dry and a rush of emotion brought a flood of color to her suddenly pale cheeks. A tense air of silence surrounded them. Andrew raised his hand as though he wanted to reach out and touch her. Instead he clenched his fist and lowered it to his side, apparently having changed his mind.

"Is Kelly ready?" he asked after a breathless moment. Jo Marie didn't move, her body blocking the front door, refusing him admittance.

She stared up at him blankly. "Ready?" she repeated.

"Yes, we're attending the opera tonight. Bizet's *Carmen*," he added as if in an afterthought.

"Oh, dear." Jo Marie's eyes widened. Kelly had obviously forgotten their date. The tickets for the elaborate opera had been sold out for weeks. Her roommate would have to go. "Come in, I'll check with Kelly."

"Andrew's here," Jo Marie announced and leaned against the wooden door inside the bedroom, her hands folded behind her.

"Drew?"

"Andrew to me, Drew to you," she responded cattily. "You have a date to see *Carmen*."

Kelly's hand flew to her forehead. "Oh, my goodness, I completely forgot."

"What are you going to do?"

"Explain, what else is there to do?" she snapped. Jo Marie followed her friend into the living room.

Andrew's gray eyes widened at the sight of Kelly dressed in her robe and slippers.

"You're ill?"

"Actually, I'm feeling better. Drew, I apologize, I completely forgot about tonight."

As Andrew glanced at his gold wristwatch, a frown marred his handsome face.

"Kelly can shower and dress in a matter of a few minutes," Jo Marie said sharply, guessing what Kelly was about to suggest.

"I couldn't possibly be ready in forty-five minutes," she denied. "There's only one thing to do. Jo Marie, you'll have to go in my place."

Andrew's level gaze crossed the width of the room to capture Jo Marie's. Little emotion was revealed in the impassive male features, but his gray eyes glinted with challenge.

"I can't." Her voice was level with hard determination.

"Why not?" Two sets of eyes studied her.

"I'm...." Her mind searched wildly for an excuse. "I'm baking cookies for the Science Club. We're meeting Saturday and this will be our last time before Christmas."

"I thought you worked Saturdays," Andrew cut in sharply.

"Every other Saturday." Calmly she met this gaze. Over the past couple of weeks, Kelly had purposely brought Jo Marie and Andrew together, but Jo Marie wouldn't fall prey to that game any longer. She'd made an agreement with him and refused to back down. As long as he was engaged to another woman she wouldn't...couldn't be with him. "I won't go," she explained in a steady voice which belied the inner turmoil that churned her stomach.

"There's plenty of time before the opening curtain if you'd care to change your mind."

Kelly tossed Jo Marie an odd look. "It looks like I'll have to go," she said with an exaggerated sigh. "I'll be as fast as I can." Kelly rushed back inside the bedroom leaving Jo Marie and Andrew separated by only a few feet.

"How have you been?" he asked, his eyes devouring her.

"Fine," she responded on a stiff note. The lie was only a little one. The width of the room stood between them, but it might as well have been whole light-years.

Bowing her head, she stared at the pattern in the carpet. When she suggested Kelly hurry and dress, she hadn't counted on being left alone with Andrew. "If you'll excuse me, I'll get started on those cookies."

To her dismay Andrew followed her into the kitchen.

"What are my chances of getting a cup of coffee?" He sounded pleased with himself, his smile was smug.

Wordlessly Jo Marie stood on her tiptoes and brought down a mug from the cupboard. She poured in the dark granules, stirred in hot water and walked past him to carry the mug into the living room. All the while her mind was screaming with him to leave her alone.

Andrew picked up the mug and followed her back

into the kitchen. "I've wanted to talk to you for days."

"You agreed."

"Jo Marie, believe me, talking to Kelly isn't as easy as it seems. There are some things I'm not at liberty to explain that would resolve this whole mess."

"I'll just bet there are." The bitter taste of anger filled her mouth.

"Can't you trust me?" The words were barely audible and for an instant Jo Marie wasn't certain he'd spoken.

Everything within her yearned to reach out to him and be assured that the glorious times they'd shared had been as real for him as they'd been for her. Desperately she wanted to turn and tell him that she would trust him with her life, but not her heart. She couldn't, not when Kelly was wearing his engagement ring.

"Jo Marie." A faint pleading quality entered his voice. "I know how all this looks. At least give me a chance to explain. Have dinner with me tomorrow. I swear I won't so much as touch you. I'll leave everything up to you. Place. Time. You name it."

"No." Frantically she shook her head, her voice throbbing with the desire to do as he asked. "I can't."

"Jo Marie." He took a step toward her, then another, until he was so close his husky voice breathed against her dark hair.

Forcing herself into action, Jo Marie whirled around and backed out of the kitchen. "Don't talk to me like that. I realized last week that whatever you feel for Kelly is stronger than any love you have for me. I've tried to accept that as best I can."

Andrew's knuckles were clenched so tightly that they went white. He looked like an innocent man facing a firing squad, his eyes resigned, the line of his jaw tense, anger and disbelief etched in every rugged mark of his face.

"Just be patient, that's all I'm asking. In due time you'll understand everything."

"Will you stop?" she demanded angrily. "You're talking in puzzles and I've always hated those. All I know is that there are four people who—"

"I guess this will have to do," Kelly interrupted as she walked into the room. She had showered, dressed and dried her hair in record time.

Jo Marie swallowed the taste of jealousy as she watched the dark, troubled look dissolve from Andrew's eyes. "You look great," was all she could manage.

"We won't be too late," Kelly said on her way out.

"Don't worry," Jo Marie murmured and breathed in a sharp breath. "I won't be up; I'm exhausted."

Who was she trying to kid? Not until the key turned in the front door lock five hours later did Jo Marie so much as yawn. As much as she hated herself for being so weak, the entire time Kelly had been with Andrew, Jo Marie had been utterly miserable.

The dinner date with Jim the next evening was the only bright spot in a day that stretched out like an empty void. She dressed carefully and applied her makeup with extra care, hoping to camouflage the effects of a sleepless night.

"Don't fix dinner for me, I've got a date," was all she said to Kelly on her way out the door to the office.

As she knew it would, being with Jim was like stumbling upon an oasis in the middle of a sand-tossed desert. He made her laugh, teasing her affectionately. His humor was subtle and light and just the antidote for a broken heart. She'd known from the moment they'd met that she was going to like Jim Rowden. With him she could relax and be herself. And not once did she have to look over her shoulder.

"Are you going to tell me what's been troubling you?" he probed gently over their dessert.

"What? And cry all over my lime-chiffon pie?"

Jim's returning smile was one of understanding and encouragement. Again she noted the twin dimples that formed in his cheeks. "Whenever you're ready, I'm available to listen."

"Thanks." She shook her head, fighting back an unexpected swell of emotion. "Now what's this surprise you've been taunting me with most of the evening?" she questioned, averting the subject from herself.

"It's about the wetlands we've been crusading for during the last month. Well, I talked to a state senator today and he's going to introduce a bill that would make the land into a state park." Lacing his hands together, Jim leaned toward the linen-covered table. "From everything he's heard, George claims from there it should be a piece of cake."

"Jim, that's wonderful." This was his first success and he beamed with pride over the accomplishment.

"Of course, nothing's definite yet, and I'm not even sure I should have told you, but you've heard me give two speeches on the wetlands and I wanted you to know.''

''I'm honored that you did.''

He acknowledged her statement with a short nod. ''I should know better than to get my hopes up like this, but George—my friend—sounded so confident.''

''Then you should be too. We both should.''

Jim reached for her hand and squeezed it gently. ''It would be very easy to share things with you, Jo Marie. You're quite a woman.''

Flattery had always made her uncomfortable, but Jim sounded so sincere. It cost her a great deal of effort to simply smile and murmur her thanks.

Jim's arm rested across her shoulder as they walked back toward the office. He held open her car door for her and paused before lightly brushing his mouth over hers. The kiss was both gentle and reassuring. But it wasn't Andrew's kiss and Jim hadn't the power to evoke the same passionate response Andrew seemed to draw so easily from her.

On the ride home, Jo Marie silently berated herself for continuing to compare the two men. It was unfair to them both to even think in that mode.

The apartment was unlocked when Jo Marie let herself inside. She was hanging up her sweater-coat when she noticed Andrew. He was standing in the middle of the living room carpet, regarding her with stone cold eyes.

One glance and Jo Marie realized that she'd never seen a man look so angry.

''It's about time you got home.'' His eyes were flashing gray fire.

"What right is it of yours to demand what time I get in?"

"I have every right." His voice was like a whip lashing out at her. "I suppose you think you're playing a game. Every time I go out with Kelly, you'll pay me back by dating Jim?"

Stunned into speechlessness, Jo Marie felt her voice die in her throat.

"And if you insist on letting him kiss you the least you can do is look for someplace more private than the street." The white line about his mouth became more pronounced as his eyes filled with bitter contempt. "You surprise me, Jo Marie, I thought you had more class than that."

Chapter Eight

"How dare you...how dare you say such things to me!" Jo Marie's quavering voice became breathless with rage. Her eyes were dark and stormy as she turned around and jerked the front door open.

"What do you expect me to believe?" Andrew rammed his hand through his hair, ruffling the dark hair that grew at his temple.

"I expected a lot of things from you, but not that you'd follow me or spy on me. And then...then to have the audacity to confront and insult me." The fury in her faded to be replaced with a deep, emotional pain that pierced her heart.

Andrew's face was bloodless as he walked past her and out the door. As soon as he was through the portal, she slammed it closed with a sweeping arc of her hand.

Jo Marie was so furious that the room wasn't large enough to contain her anger. Her shoulders rose and sagged with her every breath. At one time Andrew had been her dream man. Quickly she was learning to separate the fantasy from the reality.

Pacing the carpet helped relieve some of the terrible tension building within her. Andrew's behavior was nothing short of odious. She should hate him for saying those kinds of things to her. Tears burned for release, but deep, concentrated breaths held them at bay. Andrew Beaumont wasn't worth the emotion. Staring sightlessly at the ceiling, her damp lashes pressed against her cheek.

The sound of the doorbell caused her to whirl around. Andrew. She'd stake a week's salary on the fact. In an act of defiance, she folded her arms across her waist and stared determinedly at the closed door. He could rot in the rain before she'd open that door.

Again the chimes rang in short, staccato raps. "Come on, Jo Marie, answer the damn door."

"No," she shouted from the other side.

"Fine, we'll carry on a conversation by shouting at each other. That should amuse your neighbors."

"Go away." Jo Marie was too upset to talk things out. Andrew had hurt her with his actions and words.

"Jo Marie." The appealing quality in his voice couldn't be ignored. "Please, open the door. All I want is to apologize."

Hating herself for being so weak, Jo Marie turned the lock and threw open the solid wood door. "You have one minute."

"I think I went a little crazy when I saw Jim kiss you," he said pacing the area in front of the door. "Jo Marie, promise me that you won't see him again.

I don't think I can stand the thought of any man touching you."

"This is supposed to be an apology?" she asked sarcastically. "Get this, Mr. Beaumont," she said, fighting to keep from shouting at him as her finger punctuated the air. "You have no right to dictate anything to me."

His tight features darkened. "I can make your life miserable."

"And you think you haven't already?" she cried. "Just leave me alone. I don't need your threats. I don't want to see you again. Ever." To her horror, her voice cracked. Shaking her head, unable to talk any longer, she shut the door and clicked the lock.

Almost immediately the doorbell chimed, followed by continued knocking. Neither of them were in any mood to discuss things rationally. And perhaps it was better all the way around to simply leave things as they were. It hurt, more than Jo Marie wanted to admit, but she'd recover. She'd go on with her life and put Andrew, the dream man and all of it behind her.

Without glancing over her shoulder, she ignored the sound and moved into her bedroom.

The restaurant was crowded, the luncheon crowd filling it to capacity. With Christmas only a few days away the rush of last-minute shoppers filled the downtown area and flowed into the restaurants at lunch time.

Seeing Mark come through the doors, Jo Marie raised her hand and waved in an effort to attract her brother's attention. He looked less fatigued than the last time she'd seen him. A brief smile momentarily brightened his eyes, but faded quickly.

"I must admit this is a surprise," Jo Marie said as her brother slid into the upholstered booth opposite her. "I can't remember the last time we met for lunch."

"I can't remember either." Mark picked up the menu, decided and closed it after only a minute.

"That was quick."

"I haven't got a lot of time."

Same old Mark, always in a rush, hurrying from one place to another. "You called me, remember?" she taunted softly.

"Yeah, I remember." His gaze was focused on the paper napkin which he proceeded to fold into an intricate pattern. "This is going to sound a little crazy so promise me you won't laugh."

The edge of her mouth was already twitching. "I promise."

"I want you to attend the hospital Christmas party with me Saturday night."

"Me?"

"I don't have time to go out looking for a date and I don't think I can get out of it without offending half the staff."

In the past three weeks, Jo Marie had endured enough parties to last her a lifetime. "I guess I could go."

"Don't sound so enthusiastic."

"I'm beginning to feel the same way about parties as you do."

"I doubt that," he said forcefully and shredded the napkin in half.

The waitress came for their order and delivered steaming mugs of coffee almost immediately afterward.

Jo Marie lifted her own napkin, toying with the pressed paper edge. "Will Kelly and...Drew be there?"

"I doubt it. Why should they? There won't be any ballroom dancing or a midnight buffet. It's a pot luck. Can you picture old 'money bags' sitting on a folding chair and balancing a paper plate on her lap? No. Kelly goes more for the two-hundred-dollar-a-place-setting affairs."

Jo Marie opened her mouth to argue, but decided it would do little good. Discussing Andrew—Drew, her mind corrected—or Kelly with Mark would be pointless.

"I suppose Kelly's told you?"

"Told me what?" Jo Marie glanced up curious and half-afraid. The last time Mark had relayed any information about Drew and Kelly it had been that they were going to publicly announce their engagement.

"She's given her two-week notice."

"No," Jo Marie gasped. "She wouldn't do that. Kelly loves nursing; she's a natural." Even more surprising was the fact that Kelly hadn't said a word to Jo Marie about leaving Tulane Hospital.

"I imagine with the wedding plans and all that she's decided to take any early retirement. Who can blame her, right?"

But it sounded very much like Mark was doing exactly that. His mouth was tight and his dark eyes were filled with something akin to pain. What a mess this Christmas was turning out to be.

"Let's not talk about Kelly or Drew or anyone for the moment, okay. It's Christmas next week." She forced a bit of yuletide cheer into her voice.

"Right," Mark returned with a short sigh. "It's almost Christmas." But for all the enthusiasm in his voice he could have been discussing German measles.

Their soup and sandwiches arrived and they ate in strained silence. "Well, are you coming or not?" Mark asked, pushing his empty plate aside.

"I guess." No need to force any enthusiasm into her voice. They both felt the same way about the party.

"Thanks, sis."

"Just consider it your Christmas present."

Mark reached for the white slip the waitress had placed on their table, examining it. "And consider this lunch yours," he announced and scooted from his seat. "See you Saturday night."

"Mark said you've given the hospital your two-week notice?" Jo Marie confronted her roommate first thing that evening.

"Yes," Kelly replied lifelessly.

"I suppose the wedding will fill your time from now on."

"The wedding?" Kelly gave her an absent look. "No," she shook her head and an aura of dejected defeat hung over her, dulling her responses. "I've got my application in at a couple of other hospitals."

"So you're going to continue working after you're married."

For a moment it didn't look as if Kelly had heard her. "Kell?" Jo Marie prompted.

"I'd hoped to."

Berating herself for caring how Kelly and Andrew lived their lives, Jo Marie picked up the evening paper and pretended an interest in the front page. But if Kelly had asked her so much as what the headline read she couldn't have answered.

Saturday night Jo Marie dressed in the blue dress that she'd sewn after Thanksgiving. It fit her well and revealed a subtle grace in her movements. Although she took extra time with her hair and cosmetics, her heart wasn't up to attending the party.

Jo Marie had casually draped a lace shawl over her shoulder when the front door opened and Kelly entered with Andrew at her side.

"You're going out," Kelly announced, stopping abruptly inside the living room. "You...you didn't say anything."

Jo Marie could feel Andrew's gaze scorching her in a slow, heated perusal, but she didn't look his way. "Yes, I'm going out; don't wait up for me."

"Drew and I have plans too."

Reaching for her evening bag, Jo Marie's mouth curved slightly upward in a poor imitation of a smile. "Have a good time."

Kelly said something more, but Jo Marie was already out the door, grateful to have escaped without another confrontation with Andrew.

Mark had given her the address of the party and asked that she meet him there. He didn't give any particular reason he couldn't pick her up. He didn't need an excuse. It was obvious he wanted to avoid Kelly.

She located the house without a problem and was

greeted by loud music and a smoke-filled room. Making her way between the dancing couples, Jo Marie delivered the salad she had prepared on her brother's behalf to the kitchen. After exchanging pleasantries with the guests in the kitchen, Jo Marie went back to the main room to search for Mark.

For all the noisy commotion the party was an orderly one and Jo Marie spotted her brother almost immediately. He was sitting on the opposite side of the room talking to a group of other young men, who she assumed were fellow doctors. Making her way across the carpet, she was waylaid once by a nurse friend of Kelly's that she'd met a couple of times. They chatted for a few minutes about the weather.

"I suppose you've heard that Kelly's given her notice," Julie Frazier said with a hint of impatience. "It's a shame, if you ask me."

"I agree," Jo Marie murmured.

"Sometimes I'd like to knock those two over the head." Julie motioned toward Mark with the slight tilt of her head. "Your brother's one stubborn male."

"You don't need to tell me. I'm his sister."

"You know," Julie said and glanced down at the cold drink she was holding in her hand. "After Kelly had her tonsils out I could have sworn those two were headed for the altar. No one was more surprised than me when Kell turns up engaged to this mystery character."

"What do you mean about Kelly and Mark?" Kelly's tonsils had come out months ago during the Mardi Gras. No matter how much time passed, it wasn't likely that Jo Marie would forget that.

"Kelly was miserable—adult tonsillectomies are

seldom painless—anyway, Kelly didn't want anyone around, not even her family. Mark was the only one who could get close to her. He spent hours with her, coaxing her to eat, spoon-feeding her. He even read her to sleep and then curled up in the chair beside her bed so he'd be there when she woke.''

Jo Marie stared back in open disbelief. ''Mark did that?'' All these months Mark had been in love with Kelly and he hadn't said a word. Her gaze sought him now and she groaned inwardly at her own stupidity. For months she'd been so caught up in the fantasy of those few precious moments with Andrew that she'd been blind to what was right in front of her own eyes.

''Well, speaking of our friend, look who's just arrived.''

Jo Marie's gaze turned toward the front door just as Kelly and Andrew came inside. From across the length of the room, her eyes clashed with Andrew's. She watched as the hard line of his mouth relaxed and he smiled. The effect on her was devastating; her heart somersaulted and color rushed up her neck, invading her face. These were all the emotions she had struggled against from the beginning. She hated herself for being so vulnerable when it came to this one man. She didn't want to feel any of these emotions toward him.

''Excuse me—'' Julie interrupted Jo Marie's musings ''—there's someone I wanted to see.''

''Sure.'' Mentally, Jo Marie shook herself and joined Mark, knowing she would be safe at his side.

''Did you see who just arrived?'' Jo Marie whispered in her brother's ear.

Mark's dusty dark eyes studied Kelly's arrival and

Jo Marie witnessed an unconscious softening in his gaze. Kelly did look lovely tonight, and begrudgingly Jo Marie admitted that Andrew and Kelly were the most striking couple in the room. They belonged together—both were people of wealth and position. Two of a kind.

"I'm surprised that she came," Mark admitted slowly and turned his back to the pair. "But she's got as much right to be here as anyone."

"Of course she does."

One of Mark's friends appointed himself as disc jockey and put on another series of records for slow dancing. Jo Marie and Mark stood against the wall and watched as several couples began dancing on the makeshift dance floor. When Andrew turned Kelly into his arms, Jo Marie diverted her gaze to another section of the room, unable to look at them without being affected.

"You don't want to dance, do you?" Mark mumbled indifferently.

"With you?"

"No, I'd get one of my friends to do the honors. It's bad enough having to invite my sister to a party. I'm not about to dance with you, too."

Jo Marie couldn't prevent a short laugh. "You really know how to sweet talk a woman don't you, brother dearest?"

"I try," he murmured and his eyes narrowed on Kelly whose arms were draped around Andrew's neck as she whispered in his ear. "But obviously not hard enough," he finished.

Standing on the outskirts of the dancing couples made Jo Marie uncomfortable. "I think I'll see what

I can do to help in the kitchen,'' she said as an excuse to leave.

Julie Frazier was there, placing cold cuts on a round platter with the precision of a mathematician.

"Can I help?" Jo Marie offered, looking around for something that needed to be done.

Julie turned and smiled her appreciation. "Sure. Would you put the serving spoons in the salads and set them out on the dining room table?"

"Glad to." She located the spoons in the silverware drawer and carried out a large glass bowl of potato salad. The Formica table was covered with a vinyl cloth decorated with green holly and red berries.

"And now ladies and gentleman—" the disc jockey demanded the attention of the room "—this next number is a ladies' choice."

With her back to the table, Jo Marie watched as Kelly whispered something to Andrew. To her surprise, he nodded and stepped aside as Kelly made her way to the other side of the room. Her destination was clear—Kelly was heading directly to Mark. Jo Marie's pulse fluttered wildly. If Mark said or did anything cruel to her friend, Jo Marie would never forgive him.

Her heart was in her eyes as Kelly tentatively tapped Mark on the shoulder. Engrossed in a conversation, Mark apparently wasn't aware he was being touched. Kelly tried again and Mark turned, surprise rounding his eyes when he saw her roommate.

Jo Marie was far enough to the side so that she couldn't be seen by Mark and Kelly, but close enough to hear their conversation.

"May I have this dance?" Kelly questioned, her voice firm and low.

"I thought it was the man's prerogative to ask." The edge of Mark's mouth curled up sarcastically. "And if you've noticed, I haven't asked."

"This number is ladies' choice."

Mark tensed visibly as he glared across the room, eyeing Andrew. "And what about Rockefeller over there?"

Slowly, Kelly shook her head, her inviting gaze resting on Mark. "I'm asking you. Don't turn me down, Mark, not tonight. I'll be leaving the hospital in a little while and then you'll never be bothered with me again."

Jo Marie doubted that her brother could have refused Kelly anything in that moment. Wordlessly he approached the dance floor and took Kelly in his arms. A slow ballad was playing and the soft, melodic sounds of Billy Joel filled the room. Kelly fit her body to Mark's. Her arms slid around his neck as she pressed her temple against his jaw. Mark reacted to the contact by closing his eyes and inhaling as his eyes drifted closed. His hold, which had been loose, tightened as he knotted his hands at the small of Kelly's back, arching her body closer.

For the first time that night, her brother looked completely at ease. Kelly belonged with Mark. Jo Marie had been wrong to think that Andrew and Kelly were meant for each other. They weren't, and their engagement didn't make sense.

Her eyes sought out the subject of her thoughts. Andrew was leaning against the wall only a few feet from her. His eyes locked with hers, refusing to release her. He wanted her to come to him. She couldn't. His gaze seemed to drink her in as it had the night of the Mardi Gras. She could almost feel him reaching out to her, imploring her to come, urging her to cross the room so he could take her in his arms.

With unconscious thought Jo Marie took one step forward and stopped. No. Being with Andrew would only cause her more pain. With a determined effort she lightly shook her head, effectively breaking the spell. Her heart was beating so hard that breathing was difficult. Her steps were marked with decision as she returned to the kitchen.

A sliding glass door led to a lighted patio. A need to escape for a few moments overtook her and silently she slipped past the others and escaped into the darkness of the night.

A chill ran up her arms and she rubbed her hands over her forearms in an effort to warm her blood. The stars were out in a dazzling display and Jo Marie tilted her face toward the heavens, gazing at the lovely sight.

Jo Marie stiffened as she felt more than heard someone join her. She didn't need to turn around to realize that it was Andrew.

He came and stood beside her, but he made no effort to speak, instead focusing his attention on the dark sky.

Whole eternities seemed to pass before Andrew spoke. "I came to ask your forgiveness."

All the pain of his accusation burned in her breast. "You hurt me," she said on a breathless note after a long pause.

"I know, my love, I know." Slowly he removed his suit jacket and with extraordinary concern, draped it over her shoulders, taking care not to touch her.

"I'd give anything to have those thoughtless words back. Seeing Jim take you in his arms was like waving a red flag in front of an angry bull. I lashed out at you, when it was circumstances that were at fault."

Something about the way he spoke, the emotion that coated his words, the regret that filled his voice made her feel that her heart was ready to burst right out of her breast. She didn't want to look at him, but somehow it was impossible to keep her eyes away. With an infinite tenderness, he brushed a stray curl from her cheek.

"Can you forgive me?"

"Oh, Andrew." She felt herself weakening.

"I'd go on my knees if it would help."

The tears felt locked in her throat. "No, that isn't necessary."

He relaxed as if a great burden had been lifted from his shoulders. "Thank you."

Neither moved, wanting to prolong this tender moment. When Andrew spoke it was like the whisper of a gentle breeze and she had to strain to hear him.

"When I first came out here you looked like a blue sapphire silhouetted in the moonlight. And I was thinking that if it were in my power, I'd weave golden moonbeams into your hair."

"Have you always been so poetic?"

His mouth curved upward in a slow, sensuous smile. "No." His eyes were filled with an undisguised hunger as he studied her. Ever so slowly, he raised his hand and placed it at the side of her neck.

The tender touch of his fingers against her soft skin caused a tingling sensation to race down her spine. The feeling was akin to pain. Jo Marie loved this man as she would never love again and he was promised to another woman.

"Jo Marie," he whispered and his warm breath fanned her mouth. "There's mistletoe here. Let me kiss you."

There wasn't, of course, but Jo Marie was unable to pull away. She nodded her acquiescence. "One last time." She hadn't meant to verbalize her thoughts.

He brought her into his arms and she moistened her lips anticipating the hungry exploration of his mouth over hers. But she was to be disappointed. Andrew's lips lightly moved over hers like the gentle brush of the spring sun on a hungry earth. Gradually the kiss deepened as he worked his way from one corner of her mouth to another—again like the earth long starved from summer's absence.

"I always knew it would be like this for us, Florence Nightingale," he whispered against her hair. "Even when I couldn't find you, I felt a part of myself would never be the same."

"I did too. I nearly gave up dating."

"I thought I'd go crazy. You were so close all these months and yet I couldn't find you."

"But you did." Pressing her hands against the strong cushion of his chest she created a space between them. "And now it's too late."

Andrew's eyes darkened as he seemed to struggle within himself. "Jo Marie." A thick frown marred his face.

"Shh." She pressed her fingertips against his lips.

"Don't try to explain. I understand and I've accepted it. For a long time it hurt so much that I didn't think I'd be able to bear it. But I can and I will."

His hand circled her wrist and he closed his eyes before kissing the tips of her fingers. "There's so much I want to explain and can't."

"I know." With his arm holding her close, Jo Marie felt a deep sense of peace surround her. "I'd never be the kind of wife you need. Your position demands a woman with culture and class. I'm proud to be an Early and proud of my family, but I'm not right for you."

The grip on her wrist tightened. "Is that what you think?" The frustrated anger in his voice was barely suppressed. "Do you honestly believe that?"

"Yes," she answered him boldly. "I'm at peace within myself. I have no regrets. You've touched my heart and a part of me will never be the same. How can I regret having loved you? It's not within me."

He dropped her hand and turned from her, his look a mixture of angry torment. "You honestly think I should marry Kelly."

It would devastate Mark, but her brother would need to find his own peace. "Or someone like her." She removed his suit jacket from her shoulders and handed it back to him, taking care to avoid touching him. "Thank you," she whispered with a small catch to her soft voice. Unable to resist any longer, she raised her hand and traced his jaw. Very lightly, she brushed her mouth over his. "Goodbye, Andrew."

He reached out his hand in an effort to stop her, but she slipped past him. It took her only a moment to collect her shawl. Within a matter of minutes, she was out the front door and on her way back to the apartment. Mark would never miss her.

Jo Marie spent Sunday with her family, returning late that evening when she was assured Kelly was asleep. Lying in bed, studying the darkness around her, Jo Marie realized that she'd said her final good-bye to Andrew. Continuing to see him would only make it difficult for them both. Avoiding him had never succeeded, not when she yearned for every opportunity to be with him. The best solution would be to leave completely. Kelly would be moving out soon and Jo Marie couldn't afford to pay the rent on her own. The excuse would be a convenient one although Kelly was sure to recognize it for what it was.

After work Monday afternoon, before she headed for the LFTF office, Jo Marie stopped off at the hospital, hoping to talk to Mark. With luck, she might be able to convince her brother to let her move in with him. But only until she could find another apartment and another roommate.

Julie Frazier, the nurse who worked with both Kelly and Mark, was at the nurses' station on the surgical floor when Jo Marie arrived.

"Hi," she greeted cheerfully. "I don't suppose you know where Mark is?"

Julie glanced up from a chart she was reading. "He's in the doctors' lounge having a cup of coffee."

"Great. I'll talk to you later." With her shoes making clicking sounds against the polished floor, Jo Marie mused that her timing couldn't have been more perfect. Now all she needed was to find her brother in a good mood.

The doctors' lounge was at the end of the hall and was divided into two sections. The front part contained a sofa and a couple of chairs. A small kitchen area was behind that. The sound of Mark's and Kelly's voices stopped Jo Marie just inside the lounge.

"You can leave," Mark was saying in a tight, pained voice. "Believe me I have no intention of crying on your shoulder."

"I didn't come here for that," Kelly argued softly.

Jo Marie hesitated, unsure of what she should do. She didn't want to interrupt their conversation which seemed intense, nor did she wish to intentionally stay and listen in either.

"That case with the Randolph girl is still bothering you, isn't it?" Kelly demanded.

"No, I did everything I could. You know that."

"But it wasn't enough, was it?"

Jo Marie had to bite her tongue not to interrupt Kelly. It wasn't like her roommate to be unnecessarily cruel. Jo Marie vividly recalled her brother's doubts after the young child's death. It had been just before Thanksgiving and Mark had agonized that he had lost her.

"No," Mark shouted, "it wasn't enough."

"And now you're going to lose the Rickard boy." Kelly's voice softened perceptively.

Fleetingly Jo Marie wondered if this child was the one Kelly had mentioned who was dying of cancer.

"I've known that from the first." Mark's tone contained the steel edge of anger.

"Yes, but it hasn't gotten any easier, has it?"

"Listen, Kelly, I know what you're trying to do, but it isn't going to work."

"Mark," Kelly murmured his name on a sigh, "sometimes you are so blind."

"Maybe it's because I feel so inadequate. Maybe it's because I'm haunted with the fact that there might have been something more I could have done."

"But there isn't, don't you see?" Kelly's voice had softened as if her pain was Mark's. "Now won't you tell me what's really bothering you?"

"Maybe it's because I don't like the odds with Tommy. His endless struggle against pain. The deck was stacked against him from the beginning and now he hasn't got a bettor's edge. In the end, death will win."

"And you'll have lost, and every loss is a personal one."

Jo Marie didn't feel that she could eavesdrop any longer. Silently she slipped from the room.

The conversation between Mark and Kelly played back in her mind as she drove toward the office and Jim. Mark would have serious problems as a doctor unless he came to terms with these feelings. Kelly had recognized that and had set personal relationships aside to help Mark settle these doubts within himself. He'd been angry with her and would probably continue to be until he fully understood what she was doing.

Luckily Jo Marie found a parking space within sight of the office. With Christmas just a few days away the area had become more crowded and finding parking was almost impossible.

Her thoughts were heavy as she climbed from the

passenger's side and locked her door. Just as she turned to look both ways before crossing the street she caught a glimpse of the dark blue Mercedes. A cold chill raced up her spine. Andrew was inside talking to Jim.

Chapter Nine

"**I**s everything all right?" Wearily Jo Marie eyed Jim, looking for a telltale mannerism that would reveal the reason for Andrew's visit. She'd avoided bumping into him by waiting in a small antique shop across the street from the foundation. After he'd gone, she sauntered around for several additional minutes to be certain he was out of the neighborhood. Once assured it was safe, she crossed the street to the foundation's office.

"Should anything be wrong?" Jim lifted two thick brows in question.

"You tell me. I saw Andrew Beaumont's car parked outside."

"Ah, yes." Jim paused and smiled fleetingly. "And that concerns you?"

"No." She shook her head determinedly. "All right, yes!" She wasn't going to be able to fool Jim, who was an excellent judge of human nature.

A smile worked its way across his round face. "He came to meet the rest of the staff at my invitation. The LFTF Foundation is deeply indebted to your friend."

"My friend?"

Jim chuckled. "Neither one of you has been successful at hiding your feelings. Yes, my dear, sweet, Jo Marie, *your* friend."

Any argument died on her tongue.

"Would you care for a cup of coffee?" Jim asked, walking across the room and filling a Styrofoam cup for her.

Jo Marie smiled her appreciation as he handed it to her and sat on the edge of her desk, crossing his arms. "Beaumont and I had quite a discussion."

"And?" Jo Marie didn't bother to disguise her curiosity.

The phone rang before Jim could answer her. Jim reached for it and spent the next ten minutes in conversation. Jo Marie did her best to keep occupied, but her thoughts were doing a crazy tailspin. Andrew was here on business. She wouldn't believe it.

"Well?" Jo Marie questioned the minute Jim replaced the receiver.

His expression was empty for a moment. "Are we back to Beaumont again?"

"I don't mean to pry," Jo Marie said with a rueful smile, "but I'd really like to know why he was here."

Jim was just as straightforward. "Are you in love with him?"

Miserably, Jo Marie nodded. "A lot of good it's done either of us. Did he mention me?"

A wry grin twisted Jim's mouth. "Not directly, but he wanted to know my intentions."

"He didn't!" Jo Marie was aghast at such audacity.

Chuckling, Jim shook his head. "No, he came to ask me about the foundation and pick up some of our literature. He's a good man, Jo Marie."

She studied the top of the desk and typewriter keys. "I know."

"He didn't mention you directly, but I think he would have liked to. I had the feeling he was frustrated and concerned about you working here so many nights, especially in this neighborhood."

"He needn't worry, you escort me to my car or wait at the bus stop until the bus arrives."

Jim made busy work with his hands. "I had the impression that Beaumont is deeply in love with you. If anything happened to you while under my protection, he wouldn't take it lightly."

Even hours later when Jo Marie stepped into the apartment the echo of Jim's words hadn't faded. Andrew was concerned for her safety and was deeply in love with her. But it was all so useless that she refused to be comforted.

Kelly was sitting up, a blanket wrapped around her legs and torso as she paid close attention to a television Christmas special.

"Hi, how'd it go tonight?" Kelly greeted, briefly glancing from the screen.

Her roommate looked pale and slightly drawn, but Jo Marie attributed that to the conversation she'd overheard between her brother and her roommate. She wanted to ask how everything was at the hospital, but doubted that she could adequately disguise her interest.

"Tonight...oh, everything went as it usually does...fine."

"Good." Kelly's answer was absentminded, her look pinched.

"Are you feeling all right, Kell?"

Softly, she shook her head. "I've got another stomachache."

"Fever?"

"None to speak of. I think I might be coming down with the flu."

Tilting her head to one side, Jo Marie mused that Kelly had been unnaturally pale lately. But again she had attributed that to painfully tense times they'd all been through in the past few weeks.

"You know, one advantage of having a brother in the medical profession is that he's willing to make house calls."

Kelly glanced her way, then turned back to the television. "No, it's nothing to call Mark about."

But Kelly didn't sound as convincing as Jo Marie would have liked. With a shrug, she went into the kitchen and poured herself a glass of milk.

"Want one?" She raised her glass to Kelly for inspection.

"No thanks," Kelly murmured and unsuccessfully tried to disguise a wince. "In fact, I think I'll head for bed. I'll be fine in the morning, so don't worry about me."

But Jo Marie couldn't help doing just that. Little things about Kelly hadn't made sense in a long time—like staying home because of an argument with

Mark. Kelly wasn't a shy, fledgling nurse. She'd stood her ground with Mark more than once. Even her behavior at the Christmas parties had been peculiar. Nor was Kelly a shrinking violet, yet she'd behaved like one. Obviously it was all an act. But her reasons remained unclear.

In the morning, Kelly announced that she was going to take a day of sick leave. Jo Marie studied her friend with worried eyes. Twice during the morning she phoned to see how Kelly was doing.

"Fine," Kelly answered impatiently the second time. "Listen, I'd probably be able to get some decent rest if I didn't have to get up and answer the phone every fifteen minutes."

In spite of her friend's testiness, Jo Marie chuckled. "I'll try to restrain myself for the rest of the day."

"That would be greatly appreciated."

"Do you want me to bring you something back for dinner?"

"No," she answered emphatically. "Food sounds awful."

Mark breezed into the office around noon, surprising Jo Marie. Sitting on the corner of her desk, he dangled one foot as she finished a telephone conversation.

"Business must be slow if you've got time to be dropping in here," she said, replacing the receiver.

"I come to take you to lunch and you're complaining?"

"You've come to ask about Kelly?" She wouldn't hedge. The time for playing games had long passed.

"Oh?" Briefly he arched a brow in question. "Is that so?"

"She's got the flu. There, I just saved you the price of lunch." Jo Marie couldn't disguise her irritation.

"You didn't save me the price of anything," Mark returned lazily. "I was going to let you treat."

Unable to remain angry with her brother for long, Jo Marie joined him in a nearby café a few minutes later, but neither of them mentioned Kelly again. By unspoken agreement, Kelly, Andrew, and Kelly's unexpected resignation were never mentioned.

Jo Marie's minestrone soup and turkey sandwich arrived and she unwrapped the silverware from the paper napkin. "How would you feel about a roommate for a while?" Jo Marie broached the subject tentatively.

"Male or female?" Dusky dark eyes so like her own twinkled with mischief.

"This may surprise you—female."

Mark laid his sandwich aside. "I'll admit my interest has been piqued."

"You may not be as keen once you find out that it's me."

"You?"

"Well I'm going to have to find someplace else to move sooner or later and—"

"And you're interested in the sooner," he interrupted.

"Yes." She wouldn't mention her reasons, but Mark was astute enough to figure it out for himself.

Peeling open his sandwich, Mark removed a thin slice of tomato and set it on the beige plate. "As long as you do the laundry, clean, and do all the cooking I won't object."

A smile hovered at the edges of her mouth. "Your generosity overwhelms me, brother dearest."

"Let me know when you're ready and I'll help you cart your things over."

"Thanks, Mark."

Briefly he looked up from his meal and grinned. "What are big brothers for?"

Andrew's car was in the apartment parking lot when Jo Marie stepped off the bus that evening after work. The darkening sky convinced her that waiting outside for him to leave would likely result in a drenching. Putting aside her fears, she squared her shoulders and tucked her hands deep within her pockets. When Kelly was home she usually didn't keep the door locked so Jo Marie was surprised to discover that it was. While digging through her purse, she was even more surprised to hear loud voices from the other side of the door.

"This has to stop," Andrew was arguing. "And soon."

"I know," Kelly cried softly. "And I agree. I don't want to ruin anyone's life."

"Three days."

"All right—just until Friday."

Jo Marie made unnecessary noise as she came through the door. "I'm home," she announced as she stepped into the living room. Kelly was dressed in her robe and slippers, slouched on the sofa. Andrew had apparently been pacing the carpet. She could feel his gaze seek her out. But she managed to avoid it, diverting her attention instead to the picture on the wall behind him. "If you'll excuse me I think I'll take a hot shower."

"Friday," Andrew repeated in a low, impatient tone.

"Thank you, Drew," Kelly murmured and sighed softly.

Kelly was in the same position on the sofa when Jo Marie returned, having showered and changed clothes. "How are you feeling?"

"Not good."

For Kelly to admit to as much meant that she'd had a miserable day. "Is there anything I can do?"

Limply, Kelly laid her head back against the back of the couch and closed her eyes. "No, I'm fine. But this is the worst case of stomach flu I can ever remember?"

"You're sure it's the flu?"

Slowly Kelly opened her eyes. "I'm the nurse here."

"Yes, your majesty." With a dramatic twist to her chin, Jo Marie bowed in mock servitude. "Now would you like me to fix you something for dinner?"

"No."

"How about something cool to drink?"

Kelly nodded, but her look wasn't enthusiastic. "Fine."

As the evening progressed, Jo Marie studied her friend carefully. It could be just a bad case of the stomach flu, but Jo Marie couldn't help but be concerned. Kelly had always been so healthy and full of life. When a long series of cramps doubled Kelly over in pain, Jo Marie reached for the phone.

"Mark, can you come over?" She tried to keep the urgency from her voice.

"What's up?"

"It's Kelly. She's sick." Jo Marie attempted to keep her voice low enough so her roommate wouldn't hear. "She keeps insisting it's the flu, but I don't know. She's in a lot of pain for a simple intestinal virus."

Mark didn't hesitate. "I'll be right there."

Ten minutes later he was at the door. He didn't bother to knock, letting himself in. "Where's the patient?"

"Jo Marie." Kelly's round eyes tossed her a look of burning resentment. "You called Mark?"

"Guilty as charged, but I wouldn't have if I didn't think it was necessary."

Tears blurred the blue gaze. "I wish you hadn't," she murmured dejectedly. "It's just the flu."

"Let me be the judge of that." Mark spoke in a crisp professional tone, kneeling at her side. He opened the small black bag and took out the stethoscope.

Not knowing what else to do, Jo Marie hovered at his side for instructions. "Should I boil water or something?"

"Call Drew," Kelly insisted. "He at least won't overreact to a simple case of the flu."

Mark's mouth went taut, but he didn't rise to the intended gibe.

Reluctantly Jo Marie did as she was asked. Andrew answered on the third ring. "Beaumont here."

"Andrew, this is—"

"Jo Marie," he finished for her, his voice carrying a soft rush of pleasure.

"Hi," she began awkwardly and bit into the corner of her bottom lip. "Mark's here. Kelly's not feeling well and I think she may have something serious. She wanted to know if you could come over.''

"I'll be there in ten minutes." He didn't take a breath's hesitation.

As it was, he arrived in eight and probably set several speed records in the process. Jo Marie answered his hard knock. "What's wrong with Kelly? She seemed fine this afternoon." He directed his question to Mark.

"I'd like to take Kelly over to the hospital for a couple of tests."

Jo Marie noted the way her brother's jaw had tightened as if being in the same room with Andrew was a test of his endurance. Dislike exuded from every pore.

"No," Kelly protested emphatically. "It's just the stomach flu."

"With the amount of tenderness in the cecum?" Mark argued, shaking his head slowly from side to side in a mocking gesture.

"Mark's the doctor," Andrew inserted and Jo Marie could have kissed him for being the voice of reason in a room where little evidence of it existed.

"You think it's my appendix?" Kelly said with shocked disbelief.

"It isn't going to hurt to run a couple of tests," Mark countered, again avoiding answering a direct question.

"Why should you care?" Kelly's soft voice wavered uncontrollably. "After yesterday I would have thought..."

"After yesterday," Mark cut in sharply, "I realized that you were right and that I owe you an apology."

His eyes looked directly into Kelly's and the softness Jo Marie had witnessed in his gaze at the hospital Christmas party returned. He reached for Kelly's hand, folding it in his own. "Will you accept my apology? What you said yesterday made a lot of sense, but at the time I was angry at the world and took it out on you. Forgive me?"

With a trembling smile, Kelly nodded. "Yes, of course I do."

The look they shared was both poignant and tender, causing Jo Marie to feel like an intruder. Briefly, she wondered what Andrew was thinking.

"If it does turn out that I need surgery would you be the one to do it for me?"

Immediately Mark lowered his gaze. "No."

His stark response was cutting and Kelly flinched. "There's no one else I'd trust as much as you."

"I said I wouldn't." Mark pulled the stethoscope from his neck and placed it inside his bag.

"Instead of fighting about it now, why don't we see what happens?" Jo Marie attempted to reason. "There's no need to argue."

"There's every reason," Andrw intervened. "Tell us, Mark, why wouldn't you be Kelly's surgeon if she needed one?"

Jo Marie stared at Andrew, her dark eyes filled with irritation. Backing Mark into a corner wouldn't help the situation. She wanted to step forward and defend her brother, but Andrew stopped her with an abrupt motion of his hand, apparently having read her intent.

"Who I chose as my patients is my business." Mark's tone was dipped in acid.

"Isn't Kelly one of your patients?" Andrew questioned calmly. "You did hurry over here when you heard she was sick."

Coming to a standing position, Mark ignored the question and the man. "Maybe you'd like to change clothes." He directed his comment to Kelly.

Shaking her head she said, "No, I'm not going anywhere."

"Those tests are important." Mark's control on his anger was a fragile thread. "You're going to the hospital."

Again, Kelly shook her head. "No, I'm not."

"You're being unreasonable." Standing with his feet braced apart, Mark looked as if he was willing to take her to the hospital by force if necessary.

"Why not make an agreement," Andrew suggested with cool-headed resolve. "Kelly will agree to the tests, if you agree to be her doctor."

Tiredly, Mark rubbed a hand over his jaw and chin. "I can't do that."

"Why not?" Kelly implored.

"Yes, Mark, why not?" Andrew taunted.

Her brother's mouth thinned grimly as he turned aside and clenched his fists. "Because it isn't good practice to work on the people you're involved with emotionally."

The corners of Kelly's mouth lifted in a sad smile. "We're not emotionally involved. You've gone out of your way to prove that to me. If you have any emotion for me it would be hate."

Mark's face went white and it looked for an instant as if Kelly had physically struck him. "Hate you?" he repeated incredulously. "Maybe," he replied in brutal honesty. "You're able to bring out every other emotion in me. I've taken out a lot of anger on you recently. Most of which you didn't deserve and I apologize for that." He paused and ran a hand through his hair, mussing it. "No, Kelly," he corrected, "I can't hate you. It would be impossible when I love you so much," he announced with an impassive expression and pivoted sharply.

A tense silence engulfed the room until Kelly let out a small cry. "You love me? All these months you've put me through this torment and you love me?" She threw back the blanket and stood, placing her hands defiantly on her hips.

"A lot of good it did me." Mark's angry gaze crossed the width of the room to hold hers. "You're engaged to Daddy Warbucks over there so what good would it do to let you know?"

Jo Marie couldn't believe what she was hearing and gave a nervous glance to Andrew. Casually standing to the side of the room, he didn't look the least disturbed by what was happening. If anything, his features were relaxed as if he were greatly relieved.

"And if you cared for me then why didn't you say something before now?" Kelly challenged.

Calmly he met her fiery gaze. "Because he's got money, you've got money. Tell me what can I offer you that could even come close to the things he can give you."

"And you relate love and happiness with things?" Her low words were scathing. "Let me tell you exactly what you can offer me, Mark Jubal Early. You have it in your power to give me the things that matter most in my life: your love, your friendship, your respect. And...and...if you turn around and walk out that door, by heaven I'll never forgive you."

"I have no intention of leaving," Mark snapped in return. "But I can't very well ask you to marry me when you're wearing another man's ring."

"Fine." Without hesitating Kelly slipped Andrew's diamond from her ring finger and handed it back to him. Lightly she brushed her mouth over his cheeks. "Thanks, Drew."

His hands cupped her shoulders as he kissed her back. "Much happiness, Kelly," he whispered.

Brother and sister observed the scene with openmouthed astonishment.

Turning, Kelly moved to Mark's side. "Now," she breathed in happily, "if that was a proposal, I accept."

Mark was apprently too stunned to answer.

"Don't tell me you've already changed your mind?" Kelly muttered.

"No, I haven't changed my mind. What about the hospital tests?" he managed finally, his voice slightly raw as his eyes devoured her.

"Give me a minute to change." Kelly left the room and the three were left standing, Jo Marie and Mark staring blankly at each other. Everything was happening so fast that it was like a dream with dark shades of unreality.

Kelly reappeared and Mark tucked her arm in his. "We should be back in an hour," Mark murmured, but he only had eyes for the pert-faced woman on his arm. Kelly's gaze was filled with a happy radiance that brought tears of shared happiness to Jo Marie's eyes.

"Take your time and call if you need us," Andrew said as the happy couple walked toward the door.

Jo Marie doubted that either Kelly or Mark heard him. When she turned her attention to Andrew she discovered that he was already walking toward her. With eager strides he eliminated the distance separating them.

"As I recall, our agreement was that I wouldn't try to see you or contact you again while Kelly wore my engagement ring."

Her dark eyes smiled happily into his. "That's right."

"Then let's be rid of this thing once and for all." He led her into the kitchen where he carelessly tossed the diamond ring into the garbage.

Jo Marie gasped. Andrew was literally throwing away thousands of dollars. The diamond was the largest she had ever seen.

"The ring is as phony as the engagement."

Still unable to comprehend what he was saying, she shook her head to clear her thoughts. "What?"

"The engagement isn't any more real than that so-called diamond."

"Why?" Reason had escaped her completely.

His hands brought Jo Marie into the loving circle of his arms. "By Thanksgiving I'd given up every hope of ever finding you again. I'd convinced myself that those golden moments were just a figment of my imagination and that some quirk of fate had brought us together, only to pull us apart."

It seemed the most natural thing in the world to have his arms around her. Her eyes had filled with moisture so that his features swam in and out of her vision. "I'd given up hope of finding you, too," she admitted in an achingly soft voice. "But I couldn't stop thinking about you."

Tenderly he kissed her, briefly tasting the sweetness of her lips. As if it was difficult to stop, he drew in an uneven breath and rubbed his jaw over the top of her head, mussing her hair. "I saw Kelly at her parents' house over the Thanksgiving holiday and she was miserable. We've always been close for second cousins and we had a long talk. She told me that she'd been in love with Mark for months. The worst part was that she was convinced that he shared her feelings, but his pride was holding him back. Apparently your brother has some strange ideas about wealth and position."

"He's learning," Jo Marie murmured, still caught in the rapture of being in Andrew's arms. "Give him time." She said this knowing that Kelly was willing to devote the rest of her life to Mark.

"I told Kelly she should give him a little competition and if someone showed an interested in her, then Mark would step forward. But apparently she'd already tried that."

"My brother can be as stubborn as ten men."

"I'm afraid I walked into this phony engagement with my eyes wide open. I said that if Mark was worth his salt, he wouldn't stand by and let her marry another man. If he loved her, really loved her, he'd step in."

"But he nearly didn't."

"No," Andrew admitted. "I was wrong. Mark loved Kelly enough to sacrifice his own desires to give her what he thought she needed. I realized that the night of my Christmas party. By that time I was getting desperate. I'd found you and every minute of this engagement was agony. In desperation, I tried to talk to Mark. But that didn't work. He assumed I was warning him off Kelly and told me to make her happy or I'd pay the consequences."

The irony of the situation was almost comical. "You were already suffering the consequences. Why didn't you say something? Why didn't you explain?"

"Oh, love, if you'd been anyone but Mark's sister I would have." Again his mouth sought hers as if he couldn't get enough of her kisses. "Here I was trapped in the worst set of circumstances I've ever imagined. The woman who had haunted me for months was within my grasp and I was caught in a steel web."

"I love you, Andrew. I've loved you from the moment you held me all those months ago. I knew then that you were meant to be someone special in my life."

"This has taught me the most valuable lesson of my life." He arched her close. So close it was impossible to breath normally. "I'll never let you out of my arms again. I'm yours for life, Jo Marie, whether you want me or not. I've had to trust again every instinct that you would wait for me. Dear Lord, I had visions of you falling in love with Jim Rowden, and the worst part was I couldn't blame you if you did. I can only imagine what kind of man you thought me."

Lovingly, Jo Marie spread kisses over his face. "It's going to take me a lifetime to tell you."

"Oh, love." His grip tightened against the back of her waist, arching her closer until it was almost painful to breathe. Not that Jo Marie cared. Andrew was holding her and had promised never to let her go again.

"I knew something was wrong with you and Kelly from the beginning," she murmured between soft, exploring kisses. Jo Marie couldn't have helped but notice.

"I've learned so much from this," Andrew confessed. "I think I was going slowly mad. I want more than to share my life with you, Jo Marie. I want to see our children in your arms. I want to grow old with you at my side."

"Oh, Andrew." Her arms locked around his neck and the tears of happiness streamed down her face.

"I love you, Florence Nightingale."

"And you, Andrew Beaumont, will always be my dream man."

"Forever?" His look was skeptical.

She lifted her mouth to his. "For all eternity," she whispered in promise.

"An ulcer?" Jo Marie shook her head slowly.

"Well, with all the stress I was under in the past few weeks, it's little wonder," Kelly defended herself.

The four sat in the living room sipping hot cocoa. Kelly was obediently drinking plain heated milk and hating it. But her eyes were warm and happy as they rested on Mark who was beside her with an arm draped over her shoulders.

"I've felt terrible about all this, Jo Marie," Kelly continued. "Guilt is a horrible companion. I didn't know exactly what was going on with you and Andrew. But he let it be known that he was in love with you and wanted this masquerade over quickly."

"You felt guilty?" Mark snorted. "How do you think I felt kissing another man's fiancée?"

"About the same way Jo Marie and I felt," Andrew returned with a chuckle.

"You know, Beaumont. Now that you're marrying my sister, I don't think you're such a bad character after all."

"That's encouraging."

"I certainly hope you get along since you're both going to be standing at the altar at the same time."

Three pairs of blank eyes stared at Kelly. "Double wedding, silly. It makes sense, doesn't it? The four of us have been through a lot together. It's only fitting we start our new lives at the same time."

"But soon," Mark said emphatically. "Sometime in January."

Everything was moving so fast, Jo Marie barely had time to assimilate the fact that Andrew loved her and she was going to share his life.

"Why not?" she agreed with a small laugh. "We've yet to do anything else conventionally."

Her eyes met Andrew's. They'd come a long way, all four of them, but they'd stuck it out through the doubts and the hurts. Now their whole lives stretched before them filled with promise.

* * * * *

Dear Reader,

Growing up in a very small town in Oregon, with grandparents, aunts, uncles and cousins abounding, I always looked forward to Christmas. On Christmas Eve, my sister and I were doted on as the only great-grandchildren on my father's side of the family. We were treated as royalty in my great-aunt and great-uncle's house. The feast and festivities—which always culminated in my great-aunt playing Christmas favorites on her organ—lasted long into the night.

The next day, it was literally "over the river and through the woods, to Grandmother's house we go...."

Obviously my sister, Mom, Dad and I packed into the old station wagon rather than a horse-drawn sleigh, but as we drove over the bridge spanning the Molalla River, I always thought of that song. The river in winter raged, the woods were stark and shimmering with snow or rain, and then, once we'd driven up a winding lane canopied by the branches of trees, we were at Grandma and Grandpa's house—a farm carved into glorious stands of old-growth timber.

We raced to the back door. Inside, the smells of roast turkey, sage stuffing and pumpkin or apple pies greeted us. The tree was aglow and there was always a boot print in the ashes of the fire, proof enough that Santa had been there.

The table wasn't big enough for everyone, so it was extended by a card table covered by a lace tablecloth. I always sat on the piano bench next to Cousin Dave, the closest thing I have to a brother to this day, and we laughed all the way through the meal.

As for this year, I hope your holiday season is filled with family, friends, music and laughter. So grab a cup of cocoa, snuggle under an afghan and turn the page....

Merry Christmas!

Lisa Jackson

SNOWBOUND
by Lisa Jackson

Chapter One

Bethany Mills looked out the window of her small house and tried to convince herself that she wasn't crazy. No one was following her; no one in Portland even knew what had happened in Boise. Now that she was in Oregon, she was safe. There was no reason to panic just because she'd received a worrisome call from her parents three days before.

But panic she did, and she couldn't pull her gaze away from the window. Her brow knit in concentration and her hazel eyes swept the hillside street in front of her home. Though she'd studied the twilight scene for ten minutes, she couldn't see any evidence of a stranger lurking under the cover of encroaching night; no one huddled against the rain; not one single pair of eyes focused on her. Yet she couldn't shake

the sensation that she was being both watched and
followed.

In the past three days, since the call from her father,
she'd felt eyes boring into her back, heard footsteps
following her and even imagined that a man was dog-
ging her as she went to work each morning.

"You're out of your mind," she said, trying to ignore the chill running up her spine. "You've just read
too many murder mysteries lately," she chided herself, abandoning her position at the window to flop
onto the worn couch and toss the book she had been
reading on the coffee table. "You'd better stick to
love stories."

Laughing hollowly at the private joke, she shook
her head and her auburn hair fell in loose curls around
her face. Love hadn't been her strong suit; in fact, if
any of her friends in Portland ever found out about
her past and her painful marriage to Grant Mills, they
would be shocked. As a kindergarten teacher at Johnson Elementary school, Bethany hardly appeared the
type to have been married to a man wanted by the
FBI for embezzlement and a list of other charges as
long as her arm.

"Maybe you should give up reading altogether,"
she told herself as she walked up the two short steps
to the kitchen and poured herself a cup of hot tea.
"Take up art, aerobic exercise, basket weaving, *anything*, but lay off the books."

She glanced nervously out the kitchen window at
the cold December evening. With only a few short
days until Christmas vacation, she should have been
happy, even ecstatic at the prospect of the holidays
and her return trip to Boise. But she wasn't, and now

she'd had to cancel her vacation plans. The hard part was still to come.

With a heavy heart, she dialed the number and tapped her fingers nervously on the windowsill as she waited for the long-distance call to connect. Her father answered on the fourth ring.

"Hi, Dad!" she said, hoping to sound cheerful.

"Bethany!"

She could hear the eagerness in his voice as he answered, placed his hand over the receiver and told his wife to get on the bedroom extension. Bethany's heart sank. Her parents had expected her to visit and she knew that holly and cedar bows, complete with bright-red trim, had already been carefully draped over the mantel and along the banister of the stairs. Probably mistletoe had been hidden in the brass and glass chandelier that hung in the entry hall, and there wasn't much doubt that her mother and aunt had already started baking pumpkin pies, Banbury tarts and cinnamon rolls, filling the farmhouse with the warm, spicy scent of yeast bread....

"When do you get in?" her father asked.

Bethany hesitated. "How about March seventeenth—spring break?"

There was an awkward silence on the other end of the line. "We were counting on Christmas together, Bethie," he said slowly.

"What? Isn't she coming home? Myron?" Bethany's mother's disappointed voice interrupted the flow of the conversation as Eleanor picked up the phone.

"Not this time, Mom," Bethany said, her voice catching just a little as she looked into her living room and surveyed the sorry-looking Christmas tree she'd put up two days earlier.

"But why not?" her father demanded. "It's not because Jim Benson's son, Harry, has been snooping around, is it?"

"No—"

"Myron, I told you not to tell her," her mother scolded.

"Really, Mom, that wasn't the only reason. I've got a lot of work to do here. This is my first year at Johnson and I really need to do a good job."

"But it's vacation!" her mother insisted, and Bethany could envision the disappointment in her mother's blue eyes.

"I know, but there'll be others. I promise. I sent your packages to you yesterday; I just hope they make it for Christmas."

"Then it's settled," her father said wearily.

"And it's only three more months," Bethany offered lamely, trying not to cry.

"Someday this will all be behind us," her mother said. "And then I'll tell Jim Benson and First Security Bank to go take a flying leap."

"It's not the bank's fault," Bethany said.

"I know, I know. But just because you married Grant, that's no reason to persecute you or your family!"

"No one's being persecuted," her father cut in sharply. "Grant took over a million dollars. Jim Benson, as owner and president of the bank, has a right to be upset!"

"But not with us! Or Bethany!"

"It goes deeper than that," Myron said. "Benson's

never trusted me. I should never have dealt with his bank in the first place.''

''What happened between you and Benson is water under the bridge,'' Eleanor said. ''It's just too bad that Grant—''

Bethany cringed.

''Never did trust that boy,'' Myron muttered, for about the thousandth time since his daughter had married Grant Mills.

There was no reason to open all the old wounds, Bethany thought sadly. ''Look, Mom…Dad…I just think it would be better for all of us if I came home on spring break.''

''It's a cryin' shame, that's what it is,'' Bethany's mother said angrily. ''And Grant Mills should be strung up by his heels, or worse.''

''Now, Mother,'' Myron cajoled her. ''Bethany's right. Spring's just around the corner and by then the orchard will be in bloom, the flowers will be out, you'll be plantin' peas and onions and we'll all feel a whole lot better.''

Bethany smiled through her tears. Her father was the right man to pour oil on troubled waters and after thirty years of marriage, Myron Wagner still knew how to smooth his wife's ruffled feathers.

''I know, I know,'' Eleanor said. ''It's just that I miss you, Bethie.''

''And I miss you, too. Both of you.''

''We'll call you Christmas morning,'' her father said softly.

''Good. And Dad?''

''Yes?''

''Thanks. I love you.''

"Oh, Bethany," her mother whispered brokenly.

"That's good to hear, darlin'," Myron said, cutting off any chance for Bethany's mother to break down on the phone. "Bye now."

"Bye."

Bethany replaced the receiver of the wall phone and wiped away her lingering tears. Crying wouldn't accomplish anything. With a sniff of disgust, she picked up her lukewarm tea, walked back into the living room and sat in a corner of the couch, staring sightlessly at the small Douglas fir with its handmade ornaments and winking lights. "It's just not the same," she said to herself, thinking back to all of the holidays she'd spent on her parents' farm; the relatives, the laughter, the tears, the love. All gone.

After swallowing a couple of sips of tea, she reached for the mystery novel that she'd tossed aside earlier. Getting lost in an adventure with detective Matt Hamilton was better than moping about the fact that once again her ex-husband had managed to put a wedge between herself and her parents. Even though Grant was gone, she couldn't escape from all the pain he'd caused her family. If only she'd listened to her father and never married Grant Mills, she might have stayed in Boise near her parents, married a man they approved of and had the couple of children she so desperately wanted. The thought of children only added to her depression. Just last year she'd thought she'd become a mother....

With a pang of regret she put down the book and ran her fingers through her hair. Thinking about the baby only made things worse and she closed her eyes, letting her head rest against the back of the couch. "Get a hold on yourself," she cautioned.

Ever since her father had called with the news that Jim Benson, president of First Security, had sent his son Harry to visit her parents' homestead and ask questions about Grant, Bethany had been on edge. Again, she wondered if she was really being followed, or if she was simply overreacting to the news that the bank in Boise was looking for Grant again.

Though his shoulder muscles ached, Brett planted his feet firmly, hoisted the ax once more, swung down and put all of his force behind the blow that finally split the last chunk of oak. The wood splintered with a satisfying crack that rumbled through the mountains surrounding his home.

The temperature was barely forty degrees, but he was covered with sweat from the effort of three hours at the woodpile, and his muscles were rebelling from the labor.

The work felt good; it helped him forget about the pain of losing Roberta and the fact that his stepfather had stolen this land from him. It had all been legal, of course; Jim Benson's bevy of lawyers had seen to the legalities, but the fact remained that Jim had married Brett's mother and when she'd died, Jim had inherited the land himself. Now, since the loss of his wife, Roberta, Brett had focused on what he had left in the world; his mother's land. He was paying to get it back—but the price was more than hard cash.

He ran a hand over his beard-stubbled chin and forehead. Wet strands of dark hair fell over his brow.

Pushing the hair from his eyes, he turned toward the cabin for a well-deserved hot shower and a drink.

He heard the car before he saw it. Stiffening, eyes narrowed and jaw tight, he looked over his shoulder and recognized Harry Benson's silver-blue BMW roaring up the long drive at breakneck speed. The car's brilliant metallic finish flashed through the thick stand of green fir and bare oak trees guarding the lane.

"Great," Brett murmured. With the corners of his mouth turned downward, he leaned on the handle of the ax and watched the sporty car approach.

"Now what?" Brett thought aloud, stretching his sore muscles and walking toward the puddle-strewn area of gravel where the BMW, with a spray of rainwater and mud, had finally halted.

"Brett! Glad I caught you!" the wiry young man with thin features, equally thin moustache and receding sandy-colored hair exclaimed as he got out of the car. Harry Benson looked around at the rustic cedar and plank cabin and attempted a faint smile. He noticed the stack of wood near the corner of the cabin and nervously jerked at the knot of his tie. "Getting your exercise, I see."

"Exercise?" Brett drawled, shaking his head. "I guess you could call it that." His steely-blue eyes sparkled with ironic amusement and the grim set of his mouth curved into a cynical smile. Leaning back against the post supporting the low-hanging roof of the porch that ran the width of the cabin, he observed the younger man. "What can I do for ya, Harry?" Brett finally asked, leaning forward on one knee. "You obviously didn't come up here for the drive. How about a beer?" One of Brett's thick brows rose and some of the lingering affection he felt for the younger man gleamed in his eyes.

"I don't think so." Harry, smug in the knowledge that he was about to drop a bomb in the other man's lap, forced a smile. "You're right. Something's come up."

"Like what?"

"Like you're back on the Grant Mills case."

"Guess again."

"I'm serious, Brett," Harry said. "Remember Billie Henshaw?"

"Yeah. What about her?" Brett asked, grimacing. Billie Henshaw had been involved with Grant Mills, and she had worked in the brokerage that transferred the bearer bonds to First Security. Without her there to destroy the records of the brokerage house before the transfer of the bonds to First Security and to her lover, Grant, the crime could never have been committed.

"Billie's dead. She was in a plane crash. It happened in the Sierra Nevadas."

Brett's grin dissolved. "What?" he demanded, his eyes glittering, his hands balling into fists as the realization of what was to come hit him full in the face.

In the attempt to get out from under his stepfather's thumb, Brett had spent months looking for Billie Henshaw as a possible lead to Mills. And now Harry was saying, "Billie and her traveling companion were killed."

"Damn!" Brett stuffed his hands into his pockets and tried to remain calm. "I don't suppose that Grant Mills was on the plane?"

"No."

Of course not. Nothing in the Mills case had been easy. Brett looked to the gray sky and silently cursed the black clouds, Grant Mills, First Security Bank and Jim Benson—especially Jim Benson. "Who was on the plane with her?"

"Jake Weathers, the pilot."

"Son of a bitch!" Brett muttered. "Just Jake? Not his brother, Karl?" The Weathers brothers had also been involved in the embezzlement. Jake had been a security guard for the bank and Karl, the younger man, had helped plan the escape. So far, none of the four-person gang had been captured.

"No. Karl wasn't with them."

"But—"

"I know, Karl usually hung out with them. Not this time. And as for Grant and Billie, who knows? Maybe they split the sheets or she double-crossed him."

"Or he's dead," Brett thought aloud, a headache forming behind his eyes. "So you still don't know where he is?"

"No."

"Or if he's alive."

"He's alive all right. Some of the stolen bonds were found in the wreckage. At this point there's no way of knowing how many of them were on board, but the FAA and the FBI are still looking into it."

Brett, recovering slightly from the bad news, began to think clearly again. "When did it happen?"

"Last week."

"Last week?" he repeated, letting out a long breath of air. "So what took you so long to get here?"

"Dad wanted to be sure that Mills was alive."

"And now he's sure?"

"Ninety-nine percent."

"And the other one percent?"

"Is one percent doubt. Obviously, Dad doesn't have much use for Grant Mills. So we're back at square one. The same place we were the day we discovered the bonds and Mills were missing."

"Holy mother of God," Brett said softly, deciding to get right to the point. Already knowing the answer to the question he was about to ask, he leaned back and stared straight into the eyes of his stepbrother. "So how does that affect me?"

"Guess."

Brett's response was brief. "I don't have time for games."

The smug look on Harry's face disappeared. He suddenly looked much younger, the way Brett liked to remember him. "Okay, I'll spell it out for you: you're on the hook again."

"I don't see how," Brett lied.

Harry shook his head and smiled. "Sure you do. Now that Billie and Jake are dead, we've lost our main leads to Mills. Karl hasn't been seen since last February. For all we know, he could have jumped out the plane with Mills."

"So?"

"So, you were the investigator who located Billie and Jake."

"And I owe First Security over a hundred thousand dollars for this land," Brett muttered. *The land that should have been mine,* he thought grimly. He crossed his arms over his chest. Dredging up the old argument wouldn't do any good. Legally, Jim Benson hadn't done anything wrong. Morally, it was another question altogether.

"Anyway," Harry continued, "Dad wants you to open the investigation again and find Mills."

"Good old Dad," Brett muttered, the cynicism in his eyes making Harry all the more nervous. "It really got to him that he got away with the money, didn't it?"

Harry looked exasperated. "Of course it did. We're talking about a million dollars, for God's sake."

"And the old man's pride is on the line."

"Dad doesn't like to lose."

Brett snorted his agreement and rubbed his stiff shoulders. How the hell had he gotten involved in this mess anyway? It was a classic example of being in the wrong place at the wrong time. Of being related to the wrong people. Brett pinched the bridge of his nose and tried to concentrate. "Look, it's over. Mills had no friends, half of his gang is dead, and the only lead to him is missing. I did my part, I found Billie. What more could I do?"

"Talk to his wife."

"No." As far as Brett was concerned, Bethany Mills was clear of any crime save that of marrying the wrong man. He would only stoop so low for his stepfather, and harassing innocent people was the limit. "We had a deal," he stated slowly.

"It's off." Harry snapped open his briefcase and pulled out a manila envelope. "Here's the information on the crash, and everything else we could pull together. I assume you've got copies of all the other information you sent to the office."

Brett's eyes flashed angrily, but he accepted the thick packet. "Just like that?"

"You didn't find Mills."

Seething, Brett rubbed a weary hand over his chin and tried to ignore the feeling that he'd been manipulated. Again. "I don't want any part of this," he said.

"As you said, we had a deal. You didn't keep your end of the bargain."

"You can't blame me because the plane went down."

"I know."

Brett walked up to Harry and towered over the younger man. His blue eyes searched Harry's face for a clue to the identity of the stranger the younger man had become. "Tell the old man that I'm out of this," he said calmly. "I'm through digging into other people's lives. I just want to be left alone."

"To drink yourself into oblivion?"

Brett laughed. So that was what Harry thought. "To damned well do as I please."

"Then you have to pay the price. Otherwise Dad will sell this land to someone else."

"Is that what he said?" Brett asked.

"In so many words."

"Great! Just great!" With a sigh, Brett ran his fingers through his thick black hair and leaned his head back as if in so doing he could quiet the rage of emotions that burned deep within his soul. He hated Jim Benson; hated working with the man; hated everything to do with him. But he didn't have much of a choice. All he had left in the world was this few acres of land, and working here gave his life a purpose and kept him sane. "I don't know—"

"Your choice," Harry said, shrugging his shoulders.

Brett clenched his jaw in frustration. He was boxed in and Jim Benson was winning; again. "If I agree to help, it'll cost more."

"Dad expected as much."

"Why didn't he come himself?"

"He knows you don't like him."

"That's putting it mildly," Brett said, his hard eyes cutting into the stylish young man who was the closest thing he had to a brother. Harry had changed over the years, but not for the better. Brett couldn't help but wonder how the innocent, happy-go-lucky child had withered into the boring little man in front of him. "So the extra money won't bother him?"

"Not too much."

"I'm surprised. I thought all your father thought about was money."

"That's because you never gave him a chance—" Harry began, some of his polished facade slipping.

"Not true, Harry. I tried." Brett rubbed his temples. "It doesn't matter, anyway. What does he want?"

Harry cleared his throat. "It's the bank's position that Grant Mills has to be found and convicted. Since that little stunt last year six other employees have tried to embezzle, and one even used the same D.B. Cooper-type tactics that Mills employed."

"But he wasn't so lucky."

"Right. The point is that First Security has become a target. All of the publicity surrounding Mills's crime and escape have made him some sort of a local hero, y'know," Harry explained. "Right now, banks aren't all that popular."

"Have they ever been?"

Harry pursed his lips and his pencil-thin moustache twitched. "Maybe not. All the banks in the area are in trouble because of the publicity surrounding the lumber mills failing in Oregon and the farm foreclosures in the Midwest...." He shrugged. "We can't afford a thief like Grant Mills being canonized or imitated."

"So what do you want me to do?"

"Find him. And this time don't stop with some frail lead."

The muscles in Brett's shoulders bunched. Billie Henshaw and Jake Weathers hadn't exactly been a "frail lead." They had both been involved in taking the bonds from the bank. Without them, Mills would never have been able to pull off the robbery. Brett had worked for many hours trying to locate them and when he had, Jim Benson had been pleased; but he hadn't released the deed to the property and now it looked as if he never would. "A deal's a deal."

Harry waved off Brett's anger. "And you didn't come through. This time, the old man insists that you go all the way—to Mills."

"Won't the FBI take care of that?"

"Maybe. But you're the one who found Henshaw and Weathers."

"So I'm the backup team."

"First Security doesn't see it that way."

Brett's eyes raked his stepbrother. "I'm through with it."

"Then Dad will be forced to sell this land."

"Forced!" Brett exclaimed, his temper snapping. "Like hell! Is that the story he peddled you?"

Harry shrugged nervously.

Brett was astounded. "You didn't actually believe it, did you? Come on, Harry, you know me—"

"You can take it up with Dad. You could call, y'know, but then you don't have a phone."

Brett tried to control the burning rage that was threatening to consume him, the rage that had been with him since Roberta had died. Roberta: the only bright spot in his miserable life.

Brett's gaze sliced into the younger man in frustration. As he saw it, there was no other choice. He hadn't done much in his life, but he planned on saving the only thing of value there was; by any means possible. "Okay, Harry," he said with a sigh. "I'll give it a shot and try to find Mills, but make sure the old man knows it'll cost him more."

"He understands. If you lead us to Mills and we capture him, your note will be considered paid."

"I want it in writing."

Harry smiled briefly. "Of course. You still don't trust Dad, do you?"

"Do you?"

"He's my father."

"That's not an answer."

Harry's eyes blinked nervously. "Of course I trust him."

"I wouldn't count on becoming president of the bank, Harry," Brett advised him. "That is what he promised, isn't it?"

Harry's Adam's apple bobbed over his tight, oxford

cloth collar. "Let's stick to the subject at hand, shall we?"

Staring at the shorter man, Brett felt a stab of self-loathing and regret. He should have helped his stepbrother years ago, before Harry had surrendered his independence and become a dead ringer of his father. Perhaps he could have made the difference...but then again, maybe not. "There *is* a chance that Mills might be dead, y'know."

"All you have to do is prove it."

Brett frowned and looked again at the pewter-colored sky. Clouds brushed the tops of the stately firs and wisps of fog had begun to settle over the foothills. "Simple enough, isn't it?"

"Should be, for you." With that, the young bank executive turned and walked to the car. He stopped at the door and paused. "Oh, and Brett?"

"Yeah?"

"Just one other thing."

"What's that?"

"Don't screw this up." With a bland smile, the son of the owner and president of First Security Bank opened the door of his car.

"I'll try not to," Brett said, his mouth relaxing into a grin at Harry's choice of words. Maybe there was still hope for the kid. "I just have one more question."

"Shoot."

Resting a shoulder on the porch, Brett asked, "What happened to you, Harry? Just what the hell happened to you? I remember a time when you liked to fish and have a beer and brag about all the girls you supposedly scored with. Now you're just like your old man, all paranoid about money and nothin' else.''

Harry hesitated and then frowned. "We all grow up, don't we?" Then, looking around at the rustic cabin, sharp ax, beat-up Jeep and Brett's dirty, sweat-soaked clothing, he added, "Well, most of us do." He slid into the creamy interior of the car and drove down the lane, disappearing through the trees.

"And sometimes it's a goddamned shame," Brett muttered to himself. Then, reaching for his jacket and slinging it over his shoulder, he walked into the cabin and stripped.

Later, after loosening his muscles in a hot shower, he twisted open a bottle of beer and finally sat down at his desk. He dumped the contents of the manila envelope onto the scratched, oak surface. Most of the information was predictable; short newspaper reports on the crash and notes, his own notes from the time when he'd been piecing the puzzle together. It had taken a while to figure it all out, Billie and the Weathers' brothers involvement. Now Billie and Jake were dead and no one knew what had become of Karl.

With a shake of his head, Brett read the reports and finally came to the last piece of evidence in the file; a picture of Grant Mills's wife, Bethany.

Crossing his legs and placing his heels on the desk, Brett leaned back in his chair, took a long swallow of beer and stared at the black-and-white photograph. Bethany Mills, whoever and wherever she was, represented his only chance to locate her husband and save this miserable piece of land.

His eyes left the photo and studied the rough interior of the cabin. Small, drafty and over fifty years old, it had been built as a summer home by his grand-parents sometime after the depression. It had been inherited by their only child, his mother, and become part of her dowry when she married into the Benson family; a family that never had really accepted her or her illegitimate son by another man. When she had died, all of her property had gone to her husband, Jim Benson, Brett's stepfather.

And now Brett was fighting to get the only thing of value in his life back where it belonged.

Feeling dissatisfied, he finished the beer and set the empty bottle on the desk, then tossed aside the photograph of Bethany Mills and felt his gut wrench. So far he'd avoided using Grant Mills's estranged wife to locate the man, but this time he had no choice. He'd leave no stone unturned. Bethany Mills included.

Chapter Two

Maybe if she hadn't been daydreaming, looking over her shoulder, wondering if she was being followed by the man she'd seen watching her in the parking lot of the grocery store, Bethany could have avoided the accident. But probably not. She was pedaling up the hill, her groceries tucked into the two saddlebags of her ten-speed, trying to ignore the pouring rain and the feeling that she was being watched when she looked up, gasped and swerved.

A small, tan dog was running along the railroad tracks that cut across the street. With the puppy was Jenny, Bethany's neighbor. When Jenny recognized Bethany, both she and the puppy stopped dead in the middle of the street, between Bethany, who was bicycling uphill, and a speeding red car that was careening full tilt down the rain-slickened road.

"Jenny! Watch out!" Bethany screamed, reaching for the child with her left arm while squeezing on the hand brakes with the fingers of her right hand. Bracing herself for the inevitable fall, fingers curling in the soft material of Jenny's worn sweatshirt and praying that both she and the child would be able to land out of the path of the car, Bethany jerked on Jenny's clothes. The bicycle wheel slipped in a puddle then caught on a railroad tie, twisting her away from the child and pitching her over the handlebars onto the grass at the side of the road. She landed with a bone-jarring thud and instinctively rolled away from the street in order to get back onto her feet and try to reach the girl. She slipped on the wet grass, her ankle gave out and she could do nothing but watch in horror.

"Jenny! Oh, God! No!"

The tires of the red sports car screeched as it slid around the frightened girl. The car's bumper caught the rim of Bethany's bicycle and flipped it into the air. Narrowly missing Jenny and the puppy, the speeding car continued onward, racing down the hill in a crazy, out-of-control pattern as the bike landed in the ditch some ten feet down the hill.

Bethany, in her dazed state, hadn't even seen the driver of the car, nor had a chance to read the license plate. She scrambled out of the ditch, ignoring the sharp jab of pain in her leg. Spitting dirt and blood from her mouth, she raced to Jenny. "Oh, honey, are you okay?"

Jenny wrapped her arms around Bethany's legs and started to whimper. "Don't be mad at me."

"I'm not, sweetheart, I just want to be sure that you're all right."

Wincing as she bent on one knee, Bethany brushed the black curls out of Jenny's face and looked into her large, tear-filled eyes. "Anything hurt?"

Jenny shook her head.

"Good. I wish I could say the same for me," Bethany said, kissing the little girl and glancing down the street at the red car. "Idiot!" she yelled angrily as the car lurched around a final curve and out of sight. Wiping the dirt from her mouth, she straightened and felt another stab of hot pain in her knee. She shifted her weight off the wrenched leg and grimaced as she surveyed the damage. Her jeans were ripped at the knee and the skin on her shin was scraped raw and bleeding. She could feel a cut on her chin and an ache in her hips, but, as far as she could tell, she'd avoided breaking any bones.

"Thank God it's not worse than it is," she murmured, pushing her hair out of her eyes and shuddering when she realized how close Jenny had come to being run over. "Does your mother know you're here?" she asked the girl.

Jenny shrugged, looking steadily at the wet ground.

"I didn't think so. I think we'd better go home and tell her what happened, don't you?"

Jenny shook her head violently.

Bethany sighed. She didn't want to get the child in trouble, but saw no way around it. Jenny could have been seriously injured or killed and the driver of the car hadn't even bothered to stop.

Why?

As she took Jenny's hand and led her down the hill

toward the bicycle, Bethany replayed the horrible scene in her mind.

She remembered the sudden rain shower as she had set out to return home and her worry that the man who had been sitting in his car and reading the paper in front of the grocery store had been waiting for her. She didn't remember much more than bending her head against the rain and feeling it slide down her neck as she'd pedaled along. The next thing she knew, she'd seen the flash of the car as it careered down the hill. There had been the sound of rock music, screaming tires and a glimpse of blond hair behind the steering wheel as the car hurtled by.

Probably some teenager afraid of getting a ticket for negligent driving. She burned inwardly, seething at the driver's recklessness. Then another, more terrifying thought struck her.

Maybe the near miss hadn't been an accident!

"Just your imagination," she told herself again, wiping the dirt from her palms and trying to clear her foggy brain. No one from First Security Bank or the FBI had contacted her lately. So why couldn't she shake the uneasy feeling that she was being watched? "You're losing it, Mills," she chided angrily.

"What?" Jenny asked solemnly. "What're you losing?"

"My mind," Bethany muttered and then seeing Jenny's confusion added, "Nothing. Really." Smiling at the child and stifling a groan as she moved toward the bike, Bethany looked around and saw that the puppy seemed to have escaped injury.

But her bike looked totaled. The front wheel was twisted and still spinning and several spokes had been broken from the rim; the chain was off, hanging loosely, and the gears were stuck in one position. The few groceries she'd been carrying in the saddlebags were strewn all over the road.

"Wonderful!" she said under her breath as she pulled herself upright. "Just wonderful." The tan puppy, tail between its legs, slunk over to her. "This is all your fault, y'know," Bethany chastised him, but couldn't stay angry with the pitiful, skinny animal. "Is he yours?" she asked Jenny.

"Can he be?"

"I don't know. Where did you find him?"

Jenny looked bewildered. "He just followed me."

"And what were you doing down here?"

"Waiting for you," Jenny said proudly. "I saw you on your bike and I knew you'd be back with your groceries."

Bethany winced. "You know you're supposed to stay in your yard."

Jenny, eyes downcast, seemed properly chastised and Bethany felt her heart twist for the child. "Let's not worry about it now. Why don't you help me get this bike up the hill, huh?"

Jenny brightened immediately. She patted the small tan-and-white puppy, who rewarded her with a wet, warm tongue against her palm.

"You'd better go home," Bethany admonished the dog, grabbing what was salvageable of the groceries and packing them into the battered plastic bicycle bags.

"He can come home with me!" Jenny announced.

"He probably already has a home," Bethany said,

though from the looks of the scrawny little dog, she doubted it.

"No, he don't. That's why he followed me."

"I think it was the other way around," Bethany reminded the child. "Besides, I'm not sure your mom would appreciate you bringing him home."

"She likes dogs!" Jenny exclaimed, calling to the skinny puppy who wagged his tail and made a beeline for her.

"I hope so," Bethany said quietly as the puppy tagged along behind them, disregarding her quiet suggestions that he go home.

Jenny's mother listened to Bethany describe what had happened and Linda Porter's eyes widened in horror. "Oh, God," she whispered, leaning against the doorjamb for support. "And the driver didn't bother to stop?"

"No." Bethany shuddered.

"All because Jenny was chasing this dog, right?" Linda asked, looking at the drenched, sorry-looking pup yipping excitedly at a squirrel that was leaping through the leafless branches of the trees near the small house.

"Can we keep him?" Jenny asked, innocently unaware of her mother's state of mind.

"Not on your life!" Linda scooped her daughter into her arms and held her tightly. "You know we can't keep a puppy. Joey's allergic to dogs and that's not the point, anyway," she reminded her daughter, her worry giving way to anger.

"But I want him—"

"We can't keep him." Jenny began to wail and

Linda rolled her eyes to the dark sky. "You ought to be ashamed of yourself, Jennifer. You knew better than to wander out of the yard! Just think, you could have been hit by that car!"

Jenny studied the floorboards of the porch and put her fingers into her mouth.

"The dog goes," Linda insisted, looking up at Bethany. "Really, we can't keep him, even if he doesn't have a home, which he probably does!"

"Probably," Bethany agreed.

"Can you come in for a cup of coffee?" Linda offered, but Bethany declined.

"I think I'd better check out the damage," she said, indicating the broken bike.

"Later, then."

"Another time." Bethany waved to Jenny, leaving mother and child and ignoring the tug at her heart as she pushed her bike the final few yards to her house. The puppy followed her, whining pitifully.

"Maybe you're lost," Bethany worried aloud once she'd wedged the ten-speed between her car and the stacked wood in her garage. The dog stood at the edge of her yard, his black-tipped ears cocked, his head angled to one side. Huddled under the leafless maple tree while rain drenched him and the cold December wind ruffled his fur, the puppy, a small, forlorn creature that apparently no one wanted, shivered.

"You'd better go home," Bethany said again, but was already unlocking the door leading from the garage to the kitchen. Once the door was open, she gave up her tough-lady act, smiled and waved at the adorable pup. "You know a soft touch when you see one, don't you? Well, come on in; you look like you could use a warm bath and a hot meal. And so could I.''

Without any further urging, the small dog bounded up the driveway, through the garage and into the kitchen.

Bethany laughed a little as she began to close the garage door and then the bothersome thought struck her again. *Why hadn't the driver of the red car stopped?* Was he, like herself, caught up in his own thoughts and distracted, to the point that his reactions had slowed? Or had the near collision been planned rather than accidental? ''You're out of your mind,'' she told herself once more, looking nervously around the stark street.

No one was in sight and yet she had the feeling that she was being watched; observed from a distance. Shivering from the bite of the wind, she studied the leafless trees, uncut grass and flowerless shrubs of the surrounding houses as she slammed the garage door shut and told herself that she was being foolish. No one was watching her. Here, in Portland, she was safe from the past and all of the pain she had suffered in Boise.

For the remainder of the weekend, Bethany experienced the same eerie feeling that she was being watched. The sensation was no more than that; just a feeling that caused her skin to prickle in apprehension. She hadn't seen anyone following her, or caught an unknown stranger staring at her from a distance, but nonetheless she hadn't been able to help glancing over her shoulder whenever she took the puppy outside.

No one had claimed the little dog and he'd made

himself right at home. Somehow, he'd managed to move into Bethany's heart as well as her house.

On Monday, she checked with the neighbors and placed an ad in the lost and found section of the local paper. However, the ad wouldn't be in print until Thursday, when the local paper was printed and distributed. Then perhaps, Bethany thought unhappily, someone would claim the scrappy crossbreed.

Wednesday was the last day of school before Christmas vacation. Bethany had finally begun to relax a little and had almost convinced herself that no one was following her.

It was dark that afternoon and, much to her students' delight, snow had been predicted.

The children had gone home and Bethany was just straightening the desks in the kindergarten room. She looked up through the long row of windows and saw a man staring at her from outside the building.

Nearly jumping out of her skin, she stifled a scream. Then, looking more closely, she realized that she'd only seen a shadow. There was no one lurking outside.

"You're getting paranoid," she said to herself as she glanced around the cheery room, which was decorated in red and green construction paper. Red Santas, green holly wreaths and brown reindeer, cut in whimsical five-year-old fashion, hung from the ceiling and white cotton snowmen lined the walls.

Glancing out the window again, she saw nothing but the first few flakes of snow sifting from the gray sky. *Snow for the holidays,* she thought distractedly, and an uncomfortable lump swelled in her throat when she reflected that, had things worked out differently, this holiday season would have been her child's first Christmas.

How different things would have been if the baby had lived!

"Pull yourself together," she whispered, sniffing back the urge to cry and yanking her coat from the closet. "You're just tired. It's over. The baby's gone. And so is Grant. You've got a new life, here, in Portland."

Pursing her lips, she slung the strap of her purse over her shoulder and reached into the bag, her fingers scrounging for her keys as Marianne, the school secretary, hurried into the room.

"Glad I caught you," Marianne said, her dark eyes dancing as she handed Bethany a brightly colored package.

"Oh. Thanks." Bethany looked at the beautifully wrapped gift before smiling into her friend's beaming face. "You didn't have to—"

"I wanted to. Besides, the cinnamon rolls you baked were out of this world. We've been eating them every morning." She rolled her eyes heavenward and smiled.

"Glad you liked them."

"Too much, I'm afraid," Marianne said with a grin as she patted her protruding abdomen. "The baby and I don't need all the extra calories."

Bethany, remembering the elation of her own pregnancy, nodded numbly and tried to push aside her lingering sadness. "Ah, well, it's only Christmas once a year. You can indulge yourself."

"My sentiments exactly! I was hoping you'd reconsider and spend Christmas Eve with Jack and me.''

''I don't think so.''

''But it's your first Christmas in Portland,'' Marianne protested, her dark brows arching quizzically. ''That is, unless you have other plans?''

Bethany hedged. ''I might go skiing.''

''With that leg? The one you nearly broke on the bicycle the other day? You've got to be joking! So what else have you got in mind?''

Her lips curving into a smile, her hazel eyes sparkling, Bethany placed the package in her bag and looked at the petite brunette. ''What is this, the third degree?''

''No, it's just that Jack and I always have a few people over during the holidays. Since both of our families are on the East coast, we like to share Christmas Eve with some of our friends who're in the same boat.''

''Meaning me.''

''And a few others.''

''Thanks a lot, but—''

Marianne touched Bethany's sleeve. ''Don't say 'No thanks.' You don't have to commit yourself right now. Just think about it. There'll be a ton of food, lots to drink, and some great people; people I think you'll really like. So, if you decide that you'd rather spend a cozy evening in front of our fire drinking hot spiced wine and singing Christmas carols instead of freezing your tail up on the slopes, just bring a bottle of wine and drop by. Dinner's at seven and the dress is casual.''

Grinning, Bethany cocked her head and her thick,

auburn curls fell across one shoulder. "You missed your calling, you know. You should have been in sales."

"I don't think so—"

Bethany winked at her friend. "You could have sold snow in Alaska."

Marianne brightened. "Then you'll come?"

"I'll think about it." Once again she began rummaging in her purse.

"There was one other thing," Marianne said, sobering a little.

"Mmm?" Bethany found her keys and pulled them out of her purse.

"There was a man here today looking for you."

Bethany's heart skipped a beat. Her fingers tightened around the cold metal key ring. "Who was he?"

Marianne lifted her shoulders. "I don't know. He said he knew you in Boise."

"But you didn't bring him into the classroom."

"I didn't think you'd want him to interrupt your party—this being the last day of school and all."

"And?"

Marianne pursed her lips together. "I told him that it was impossible for you to see him and he said he'd wait. When I pointed out that he couldn't just hang around the school, he smiled and said he understood."

"And then?" Bethany asked.

Marianne shrugged. "He left."

"Good." Bethany glanced nervously at the window. "Did he tell you his name?"

"No. When I asked for it, he gave me an incredible

smile and said he wanted to surprise you. He acted
like he was one of your best friends.''

''I don't have many friends in Boise,'' Bethany
whispered almost to herself as she pulled on her
gloves and wrapped a warm scarf around her neck.

''I think you'd remember this one.''

''Why?''

Marianne stared straight at Bethany. ''Because he's
memorable. There's something about him...an aura
of power, you might say.''

Bethany laughed despite the tension tightening her
shoulders. ''I'd *never* say that about anyone.''

''Wait till you meet him.''

''I hope I don't.''

''He didn't look like he'd be easily put off.''

''Because of this 'aura of power'? Even J.R. Ewing
meets his match occasionally.''

''Sometimes, Ms. Mills, you're impossible!'' Marianne teased as she started to leave the room.

''But not always, right?''

Looking over her shoulder at Bethany, Marianne
offered a sincere smile. ''Look, if you ever want to
talk about what happened in Boise...''

''You'll be the first to know; I promise.''

''Okay.''

''Marianne?''

''Yeah?''

''Thanks again for the gift. And Merry Christmas.''

''You, too. See ya Wednesday night,'' Marianne
said, waving as she walked out the door and through
the primary wing of Johnson Elementary.

''I don't think so,'' Bethany said to herself, switch-
ing off the lights in the room and, carrying all of her

books, packages and purse, slowly making her way
out of the building. This was one Christmas she
planned to spend alone. And to start it off, she intended to feed the dog as well as herself, take a long,
hot bath and then settle into bed with a good book.

It was nearly dark at four-fifteen and the wet snowflakes melted the minute they hit the ground. A cold
east wind, blowing down the Columbia River Gorge,
cut through Bethany's wool coat. Waving and shouting "Merry Christmas!" to some of the other teachers
leaving the school, she ducked her head against the
gale and walked across the parking lot to her car.

The man was already there. He was lounging
against the back of her small Toyota wagon, as if it
were a brilliant spring day instead of the dead of winter.

Bethany stopped short, her heart nearly missing a
beat. Despite his casual stance, an inner tension radiated from him.

"Bethany Mills?" he asked, pushing himself up
from the car with his elbow.

The blue cast from the security lamps shadowed
the slightly uneven features of a hawkish nose, deep-
set blue eyes, thick brows and thin lips. His hair was
black and windblown and he wore a thick suede coat
and faded jeans. With his lean, angular features he
looked leather-tough.

Bethany had never laid eyes on him before.

Her gaze locked with his and she realized that he
already knew who she was. A sinking feeling took
hold of her, but since the parking lot was far from
empty, she felt somewhat safe. "Yes?"

He smiled. Warm and lazy, it softened his features

with its off-centre charm and somehow managed to take the chill out of the evening. "I've been looking for you. The name's Hanson; Brett Hanson." He extended his hand.

Juggling her books, bag of packages and purse, she accepted his handshake. Even through her gloves, his hand was warm.

"What can I do for you, Mr. Hanson?"

Again the devastating smile. "It's what I can do for you, Mrs. Mills. I think I can locate your husband for you."

"What?" Bethany felt her face grow white and she nearly dropped everything she was carrying.

"I said, that, with your help, I think I can locate Grant."

Shocked, Bethany stood rooted to the ground, not noticing that the wind had caught in her hair and whipped it over her face. Swallowing hard, she pushed the dark strands aside and shivered. "I don't want to find my husband, Mr. Hanson. We were divorced at the beginning of the year. If you'll excuse me—" She pushed her key into the lock of the Toyota, but Hanson didn't move.

"Wait a minute. I think you should hear me out."

"Not tonight."

"When?"

"Never."

He offered her a charming smile that was offset by the cold glint in his eyes. "I just want to talk to you," he insisted.

"Why?"

"I think maybe I can help."

"I don't need any help, Mr. Hanson! And I don't

want it." Bethany opened the back of the wagon and placed her books and bag of Christmas gifts inside before realizing just how angry and scared she must have sounded. Straightening, she met his sharp gaze. "Look, I didn't mean to come off so hostile," she said as she slammed the tailgate shut, "but what happened in Boise is behind me."

"You're sure?"

"Positive." She sidestepped a few puddles as she walked to the driver's side of the car. "I'm not interested in finding my husband," she said softly, wondering why talking about Grant still bothered her.

"Maybe you should be."

"No."

"Even if you don't want to locate Grant, there are other people who want to see him brought to justice."

"It doesn't affect me," she lied, unlocking the car door.

His voice was calm but determined. "Anything your husband did affected you."

"Not anymore." Gazing directly at him, Bethany hoped she looked stronger than she felt. "Why are you involved?"

"Business."

"Come again?"

"I'm an investigator—for First Security."

"I see," she said tightly. First she'd been grilled by the bank auditors, then the FDIC and the FBI as well as the local police. Next the reporters had taken their turn.... "I already talked to the auditors. Surely you have a file."

He nodded and rubbed his chin. "Incomplete."

"I can't add anything more—" Bethany stopped

in midsentence and reevaluated the man standing near her car. "Wait a minute, Mr...."

"Hanson. Call me Brett."

She studied him carefully. "I think you'd better leave me alone. First of all you don't look like any banker I've ever seen." She took in his worn jeans and suede jacket, his unruly hair and lack of suit and tie.

"I don't work for the bank, not as an employee."

"I don't suppose you have some credentials?"

"In my Jeep."

Sure. "You don't mind if I see them?"

He offered her the same lazy, slanting grin. "I'd expect that you'd want to."

"I do." He'd already started to turn toward the Jeep parked near her car when she changed her mind and waved her hand in the air with sudden decision. "No, never mind. I don't want to talk to you. You call your head office and talk to Bill Standish, the head auditor, he's the man I spoke with. If that isn't good enough, talk to the president of the bank. Mr. Benson."

"He's the guy who sent me."

Dear God. "Why?"

"I'll explain all that when we talk." He eyed the dark sky. "We can go to a restaurant in town—"

Bethany shook her head. "I don't have anything more to say. Can't you go read the reports or listen to the tapes of the conversations I had with the auditors?"

"I already have."

Exasperated, she leaned against the car. "And you decided that you needed more information."

"They decided."

"By 'they' you mean Benson?"

"Right."

"So it's the old feud again."

"What?"

"Nothing. Benson's not too crazy about my dad, but it doesn't matter. The feeling's mutual."

"Maybe you'd better tell me about it."

Bethany shook her head. The nightmare was starting all over again. Inside her gloves, Bethany's palms began to sweat. "Ask Jim Benson. There's nothing I can say to help you."

"I just want to ask you some questions."

"Look, Mr. Hanson, I'm tired and I want you and the rest of the world to leave me alone. I've cooperated with the bank and the insurance company and the FDIC and the FBI. They questioned me for days on end, threatened me with jail and my parents with scandal. They kept at me, determined that I was involved in what my husband did! Now I think I deserve some peace and quiet. In case you've forgotten, it's nearly Christmas."

"I understand," he said.

"Do you?" she asked, her eyes bright.

"Yes."

"Good."

"I'd just like to know why you ran away."

"Ran?" she echoed, her eyes widening at the audacity of the man. Anger and frustration burned in her veins. "I stayed there, in Boise, while everyone assumed I had something to do with the embezzlement. I didn't run, Mr. Hanson; I was forced out of town. Now, I'm not about to stand out here and freeze talking about Boise or my ex-husband. I'm really not sure what you're peddling, but I'm not interested.''

"Even if it would clear your name?"

"*My* name is clear."

"There are still people who think you were involved."

"That's their problem."

"And mine."

"But not mine," she reminded him. "I did what I had to do and now it's over. The police and the FBI know I wasn't involved in what my husband did at the bank." She jerked open the door and slid inside. She was shaking and couldn't decide if it was from the cold or from facing the past. Probably a little of both. "Good night, Mr. Hanson. And, I'd appreciate it if you'd quit following me."

"I haven't been."

"Give me a break." But the intense look he sent her was filled with honesty. Swallowing hard, she asked, "Weren't you looking through the kindergarten room window a little while ago?"

"No."

She believed him. Something in his steely-blue eyes convinced her that he wasn't lying. So maybe the man had been a figment of her imagination, after all. "I'm sorry. There's nothing more I can tell you." With a jerk, she slammed the car door shut, pushed the key into the ignition and, with trembling fingers, started the car. Forcing herself to count to ten, she tried to calm down before she put the Toyota into reverse and then drove out of the parking lot. In the rearview mirror she could see him, still standing under the ghostly security lights.

Why now? she wondered. Just when she was getting her life back together, why did this stranger have to appear and dig up the past?

Brett stared at the retreating taillights. He'd blown it. No doubt about it. Forcing his frozen fingers deep into the pockets of his jeans, he walked back to his Jeep and slid inside, cursing himself.

He started to put the vehicle into gear, then paused and clicked open the briefcase on the passenger seat. The manila folder was just where he'd hidden it. Frowning, he dumped the contents of the packet into the case. Several documents fell out. He ignored them and picked up the picture of Bethany Mills.

In glossy black and white, she seemed flat and lifeless. But the real woman he'd met was just the opposite; full of fire and life.

His lips twisted cynically as he stared at the photo and colored it from memory. Rich, brown-red hair cut in several layers framed an oval face with burnished curls. Her deep-set, widely spaced eyes were a unique shade of hazel hovering between green and gold, and her high cheeks, pink from the bite of the wind, rounded over a small, full-lipped mouth.

Nope, Bethany Mills wasn't what he'd expected. Not by a long shot. The black-and-white photo didn't do her a bit of justice.

With a grimace of frustration, he tossed the picture back into the envelope, snapped the briefcase shut and shifted into reverse. *Well, Mrs. Mills,* he thought to himself, as he wheeled out of the parking lot, *unfortunately for both of us, you haven't seen the last of me!*

Chapter Three

Bethany awoke slowly, vaguely aware of a noise that was disturbing her dreams. As she opened her eyes, the pounding got louder and Winston, the puppy no one had yet claimed, barked and growled at the foot of the bed.

"What now?" she asked, grabbing her robe and glancing at the clock. Who in his right mind would be banging on her door at eight in the morning on the first day of vacation?

The puppy growled again and Bethany laughed. Winston bounded onto her stomach and washed her face with his warm, wet tongue. "Ugh. Give me a break," Bethany moaned, petting him before she sat up, wiping her face and rubbing her eyes. "Feeling pretty territorial, aren't you? For all we know, the person knocking on the door could be your owner.

And if he is, I'm going to give him a piece of my mind!"

The knocking continued and in her mind's eye, Bethany pictured the man in the parking lot, Brett Something-or-other. "I'm coming!" she yelled, pushing the hair out of her eyes and cinching her robe around her waist as she hurried down the hall.

Yanking open the front door she discovered Jenny standing on the small front porch. Rosy cheeks, curly black hair and sparkling green eyes were all that were visible of the child. The rest of the round four-year-old was covered in gloves, hat, ski jacket, trousers and boots.

"Hi!"

Bethany leaned against the opened door, crossed her arms over her chest and looked suspiciously at the child. "What're you doing up so early?"

"It snowed!" Jenny gestured expansively at the white-flecked greenery surrounding Bethany's small cottage on the hill.

Still rubbing the sleep from her eyes, Bethany yawned and couldn't suppress a grin. She'd always loved the first snow of winter. "That it did. In spades."

"What?"

"Nothing." Bethany waved aside the question. "It's just a bridge quote, an expression adults use, like raining cats and dogs." Seeing that she'd completely confused the child, Bethany started again; this time on a different subject. "Does your mother know you're here?"

"She's still in bed."

"I see. But, she, uh, knows you're outside?"

"Yeah. I thought maybe you'd wanna sled down the hill."

"Not just yet," Bethany said, opening the screen door and stepping back to allow the excited child inside. "How about a cup of cocoa while I wake up?"

"Yummy!"

"I remember how it warms you up," Bethany said, thinking back to her own childhood on the farm outside of Boise. Piled, drifting snow, red-checkered oilcloths on the kitchen table, icicles hanging from the eaves of the house to glisten in the sun, the smell of coffee and hot chocolate and her mother's soothing voice. Winter had been harsh but beautiful. Bethany had loved it and still missed the early mornings when she'd been up at five to help with the chores. How long ago it seemed.

Putting aside the vivid memories, Bethany called to the pup and let him out to romp in the snow.

Jenny squealed with delight as the dog shot down the hall and out the front door. "Can we go sledding?" she asked, taking off her boots and climbing into a cane back chair near the kitchen table.

"Maybe." Bethany poured a cup of milk and placed it in the microwave. Then, stretching to reach into the uppermost cupboard over the stove, she pulled down the package of cocoa that she saved for Jenny. "If your mom says it's okay."

"She don't care."

"She might," Bethany replied, stirring the chocolate powder into the warm milk. Jenny's mother was divorced and worked at two jobs to make ends meet. Though it really wasn't Linda's fault, Jenny and her older brother Joey sometimes got lost in the shuffle.

Play TIC-TAC-TOE and get FREE GIFTS!

HOW TO PLAY:

1. Play the tic-tac-toe scratch-off game at the right for your FREE BOOKS and FREE GIFT!

2. Send back this card and you'll receive TWO brand-new Silhouette Romance® novels. These books have a cover price of $3.50 each in the U.S. and $3.99 each in Canada, but they are yours to keep absolutely free.

3. There's no catch. You're under no obligation to buy anything. We charge nothing — ZERO — for your first shipment. And you don't have to make any minimum number of purchases — not even one!

4. The fact is, thousands of readers enjoy receiving books by mail from the Silhouette Reader Service™ months before they're available in stores. They like the convenience of home delivery, and they love our discount prices!

5. We hope that after receiving your free books you'll want to remain a subscriber. But the choice is yours — to continue or cancel, any time at all! So why not take us up on our invitation, with no risk of any kind. You'll be glad you did!

YOURS FREE A FABULOUS MYSTERY GIFT!

We can't tell you what it is…
but we're sure you'll like it!

A FREE GIFT —
just for playing

TIC-TAC-TOE!

DETACH AND MAIL CARD TODAY!

With a coin, scratch the gold boxes on the tic-tac-toe board. Then remove the "X" sticker from the front and affix it so that you get three X's in a row. This means you can get TWO FREE Silhouette Romance® novels and a **FREE MYSTERY GIFT!**

PLAY TIC-TAC-TOE

YES! Please send me the 2 Free books and gift for which I qualify. I understand that I am under no obligation to purchase any books, as explained on the back of this card.

315 SDL CX7Y

215 SDL CX7S
(S-BR2-12/99)

Name: _____

(PLEASE PRINT CLEARLY)

Address: _____ Apt.#: _____

City: _____ State/Prov.: _____ Zip/Postal Code: _____

The Silhouette Reader Service™ — Here's how it works:

Accepting your 2 free books and gift places you under no obligation to buy anything. You may keep the books and gift and return the shipping statement marked "cancel." If you do not cancel, about a month later we'll send you 6 additional novels and bill you just $2.90 each in the U.S., or $3.25 each in Canada, plus 25¢ delivery per book and applicable taxes if any.* That's the complete price and — compared to the cover price of $3.50 in the U.S. and $3.99 in Canada — it's quite a bargain! You may cancel at any time, but if you choose to continue, every month we'll send you 6 more books, which you may either purchase at the discount price or return to us and cancel your subscription.

*Terms and prices subject to change without notice. Sales tax applicable in N.Y. Canadian residents will be charged applicable provincial taxes and GST.

If offer card is missing write to: Silhouette Reader Service, 3010 Walden Ave., P.O. Box 1867, Buffalo, NY 14240-1867

BUSINESS REPLY MAIL

FIRST-CLASS MAIL   PERMIT NO. 717   BUFFALO, NY

POSTAGE WILL BE PAID BY ADDRESSEE

SILHOUETTE READER SERVICE
3010 WALDEN AVE
PO BOX 1867
BUFFALO NY 14240-9952

NO POSTAGE
NECESSARY
IF MAILED
IN THE
UNITED STATES

"You drink this while I take a shower and get cleaned up. Then we'll talk about sledding. Okay?"

"Okay. Oh, you forgot the marshmallows."

Bethany laughed. "You know where they are, you can help yourself."

By the time that she'd showered, dressed, pulled her hair away from her face and put on a little makeup, Bethany wasn't surprised to find that Jenny was finished with her cocoa. She was standing with the front door wide open and calling to the dog.

"That didn't take long," Bethany observed, eyeing the opened bag of marshmallows on the counter. "Have you had breakfast?"

"Not yet."

"Well, let me make us both a piece of toast and then we'll go outside."

Jenny looked contrite. "Mom says I shouldn't eat over here."

"But hot chocolate is okay?"

Jenny shrugged and looked decidedly guilty. "I think so."

Bethany got down on one knee so that she was eye to eye with the little girl. "And I think it's okay for you to have a piece of toast and an orange. I'll talk to your mom about it later. Okay?"

"Okay." After closing the door, Jenny took her usual place at the table and scooted the poinsettia aside so she could have a better view out the window. Bethany served them both and sat at the table with the bright-eyed child. "How come you don't have a husband?" Jenny asked, once she'd devoured the last crumb of toast and raspberry jam.

Surprised, Bethany took a sip of her coffee and lifted a shoulder. "I did."

"Where is he?"

"We're divorced."

"Oh. Like my mom and dad."

"I guess so."

"Do you see him?"

Bethany picked up the crumbs of toast with her finger. "No. I haven't seen him for a long time. I...I thought he might be dead," she admitted, wondering why she could talk to a child and no one else.

"Why?" Jenny asked innocently.

"Because he's been missing, er, gone for a long time."

"But he's not dead, is he? Not really."

"I don't know."

Jenny frowned. "That's sad. Do you miss him?"

"Sometimes," Bethany admitted, though she knew that what she missed was the companionship that had been part of her marriage, not her husband. Grant hadn't been much of a husband, but he'd been someone to come home to, someone to dream with, someone to worry about....

"I bet he misses you a lot."

"I don't know about that." Bethany stacked the dishes in the sink and then put on her ski jacket and wool scarf. "Okay, let's go tackle that hill before all the snow melts."

"It won't melt," Jenny said with all of the wisdom of her four years. "It can't. It isn't even Christmas yet!"

"But it will be soon."

"I can't wait! This year I'm gonna see Santa Claus!"

"Are you?"

"Uh-huh! Mom said we could bake him some cookies and leave them on the heart."

Bethany smiled down at the excited child. "Hearth."

"Uh-huh."

"That sounds wonderful." While she waited for Jenny to put on her boots, Bethany looked at the solitary fir tree standing in a corner near the window. It somehow looked small and lonely in the living room with the high ceiling and brick fireplace.

"Come on," Jenny insisted, tugging on Bethany's arm. "Do you have a sled?"

"Just a saucer."

"Will it work?"

"You bet it will." Bethany closed the door behind her, walked to the garage and picked up the round plastic disk.

"I don't think we'll both fit on that," Jenny stated.

"Sure we will. We'll just have to squinch."

"Squinch?"

"You know, huddle close together."

"I'd like that," Jenny decided with a wide grin.

"And so would I."

"Can Winston come, too?"

"Not in the saucer. But he can run alongside."

"Why'd you name him that?" the child asked as they walked through the garage to the pristine outdoors. Other children were already laughing and squealing as they swooped down the hill on every-

thing from giant inner tubes to plastic garbage can
lids.

"Why'd I do what? Oh, you mean name him Winston?"

"Yeah. It's a funny name. Mom says you named
him like a cigarette."

Bethany chuckled and brushed the snow from her
face. "Not really. I named him after a very famous
British prime minister. I didn't think about the cigarettes. Don't you like the name?"

"No."

"Then how about Unlucky?"

Again, Jenny shook her head.

Bethany smiled. "Maybe I should have named him
Lucky, like the rest of the population would have.
After all he did survive—"

"Survive what?"

Bethany looked down at the suddenly sober child.
"Nothing," she said. "Come on. You hop on first."

They settled together in the red disk and, holding
Jenny tightly, Bethany lifted her feet and pushed off.
They flew down the hill. Snow sprayed upward, covering them both as Jenny and Bethany landed at the
bottom of the cul-de-sac against a snow-covered pile
of dead leaves. Bethany was breathless, but Jenny,
mindless of the snow and leaves on her face, was
giggling and eager to do it again.

"You're sure?" Bethany asked, picking a dead
twig from Jenny's stocking cap.

"Oh, yes. Please! Come on!"

Bethany, once she discovered that she hadn't rein-
jured her ankle, was glad to accommodate the enthusiastic child.

"Did that man find you?" Jenny asked as they trudged up the hill together.

Bethany nearly stopped short. "What man?" she asked, trying to control the thudding of her heart.

"The man that was here the other day."

"Here where?"

"At your house. I told him you were at school."

"Oh, honey, you know you shouldn't talk to strangers." Seeing the wounded look in Jenny's eyes, Bethany took the child's gloved hand in hers. "It's just not safe."

"But he said he knew you!"

"Did he tell you his name?"

Jenny shook her head. "Can you tell me what he looked like?"

"A man."

"A tall man?"

"Uh-huh."

"What color of hair did he have?"

"I don't know," Jenny said, looking at the ground. "He was just a man." Tears were beginning to well in the child's eyes and Bethany knew she'd pressed too hard.

Ignoring the worry nagging in her mind, she smiled down at the girl. "Listen, sweetheart, let's forget about him for a while. Okay?"

"Okay."

For the next hour Jenny and Bethany shot down the hill in front of Bethany's house. They spun on the disk as it careened down the hill and once they flew off into the pile of leaves and snow.

"We were lucky that time," Bethany said, rubbing her hip and realizing how dangerous sledding with

Jenny might be. Jenny's mother, Linda, was a likable person who didn't object to the friendship that had formed between her daughter and Bethany, but Linda wouldn't be so pleased if Jenny got hurt. "We'd better call it quits for a while."

"Do we have to?" Jenny protested as they climbed back up the hill.

"I'm afraid so. At least until I talk to your mom."

"But she doesn't care—"

"Sure she does. And I don't want you to get hurt. Now, you go on home and I'll see you later."

"Promise?"

"Promise."

Jenny threw her chubby arms around Bethany's neck and then she was off, slipping and sliding down the snowy hill, chasing her brother and his friends as they sped past Bethany on a battered toboggan.

Bethany stared after the child and then again experienced the uneasy feeling that she was being observed. Dusting the snow from her ski pants and looking around, she started when she recognized the man from the parking lot leaning against the telephone pole at the bottom of the street, not far from where Joey and his friends had landed.

When Brett's eyes locked with hers, he straightened, then began walking up the hill. Bethany felt her throat tighten and her heart flutter with dread as he approached.

"Mornin'," he drawled once he was within earshot. Offering her a lazy, slanting smile that softened his harsh features, he pushed his hands deep into the pockets of his pants. He was dressed just about the way he had been the night before: old jeans, faded shirt and heavy jacket. He'd rammed a Stetson onto his head and his black hair poked out beneath the brim, so that he looked rather like a world-weary cowhand straight out of a Hollywood set.

Bethany ignored his greeting and didn't bother returning his smile. "You certainly don't know how to take a hint."

"Not until I get what I want."

Eyes narrowing, she asked, "Which is?"

"Just to talk to you."

"We talked last night."

"Not enough." He smiled again, his gray-blue eyes searching the hilly, snow-covered neighborhood of small homes clustered on the wooded slopes. Douglas fir trees, their green-needled boughs heavy with snow, stood near naked maples and alders and the quiet morning air was disturbed only by the shouts of happy children or the occasional whine of tires slipping on the icy street. "I think you should hear what I have to say."

"And I don't think I want to. What happened in Boise is all in the past. I've got a new life now," she said.

He lifted his hat from his head and smoothed his hair with his hand. "You just can't forget what happened."

"I can try!"

"Please, Mrs. Mills. Just hear me out. I'm not here to hurt you, I just need to sort out a few facts."

"So that you can file a report with the bank."

He snorted. "'Fraid it won't be that simple."

"I thought the bank auditors were satisfied."

"They were."

"But?"

"Jim Benson isn't."

"Him again. Doesn't he ever give up?" Her chest began to tighten.

"He feels that First Security has become a target. Ever since your husband's heroic embezzlement—"

"Heroic?" she echoed, sick to her stomach.

"That's the way some of the people see it. Not only did he swindle a bank out of a million dollars—a bank that's had to foreclose on businesses and homes in the area—he did it with style."

"If you call it style to jump out of a plane in the middle of the night wearing only a single parachute. I call it crazy!"

Brett shrugged. "Nonetheless, he's become some-what of a legend around Boise."

"And he's probably dead," Bethany whispered.

"That just adds to the mystery."

"Dear Lord."

"So, every Tom, Dick and Harry who has a grudge against the bank has tried to rip off First Security. Obviously that doesn't sit well with the board of directors. The bank has become a target and a laugh-ingstock. Jim Benson doesn't like it."

"So how does that involve you?"

"Benson wants me to find your husband."

"That's impossible."

"I don't think so."

"Grant's probably dead," she muttered, ramming her hands into the pockets of her jacket.

"Maybe not."

The children had come up the street again and while they climbed onto their sleds and inner tubes,

Bethany stood silent. Only when the shouts faded and the children were far down the hill did she turn her worried eyes back to Brett. "Why should I trust you?" she asked.

He glanced around the street and frowned. Realizing that he hadn't convinced her that she should help him, he reached into his back pocket, withdrew his wallet and handed her a business card.

Though old and faded, its message was clear: Brett Hanson, Private Investigator. The address was an office building in Boise.

Bethany read the card, curled it into her fist and pursed her lips. "Okay, Mr. Hanson. We'll talk, if that's what you want. But I can tell you right now that I'm not really interested in any investigation." She began walking up the drive, carrying the red disk, trying to still the hammering of her heart.

"Not even if I can prove that your husband is alive?"

Bethany swallowed hard, remembering all of the pain and humiliation she'd suffered at Grant's hand. "No," she whispered, feeling the lie getting stuck on her tongue.

"But surely—"

Closing her eyes for a second, she took a deep breath. "What Grant did or didn't do isn't really any of my concern. Not anymore. We've been divorced for a long time." She reached the front door and opened it, set the disk inside the house, then stomped her boots on the outer mat before finally slipping them off.

Brett followed suit, leaving his boots on the porch before he entered the house and took off his hat. His

eyes scanned the interior of the small home. Hardy
green plants, bookcases filled with paperbacks and
reference books, worn but comfortable furniture and
a colorfully braided rug gave the living room life. In
a corner near the brick fireplace stood a small Christmas tree, its lights winking brightly in the morning
light, filling the house with the scent of fir.

Bethany slung her coat over one of the rails of a
brass hall tree and Brett, feeling awkward in his
stocking feet, did the same.

"Please, sit down," Bethany offered, perching on
her favorite ottoman and observing him through suspicious green-gold eyes.

Brett sat on the couch, his long, jean-clad legs
stretched in front of him, his elbows resting on his
knees as he stared at her and wondered what the hell
had possessed him to take this case. Thirty acres in
the mountains, he told himself; his mother's land. He
had to keep the property in mind as he looked at the
beautiful, defiant and slightly frightened woman facing him. She was near enough that he could touch her
easily....

"Okay, Mr. Hanson—"

"Brett. Remember?"

"Right. Brett. Why don't you start at the beginning?" His presence in her house made her uncomfortable, so, to avoid seeming nervous, she crumpled
pages from a newspaper and began building a fire.

He gestured to the wood. "I can do that."

"It's all right. I need to keep busy. I'd be lying if
I didn't admit that your being here is upsetting," she
said with a sigh. "Let's keep this to the point; just
tell me what you want from me."

"I want you to help me find your husband."

Bethany's heart stopped. She hesitated, wiped her sweating palms on her pants and then continued arranging the kindling and logs on the grate. "So you really do think he's alive."

"It's not something I'd joke about. Some of the bonds he stole have turned up."

"Oh, God," she whispered, her throat thick. "Where?"

"California."

She struck a match with shaking fingers and waited until the kindling caught and began to crackle, before she finally trusted her voice enough to turn and face the stranger in her home. "And you people thought I just might know where he was."

He smiled.

Damn him and that ingratiating grin on his face, she reflected bitterly.

"It's happened before."

"Not this time." She stood and met his gaze squarely. "I don't know why my husband took off with the bearer bonds. We were divorced at the time."

"He did it because he needed a large sum of cash to start over. He'd been embezzling for years, but only small sums."

Bethany closed her eyes. "I never saw any of the money," she said. "Honestly. I know what the bank thinks: that Grant and I spent all of the hundred thousand he took over the previous four years, but I didn't know a thing about it. As far as I was concerned, we lived off his salary and mine. I didn't see any of the extra money."

"I know."

She stiffened. "You do? How?"

"Because there was another woman involved."

Bethany closed her eyes and clamped her teeth together. The old wound was still raw. Having tried to convince herself for over a year that what Grant had done during their marriage no longer affected her, she came face to face with the fact that Grant's betrayal still hurt. "Grant had several affairs while we were married," she said, nervously stuffing another piece of newspaper onto the grate and watching the hungry flames devour the crumpled pages.

"I know."

Whipping her head around, Bethany stared straight at him. "Is there anything you don't know about me, Mr. Hanson?"

A touch of regret softened his gaze. "Brett. And I don't know where your husband is right now or who he's with."

"I don't see how I can help you."

"You haven't heard from him?"

"Of course not! I—I was under the impression he'd died while jumping out of the plane…like that D. B. Cooper person."

"They never found him, either." Brett's eyes pierced hers and Bethany felt her pulse begin to accelerate. "Besides, we're talking about an entirely different situation. Your husband had help—as far as Cooper went, he probably worked alone. And your husband didn't jump out of a commercial airliner; he leaped out of a Lear airplane owned by one of his friends."

"Who didn't know anything about it."

"He claimed. Remember, he was a security guard for First Security. Grant couldn't have done the job alone."

"Jake Weathers was put through the wringer, just like me. They had a hearing, but the grand jury wouldn't indict him. There just wasn't enough evidence...." She stopped talking and swallowed hard under Brett's gaze. "But you know all that, don't you?"

"And more."

"I don't think I want to hear it." She stood and warmed her legs against the flames.

"Don't you want to know the name of the woman your husband had working with him?"

"I've heard it," she said dryly. "Look, Grant and I were divorced over a year ago, before all of this embezzlement fiasco. He left me for...other reasons. Personal reasons..." She felt her chest go tight at the memory of her pregnancy, the sharp continual pains of labor on the icy road to the hospital, the sickening sensation when the car had slid into the ditch and then, hours later at the hospital, the eventual delivery of the stillborn child....

"Bethany?"

Looking up, Bethany was surprised to find Brett beside her, his hand resting on her shoulder.

"Are you okay?" His blue eyes were warm, suddenly filled with compassion.

As if warding off a chill, Bethany rubbed her hands over her upper arms and took a step away from him, breaking the intimacy of his touch. "Yes. I was just...thinking back; memories, you know... Look, I don't really want to dwell on the past, okay?" Forcing a cheerful smile she didn't feel, she lifted her chin. "How about a cup of coffee?"

His thick brows continued to beetle over the steely blue eyes that reached through her defenses and slipped past her facade. She could feel him reading her mind, stripping her bare. Lord only knew what he'd already learned about her.

"I don't want to impose—"

"My eye," she said softly. "You've imposed from the minute I met you last night. One cup of coffee won't make a whole lot of difference one way or the other."

He grinned, and the smile sliced across his tanned face to make it appear handsome rather than rugged. "Then I don't mind if I do."

"Good." With a sense of renewed purpose, to give him the coffee and then as quickly as possible shove him out the door, Bethany walked up the two steps to the dining room and into the kitchen. Once there, she poured coffee into two enamel mugs.

"Sugar or cream?" she called over her shoulder.

"Black."

Of course. Just the way they drink it on the range. She stirred a little milk into her coffee and frowned. With any luck, she could give Brett the hot drink, some quick answers, a firm "No way," when he asked for her help and then he'd be off. On his own. Out of her calm, quiet, predictable life. Forever.

Setting the spoon in the sink, she stared at her still swirling coffee. Why would the thought of Brett leaving bother her? The man was a royal pain in the neck and he seemed hell-bent to upset her life.

"Thanks." Brett grabbed his cup from the counter and took a long swallow.

Bethany nearly jumped out of her skin. She hadn't heard him come into the kitchen. "You're welcome," she replied, quickly picking up her cup and blowing across the hot liquid. "I didn't hear you walk in. That's the second time you sneaked up on me. I don't know how you do it."

"Practice," he admitted, grinning cynically. "Old habits die hard. And I didn't sneak up on you; you were lost in thought."

"Is there anything you don't know about me?"

"A lot."

"I doubt it."

"But I'd like to know more." His voice was low and sounded a little reluctant.

"Why?"

Gazing into her eyes, he lifted a hand to touch her chin, but let it drop. "It's my job."

"Oh, right. The bank."

Looking past her, out the window to the snow-covered trees, he scowled. "Yeah, right. The bank." *And Jim Benson; good old stepdad with his iron fist and cash register for a heart.* He slowly uncurled his clenched fists, willing the anger and bitterness aside. "What do you know about Billie Henshaw?"

"Nothing. Just what I read in the papers."

"Your husband was supposed to be involved with her."

"That's probably true," she admitted. "I don't know. We were divorced and didn't see each other. What he did in his personal life..." She shrugged her shoulders as if Grant's betrayal hadn't hurt, but her fingers took a firmer hold on her cup. "It...it really had nothing to do with me."

"I'm sorry," he said, seeing her pain.

Looking up sharply, she said, "It's not your fault. No reason to be sorry." Squaring her shoulders, she tilted her chin upward and met his gaze. "I never met this Billie Henshaw, or whatever her name is." Her stomach twisted painfully, but she took a sip of coffee anyway. "Look, there really isn't much more I can tell you. I don't know anything about the embezzlement, never saw any of the money, and once we were divorced, I really didn't keep tabs on Grant." Placing her cup carefully on the counter, she faced him once again. "I can't really help you, Mr. Hanson. It's not that I don't want the bank to recover its money, but I don't know anything! Maybe you should be talking to Billie Henshaw."

"I can't," Brett explained.

"But surely she knows more than I do."

"Not anymore," he said evenly, setting his cup in the sink before turning around again. "Billie Henshaw is dead. She and Jake Weathers died when the Lear jet they were riding in went down in the mountains just west of Reno. It was the same plane that your husband jumped out of."

Bethany blanched.

Brett sighed and muttered under his breath, "So much for Jake Weather's story."

"So you think he lied to the police?"

"No doubt about it. Jake, as well as Karl, insisted that he didn't know that your husband had the bonds from the bank or that Grant intended to jump from the plane. Now Jake's body has been found with some of the stolen bonds. The way I see it, Jake's story has just been blown to hell.''

Bethany braced herself against the counter. Her peaceful life was about to be torn apart, again. And there was nothing she could do to stop it from happening.

"The plane burned, of course, but part of the fuselage was intact and several things were recovered from the crash site."

"I'm sure you're leading up to something."

"Billie Henshaw's purse. Not only was she carrying a picture of your husband in her wallet, but she also had several of the bonds on her."

"So that makes you believe that Grant is alive and has the rest of the bonds."

"It's a possibility."

"I see," Bethany said, her voice surprisingly even. "And now you think I can help."

"I hope so."

"Look, I've told you it's not that I don't want to," she said, her fingers gripping the edge of the sink.

"But?"

"There's nothing I can do or say that I haven't said or done before." Shaking her head as if to clear it, she looked out the window and said, "My life in Boise, the life I had with Grant, is over. I came out here to start fresh; I have a new job, new friends, everything. Very few people have any idea what happened in Idaho and that's the way I like it. So what you're suggesting now, that I dig it all up again, is impossible and futile. My story hasn't changed and it's all in the file—with the police and the FBI and the bank and the Associated Press. You'd probably learn more from going to the library and reading the old newspaper reports than talking to me.''

"I've already done that.''

Bethany pushed the hair out of her face and smiled sadly. "Well, if nothing else, you're efficient,'' she murmured. "No wonder Jim Benson hired you.''

Brett's eyes glittered, but he didn't respond.

Sighing, Bethany said, "That's all I have to say. I think you'd better go now.'' She was surprised when she felt his hand on her shoulder.

"What do I have to do to convince you to help me?''

"You can't.'' She shrugged off his hand when he didn't move.

Resting his hips against the counter, he crossed his arms over his broad chest, tilted his head to one side and stared at her. "I don't know what you're running from, but you can't hide forever.''

Defiantly, she stared up at him. "And I don't know why you're so involved in this case. But I'm out of it.''

"I don't think so. Whether you like it or not, you're right smack-dab in the middle.''

"I was. Not anymore.''

"When that plane went down, all the rules changed.''

"Great,'' she said with a weary sigh. "I suppose I'm a suspect again.''

"I wouldn't go that far—''

"Then just how far would you go, Mr. Hanson?''

"Far enough to convince you to help me.''

"But I can't! I told you—''

"I think you can,'' he cut in angrily. Bethany Mills

had to help him. She was his only lead. Much as Brett hated to admit it, he'd run out of options since Karl Weathers had gone into hiding. "It's important," he said quietly.

"To you?"

"To all of us."

"I don't know..."

"Help me, Bethany," he said. "I need it."

Staring into his silvery-blue eyes and swallowing with difficulty, she asked, "And just what is it I have to do to make you go away and leave me alone?"

"Just help me track down your husband."

"If he's alive."

"Even if he isn't."

Bethany shuddered. "Oh, God, I—I don't know."

"Help me; we can put it to rest."

"I'm on vacation."

"I know. And you don't have any plans."

Narrowing her eyes, she felt the anger surge in her veins. Was there anything he didn't know about her? "You really are a bastard, aren't you?"

"I've been called worse."

"I'll bet."

"But I thought that you could help me, now, when you're off work for two weeks and no one would know. We wouldn't disturb your life."

"Just turn it inside out."

He held up two fingers. "Two weeks, that's all. And if we can't find him by then or have a helluva good idea where he is, well, I'll keep trying on my own."

"Why is it so important to you?"

The skin over his cheekbones grew taut. "It's just business."

"You really don't expect me to believe that, do you?" she asked, shaking her head in disbelief. "Look, I don't know about all this." Her stomach twisting with apprehension, she stared into his cold, steel-blue eyes. "What's in this for you, Hanson?"

"Freedom," he answered honestly. "For both of us. Freedom from the past."

"And when it's over…sometime in the next two weeks, you'll go and leave me alone."

"Yes."

Setting her jaw, she said, "Okay, Mr. Hanson, you've got yourself a deal. The only thing I want from you is Jim Benson's word, in writing, that after I help you, he, you, and everyone associated with First Security will stay out of my life, and my parents' lives forever!"

Smiling with inner amusement at the fire in her eyes, Brett extended his hand. "That, Mrs. Mills, is a promise!"

Bethany wondered if she was about to make the biggest mistake of her life. She shook his hand, feeling his large, warm fingers surround her own.

"So what now?" she asked, retrieving her hand and trying to ignore the warmth and satisfaction she saw in his eyes.

"Nothing more for now. I'll be back later, after I've done some research."

"On what?"

"The whereabouts of Jake Weather's brother, Karl. He was on Jake's plane when your husband jumped. His story corroborated his brother's. Now that Jake's body has been found with some of the stolen bonds, Karl's alibi doesn't hold much water.''

''And you think he knows where Grant is.''

''Maybe. He's been in hiding. Didn't even show up for his brother's funeral. That's unusual unless he has something to hide. He and Jake were very close. I've been looking for him.''

''And when you struck out with Karl, you came here.''

He nodded. ''Grant didn't have a lot of friends, unless you know of some that I don't.''

''I doubt that.''

''Didn't think so.'' Brett walked back to the entry hall and tugged on his boots before shrugging into his jacket. ''I'll be back,'' he said, ramming the Stetson onto his head.

And what then? Bethany wondered. ''When?''

''Later.''

And then he was gone. As quickly as he'd come into her life, he left. *But not for long,* she reminded herself and tossed another chunk of cedar onto the fire to ward off a sudden chill.

Freedom, he'd promised. Well, Brett Hanson had damned well better be as good as his word!

Chapter Four

Y ou're an idiot, Bethany told herself later as she placed the last batch of cookies in the oven. "Why in the world did you trust that guy? Stupidity, Bethany, sheer stupidity."

She was still muttering to herself when the doorbell rang. Her heartbeat quickened. Half expecting to see Brett standing on the porch, she jerked open the door to find Jenny, red-faced and snow-covered, holding Winston in her arms. "I thought maybe he was getting cold," Jenny explained.

Bethany laughed and stepped out of the way. "Thanks, Jen. I hate to admit it but I forgot all about him."

"Why?"

"I guess I'm not used to owning a pet quite yet. Bring him in and have a couple of cookies."

Jenny didn't need any more encouragement. She let Winston down and he took off like a streak, racing down the short hall and back again, romping over the couch and running in circles in the living room.

He dashed through the living room just as Bethany was closing the door. "Watch out," she called, but it was too late. The puppy circled the Christmas tree and nearly knocked it down.

Kicking off her boots and unwrapping her scarf, Jenny shook her pigtails free and giggled as she watched the spunky little dog's antics. "What's he doing?"

"I don't know the technical name for it. But my dad used to call it a crazy streak."

"Your dad has a dog?"

"Usually two or three," Bethany said, heading for the kitchen with Jenny on her heels.

"Three dogs?" Jenny looked at Bethany suspiciously.

"Sure. He lives on a farm, a big one. He usually keeps a hunting dog and a sheepdog and any other stray that wanders onto the place."

"Did you live on the farm, too?"

"Sure did." Bethany set a plate of frosted Christmas cookies on the table and took a chair near the window.

"I bet you liked it."

"I did."

"Did you have a horse, too?"

Bethany grinned. "Several. My first one was a little pony that would be just about your size."

Jenny's eyes rounded. "For real? A pony?"

"Yep. His name was Doc and he was the meanest little horse you'd ever want to see."

Jenny frowned. "Didn't you like him?"

"Of course I did."

"But you said he was mean."

"He was." Bethany laughed as she remembered the feisty little Shetland. With his ears flattened against his head, his eyes turned angrily on every potential rider, he had more tricks than a circus clown. "But he had personality. Lots of it. And we got along just fine."

"I wish I lived on a farm."

"It was great," Bethany said, breaking a cookie in half and giving part of it to Winston. The puppy snatched it away and begged for another treat. "And Christmas was the best time of the year on the farm. My mom always went all out. Dad and I had to go and find the biggest tree on the place, cut it and drag it home while Mom and my aunts made more food than an army could eat. We sang Christmas carols at the old piano and hung mistletoe, holly, red ribbon and lights all over the house!"

Jenny squirmed in her chair and looked at Bethany. "So what happened?"

"What do you mean?"

"Why did you move away?"

"Oh." Bethany sighed and looked out the window to the drifting snow. "Remember I told you I got married?"

"Yeah."

"Well, my husband and I moved away into the city once we were married. It wasn't that far from Mom and Dad's and we visited the farm a lot. At least we did at first."

"Until your husband left?" Jenny asked.

Bethany nodded. "Yes. And then I moved here."

"But you can still go back, can't you?"

Bethany thought about her canceled vacation plans and she had to fight to overcome the awful sadness that had been with her since she'd called her folks. "Of course I can go back, sweetheart. Any time I want. But this year I thought I'd better stick around— get some work done over vacation. It's my first year on the job, you know."

Jenny's face brightened and she turned her attention to the plate of decorated cookies on the table. "Can I have another one?"

Glad for a turn in the conversation, Bethany handed the girl a star-shaped sugar cookie. "Here, and before you go, we'll pick out a dozen of these—" she pointed to the cookies cooling on the counter "—and you can take them home to your mom and Joey."

"Really?"

"Really."

Jenny stood on a chair to look over the decorated snowmen, reindeer and Santas. "I want this one and this one, and how many is a dozen?"

"Usually twelve, but let's make it a baker's dozen. That's thirteen."

"Okay." Jenny studied them all and pointed out the cookies she liked best while Bethany carefully placed them on a platter and covered it with red plastic wrap. "Where's that man that was here today?" Jenny asked as she climbed down from her chair.

The thought of Brett killed Bethany's Christmas spirit. "He had to leave."

"Is he coming back?"

"I think so."

"I think so, too."

"Oh you do, do you? Why?"

"'Cause he's been here before."

Bethany nearly dropped the platter of cookies. "He has?"

"Um-hum. Lots of times."

"You saw him?"

"Yes," Jenny said, looking strangely at Bethany. "I told you I did."

"When? When was he here?"

The child shrugged. "Don't 'member."

"Yesterday? The day before?"

Jenny's little face drew together in concentration, but she lifted her palms to the ceiling. "Don't know," she said, pouting a little.

"It's all right," Bethany said, trying to calm her suddenly racing heart and reassure the child at the same time. "It really doesn't matter." She helped Jenny with her coat and tucked the scarf around her neck. Jenny tugged on her boots and Bethany handed her the plate of cookies. "Are you sure you can carry this to your house without slipping?"

"I can do it," Jenny said confidently as she walked onto the front porch and picked her way down the stairs.

"Be careful," Bethany warned, cringing each time Jenny took an unsteady step.

"I will!"

Closing the door, Bethany watched from the window as Jenny carefully walked down the hill to her mother's driveway.

"So Brett Hanson has been here snooping around," she whispered to herself. "Maybe that's why you felt like you were being followed." Angry at herself as well as Brett, she went back into the kitchen and started cleaning the dishes. "Well, Mr. Hanson, if and when you decide to return, you'll have to do some fast talking!"

Brett slammed down the receiver. "Damn!" he swore, kicking at the snow as he left the phone booth. He'd used the outside booth for its privacy and now he was cold to the bone and mad as hell!

He balled his fists, stuffed them into the pockets of his down jacket and walked down the windy Portland streets as he thought about his conversation with Harry.

"Press her, Hanson," Harry had insisted when Brett had reported on his first meeting with Bethany.

"I don't think that'll work."

"Well, something's got to. She's our only lead to Mills. Lean on her if you have to!"

"Lean on her?" Brett had repeated. "Come on, Harry, this isn't some late-night detective show; we're talking about a real woman!"

"Yeah. A woman who was married to the man responsible for taking First Security to the tune of a million big ones!"

"She didn't know anything about it!"

"How can you be so sure? She was married to the bum, for God's sake."

"That was before the theft."

"Mills was on the take for years."

"She didn't know about it."

"Sure, she didn't. Look, Hanson, Bethany Mills doesn't strike me as the dumb-bunny type. She had to have known that he had more money than he made here."

"Not to hear her tell it," Brett had replied, his anger beginning to get the better of him. "Besides, you guys got your money back. The insurance company—"

"Hasn't paid a dime and doubled our premiums! Now listen to me, Brett, don't let your emotions get in the way—not the way you did when Roberta died."

Flinching, Brett had hung up on his half brother.

"You're lucky I haven't wrung your miserable neck, Harry," he muttered at the phone as he bunched his shoulders and walked along the waterfront. The gray Willamette River was moving sluggishly under the Hawthorne Bridge and thousands of icicles hung like crystal cones from the seawall.

The city of Portland was practically immobilized. Snowplows, sanders and workmen struggled against the biting wind and piling snow that threatened power lines and crippled traffic.

He met a few other pedestrians on the slippery sidewalks as he walked, head bent against the wind. Stopping at one of the waterfront bars near the section of the city known as Old Town, he shouldered his way inside.

Brett returned just before seven. Bethany heard his Jeep grind up the hill and then come to a stop in her driveway. Heart thudding, she met him at the door before he had a chance to knock.

"You were expecting me," he guessed with a smile. He stood, with his hat in his hand, on the porch. The porch light smoothed his rough features, made his blue eyes sparkle and caught in his jet-black hair. Handsome and dangerous, he touched a very private part of Bethany that she preferred to keep hidden—even from herself.

"You said you'd be back," she pointed out, standing out of his way as he entered.

"I know, but I didn't expect you to be waiting." He placed his boots inside the door and hung his hat and jacket on the hall tree.

"It's not exactly a welcoming party."

"Oh?" He walked into the living room, bent down and warmed his hands over the fire. The corduroy stretched over his slim buttocks and his sweater tightened over his shoulders. "Something bothering you?" he asked, after putting more logs on the fire and watching the flames catch and crackle against the dry wood.

"Something? How about a basketful of things?" She took a seat on the couch, leaned back and crossed her arms over her chest.

"Okay. What is it? Shoot."

"One of my neighbors said you've been up here before."

"That's true." He turned to face her before sitting on the hearth and pinning her with his eyes.

"But you didn't come to the house."

"Wrong. I did. You weren't home. And it wasn't just once. I was here twice."

"Twice?"

"That's right." His lips twitched and his eyes twinkled as if at a private joke. "Don't tell me; this neighbor who's spying for you is about three feet tall, wears pigtails and is wise beyond her years—all three of them."

"Four," Bethany corrected, laughing as some of her anger dissipated.

"All this time I thought she was just a cute little girl."

"She is; but she keeps her eyes and ears open. Nothing gets past Jenny."

"A live wire?"

"Definitely."

"I'll bet." He chuckled and rubbed his hands together.

Bethany grinned. When Brett Hanson wasn't poking his nose where it didn't belong he could be an interesting, even charming, man. "Have you eaten?" she asked.

"Not since lunch."

"All I've got is homemade soup and Christmas cookies. But you're welcome to both."

He hesitated, but couldn't resist. "That's the best offer I've had all day."

"Come on then. It'll only take a minute to warm the soup."

While Brett stood at the kitchen window staring at the black night, Bethany heated the leftover chicken and noodle soup and told herself she was acting like an idiot. Cooking and making Brett feel at home was as stupid as sleeping with the enemy, she told herself. Brett Hanson worked for Jim Benson and the owner and president of First Security would like nothing better than to pin Grant's embezzlement on his ex-wife.

"This is great," Brett said twenty minutes later as he finished a large bowl of the soup. "Where'd you learn to cook like that?"

"On a farm in Idaho," she replied, shifting uncomfortably in her chair. To avoid his gaze, she picked up some of the dirty dishes and carried them to the sink.

"You live there all your life?"

"Most of it." She put the dirty dishes in the dishwasher and then poured them each a cup of coffee. "But you already knew that, didn't you?"

Scowling, he grabbed a cookie from the platter on the table and ate it slowly. "I'm not here to crucify you, you know."

"You can't! I'm innocent!"

"All I want to do is find your husband."

"My *ex*-husband!" She slammed the door of the dishwasher. Eyes gleaming indignantly, she handed Brett a ceramic mug. "And don't lie to me. If Jim Benson thought he could pin Grant's crime on me or anyone else in my family, he would. His pride's on the line."

Brett's lips twisted cynically. "I take it you know the man."

"You could say that. Dad and he have never gotten along. They knew each other in school and were always rivals. Then Mom decided to marry Dad instead of Jim. But that was years ago."

"And Jim never forgave either of them."

"I don't know. I guess not. He did give Grant a job...." She looked up suddenly and caught Brett watching her. "I don't need to be telling you all of this; it's water under the bridge."

Seething, she walked into the living room and sat on the hearth. Cradling her cup in her hands, she blew at the steaming coffee and tried to quiet the rising anger that swept through her when she thought of the injustice of it all. "You know, if I had any brains at all, I'd tell you and First Security to go take a flying leap and then I'd get on that plane to Boise tomorrow and visit my folks. But instead I'm cowering here in Portland, hoping the whole world doesn't find out about Grant, afraid to go home because of all the publicity and embarrassment it would stir up again. My folks have been through hell already." She took a sip of coffee. It burned her throat but she barely noticed. "You know, before you came here and Harry Benson went out to visit Mom and Dad, I had the crazy notion that I could lead a normal life again."

"You can," he said gently.

"When?"

"When we find Grant."

"But I didn't have anything to do with what he did. Why should I be punished? And my folks—it's just so damned unfair."

"Guilt by association," he said, trying to lighten the mood.

"Exactly! And it stinks!"

"Can't argue with that," he admitted, crossing to the couch and stretching his long legs out in front of him as he sat. "But maybe when we find Grant, we can clear everything up."

"*If* you find Grant."

Brett's jaw hardened and his eyes glittered with

renewed determination. "Oh, I'll find him," he promised, lifting his cup in a mock toast. "It'll just take a little time."

"And cooperation from me."

"Yes."

She held his gaze but frowned. "I really don't think I can help you."

"Maybe it would help if I explained what I've already done."

"That would be a start." She settled back against the warm bricks and watched as his face hardened in the glow from the fire.

"You know that I'm a private investigator."

"So you said."

"Well, I'd just about given it up, but I owed Jim Benson a favor."

"Bad move."

He smiled tightly. "Right. Anyway, I agreed to find Grant several months ago."

"Why? What was the favor?"

Brett thought about his mother's cabin in the woods in Washington, about the fact that Jim Benson was his stepfather, about the fact that there was no love lost between Jim and himself, about the fact that since Roberta's death, he'd had no ambition in life except to live like a hermit on his mother's land and said, "I owed him some money."

"You and the rest of the population of southern Idaho."

Brett lifted a shoulder. "Anyway, I managed to track down Billie Henshaw. She'd helped Grant by fouling up all the documentation on the bonds when they were shipped from the brokerage house to the bank. Without her, Grant would have had a helluva lot of trouble cashing those bonds.''

"He probably did anyway.''

"Anyway, once I'd located Billie, I thought I was out of this deal with Jim Benson, because I was sure she would lead the FBI to Grant either inadvertently or by turning state's evidence.''

"But it didn't work that way.''

"Nope. Before they were brought in, she and Jake Weathers died in the plane crash. That brought the investigation back to square one.''

"Meaning me?''

"Meaning Karl Weathers.''

"I have no idea where he is.''

"I know.'' He placed his empty cup on the table, stood and stretched. His sweater climbed up and exposed a flat portion of his abdomen just above the waistband of his jeans.

Before she could look away Bethany got a glimpse of his navel and the swirling dark hair surrounding it. Swallowing against a suddenly tight throat, she shifted her gaze to his face.

If he was aware of the blush rising in her cheeks, he didn't show it. ''But Karl is the only living person who knows the whereabouts of Grant, if Grant's still alive.''

Shivering over the fate of the man she'd once loved, Bethany stared into her cup and nodded.

"So I'm hoping that once I locate Karl, he'll lead me to Grant and the stolen bonds.''

"Except that Grant may not be alive. He may have died jumping out of the plane—''

"But they found some of the bonds on Billie Henshaw."

"Maybe she took her cut before Grant jumped."

"Maybe."

"So this could all be a wild-goose chase," she said.

"God, I hope not. We're working on the assumption that Mills is still alive. That's why I need your help." His eyes, dark blue and brooding, searched her face.

Bethany's heart fluttered stupidly. She cleared her throat and broke away from that knowing, almost possessive stare. "Okay. So where do I fit in?" she asked.

"For now, all I want to do is go through every scrap of paper you have from your marriage to Grant. Checking account statements, loans, real estate deeds, letters, insurance papers, the works."

"It's already been done."

"I know. But not by me. And I want everything. Old address books, phone bills, old mail and receipts."

"The FBI and the bank have already been through everything."

"But it's just possible that they missed something. I just want to double-check. Okay?"

Bethany sized him up. Unfortunately, she liked what she saw. It would be so much easier if she could just despise him. "Whatever hold Jim Benson has on you must really be something," she guessed.

Brett's stomach muscles grew tense. "I thought I told you I owe him money."

"A lot?"

"Enough."

"And finding Grant will pay off the loan?"

"Yep."

"So your motivation is purely mercenary," she said, feeling a sense of disappointment.

"I guess you could say that," Brett lied. Telling her some maudlin story about his mother's land wouldn't serve any purpose. Let her think what she wanted.

"Okay," she said, standing. "At least we understand each other." She tossed her rich, red-brown hair away from her face. "Now, I just have one question for you."

"Shoot."

"Why have you been following me?"

He didn't move. "I haven't."

"I thought we were going to be honest with each other."

His blue eyes grew cold. "I am. I haven't been following you. I just came up to the house looking for you."

"What about one of your men?"

"I don't have any."

Unnerved, she pushed her shaking hands into the pockets of her jeans. "Well, someone has been, and unless it's one of Jim Benson's people or you or the FBI..."

"You're sure you're being followed?" he cut in, walking over to her and placing his hands on her shoulders.

His hands felt large and warm and comforting and some of the tension left her body. "It's just a feeling I've had."

"How often?"

Standing, he walked to the front door and slipped on his jacket. "I'm going to go outside, look around."

"You won't find anything."

Casting a glance over his shoulder, he smiled. "Let's hope not." He tugged on his boots, placed his felt Stetson on his head and then walked through the kitchen to the garage before slipping outside into the darkness.

"This is madness," Bethany told herself once again as she carried the cups into the kitchen, "sheer, unadulterated madness!"

Brett's eyes grew accustomed to the darkness. Walking stealthily through the shadows, he watched and waited, staring at the snow-covered landscape. The only illumination came from a solitary street lamp and the colorful Christmas lights from windows of neighboring houses. In the distance a train whistled and was answered by the gruff bark of a dog. He heard the sounds of traffic on a faraway road that had been plowed, but up here, on the hill, all was quiet. Peaceful. Deceptive.

He thought about his mother and her marriage to Jim Benson; considered the fact that his stepfather would be just sleazy enough to hire another detective to watch over him and cheat him out of his land. Gritting his teeth, Brett slipped beneath the lowest branches of a fir tree and watched Bethany's small cottage.

Occasionally she would pass in front of the window and he would catch a glimpse of her profile. The sight

"I don't know. Maybe once a day; maybe m

"*Once a day?* For how long?"

"A couple of weeks."

"About as long as it's been since Billie Hens
and Jake Weathers were killed." His eyes narro
speculatively and a cold, hard look made his rug
features more pronounced. "Where and when?"

"Anytime," she admitted with a shrug. "Son
times when I'm here alone in the house, or at t
grocery store, or at school. I haven't really caug
anyone, but I can't shake the feeling either. I though
it was you."

He shook his head and looked directly into her
round, hazel eyes. "Sit down," he said, pressing
gently on her shoulders so that they both took a seat
on the edge of the couch. "Tell me everything."

At first she was reluctant, but once she started, the
dam of silence broke and the waters came rushing
through. She explained about the biking accident as
well as the premonition that she'd been watched.

Brett listened quietly, his countenance darkenin
with each added detail of her story.

"It's probably just my imagination," Bethany
nally concluded.

"I don't think so."

She stared at him and saw worry contract the
over his cheekbones. "What are you talking ab
she asked. "Do you know something I don't?"

"No, but I learned long ago to trust my in
And I think we should trust yours. If you've
you're being followed or watched, there's pr
reason for it."

"That's comforting," she murmured sarc

of her busy in the house, worried about events out of her control made his gut twist.

Damn you, Grant Mills, you miserable son of a bitch, I'll get you if it's the last thing I do.

Chapter Five

Over an hour after Brett had gone outside, he knocked on the door to the garage.

"Well?" Bethany asked, trying to hide her case of nerves as she let him inside.

Brett met her worried gaze with one of his own. His skin was flushed from the cold, his eyes dark with the night. "Nothing." He knocked the snow off his boots in the garage and left them there.

"I told you it was probably my imagination."

"And I told you to trust your instincts."

"What if I'm wrong?"

"Nothing's lost. But better safe than sorry, don't you think?" He took off his jacket and placed it over the back of one of the kitchen chairs before walking to the stove and pouring himself another cup of coffee. The hot liquid warmed him from the inside out.

"So now what?" Bethany asked.

"I think I'd better spend the night."

"You think *what*?"

"Just in case you're right and someone is watching you."

"Now, wait just a minute," she said, shaking her head in disbelief. "You can't stay here!"

"Why not?"

"*Why not?* Because I'm a single teacher in this community. I can't take a chance that someone will find out you were here and misconstrue it!"

Brett's lips twitched in amusement. "We aren't exactly living in the Dark Ages, you know."

"Tell that to my superintendent! Look, I've spent the last year trying to live down the past and I've managed to do it by moving here and making a fresh start. I can't afford to have you or Grant or First Security ruin it for me!"

"No one will know."

"The truth has a habit of turning up."

"Think of me as your bodyguard."

"I don't need one!" Flushed and furious, she walked over to him and looked him straight in the eye. "I've lived here by myself for nearly a year. Back in Boise I stood up to the press, the FBI and the bank. I don't need you or anyone else to take care of me! And then there's Winston: he'll bark if someone's out prowling around."

Brett laughed and glanced at the scrawny pup. "That mutt?" he said, bending down and scratching the dog behind his ears. "If Joe Burglar broke into your house, this guy would probably wag his tail, jump up and lick him right on the ski mask!"

"Very funny," she said, but couldn't help but smile. As a watchdog, Winston was a big fat zero.

Brett straightened, finished his coffee and set the cup in the sink. Leaning against the counter and eyeing her curiously he asked, "Just what is it you're afraid of?"

You, she thought, but closed her mind to the admission. Finding him fascinating was dangerous and she had to fight her feelings. "I'm afraid of losing everything I've worked so hard to keep," she replied, knowing it was only half the truth. But she couldn't let herself become involved with a man she knew nothing about; a man who was being paid to hunt her ex-husband; a man linked with the bank that would like to see her thrown in prison for a crime she hadn't committed.

Brett ran his hand over the dark stubble that was beginning to show on his chin. "You're a very stubborn woman, you know."

"So I've been told."

"I think it's a good idea for me to stick around, watch the place," he said, walking across the linoleum to stand close to her. She had to lift her eyes to meet his gaze. "What if I gave you my word that nothing will happen?" he asked softly, touching her chin and forcing her to meet his steady blue gaze.

"I don't know if I'd believe you," she admitted.

"Why not? Don't you trust me?"

"Not really." *And I don't trust myself when I'm around you*, Bethany thought. Grant had taught her about men; she didn't need another lesson from Brett Hanson. "I'm not ready for any kind of relationship with you."

"This is strictly business," he said, cringing inwardly at the lie.

"Business? Well, I hate it! I hate the intrusion into my life! I hate the fact that I have to go through everything I've ever done and have it looked at through a magnifying glass, I hate not being able to sit in my house without someone insisting that he should stay here for my protection!"

Brett sighed and raked his fingers through his hair in frustration. "I don't like it any better than you do, but it's my job and I'm here and short of calling the police and throwing me out, you're stuck with me."

"You know I can't do that," she whispered, her gold-green eyes flashing angrily.

"Then we'd better make the best of a bad situation," he suggested. "If it offends your sense of morality for me to sleep in the house, I'll camp out in the Jeep."

"You wouldn't!"

"Try me." With an off-center smile and a cynical gleam in his eyes, he put on his coat, walked out the back door and slipped into his boots. "You know where I am if you need help." Stuffing his hat onto his head, he closed the door behind him and, cursing to himself, walked out to his Jeep.

"Of all the despicable, arrogant, self-serving bastards!" she muttered, watching from her window as he took up his vigil in the frost-covered vehicle. "It would serve him right if he froze out there!"

But she couldn't quiet the little doubt that kept nagging at her, telling her she should have had the decency to let him sleep on the couch.

"Never!" she swore, changing into her nightgown

and slipping under the thick down cover on her brass bed. Winston curled up at her feet and the warmth of the small house surrounded her with a feeling of guilt. "His choice," she muttered to herself, but she couldn't help thinking of Brett sitting outside in the cold with nowhere to stretch his legs.

Brett stared through the ice clouding the windshield and sipped lukewarm coffee from a thermos. It was bitter and didn't take the chill off much. Even the down-filled sleeping bag he'd thrown over his legs didn't keep out the cold Oregon winter at three in the morning.

"I thought it was supposed to rain here all the time," he grumbled to himself as he swallowed the final dregs from his cup while searching the quiet street with his eyes. Nothing disturbed the silence or stopped the snow as it continued to fall from the night-darkened sky. "Great," he muttered sarcastically, as he slid lower on his back and shifted his legs. The brim of his hat slipped over his nose. "This is just great."

Bethany was already frying bacon when she heard the thudding on the back door. "Just a minute," she called as she unlocked the door and let Brett inside. "How'd you sleep?"

"I didn't," he grumbled.

"Am I supposed to feel sorry for you?" She smiled up at him with warm hazel eyes.

"It would help," he admitted, stretching to release the cramps from his back and legs.

"Okay. I'm sorry you camped outside in the cold, but it wasn't my idea."

"Just part of the job, ma'am," he said with a grin when she handed him a fresh cup of coffee. "All in the line of duty."

"Sure." She walked back to the stove, placed the bacon on a platter and began frying eggs. "Hungry?" she asked over her shoulder.

"Starved."

"I suppose that sitting out in the cold all night does create quite an appetite."

"You suppose right."

Glancing in his direction, she set about making pancakes and hash browns. "And I guess the least I can do is feed you. Have you got a change of clothes?"

"In the Jeep. Why?"

"Because I thought you might want to take a hot shower and warm up. When you get out, breakfast will be just about done."

Brett arched a surprised brow and couldn't hide the devilish glint in his eyes. "What's this, a turnabout? Aren't you the lady worried about her pristine reputation?"

"It's just a shower, isn't it?" she snapped, hating to admit to herself that she liked having him around. Maybe the risk of her reputation was worth an involvement with him. Certainly her relationship with him was innocent...so far. "It's no big deal."

"It certainly was a big deal last night," he pointed out.

"That was different."

"How?"

She looked at the ceiling and made a face. "Well, maybe it wasn't. Anyway, I didn't sleep much either last night and I decided that if I work with you rather than against you, we might get through this a whole lot quicker."

Brett grinned, that dazzling grin that sent her senses reeling. "I knew you had a brain in that pretty head of yours; I'm just glad you finally found it!"

"Get out of here," she said, but laughed and pointed at the linen closet. "You can find fresh towels in there and the shower is in the bathroom right across the hall from the closet."

Within minutes she heard the sound of water running as the hotcakes sizzled on the griddle. Bethany hummed as she set places for two and wondered why just having Brett in the house made her feel so safe. "Because you're a fool," she told herself as she plucked a shriveled petal from the poinsettia sitting in the middle of the kitchen table. "A lonely fool who needs a little romance in her life at Christmastime."

The bathroom was still filled with steam as Brett squinted into the mirror and tried to shave. He cut himself twice on the dull razor; when the mirror cleared and he stared at his reflection, he stopped wiping the excess shaving cream from his face.

"What're you doin'?" he asked the tall man in the mirror. "And why?" Sure, he could rationalize that he was trying to protect Bethany. He wasn't sure he understood what was going on and if she honestly thought she was being followed, it was in his own best interests to protect her. But it was more than that. He was here, in her house, because he wanted to be;

because she intrigued him. "So Harry was right," he accused the damp image. "You are letting your emotions get in your way." He stared straight into his own blue eyes. "You poor, miserable bastard," he whispered, angry with himself as well as the world.

Bethany turned when she heard him walk down the hall. Her pulse leaped crazily at the sight of him. He was stripped to the waist and was towel-drying his dark hair. Drops of moisture clung to his face and neck and he wiped them away with the towel. Near-black hair swirled over a muscular chest before narrowing to the waistband of his faded jeans.

Her own heart began to beat traitorously.

His gaze caught in hers, lingered a minute and then he looked away, to the table. "That looks great," he said, his voice rough as he stared at the hearty breakfast. "What do you want me to do with this?" He held up the wet towel.

"Just toss it over the shower stall."

He walked back into the bathroom and Bethany's gaze followed him, focused on the play of rippling muscles as he folded the towel, noticed the hard strength of his shoulders when he shrugged into a clean flannel shirt.

"Every muscle in my body aches," he admitted as he sat at the table.

"Maybe you need hot food."

He nodded in assent, looked up and smiled. "Thanks," he said.

Bethany blushed. "It's no big deal. Go on, help yourself."

She sat across from him and ate silently, feeling his gaze on her face.

"I'm sorry that you had such a rough night," she said.

He shrugged, finished a last bite of toast and sipped his coffee, staring at her over the rim of the enamel cup.

"But maybe you just got what you deserved for being so mule-headed last night."

"Maybe."

"And, just maybe you blew everything out of proportion."

"Or maybe you did," he said, pushing away from the table, but never letting his eyes drop.

"I suppose that's possible," she admitted as she cleared the table and stacked the dishes on the counter. "So, what do we do now?"

"Show me everything I asked for last night—the old receipts and papers—and let me go through them. You can go about doing whatever it is you planned to do today."

"I didn't really have any plans," she admitted.

"Then try and pretend that I'm not around."

Easier said than done, she thought as she took him into the second bedroom that she used as a den and showed him all the scraps of paper from her marriage to Grant. Brett sat at the rolltop desk, meticulously going over each piece, checkbook entry, address, or phone number as if he actually expected to find the clue to what had happened to Grant.

"These things have been looked at over and over again," she said. "They've been copied, studied and questioned by the police and the bank auditors. I don't know what you can possibly hope to find."

"Something they missed."

"Good luck," Bethany whispered, leaving him alone in the room.

The afternoon passed quickly, but Bethany couldn't forget that Brett was in the house. She noticed him whenever she walked down the short hall. While he worked, she spent the day straightening the house and washing clothes and trying not to remember that she would already have taken a plane to Boise—if only things had been different.

Brett asked a few questions, made a couple of phone calls, but for the most part remained glued to the chair at the desk in the den.

His presence in the house would have bothered her, Bethany supposed, except that a tiny, foolishly feminine part of her enjoyed being with him. He appreciated the coffee she brought him, smiled whenever she poked her head into the room and brooded when he asked her a personal question about her marriage to Grant.

She was amused by his dry wit and decided that when he wasn't being so dead serious, Brett Hanson could be a devastatingly handsome and charming man.

Late in the afternoon, the doorbell chimed. Bethany opened the door to find Jenny, as bright-eyed as usual, standing on the porch.

"I'm 'sposed to say thank you for the cookies," the little girl announced.

"You're welcome."

"And Mama wanted me to give you this." She held out a jar of blackberry jelly in her mittened hand.

"You tell your mom 'Thanks.'"

"I will." Jenny craned her neck to look inside for the little dog.

Winston was right by the door, wagging his tail furiously.

"Would you like to come in for a while?" Bethany asked.

"Sure!" Jenny was through the door before she answered. "You makin' cookies again?"

"Not today," Bethany said, reading the disappointment in the child's eyes. "But I still have a few left. Want one?"

"'Course I do." Jenny climbed into her favorite chair and waited expectantly. "Can we make some together?"

"Sure, but not today. How about tomorrow?"

"I'll go tell my mom." She bounced off the chair then halted in her tracks, eyes wide, when Brett walked into the kitchen.

"You can wait to tell her until later. How about some hot chocolate with your cookie?" Bethany asked.

Jenny, still staring openly at Brett, nodded.

"How about you?" Bethany smiled at Brett.

"Why not?" Brett sat down at the table and introduced himself to the little girl, who settled back down in her chair. While Bethany placed a platter of cookies on the table, Brett and Jenny talked like long lost friends.

"Will you take me sledding?" Jenny asked as she

finished a frosted snowman and reached for another cookie.

Brett grinned but shook his head. "Haven't got a sled."

"Bethany's got a saucer!"

"Is that right?" He lifted his eyes to Bethany. She was leaning against the counter and watching the exchange.

"Uh-huh. And she'd let us use it, wouldn't you, Bethany?" Jenny turned eager eyes in Bethany's direction.

Bethany placed two steaming mugs of cocoa on the table. "One lump or two?" she asked Jenny as she held a handful of small marshmallows over the child's cup.

"Five!"

"Five it is."

Jenny wasn't about to be deterred. "But it's okay if we use your saucer, isn't it?"

"If your mom says it's all right."

"Oh, it's okay with her. She don't care, just as long as I stay out of her hair."

Bethany bit into her lower lip. "Maybe some other day, Jen. Mr. Hanson has a lot of work to do."

"Not that much work," he said, pushing away from the table. "You know what they say about all work and no play?" Winking at Jenny, he asked, "Where's the saucer? In the garage?"

Bethany nodded and folded a dish towel. Then, deciding that Jenny was her responsibility and that she didn't know Brett well enough to trust him with someone else's child, she grabbed her coat, gloves and scarf and followed them outside.

Winston bounded through the freshly fallen snow and children squealed as they raced down the hill on sleds, saucers, and inner tubes.

"Is this the way you remember Christmas?" Brett asked, watching Jenny spin down the hill.

"It was different. Quieter on the farm," Bethany said. "The nearest neighbor was half a mile down the road. Once in a while we'd meet at Taylor's hill and slide down in our toboggan, but most of the time it was business as usual at the farm. You know, cows to be milked, eggs to be gathered, chickens and pigs to be fed."

"Do you miss it?" Brett asked. Standing so close to her, looking down into the sad depths of her eyes, he felt an overpowering surge of possessiveness pass through him. The feeling was absurd; totally out of line. He'd only felt it once before. With Roberta.

"Miss the farm?" she repeated. "Yeah, sometimes. Especially around the holidays. What about you? Where's your family?" she asked.

His gaze shifted from her face to the tall stand of firs at her back. "They're all gone," he said. "My mother died when I was quite a bit younger."

"And your father?"

Brett glanced back at her, his face tense and strained. "I never knew him."

"Oh." Bethany shivered from the cold. "I didn't mean to pry."

"It's all right," he assured her, placing an arm over her slim shoulders. "Tit for tat, wouldn't you say?"

She smiled sadly and nodded. "Okay. I guess we're even. Except for one thing."

"Which is?"

"You know all about my marriage. What about you?"

He hesitated and his eyes became dark as he looked away from her and at the pewter-colored sky. "I was married once," Brett admitted, his eyes growing distant as he remembered Roberta's beautiful face, her trusting brown eyes and easy smile. Over the years her image had begun to fade from his memory and he hated the loss.

"What happened?" Bethany asked, sensing his sadness but wanting desperately to know about him.

"It was a long time ago. She was killed by a hit-and-run driver."

Shaken, Bethany didn't know what to say. "I'm sorry," she whispered.

"It's over," he said angrily.

"Then the driver of the car was convicted."

"Nope." Brett rubbed the tired muscles of his shoulders and frowned into the gathering night. "The bastard got away."

"It's been hard on you, hasn't it?"

"Like I said, it's over." His jaw tight, he turned and strode back into the house.

An hour later Bethany sent Jenny home and put the disk away. Then she whistled to Winston and walked through the garage and into the kitchen. The house was quiet. Only the soft ticking of the clock on the mantel and the gentle hum of the refrigerator made any noise.

The door to the study was closed, and Bethany didn't dare knock on it. Brett obviously needed time alone and she was more than happy to give it to him.

After lighting the fire, flipping on the switch that illuminated the tree and turning on the radio, she went to work in the kitchen, baking corn bread and making clam chowder.

The warm scents of baking bread and simmering soup filled the house while the fire crackled against the pitchy cedar and soft music filled the tiny rooms. With Brett in the study and Christmas in the air, Bethany couldn't help but smile.

She knocked gently on his door and heard him grunt in reply.

Opening the door a crack, she stuck her head through. "Is it safe to come in here?"

He turned and forced a smile. "I didn't mean to growl at you earlier."

"No harm done," she said, slipping into the room. "I was just going to offer you an eggnog as sort of a peace offering."

"A truce?"

"Uh-huh. What d'ya say?"

"Sounds good."

"It'll be just a minute." She hurried out of the room, poured them each a glass of eggnog, added a little brandy and sprinkled the foaming liquid with nutmeg. By the time she was finished and had set the tall glass snifters on a red tray, Brett had come into the kitchen.

"Cheers," she said, handing him his glass and touching it with her own.

"Cheers," he agreed. His gaze held hers for a heart-stopping moment, then he looked away.

"Come into the living room," she invited, knowing she was flirting with danger and not really caring.

Having Brett around added a sparkle to her life that she hadn't felt in years. Not even with Grant.

He looked at the winking Christmas tree and sat on the edge of the hearth. "You know," he said, almost to himself, "I think that ex-husband of yours must have been out of his mind."

"Why?"

His blue eyes sober, he searched her face. "Because if I ever found a woman like you, I'd never let go."

Warm from the liquor and the compliment, Bethany blushed and looked at the Christmas tree. "I think maybe we'd better eat," she said, finishing her drink and starting for the kitchen.

"Bethany?" His voice was low and hoarse. The sound of her name, whispered across his lips, made her heartbeat quicken.

She turned and looked over her shoulder, waited as he approached, felt his fingers grasp her shoulder. "I meant it when I said I'd keep our relationship professional," he whispered, one hand climbing her throat to touch the soft underside of her chin. "But it's going to be hell."

Deep in his gaze, beyond the reflection of the lights on the tree, she recognized the dilation of his pupils, the smoldering desire he fought to control.

"I know," she whispered, unconsciously licking her lips.

"I'll try to keep my distance, but you can't be tempting me."

"I'm not—"

"You are!" The fire leaped in his eyes. "Don't be too kind to me, Bethany. Don't try to seduce me with bright smiles, soft music and intimate rooms just oozing with Christmas spirit.''

"I didn't mean to.''

"Maybe not. But I'm warning you,'' he said, fingers caressing the soft skin of her throat. "You might just get more than you bargained for.''

"I already have!'' she said, furious at herself and him. "I didn't want you here in the first place!'' Struggling, she broke free of his grasp and rubbed her arms. "You can read anything you want into this, mister, but all I'm trying to do is make the best out of an awkward and uncomfortable situation. The least you could do is appreciate that fact!''

She turned on her heel and stormed into the kitchen, rattling the bowls as she set the table. Brett followed her and propped one shoulder against the wall, watching as most of her anger was vented on the silverware.

"I didn't mean to make you mad.''

"Well, you did. Why don't you just sit down and eat?'' She glared at him and waited for him to take his seat. Then she ladled them each a bowl of chowder and placed the bread and salad on the table.

They ate without saying a word.

"Best meal I've had in years,'' he said once he'd finished.

"Just soup.''

"Yeah, well, it beats the canned stuff that I feed myself. Thanks.'' After clearing his dishes, he retreated to the den and Bethany tried to forget their earlier argument. Though she was loath to admit it, even to herself, she had been secretly falling for him;

flirting with the idea of what it would be like to make love to him.

"So you got what you asked for," she told herself.

She was reading when he finally came out of the den and joined her in the living room. She looked up, pushed her glasses off her nose and watched as he withdrew a small brown book from his back pocket.

"Are you sure this is the only address book you had?" he asked, holding up the battered little book.

"Positive."

"What about for his work?"

"They confiscated everything he left in his desk at work, which wasn't much."

Brett knew that and more. Grant had been clever enough to take his desk calendar, address file and any personal papers with him on that Friday afternoon when he left the bank with a million dollars' worth of bonds in his briefcase.

Bethany tossed her paperback onto the coffee table. "You find anything?"

"Nope. But I'm only about a third of the way through everything in there." He nodded toward the den.

"And if you don't find anything, what then?"

"Then I look harder," he said.

"What if you don't find anything that helps you?"

He rubbed the bridge of his nose between his thumb and forefinger. "I guess I'll cross that bridge when I come to it. But not tonight." He stretched his arms high over his head. "Tonight I'm done."

"Then you're leaving?"

He shook his head. "Nope."

"You're not staying here!"

"And you're still mad."

She squinted up at him. "I just don't like being accused of tempting you." Picking up her novel, she opened it and without looking up said, "Good night."

"I'm not leaving."

"And I'm not having the same argument that I had with you last night. Certainly there's somewhere you can go—"

"Not until I've found what I'm looking for. Besides, I don't think it's safe for you to stay alone."

She slammed the book down. "Great! Just great! You come barging into my life and expect me to do exactly whatever you tell me—and if I try to make you more comfortable, you get angry. On the other hand, you want to spend the night in my house. Well, forget it, Hanson. You're not welcome!"

"If you had any sense—"

"I'd call the police. But we both know I can't do that, don't we?"

The muscles in his face grew tense. Then, without a word, he walked into the kitchen, rinsed out his thermos and poured hot coffee into it. He heard her follow him and looked over his shoulder to see her standing with her arms crossed firmly over her chest, her eyes bright with challenge.

"What're you doing?"

"Letting you have it your way."

"You're not sleeping in that Jeep again!"

His lips twisted scornfully. "I told you I didn't sleep last night."

"Why are you doing this to me?"

He missed a beat while he willed the anger out of his voice. "I'm not doing anything."

"You are! You're turning my life upside down and inside out!"

He turned slowly, forcing a tired smile. "Believe me, I didn't mean to," he said, running a hand over his stubbled chin. The grooves around his eyes seemed suddenly deeper and there was a weary slump to his shoulders.

Bethany's heart went out to him. "I get the feeling that you were coerced into coming here."

Shrugging, he poured himself a cup of coffee and took a long drink. "Doesn't matter. I'm here."

"Just what is it that Benson's got on you?" she asked once more.

"What's he got on anybody? I owe him some money and I don't like owing."

"Especially Benson?"

He drained his cup. "Right. Especially Benson." Screwing on the plastic mug of his thermos, he grabbed his jacket and headed for the back door.

"Brett—" she said impulsively, her heart stopping when he turned to face her.

"Yeah?"

"You can stay inside...on the couch."

He eyed her steadily. "I don't think so."

"I mean it," she whispered. "I don't want you sleeping out there again."

"You're sure?"

"As sure as I am about anything right now," she said, biting her lip and returning his stare before shutting off the kitchen lights, walking into her bedroom and closing the door firmly behind her.

Chapter Six

Bethany's thoughts kept her awake most of the night. Knowing that Brett was lying in the living room was more than she could bear. She tossed and turned until well after one and then, because she couldn't stand rolling restlessly around in bed any longer, she grabbed her robe, pushed her arms through the sleeves and quietly crept down the hall.

She stopped near the living room and stared at the cozy sight. The lights from the Christmas tree were still winking and the coals in the dying fire glowed scarlet. Brett was sprawled on the couch entangled in a couple of blankets. "Some bodyguard," she murmured, a smile playing on her lips as she walked into the room and looked down at him.

One of his arms had flopped over the back of the couch and his face was partially buried in the pillow.

His black hair fell over his eyes and his features were shadowed as he breathed deeply under the blankets.

Bethany unplugged the tree and then walked back to the couch. Very carefully she leaned forward and straightened the blanket under his chin.

His hand reached forward and captured her wrist as his eyes slowly opened.

Horrified that he'd caught her fawning over him, she blushed. "You weren't even asleep!" she charged as his fingers tightened over her arm.

"What do you think you're doing out here?" he asked, rubbing his face with his free hand.

"I...I couldn't sleep. I saw that the lights were still on and I thought I'd turn them off."

"And check up on me." He grinned, teeth flashing white against his skin.

"Maybe."

His blue eyes glittered. "I told you this wouldn't be easy," he said, steeling himself as his gaze drifted downward to the lapels of her robe where the red velour gaped open. White eyelet peeked between the red folds and beneath the flimsy lace, Brett saw the dark hollow between her breasts.

Embarrassed beyond words, Bethany bunched the robe together with her free hand, but not before his gaze had burned through the white lace to touch her bare skin. Her chest suddenly felt constricted and she found it difficult to breathe, impossible to break away from the seduction in his eyes. "I—I didn't mean to—"

"To what? Tempt me?"

"No, but I... Oh, God, just let go of me. I should never have come out here."

"You're right about that," he agreed, pulling her gently forward so that she tumbled onto him. His strong arms surrounded her, held her tight.

"Brett, please," she whispered, her throat aching. "Don't—"

But it was too late. Her pleas fell upon deaf ears. Waking to find her near him, her long hair framing her face in thick, wild curls, her creamy skin peeking above the lace of her nightgown, he couldn't stop himself. Dragging her slowly on top of him, he tangled his fingers in her hair and pressed his lips to hers, molding his mouth against the softness and warmth of her skin.

She tried to struggle, but only for a minute and then she surrendered to the power of his kiss.

"Bethany," he groaned, gasping for air.

Again she tried to free herself, but couldn't move. The strength in his arms was overpowering and she was pinned to the hard wall of his chest. Her hair fell forward, brushing against his shoulders, and her breath was caught somewhere between her lungs and mouth. "I...think you'd better let me go," she said, trying to push away. "You're the one who didn't want to be tempted, remember?"

"I didn't say I didn't want it; I said you shouldn't do it."

"I didn't intend to."

"Like hell! Coming in here, parading around in your nightgown and you didn't think I'd notice?"

"I came in to shut off the lights!"

"Sure." He grinned and his blue eyes gleamed. With one finger, he traced the gentle curve of her jaw. "And I really was asleep."

"You deliberately tricked me!"

He held up her wrist, his fingers still wrapped securely around her small bones. "You were the one who started it."

"I just wanted to…"

"To what?"

"Make sure that you were comfortable."

He couldn't help but laugh. Shifting on the couch, so that she was lying beside him rather than on him, he shook his head. "With you around? Impossible!"

"But you looked so…cold."

"Cold? Oh, lady," he whispered, "if you only knew!"

Her own blood was warm, pumping heatedly through her veins, and when he brushed his lips gently over hers, all the doubts in her mind scattered like dry leaves in the winter wind. She felt him tug the blanket over both of them and then she was pressed against the length of his body, his skin hot against the thin fabric of her nightgown.

"I think I should go back to bed," she said, licking her lips nervously.

"Stay with me."

"I don't know if that would be such a good idea."

"Shh." He kissed her hair, his breath warm and soft against her skin. "Be quiet." His lips pressed against her temple, her eyelids, her cheeks.

"I thought we were going to keep our relationship professional."

"We will." His hands slid around her waist, bunching the nightgown and burning her skin. "Later…much later." His mouth came back to hers as he kissed her leisurely, openly, the warmth and

desire in his blood flowing from his body to hers as
his tongue slipped through her parted lips to touch
and parry her own.

Closing her eyes, she tried to think beyond the feel
of his skin against hers, past the warmth radiating
from deep inside her. His hand moved upward, un-
tying the belt of her robe, pushing the soft fabric over
her shoulders until her arms were bare, then he slid
one lacy strap across her shoulder and placed his wet
lips against her throat.

Her skin tingling, she let her head fall away as his
lips pressed warm and hard against her, searing her
flesh, heating her blood even more. "Let me love
you," he whispered hoarsely and his hot breath
seeped through the thin lace to tantalize a nipple.

"I can't…please, Brett…"

But the thin nightgown slid lower, exposing the top
of one breast to his hungry lips and tongue. Her
breath shallow, her heart pounded wildly as slowly,
so slowly, he pulled on the fabric, and her breast
spilled over the lace, the peak hard with waiting.
Gently his lips rimmed the dark bud and Bethany
couldn't resist him.

His tongue and teeth played with her nipple, teasing and laving it gently as he tugged on the nightgown again, pulling it slowly over both shoulders,
down past her waist, crumpling the white cotton as it
slid past her hips.

"Brett," she cried, her breath a hoarse whisper.
"Oh, love," she said, as his rough chin slid lower,
down her ribs to rest against her abdomen. Her fingers
curled in the thick strands of his hair and her body
arched closer to his until she could feel his muscled

thighs pressed hard over her legs and the wicked torment of his tongue as it circled her navel.

His big hands closed around her. "God, I want you," he whispered, burying his face in her skin before slowly lifting himself up and kissing the hard trembling points of her breasts and looking into her eyes. "I want you more than any sane man should want a woman," he said, smiling a little at the irony of it all as he moved on and upward, twisting his fingers in her hair and drawing her face to his.

"And I want you," she admitted, frightened of the emotions grappling within her. Desire, hot and wanton, flowed through her veins, controlling mind as well as body. Trembling, she held him close, pressing her cheek into the soft mat of dark hair covering his chest.

"But?"

She tried to concentrate on slowing the beat of her heart and thinking rationally. "You were the one who didn't want to get involved."

"I know."

She looked up at him. "Have you changed your mind?"

Shaking his head, he sighed and looked up at the shadowed ceiling. "No."

"Well, neither have I."

"Just stay with me for a little while."

"Do you think that would be a good idea?"

"Good? Probably not." He held her tight, smelling the scent of her hair, the feminine fragrance of her skin. "But one I can live with."

"You're sure?" she asked, snuggling closer.

"Yes," he lied, ignoring the throbbing deep in his loins. "I'm sure."

Bethany didn't argue. Instead she listened to the rapid beat of his heart, the unsteady sound of his breathing. It was stupid to stay with him and she knew it, but she closed her eyes and slid her arms around his waist, her head cushioned by his chest. "Good night," she whispered, sure neither one of them would sleep.

"Night."

She didn't move, but closed her eyes and felt the warmth of his body next to hers. Concentrating on the sound of his breathing she slowly relaxed; within fifteen minutes exhaustion overtook her and she fell asleep.

Brett lay on the couch, entangled in her, wanting her more than he'd ever wanted a woman since Roberta. Her scent filled his nostrils and her warm body cuddled against his made him ache with desire. He stared at the ceiling and cursed his luck. Of all the women in the world, he was attracted to Bethany Mills, with her green-gold eyes, dimpled smile, and sweet-smelling skin. And Bethany Mills was strictly off-limits.

So why had he insisted that she spend the night with him? Just to torture himself? She moved, her lips brushing against his chest.

Stifling a groan and the urge to wake her and take her without regard to anything other than the male urge to claim her as his own, he kissed her forehead and tried to ignore the god-awful, cursed blessing of sexual need that was keeping him awake.

* * *

Bethany awoke with a crick in her neck and the sensation that something was terribly wrong. Stretching, she opened her eyes and found herself staring into Brett's blue eyes.

"Mornin'," Brett drawled, pushing a lock of hair out of her eyes.

"Oh, no," she groaned as the cobwebs in her mind disappeared and memories of the night before brought her crashing back to the reality that she'd spent the entire night sleeping in Brett's arms. Not only that, but she'd almost pleaded with him to make love to her. "Oh, God. I really didn't sleep here all night," she whispered, hoping that he would lie to her.

"You sure did," he taunted, grimacing. "All of you. Good thing I was a perfect gentleman."

Casting him a disparaging look, she yawned. "A gentleman?"

"But you weren't much of a lady."

"*What!*"

He laughed and released her. "Don't have much of a sense of humor in the morning, do you?"

She climbed off the couch and blew a wayward strand of hair from her face. "Not when I'm insulted."

He smiled seductively. "Me? Insult you?"

"Ooh. I knew you were trouble the minute I laid eyes on you," she gasped, snatching her robe, wrapping it around her and marching down the hall to her bedroom. Once there, she stripped, walked into her bath and spent twenty minutes under the shower, hoping the hot spray would soothe her tense muscles and relieve the ache in her neck. "Now, what do I do about that pain in my backside?" she muttered, thinking about Brett and wrapping a bath sheet around her before dressing in her favorite cords and a sweater.

By the time she'd put on some makeup, tied her hair back in a ponytail and walked into the kitchen, Brett was already there. Offering her a cup of coffee, he smiled that damned, disarming, slightly crooked grin. "It's Christmas Eve. Let's not fight."

"Christmas Eve?" she repeated.

"Yep. Comes every year about this time."

"Of course," she whispered, thinking about her family in Idaho and feeling sadness steal into her heart. "Mom and my aunt are probably already cooking for dinner...."

He rested a hip against the counter. "You miss your folks, don't you?"

Blowing on her cup, she nodded. "We're very close. The only real big fight we ever had was over Grant."

"When he stole the bonds?"

Shaking her head, she looked past him, out the window to where the snow-laden fir branches blocked the view. "When we got married. Mom and Dad were against it."

"Why?"

"They didn't trust him," she admitted, her lips twisting into a sad smile. "Ironic, isn't it? They were right all along, but I didn't believe them."

"Because you loved him." Brett had to force himself to say the words.

"I thought I did. I was pretty young at the time; not even through college. I'd gone with Grant ever since high school and I wanted to get married. Mom and Dad wanted me to wait, but I wouldn't listen."

"So then what happened when he took off with the bonds?"

She sipped her coffee and felt tears burn her eyes. "They were great. No 'I told you so;' nothing like that. They were wonderful; the only people in town who believed I was innocent."

"They sound too good to be true."

"They are," she said wistfully. "I was supposed to go back home for the holidays, you know, but Harry Benson drove out and harassed them."

"So you stayed here."

"I didn't think they needed me to drag both you and the press back on their doorstep. And that's what would have happened, wouldn't it? You would have followed me to Boise if I'd gone."

"Probably," he conceded, compressing his lips.

"I didn't think that Mom and Dad would appreciate me bringing home an investigator from First Security for Christmas!"

"But they don't blame you for what happened."

"Of course not! They blame Grant *and* Jim Benson!" Bravely, she fought the urge to break down and cry. "It's all so damned unfair! I wish…"

"You wish what?" he asked, when she didn't finish.

"I wish I'd never married Grant and that he'd never taken a job at the bank. Dad warned him about Jim, that he might be hard on him."

"Was he?"

Bethany shook her head. "I don't think so. Grant worked there a few years and didn't have much contact with the president of the bank. Oh, God, it's all such a mess!"

Brett swallowed his coffee and threw half of the dark liquid down the sink. *Damn Jim Benson and Grant Mills!* "Maybe it will be over soon."

"It had better be!"

"Didn't I promise?" he asked grimly.

"Yes, but I'm not sure I can believe you."

"Why not?"

"You don't know my husband. He fooled me and the bank for years, and then he masterminded the theft of the bonds." She shook her head and frowned. "He's very good. If he's not dead, he's hiding out, and if he's done it for this long, no one, not even you will find him."

"Oh, I'll find him all right," Brett said, his eyes growing cold and hard. "If it takes forever."

"I don't want my life torn apart forever."

He saw the worry in her gaze and smiled. "It won't be. Now, come on"—he touched the underside of her chin—"don't borrow trouble.'

"I didn't. You brought it."

His expression softened. "Lighten up, okay? It's Christmas Eve and I'm starving. How about breakfast?"

"You're cooking?" she asked dubiously.

"If you can call it that. Where's a frying pan?"

She pointed to the drawer under the stove.

"And the toaster?"

"Right here." Opening a cupboard, she pulled out the toaster, plugged it into the nearest outlet and stood aside. "Voilà!"

"Good. Now, if you could set the table, I'll make you the best Spanish omelet this side of the Rio Grande."

"The best?" she asked dubiously. "You know you're talking about the entire continental United States, including Texas."

"That's right."

"This I've got to see. It's a deal." She thought about the cinnamon rolls and eggs benedict that her mother always cooked on Christmas morning, then told herself that variety was the spice of life. And she was stuck with Brett Hanson and his Spanish omelet whether it was Christmas or not.

Harry Benson was cold. And mad. His father had sent him out to the Wagner farm again and he resented it. As far as Harry could see, he had no bloody reason in hell to be out there. It was Christmas Eve, for crying out loud, and dealing with anyone associated with Grant Mills was Brett's job.

"I just want to make sure Hanson's handling the job," his father had explained earlier, when Harry had complained about visiting Bethany's folks.

"Don't you trust him?"

Jim had looked over the frames of his glasses. "About as far as I would a grizzly bear. Now, go on, see the Wagners, just to make sure that Mills's wife didn't come home visiting for the holidays."

"Why do you care?"

Jim had leaned back in his desk chair and tugged at his tie, the old resentment welling up. He'd never liked Myron Wagner and the fact that he'd once been engaged to Myron's wife, Eleanor, still rankled him. Jim had since been married twice. He had looked blandly at his boy. "I really don't give a damn one way or the other about Bethany Wagner Mills, but I just want to check up on Hanson. This is the easiest way."

"So you think Brett's up to something?"

Jim had grinned without any amusement registering in his eyes. "I don't know. He's hard to read. Always has been. And there's certainly no love lost between us. I know that he wants that worthless piece of land in the Cascades, and badly. But I talked to him last night and he sounded as if he was drifting. Losing sight of his goal. He damned near made me promise to write this Mills woman a letter—something to the effect that if he found her husband, we'd leave her and her family alone." Disgusted, Jim had gotten up and poured himself a drink from the bar in his den.

"You think he's overprotective of Bethany Mills," Harry had commented.

His father's jaw had gone rigid and he'd downed his gin and tonic in one gulp. "Right."

Harry hadn't disagreed with his father. He'd received the same mixed messages when he'd talked to Brett himself. But it still didn't make it any easier to barge in on a family on Christmas Eve.

The wheels of the BMW spun on the wet snow as he turned down the long lane leading to the Wagner farm. A few cattle dotted the snow-crusted landscape and a weathered, once red barn contrasted with the gray sky and white fields. There were several cars parked in front of the farmhouse. As Harry braked to a stop and got out of the car, he heard the sound of laughter and music filling the air.

Gritting his teeth, Harry climbed the slippery steps and after a moment of hesitation, knocked loudly on the door.

* * *

Brett stretched and rubbed his lower back. He wasn't used to sitting at a desk all day and his muscles ached from their cramped position. Blinking, he glanced at his watch. It was after five and he hadn't taken a break. Worse yet, he hadn't found anything, not one clue to Grant Mills's whereabouts. Maybe this whole thing was nothing more than a wild-goose chase....

With a groan, he got out of the chair, stretched again, and walked through the house to find Bethany digging through the drawers of an antique sideboard in the dining room. There were pictures and old papers spread all over the dining-room table.

"Find anything?" he asked, eyeing the growing mound of papers.

"Just warranties for appliances that I don't have anymore," she said. "I don't know why I never threw any of this stuff away."

"Maybe it's important to you." He picked up a photo of Bethany; she was younger, her hair was cut short and she was standing arm in arm with her husband, a bearded, bespectacled outdoorsman. Dressed in cutoff jeans and sweatshirts, a roaring mountain stream behind them, Bethany and Grant looked the perfect couple. His gut reflecting his inner tension, Brett dropped the photo back onto the table and began searching through other pictures that were just as irritating.

"Hey, you don't have to look through those."

"I think it would be a good idea."

"Why?"

"Maybe there's some clue here. What's this?" He took an old book from the pile. It smelled musty.

"Nothing. Just my yearbook, from high school."

Brett began leafing through the pages.

"Really, there's nothing in there."

He looked up. "The police or FBI look through this?"

Sighing, Bethany crossed her arms over her chest. "I don't think so, but I don't know. It's really not important."

"Is that you?" He pointed to a black-and-white photo and Bethany groaned. The picture showed her on horseback, a wide smile on her girlish face, a first-place ribbon in one hand.

"4-H club," she said wistfully.

He flipped through the pages until he came to Grant's picture. It didn't look out of the ordinary.

"Who are all the people who signed this thing?" Brett asked.

"Come on, nobody. It was *years* ago. I don't even know those classmates."

Brett ignored her. "Who is Mary Alice Wilson?"

"An old girlfriend."

"And Bob Patterson?"

"Just a kid I knew."

He twisted the annual sideways. "How about Howie Sparks?"

"Howie? Oh, that was Grant," she said softly, thinking back to high school. "A name he used… kind of a joke."

"A joke?"

"Yes," she said, shaking her head at the memory. She and Grant had been so young. "A practical joke on one of the teachers he didn't like. During his free period, he went to her class and signed up as Howie, er, Howard Sparks, and spent three weeks as this kid.''

''But he got caught?''

''Eventually.''

''What happened?''

Bethany thought back. ''I don't remember. But I don't think he got suspended, maybe just reprimanded. It doesn't matter. It was over ten years ago.''

Brett leafed through the album and put it aside. Then he started looking through the pictures for a clue, any clue to Grant's whereabouts.

Pointing to a photo of Grant rock climbing, he asked, ''Where is this?''

''I don't know. Somewhere in Oregon or Washington, I think.''

''Who took the picture?''

''A friend of his, I guess.''

''You can't remember?''

''I wasn't there.'' Bethany looked at the table and waved at the stack of photographs. ''Look, none of this is going to help, you know.''

''Never can tell,'' he murmured. ''Where, exactly were these taken?'' He picked up seven or eight shots of Grant mountain climbing.

''I said I don't know. The Cascades, I think.''

''What state?''

She shook her head. ''I said I can't remember!''

He rubbed his chin. ''Look, Bethany, this might be important!''

''Give me a break!'' she said, shaking her head again and frowning. ''These are just old pictures that I should throw away or burn!''

Brett pulled out one of the chairs at the table and sat down. "Tell me about them," he suggested.

Bethany shook her head. "I don't want to."

"Why?"

"They're personal.... Look, this is hard for me; very hard. I feel like my entire life is an open book and you're turning each and every page, looking it over, checking for flaws."

"I just want to find your ex-husband."

"Well, maybe I don't."

"We had a deal, remember?"

Bethany looked away. "Maybe the deal should be called off!"

Brett placed his elbows on the table. Pictures scattered and fell to the floor. "And then you'd be running, looking over your shoulder for the rest of your life. Is that what you want?" He stared straight at her, steel-blue eyes delving deep into hers.

"I just don't think you'll be able to find anything."

"We've just started."

"But it's been so long." Shrugging her shoulders, she picked up a picture of Grant that had been taken when they were first married. How young and naive she'd been all those years ago!

The telephone rang and she dropped the photograph, but Brett picked it up and stared at the man Bethany had loved; the man he'd vowed to bring to justice. Gritting his teeth, he began sorting through the pictures, trying to ignore the jealousy that twisted his stomach every time he saw a picture of Bethany and Grant together.

He worked quickly until he heard the click of the phone. When he looked up, she was standing in the door between the dining room and kitchen, her hazel eyes bright with tears. "That was Dad," she said angrily.

"And?"

"And Harry Benson just dropped by."

Brett froze. *"What?"*

Angry and frustrated, Bethany wiped away her tears. "It wasn't to wish my folks Merry Christmas. He was looking for me."

"Why?"

"You tell me."

His eyes narrowed and every muscle in his body tensed. Planting his hands on the table, Brett slowly rose. "I don't know."

"Sure!"

"But I intend to find out!" He strode over to the hall tree and jerked his jacket off one of the brass spokes.

"Do that," she said. "And tell him to leave my family out of this! It's bad enough that I've been dragged into this mess, but I don't want Mom and Dad involved!"

"Don't worry; I'll give him the message!" He walked to the door, looked around and saw her standing in the dining room, her arms wrapped around herself, her cheeks burning with indignation. "Will you be okay here?"

"I'm fine," she lied. "But I think it would be best if you left and didn't come back. I don't want anything more to do with Grant. It's over and that's all there is to it."

"Not to Jim Benson."

"Jim Benson can go to hell!" Casting him an angry glare she walked back into the kitchen, took hold of the counter and leaned over the sink, trying to calm the anger that surged through her in hot, furious waves.

"He's no friend of mine, either," Brett said softly. He'd followed her into the kitchen and was staring at her as she slumped against the counter.

"So why are you so hell-bent to help him?" Before he could answer, she held up her hand. "Oh, yeah, I remember. You owe him money. Well, so do a lot of people! But they don't go around tearing up people's lives because of it!"

"Bethany—"

"Just leave!" She closed her eyes and took a long breath, listening for the sound of his retreating footsteps. Instead, he came closer, spun her around to face him, and then, while she was still sure she hated him, he kissed her, long and hard and fiercely, his mouth pressing over hers possessively, almost angrily. Her heart raced and blood pulsed rapidly through her veins, heating her from the inside, betraying the desire that was beginning to throb deep within her. "Don't—" But her pleas were cut off as his arms enclosed her.

"Just believe that I never intended to hurt you," he whispered against her hair. "Never."

"It's so hard."

"I know. But we'll get through it." With a groan he released her and then, after one last searching look in her direction, he opened the door to the garage and was gone.

Bethany stared at the door for a long time. She

touched her lips, felt them still hot and swollen and
listened as she heard Brett's Jeep roar down the hill.
"Merry Christmas," she whispered despondently,
"and peace on earth."

Chapter Seven

Bethany sat at the dining-room table and stared at the single red candle, watching the wax drip slowly down the brass candlestick. Winston was curled at her feet and she could hear the distant chime of church bells.

Brett had been gone nearly three hours and the house seemed empty and cold without him. She thought about her parents, who were probably gathered around the table, carving a plump turkey and laughing with all of the relatives, thought about last Christmas, before she'd lost the baby and Grant had divorced her, and she thought about all of the Christmases looming in her future. "I wonder if they'll be as lonely as this one?" she asked, as the puppy lifted his head and wagged his tail.

Absently she scratched Winston behind the ears

and looked at the clock for the twentieth time in fifteen minutes. "No use sitting around and brooding, is there?" she told the bright-eyed dog. "Not when there's Christmas cheer and friends who claim they want to see me."

She'd been toying with the idea all day. And now that Brett was gone she decided to take Marianne up on her offer. Before she could talk herself out of it, she changed into a pair of black slacks, boots and a warm, cowl-necked sweater. Then she twisted her hair up, dabbed on some fresh lipstick, grabbed her coat, a plate of cookies and a bottle of wine and headed for the door. "Maybe it's not Christmas at the farm," she said to herself. "But it'll just have to do!"

The party was in full swing when she arrived and rang the bell.

"Bethany!" Marianne exclaimed in surprise. "I'd just about given up on you. Come in, come in!"

"Better late than never, right?" Bethany asked as she stepped inside the cozy cottage.

"Right!"

The smells of scented candles, cinnamon and burning wood filled the small house. Laughter, soft music and the muffled hum of conversation surrounded her as she followed Marianne through the dining room.

After setting the wine and cookies on an already overflowing buffet, Marianne introduced her to the small group of people who were clustered in the living room. Bethany already knew a few teachers from school, but the majority of the guests she'd never seen before.

"I was just about to send Jack out looking for

you," Marianne teased, her dark eyes gleaming. "What happened to your big idea of going skiing?"

"Too much snow right here in the city. No reason to go all the way to the mountains," Bethany said with a smile. "I almost had to ski to get over here. I don't think the Toyota would have made it to Mount Hood."

"Well, I'm glad you came whether you drove, skied or used a dogsled," Marianne said. "Come into the kitchen and help yourself."

Bethany sampled the hors d'oeuvres and accepted a cup of hot spiced wine from Marianne's husband, Jack. He was short, had thinning red hair and an easy, glad-to-meet-you smile that constantly curved his lips as he watched his wife play hostess.

"Can I get you anything else?" he asked.

"No, really. This is enough."

"Too bad," he said regretfully, gesturing at the filled table. He glanced at Marianne who was flitting from one knot of people to the next. "You know Marianne, she makes enough food for the entire third battalion! We'll be eating these things clear into next year."

"What're you griping about now?" Marianne teased as she returned.

"He seems to think you went overboard on the food."

Marianne eyed the table and groaned. Every inch of the linen cloth was covered with delicacies. "Remember, I'm thinking like a pregnant person."

"Let's just hope the guests eat like pregnant people or you'll have to wean the baby on shrimp roll-ups or whatever you call these things,'' Jack said as he popped an appetizer into his mouth.

''Be serious.''

''Not a chance.'' With a devilish smile, he grabbed Marianne with one arm while holding a tiny sprig of mistletoe over her coffee-colored curls with the other.

''Wait a minute...Jack—''

''Gotcha!'' He smothered Marianne in a playful kiss and then released her.

''Just as long as you don't use that on anyone else,'' she said breathlessly, her face flushed, her dark eyes gleaming.

''Never!'' Jack replied, winking broadly at Bethany before refilling his glass and mingling with the other guests.

''He's crazy about you,'' Bethany said.

''Or just plain crazy!'' Marianne watched her husband joke with a couple of friends. ''Maybe a little of both,'' she admitted and plopped down into one of the maple chairs at the kitchen table. ''My feet are killing me!'' Slipping off her shoes, she sighed. ''So what happened to the mystery man from Boise?''

Bethany nearly dropped her cup, but managed to recover herself. The last thing she wanted was any questions that might link her to Brett and his investigation. Shrugging she said, ''Oh, I met up with him in the parking lot on the last day of school.''

''And?''

Hating to lie, Bethany decided to avoid the subject. ''He was just looking for a mutual acquaintance of ours.''

''And he thought you could locate this guy?''

"Mmm-hmm." Uneasy, Bethany walked over to the stove and ladled some more hot wine into her cup.

"Well, could you?"

"Find him? No. I haven't heard from the guy in years," Bethany said, her eyes dark as she remembered Grant walking out on her. All for the best, she told herself now, though his leaving had been painful at the time.

"And so the mystery man just jumped on his white steed and was swallowed up by the night?"

Bethany chuckled. "Actually, it was a Jeep, I think."

"Oh, that's right," Marianne said, smoothing the silky fabric of her dress over her protruding abdomen. "This is the 1980s."

"Right. So, from what I understand, Brett—"

"Wait a minute. Who's Brett? The guy that came looking for you or his friend?"

"They're not exactly friends," Bethany admitted, thinking about Grant and the fact that Brett had been hired to track him down and bring him to justice, if, indeed, he was alive. "But Brett's the man I met in the parking lot and he gave me the impression that he's still looking for this other guy."

"The one you knew?"

"Yes."

Marianne placed her fingers on her temples and shook her head. "This is all too confusing to me."

You and me both, Bethany thought, wondering about Brett; where he was, whom he was with, how he was connected, really connected, to Jim Benson and First Security Bank and why she even cared.

"Well, let me tell you," Marianne said, grinning

slyly and winking. "If I were still single and a good-lookin' guy like that came lookin' for me, I'd sure let him find me."

"Oh, you would, would you?" Jack said, walking into the kitchen and hearing the tail end of the conversation. "I wonder why I had to chase you to the ends of the earth, hmm?" He leaned over and kissed her dark curls. "Come on, Mata Hari, get your shoes on. It's show time!"

"Can't I play without them?"

Jack laughed. "Your choice."

Grumbling as she slid into her pumps, Marianne smiled at Bethany. "Remember what I said; I wouldn't let that one get away without a fight."

Shaking his head, Jack led Marianne into the living room and placed her solidly on the piano bench. "How about some carols?" he asked and a few of the more vocal of the group gathered around as Marianne started playing "Deck the Halls."

Leaning against the brick fireplace, Bethany sipped her hot wine, stared at the fire and listened to the music as Marianne played requests from the crowd. Trying not to think about Brett and the way he'd bulldozed himself into her life, Bethany hummed the familiar Christmas songs, but her mind continued to return to the past few days and the secret happiness she'd felt whenever he was around.

She wandered back into the kitchen and picked up a couple of appetizers. "You're a dolt," she muttered to herself, "acting like some adolescent schoolgirl! You don't know a damned thing about him!"

Sampling the salmon pâté, she wondered just how far she could trust Brett and why she still felt that he was hiding something from her—something important.

What does it matter? she thought, sighing and setting her cup in the sink as she heard the first few notes of "God Rest Ye Merry, Gentlemen." She went back into the living room just as Marianne was begging off.

"Come on, just a couple more," one of Marianne's closest friends insisted.

"Maybe later."

"You love it and you know it," Jack teased and a gale of laughter swept through the crowd just as the doorbell rang. "I'll get it, honey, you play. And that's an order!"

Marianne made a face at her husband but turned back to the piano and Bethany forced herself to get into the party spirit.

She felt a tap on her shoulder and turned to find Jack's worried face close to hers. He cupped a hand to her ear, so that she could hear him over the music. "There's a man here, guy by the name of Hanson— Brett Hanson. Says he needs to see you right away."

Surprised, Bethany felt her heart begin to pound. "He's here?"

"You want me to get rid of him?" Jack asked. His kind face was worried, as if he expected trouble.

"I doubt if anyone could."

"I'd sure give it my best shot."

"No, no, I'll talk to him," she said, getting a hold on herself. Why was Brett here? How had he known where she was? Looking over Jack's shoulder, she saw him.

He was standing between the living room and the

entry hall, his features hard and grim, his cold eyes trained on Bethany. Relief spread over his face for a second when he caught her gaze, and then his expression became hard again. He hadn't bothered to take off his heavy jacket or his hat. Dressed in jeans and the thick suede jacket, he looked completely out of place in the festive, holiday-spirited crowd.

"This'll just take a minute," Bethany whispered to Jack, praying that Marianne would keep playing and that Brett wouldn't cause a scene she couldn't explain.

"What're you doing here?" she asked, once she'd reached his side.

"Maybe I should ask you the same thing."

"I was invited."

Brett's mouth compressed angrily and he made a sound of disgust. "It doesn't matter anyway. Maybe it was best that you weren't home."

"What do you mean?"

He looked past her to the group of people clustered around the piano and his blue eyes narrowed suspiciously. "Who knew you were coming here?"

"Just Jack and Marianne. Wait a minute, what's going on?"

He turned his attention back to her. "We're leaving."

"You mean *you're* leaving."

His jaw set inflexibly, he took her arm. "Both of us. Come on."

"I'm not going anywhere—" But the look in his eye stopped her. Cold and assessing, his gaze cut her to the bone. When he took hold of her arm, she tried to jerk away, but couldn't shake off the hard manacle of his hand.

"Where's your coat?"

"Let go of me," she warned in a hushed whisper.

"First we get your coat. Where is it?"

"In the front closet, but—"

"Get it."

"Brett—"

"Any trouble here?" Jack asked, coming up to Brett and Bethany and searching Bethany's face.

"No," Bethany replied and Brett released her arm. Shooting him a furious glance, she kept her voice even for Jack's sake. "I think I'd better go now."

"You're sure?" Jack asked looking from Bethany to Brett and back again.

"Yes."

The music stopped and the group of people at the piano clapped before breaking up into small clusters. Marianne climbed off the bench, took one look at the angle of Jack's jaw, and hurried over to diffuse the fight she sensed was brewing.

Seething, Bethany shrugged into her coat.

"You can't leave yet," Marianne protested, darting a look of recognition at Brett.

Bethany forced a smile. "Sorry, it's been a great party."

"And it's not over! I've got tons of food! You're welcome to stay, too," Marianne invited, offering a smile to Brett.

"Some other time," Brett said.

"But it's Christmas! Bethany?"

"I'll call you later in the week, okay?" Bethany said, anxious to leave before Brett managed to cause such a stir that people she knew from school would begin asking questions about him and how she'd become involved.

"If you're sure," Marianne said, walking them to the door.

"I'm sure."

"Well, Merry Christmas." She grabbed her husband's hand as Jack held the door open.

"Same to you," Bethany replied, stepping outside to the bitter cold as Brett took hold of her hand and shut the door behind them. She saw Marianne still watching them through the window. Scowling with worry, Jack stood next to his wife, his arm settled comfortably across her shoulders. Bethany grinned and waved, hoping she didn't appear as anxious as she felt.

"You've got one helluva lot of nerve," she said, turning on him. "What's the meaning of dragging me out of a party on Christmas Eve?"

"Had to."

"Had to?" she repeated. "Give me a break. I don't know what your game is, Brett, but I'm tired of playing it." She stopped near his Jeep and turned furious eyes up at him. Her chin stuck out in the frigid night air, her face was flushed from anger as well as the cold, and she looked as if she were ready to tear him limb from limb. She was. "You'd better explain yourself."

"Later."

"Wonderful. I'm having the worst Christmas of my life and you're keeping secrets!"

Brett sighed. "Humor me, Bethany. *Please.* It's important. Come on. Get in the Jeep."

"Thanks, but I have my own transportation," she hissed. She started for her car, but Brett put his hand on her shoulder. "Can you leave it here?"

"No."

"Really, Bethany, I'm serious," he said, his voice calm. She turned and faced him and for the first time noticed the worry in his expression. "Can't you leave the car?"

"Well, I suppose so, but I'd have to ask and that would cause a whole lot of questions that I don't want to answer right now. Look, I'd just like to know what's going on."

"So would I," he said eyeing her car and frowning. "So would I. Is there anywhere near here that you can leave it?"

Crossing her arms over her chest, she shook her head. "No."

"All right. I'll follow you and explain everything when we get to your place."

"Forgive me if I don't say 'fair enough!'" she said, climbing into the Toyota and forcing the key into the ignition.

The drive seemed to take forever. Though the streets were nearly deserted, the snow that had begun to melt during the day had now turned to ice. Where the roads were sanded, Bethany was able to drive without much of a problem, but once she started climbing the hill on which she lived, her car spun and skidded on the rutted snow and ice.

"Great," she muttered, sliding sideways as she tried to turn sharply. "Just great." She'd driven in snow as long as she could remember. But that had been in Boise, where the land was flat and the snow-plows were able to take care of keeping the roads clear. Portland didn't have the equipment or the man-power to keep the smaller hillside streets clear.

When her wheels spun out of control and she started slipping down the hill while still in first gear, she gave up and parked her car on one of the side streets. Then she trudged through the snow to Brett's idling Jeep. "I guess I'll have to leave it here for the night," she decided as she climbed inside. "I'll get it in the morning."

"Or maybe later." He put the Jeep into four-wheel drive and started up the twisting road to Bethany's house.

"What's that supposed to mean? And what was the idea of crashing Jack and Marianne's party!"

"I had to find you."

"Why?"

He looked at her furious face, the anger in her wide eyes. "Because I was worried sick. I thought maybe you'd been kidnapped."

"Kidnapped!" Bethany laughed and cleared a spot on the window as the Jeep twisted and turned through the final bend to her driveway. "Are you out of your mind?"

"I wish I was. I came back here about an hour ago. You were gone, but I let myself in."

"You broke in?"

"The door was unlocked."

"But...I locked it."

"It had been forced," he said, the corners of his mouth pinching. "And the whole place had been turned inside out. Ransacked."

"My house? Why?"

He jerked on the emergency brake and parked in the driveway. "Your guess is as good as mine, but I imagine it had something to do with Grant."

"But why?"

"I don't know. Maybe you were right; maybe someone was watching the place and waited until he saw you leave. Hell, maybe someone was following *me*."

"I can't believe it."

He opened the door for her and helped her down. "Believe it," he suggested, his voice cold as they walked through the front door.

Bethany snapped on the lights and then had to lean against the wall when she looked around her house. Drawers had been dumped on the floor, furniture overturned, papers strewn all over the house, windows left open and closets emptied. Flour, beans, sugar and pasta had been jerked out of the pantry and were now spilling out of broken sacks in the middle of the kitchen floor.

In the living room, the Christmas tree was overturned and all the packages had been stripped open, bright bows and paper still clinging to cardboard boxes. The bentwood rocker had been smashed against the fireplace and the basket of kindling overturned, spilling splintered cedar and dry moss onto the floor.

"Oh my God," Bethany whispered, walking room to room. In her bedroom, her lingerie had been thrown on the floor, her shoes spread out, the mattress and bedding strewn about the room.

Fuming, Bethany walked into the bathroom. Broken bottles of makeup, perfume, bath oil and cleaning supplies filled the small room with a concoction of odors that was stifling.

"Who did this?" she demanded.

"Someone who knew you weren't here," he said, eyeing the mess. "Tell me about Jack and Marianne."

"The Selbys?" Whirling to face him, she almost laughed. "They're two of the nicest people anyone would ever want to meet! They couldn't have had anything to do with this." She looked at the mess and shook her head before lifting her suspicious gaze to meet his. "How did you know where I was?"

"It wasn't easy," he admitted, recalling how frantic he'd been when he couldn't find her. "But I remembered a party invitation I'd found when I was looking through your things. I managed to find it again and tried to call the R.S.V.P. number, but no one answered."

"That's because it's the number of the school. Marianne works in the office."

"I know. When I couldn't get hold of you on the phone, I drove over to the address on the invitation. Fortunately, you were there."

"And if I hadn't been?"

"I'd have called the police."

"I don't want the police involved in this!" Bethany said.

"You don't have much of a choice. Your insurance company will demand an investigation."

"And then it will all come out about Grant; my marriage to him and the fact that he stole all that money from First Security Bank."

"Eventually." Brett opened the closet door, found a suitcase and threw it onto the floor. "Put some things together—warm clothes—we're leaving."

"I can't leave!"

"You damned well can't stay," he said, his anger finally exploding as he gestured at the disaster in the middle of the floor. "Whoever did this means business, Bethany. You can't just stay here and invite trouble."

"What's that supposed to mean? That I'm going into hiding?"

"For the time being."

"Out of the question."

"Damn it, woman!" Brett said, striding over to her and taking both her shoulders in his hands. "Don't you see that this has become something more than just an idea? You thought you were being followed. Now it looks like you were right. Are you going to just sit here and wait for him?"

"This is my home," she said staunchly, ignoring the sick feeling in her stomach and the fear that was spreading slowly through her body.

"And right now it's not safe!"

"You don't know that!"

"For crying out loud, Bethany! Look around!" He went over to a pile of clothes on the floor and tossed them into the suitcase. "The first thing we're going to do is call the police, then you're going to get packed and we're going to hightail it out of here. Got it?"

"You can't call the police—"

"*Got it?*" he demanded, walking over to the phone and dialing the emergency number.

"But my whole life—"

"Will probably be thrown open for public inspection again, but that's the breaks."

"You did this, you know!" she shouted, throwing a pair of jeans into the suitcase and feeling so mad she wanted to scream, but Brett held up his hand, cutting her off as he connected with the police. He explained who he was, who Bethany was and what had happened.

Shaking, Bethany wanted to dive into the bed and hide—only the bed and everything else in the room had been torn apart.

"It'll be a while," he said, once he hung up. "Christmas, y'know."

"Right. Christmas. A time of joy to the world and peace on earth. Everywhere but here!" Angry sobs filled her throat and tears burned at her eyes as she looked at the shambles that had once been her tiny cottage on the hill, her haven from the past.

His fear slowly subsiding, he walked over and lifted her chin with one finger. "It could be worse," he offered.

"How?"

"Could be raining."

"That would be an improvement!" But she managed a thin, sad smile and swallowed back her tears when he bent down and brushed his lips tenderly over hers.

"I was worried sick," he admitted.

"About me?"

"Yes, about you." Pushing his fingers through his hair, he looked at the ceiling. "I thought that whoever did this had gotten to you." His blue eyes flicked back to hers. "I thought I'd lost you," he said softly. "And it scared me. It scared the hell out of me." Gently, he folded her into the circle of his arms. "I'm not going to let that happen again."

Warmed by his words and the strong arms holding her close, Bethany clung to him, glad for his strength and calm when she felt like falling apart inside. "Did you get hold of Jim Benson?" she asked.

The tense line of Brett's mouth became severe. "He's out for the day because of the holiday."

"What about his home?"

"No answer." Brett's thoughts hovered on the hatred he felt for his stepfather and somehow he couldn't shake the feeling that Benson was behind all of this. Deep inside, he vowed he'd get his revenge. "Has anything like this ever happened before?"

Bethany shook her head, extricated herself from his embrace and wandered down the hall to the kitchen. In the nook, she righted a picture on the wall, then made a sound of disgust when the photograph fell to the floor, the glass breaking into thin shards. "Nope.... Well, there was the accident..."

"Accident?"

"You know, when I was biking up the hill and saw Jenny and Winston. Where is he? I left him here." She started running through the house, calling for the little dog, frantic that he'd been lost in the confusion.

"Hey, hold on! He's fine. At least he was when I left."

"Where was he?"

"In the garage."

Bethany picked her way through the kitchen and opened the door to the garage. "Winston!" She heard the puppy's familiar whine and bent down so that he could dash into her arms. "Poor baby, I bet you were scared out of your mind," she said, holding onto the wriggling mass of thick fur as Winston tried to wash her face with his wet tongue.

Brett jammed his hands into the back pockets of his jeans and waited impatiently. Someone was after Bethany, either to scare her or to locate something important, something that would help them get to Grant Mills. But who? And what were they looking for?

The police arrived in a flurry of sirens and flashing lights. Two officers knocked on the door and Brett let them inside. Muttering to each other as they poked through the mess, the two officers took pictures, scribbled notes and asked more questions than Bethany wanted to answer. Under Brett's wary eye, she told them exactly who she was and how she was connected to Grant Mills.

"*The* Grant Mills," the younger officer, a man by the name of Andrew Daniels, guessed as he pushed his hat back on his head.

Cringing inside, Bethany met the young officer's gaze. "The same."

"Does the FBI know about this?"

"Not about what happened tonight," Brett said. "Not yet."

"We'll have to inform them," Officer Donaldson, the older of the two men, said. With weary eyes, he looked at the overturned furniture and smashed Christmas tree. "I'd appreciate it if you would leave everything just the way it is."

"I can't live in this mess——" Bethany began, but Brett cut her off.

"We intend to." While the policemen completed their reports, Brett explained his position with First Security and the fact that he was still working on the Mills investigation.

"So you think there's a chance that he's alive," Donaldson surmised with a long, low whistle.

"A good chance," Brett said, seeing Bethany pale. "Now, if you're finished, we'd like to get out of here."

"You'll leave an address and number where you can be reached."

"Wait a minute," Bethany said, "I'm not going anywhere."

"Sure we are," Brett said, his voice edged in steel and his eyes cutting her to the quick. "Just until the FBI have checked this out and we can come back and clean it up." Then he turned his gaze on the two officers, scratched the address of his cabin on an old business card and handed it to the officers.

"They'll want to talk to you, you know," Donaldson said. "Maybe you'd better stick around a while."

Brett agreed with them, and he and Bethany nervously paced the rooms until the FBI arrived an hour later. Bethany then answered the same questions that Officers Donaldson and Daniels had asked.

When the men left after another two hours, Bethany was livid. "I am sick and tired of you railroading me into doing things I don't want to do!" she said, her chin jutted in defiance.

"You don't have much of a choice."

"The last I heard this was still a free country."

"Cut it out!" Brett said, marching back into the bedroom and pointing at the suitcase. "Is that thing packed?"

Fuming, Bethany didn't answer.

Brett's eyes narrowed and he closed the case. "Good enough, then. Let's get going."

"Where?"

"To my place."

"In Boise?"

"Of course not. That's the next place whoever did this will look."

"So where, then?"

"I've got a mountain cabin not too far from Seattle."

"Seattle?" Shaking her head, she took a seat on the edge of the box spring and looked at the mess strewn all over her bedroom carpet. "I'm not going anywhere. This is my home and there's just too much work to be done to go traipsing off to Seattle or wherever!"

"You want to stick around and answer more questions from the FBI and the press?"

Groaning, Bethany shook her head. "Do I have a choice?"

"I'm giving you one."

"I'll have to talk to them sooner or later."

"Let's make it later. Okay? Look, there's no time to argue right now. We don't know if whoever's behind it will be back or not. It looks like a burglary, but nothing seems to be missing to me—what about you?"

"I already told you and the police that I think most everything's here."

"Then how do you know that the man who did this isn't after you? How do you know that it isn't the same guy that nearly ran you over a couple of weeks ago? And how do you know he won't be back?"

"This is my home—"

"Not for the next couple of weeks," he said, his jaw set in determination. "You're coming with me if I have to carry you across the Columbia River myself!" The gleam in his eye suggested that he was dead serious.

Relenting slightly, she picked up her favorite pair of jeans, several sets of underwear and two heavy sweaters. "Okay. You win. For now."

"Thank God for small favors," he muttered, opening the suitcase and watching as she folded a few other clothes and tucked them inside. When she was done, he snapped the case shut. "All set?"

"As ready as I'll ever be," she said, whistling to the dog. "One more thing."

"What's that?"

She bent down and the gangly pup climbed into her arms. "Winston goes with us."

In no mood to argue, Brett nodded his head. "Fair enough." He took the suitcase and Bethany's purse and she followed him outside and climbed into the Jeep. Then he returned to the house, threw a few papers, pictures, scrapbooks and pieces of Bethany's jewelry into a large box and brought it to the Jeep.

"I hope you know what you're doing," Bethany said, shooting a glance at him as he got in and put the Jeep in gear.

His features hard, he muttered. "I hope so, too. I hope to God I know what I'm doing."

Chapter Eight

Brett was silent as he drove through the quiet streets of Portland. Colored lights winked from some of the skyscrapers along the waterfront and street lamps reflected in the piled snow and slush on the sidewalks.

He drove slowly, checking his rearview mirror. None of the bright pairs of beams behind him looked like a tail. Maneuvering the Jeep through side streets, he relaxed a little. No car followed. Letting out a long sigh, he snapped on the radio.

"So far, so good," he muttered, shifting down and weaving into the traffic as it crossed the Hawthorne Bridge before heading north.

"Thank God for small favors," Bethany murmured, looking through the steamy windows and watching warily. Ever since leaving the house, she'd been on edge, sure that whoever had been tracking her for the past few weeks would be after them. "So where are they? The people that ruined my house?"

"Let's hope in Timbuktu."

A smile curved over her lips and she yawned. "Come on, Brett. Tell me: where do you think they are?"

"I wish I knew," he admitted. "Maybe I scared them off by coming back. My guess is that they knew you were going to that party."

"Impossible," she said. "Even Marianne and Jack didn't know I'd show up. On the last day of school I told Marianne that I'd probably go skiing instead."

"And the other people at the party?"

"I only knew a few of them. They're elementary school teachers, Brett," she pointed. "Not exactly the criminal element."

His fingers tightened over the wheel. "Don't get your back up. I'm just trying to figure this thing out."

"So am I," she said, glancing angrily at him. "You know, if I had my guess, I'd blame Jim Benson."

"He's in Idaho."

"You think. Besides, he wouldn't get his fingers dirty by doing it himself. He'd hire it done."

"But why?" Brett demanded.

"How should I know? He sent you, didn't he? And he sent his son out to harass my folks this morning. And he's the guy with the motive: revenge. Not only does he hate my dad but he blames me for everything Grant did!"

Brett shifted lanes and checked the rearview. No car lights followed. Ahead, across the black waters of the Columbia River was the city of Vancouver, the first milestone of their journey northward through Washington. "I guess I wouldn't put it past Benson."

"How well do you know the man?"

Brett's shoulders tightened. "Well enough."

Bethany leaned back in the seat. "There you go," she said, burrowing deep into her jacket and closing her eyes, "I bet he's behind it."

They drove in silence for a while. Bethany leaned her head against the window of the car and tried to tell herself that she could trust Brett; somehow he'd make everything right. But the image of her home, the smashed Christmas tree, broken ornaments, papers and clothes strewn throughout the small house made her shudder. All her fears of the past few weeks crystallized and she wondered if she'd ever be able to put the past behind her.

"Do you have any enemies?" Brett asked.

"Only Benson."

"What about the Weathers brothers?"

"Never met either of them."

"You're sure?"

"Yes, I'm sure; I never even saw Jake at the bank," she said through clenched teeth. "How many times do I have to tell you?"

"I just wanted to get it straight."

"I never met anyone associated with the theft, okay?" She tossed out the words, staring into the dark night. Rows of taillights gleamed up ahead as far as she could see. "And that includes Karl and Jake Weathers and that Henshaw woman. And why are you so sure what happened tonight is connected with Grant? As far as you know it might just be a simple case of vandalism."

"Unlikely."

"So we're back to Grant or someone associated with him." She stretched and closed her eyes again. "And we don't even know if he's alive." Trying not to think about the fact that her life had changed forever, she huddled in the corner of the Jeep and held Winston on her lap. "How long, exactly, is it to this cabin?"

"A few hours," he replied. The Jeep hit a patch of black ice and fishtailed for a second.

Bethany's stomach lurched and she gripped the armrest until the vehicle was back in control. "A few hours," she repeated. "That could be anything from two to twenty!"

"Not that long, I promise." He grinned and glanced at her. He couldn't really blame her for her resentment; so far all he'd managed to do was to throw her life into emotional turmoil.

As she closed her eyes, he listened to the strains of Christmas music on the radio. Had Jim Benson set him up? Brett's eyes narrowed suspiciously. If Benson was behind the ransacking, it wouldn't take him long to figure that Brett had taken Bethany to his cabin in the mountains.

His lips compressed, Brett tried to convince himself that what had happened to Bethany's house had been a simple case of vandalism, but he couldn't shake the feeling that he'd led whoever had torn apart her house straight to her door. Glancing over at her, he saw that she was asleep. He reached behind the front seat, grabbed an old wool blanket and, with one hand on the wheel, spread the blanket over her and the small dog.

"Merry Christmas, Bethany," he whispered as he turned his concentration back to the long, dark road ahead.

Bethany was jostled awake as one of the Jeep's tires caught in a pothole and the rig jerked to one side. Her eyes flew open and she realized that it was dawn and they were somewhere in the mountains. The first rays of pale sun were filtering through the thick stands of snow-encrusted Douglas fir trees.

"Just about there," Brett said, glancing at her.

"You drove all night."

"All morning. We didn't leave your place until after one."

"Don't remind me," she muttered, shuddering. Absently, she scratched Winston behind the ears, trying not to think about the mess she'd left behind.

"You rent that place, don't you?" Brett asked.

"Yes."

"How come it's so cheap?"

"What?"

"The rent—it's not much."

"How do you know?" she asked crossly, and then waved aside his explanation. "Oh, the checking account statements you've been digging through. The house is owned by my uncle."

"Does he live in Portland?"

"No. He's in Idaho. He inherited the place and when I needed a house in Portland, he agreed to rent it to me to help me out." She looked out the window to the snow-covered ground and thought about her smashed furniture, broken windows, and ruined carpet. "I don't even want to think about telling him what happened."

"The police will take care of that."

"I guess that's good," she muttered, feeling a twinge of guilt.

"You don't think the vandalism was aimed at your uncle?"

"Do you?"

"No, but I'm trying not to ignore any possibility. Here we are." He guided the Jeep into a clearing.

"This is where you live?" Bethany asked, staring at the small cabin with the sagging front porch. Built entirely of wood that had bleached and stained through the winters, the house looked as rugged and weathered as the man who owned it.

"Yep."

"Wait a minute," she said, turning serious eyes on him, "maybe I'm a little dense, but I don't understand how you run a private investigation practice in Boise from here."

"I don't. I'm semiretired."

"And you just came out of retirement to track down Grant because you owe Jim Benson some money?"

He parked the Jeep, grabbed her bags and opened the door. "That's a little simplistic, but you've got the basic idea." He came around to her side of the Jeep and helped her out. Winston jumped off her lap and landed in a drift of snow that covered him.

"Whoa, fella," Brett said, picking up the little dog and brushing the white powder from his fur. "Slow down."

Bethany grabbed her suitcase and walked through

the knee-deep snow in silence as she looked at the clearing in the woods. The setting was beautiful. Winter sunlight spilled over the small cabin set on the side of a forested mountain. Giant firs, their branches drooping from the weight of the snow, knifed upward to jut against a clear blue sky.

"It's gorgeous up here," Bethany admitted. "Like one of those picture postcards we used to get at Christmas."

"I like it," Brett replied. He climbed the two steps to the porch and stomped the snow from his boots. Unlocking the door, he held it open, letting Bethany walk inside. As she slowly unwrapped her scarf, she stared at the barren dwelling that Brett called home. Her breath hung in the air and she shivered from the cold that seeped through her clothes.

The interior was stark, almost bare. Sparse, worn furniture sat on an ancient braided rug that partially covered the plank floor. The kitchen, dining and living areas of the house were really one big room, heated at one end by a stone fireplace and at the other with a wood stove that was obviously used for cooking. Overhead was a loft with a ladder for access.

Winston was everywhere at once, running from one end of the cabin to the other, sniffing in the corners and whining as he passed Bethany.

"You'll get used to it," she said, petting him and watching his tail wag furiously. "We all will."

Brett set her suitcase near the front door and finished unloading the Jeep. Once back inside he rubbed his hands together and pointed toward the kitchen. "The bathroom's off the kitchen, near the back porch. The shower is heated with propane, when I remember to buy it. A few years ago, I had the electric company hook me up, so we have lights.''

"But no heat."

"Haven't got around to adding a furnace yet."

"Great."

"It's not that bad." When she looked at him dubiously, he forced a tired grin. "Even when the electricity goes out, we've got lanterns for light and the wood stove does a decent job of heating this place. Someday I'll buy an electric water tank and stove."

She walked around the rooms and stared at the chipped wood and old, paned windows. "How'd you ever find this place?"

"It was my mother's."

"Oh. I see." Bethany said, noticing that his expression had grown tense again. "So you live up here like some kind of hermit?"

"Some people think so." He walked over to the wood bin and began piling kindling into the stove. "I like it." Then, frowning, he stood and dusted his hands. "Look, why don't you go and clean up? I'll get the fire going and fix us something to eat. Fair enough?"

"I guess," she said, dragging her suitcase into the bathroom and stripping off her clothes. She looked down at her slacks and angora sweater and laughed at herself. There wasn't much room for fashion here—wherever here was.

By the time that she'd showered and changed, the cabin was beginning to warm. The smell of burning wood and the sizzle of frying bacon greeted her when she walked into the kitchen. Brett was standing over the stove, carefully watching two cast-iron pans.

"Where'd you get that?" she asked, eyeing the strips of slab bacon.

"The freezer. When you live up here, you've got to be prepared just in case you get snowed in."

"Does that happen often?"

"Often enough," he said, shrugging.

She stared at the pan biscuits in the other skillet. "I can take over if you want a turn in the shower."

Rubbing the kinks from his neck, he smiled wearily. "You're on, lady," he said with a wink, and Bethany's heart fluttered.

By the time the food was cooked and the coffee perked, Brett had showered and shaved. Wearing a faded blue flannel shirt and worn jeans, he fitted the image of a mountain recluse. He put a couple of chipped plates on the small table.

"I don't get it," Bethany said, once she'd sat down in a beat-up wooden chair.

"Get what?"

She spread butter over her biscuit, then looked at him. "What's a private investigator from Boise doing up here?"

"Hiding." He grinned again and she had to laugh.

"I mean the rest of the time."

"I told you—"

"I know. A semiretired hermit. A thirty-five-year-old recluse."

"Thirty-six." He set his elbows on the table and sipped his coffee.

"So how do you make a living?"

"Once in a while I take a case, like this one."

"And the rest of the time?"

"I live here. I don't need much."

"Except that you owe Jim Benson."

Brett grimaced, but nodded as he scraped his chair back and cradled his coffee cup in his hand.

"How?"

"How what?"

"How'd you get into debt? The Jeep? Your practice? What?" she asked, still feeling as if he were holding out on her, hiding something.

Brett eyed her for a minute. "A combination of things really. Debts my mother had when she died, property taxes on this place."

She pulled off a piece of biscuit and ate it. "And you never heard from your father?" she asked, and saw the familiar tightening of his face muscles.

"Nope. Took off when Mom found out she was pregnant. They weren't married."

"Oh…I'm sorry," Bethany said, suddenly feeling as if she'd pried.

He lifted a shoulder. "It was hard on my mother. In those days it wasn't popular to keep illegitimate children. Fortunately my grandparents were ahead of their time in their thinking. They didn't condemn her and she inherited this place from them."

"And your mother didn't ever marry?"

Brett's eyes darkened. "Years later. My stepfather and I never got along."

"That's a shame," she murmured, thinking of her own near perfect childhood on the farm.

"I don't think so. There's no love lost between my stepfather and me and that's the way I like it. The less I have to do with him, the better."

"So you never see him?"

"Only when I have to." His shoulder muscles were

so tight they ached. He stood and walked to the fireplace. Once there he finished his coffee and tossed
the dregs into the fire. The flames flickered and
hissed.

Bethany cleared the dishes from the table while
Brett continued to stare into the bright yellow flames.
When she was just about finished in the kitchen, he
grabbed his denim jacket and called over his shoulder,
"I'll bring some more wood inside." And with that,
he was out the door.

The rest of the morning Bethany busied herself by
cleaning the three rooms until they shone and then
she made lunch. Brett piled wood in the living room,
fixed the hinges on the door and spent a lot of time
staring out the window, as if he really expected that
someone had actually followed them.

After lunch, she thought about dinner—Christmas
dinner. Brett's freezer was well stocked. And though
there was no turkey or goose inside, she did find a
beef roast that she managed to thaw and place into
the oven. She discovered onions, potatoes, apples and
oranges in boxes on the back porch. "No roast goose,
Waldorf salad or cranberry sauce, but we'll get by,"
she told herself, hoping that she could master working
with a wood-burning oven.

After she'd finished in the kitchen, she polished a
kerosene lantern, lit the wick and set the lamp in the
middle of the table.

"Something smells great in here," Brett said as he
walked through the kitchen to put his tools on the
porch.

Blushing at his compliment, she smiled. "Thanks.

I don't suppose you have a bottle of champagne?"
she asked.

"Sorry."

"Wine?"

Shaking his head, he frowned. "If you're desperate, I could probably dig up a bottle of Scotch—"

"Not that desperate," she said with a laugh.

"Well let's see..." He opened a cupboard and poked around inside. "How about this?" Pushing some bottles aside, he pulled out a nearly full fifth.

"What is it?"

"Brandy."

"For after dinner," Bethany said, nodding. "Perfect."

The meal was a success, and if the onion gravy, sliced apple and orange salad and slightly charred roast weren't traditional, at least they were tasty.

Bethany spent the rest of the evening sitting on a lumpy, overstuffed couch with her feet propped against the hearth. Brett sat on the hearth and insisted on making popcorn. Sipping brandy, staring into the fire and munching on the puffed kernels, Bethany felt warm and secure. They talked and laughed together, while outside snow collected in the corners of the windowpanes.

"I don't suppose you have a phone," she said.

"Nope."

"Too bad."

"You need to call someone?"

"Not right this minute. But I really should let Mom and Dad know where I am."

"Why? Do they check up on you?"

"Sometimes," she said, with a little laugh. She

stared into her glass and watched the reflection of the flames dance in the amber liquor. "Especially this year. They knew I was disappointed when I couldn't come home for the holidays. And now that Harry Benson's been nosing around, Mom and Dad are worried. When they try to call me at home—" she shrugged and her smooth brow furrowed.

"What will they think?"

"I don't know."

"Probably that you've gone skiing."

"Maybe. Unless the police call my uncle about the damage to the house. Then he'll probably call Mom."

"That could be a problem," he thought aloud. "We can't do anything about it tonight, but I'll see that you get to a phone as soon as we go into town."

"I'd appreciate it," she murmured, sipping her drink.

"They don't have any reason to think you're in danger, do they?"

"No." She shook her head. "Not unless Harry Benson scared them or my uncle called."

"Then don't worry." He walked over to the couch and sat beside her. "Harry Benson couldn't scare anyone." His arm encircled her shoulders. "In a few days we'll go into town and give your folks a quick call. You can tell them that you decided to hit the slopes."

"Lie?"

"Not exactly. You are up in the mountains."

"But—"

"Besides, would you rather tell them what happened?"

"I guess not, but I might have to." She frowned into her glass and took a drink.

"Then we will," he decided. "Now cheer up, it's Christmas."

"How could I forget?"

Noticing the sadness in her eyes, he drew her close and stroked her cheek with his finger. "This will all be over soon," he said.

"How can you be sure?"

"Because I made a promise to you that it would be one way or another, didn't I?"

"I...I guess so."

"Oh, by the way, I have a Christmas present for you."

"You do?" She looked up and caught the twinkle in his eye.

"Yep." Stretching, he got off the couch, went over to his briefcase and extracted a long, white envelope. "Your guarantee."

"Guarantee?"

"Didn't you insist on having Jim Benson's promise, in writing, no less, that if you cooperated with me, he would leave you and your parents alone?"

"This is it?" she asked.

"Yep. Proof positive that he means what he says," Brett said sarcastically. He handed her the letter and she read it eagerly.

"When did you get this?"

"I had him express it to me."

She looked at the formal document. "Do you think he'll be as good as his word?"

"Sure of it," Brett said, his eyes growing that cold,

cold shade of blue that made Bethany shiver. "If not, he'll have to answer to me."

"Maybe he already has," she said softly, thinking back to her smashed home. "Maybe whoever ruined my house is connected with him."

"I don't think so." Brett walked over to the stove and stoked the fire. "I'm not saying he's not capable of having your place vandalized, but I don't think he'd do it—not now. Right now you and I are both too important to him and he wouldn't want to do anything that might stop us from tracking down Grant."

"Is that what we're doing?"

Brett nodded and rubbed his chin. "I admit that we've been sidetracked a bit, but only for a little while."

"Until?"

"Until I find out who was behind what happened."

"And how do you expect to do that from here?"

Brett turned and smiled lazily. "Connections. I didn't spend twelve years as a private investigator without making a few connections along the way. Tomorrow morning we'll go into town, call the police, see what they've come up with and then I'll start snooping on my own."

"Up here?"

"Nope. I've got a friend in Portland who owes me a favor. He has his own investigation business. I think I can convince him to do some poking around."

"And if he doesn't find anything?" she asked. She stood and walked to the stove, extending her palms to warm her hands.

"Then we'll do something else. Unfortunately, we have to take this thing one step at a time."

She wrapped her arms around her chest and sighed. "I just wish it were all over," she whispered. "Over and done with."

The brackets around Brett's mouth deepened. He finished his drink and set down the empty glass. "I'll do the best I can," he promised, staring into the black, starless night. "In the meantime, maybe we should think about bed." He glanced back at her and then looked away again. "Go on, take the loft. I'll camp out down here—the couch folds out—and make sure the fire keeps going."

"I don't want to kick you out of your own bed," she said.

He lifted a thick dark brow. "Don't tell me you're interested in sharing it with me?"

"What!"

He turned and faced her, placing his hands on the windowsill and leaning back. His expression was as bland as he could make it, though thoughts of the night before and the feel and smell of Bethany as she lay with him ruined his concentration. "I just asked if you wanted to sleep with me."

"I don't think that would be such a good idea."

He nodded once and reached for the bottle of brandy to pour himself another drink. "Neither do I," he lied, filling his glass and then tossing back the drink in one swallow. "So go on upstairs."

Wanting to argue, but knowing it would only make the tension between them worse, Bethany grabbed her suitcase and lugged it up the ladder to the loft. Once there, she undressed quickly and discovered that she hadn't brought a nightgown.

"It figures," she muttered to herself while tossing

an oversize sweatshirt over her head. Braiding her hair away from her face, she sat on the edge of the bed and looked around the room. The furniture had definitely seen better days. A scratched table sufficed as a nightstand. A bureau was pushed against the far wall and the closet was just a rail. There was a single window in the wall opposite the bed. The remaining wall was only hip level. Standing over it, she could look into the living room.

"Hey!" Brett shouted. "You forgot your friend."

Bethany looked down and saw Winston at the bottom of the ladder. At the sight of her, the puppy whined loudly and his fluffy tail wagged, sweeping the floor.

"Poor baby," she said with a smile. "Come on."

Brett had to carry the small dog to the top step. "There you go." He put the dog on the floor of the loft and then looked up, past the length of Bethany's legs, over the gentle curve of her bottom and the lacy underpants peeking beneath the sweatshirt, then upward past the rounded swell of her breasts to her eyes, wide and hazel, looking at him with a combination of innocence and seduction.

"Thanks," Bethany said, conscious that her voice had deepened.

"No problem." He offered a tentative smile that nearly took her breath away. "Good night."

"Night," she whispered as Winston made himself at home on the foot of the bed.

"See you in the morning." His blue eyes searched her face.

"Right. In the morning," she whispered, her heart racing as she watched him slowly climb down the ladder. When he reached the floor below, she let out her breath and remembered how warm and safe she'd felt in his arms—Good Lord, had it only been a few hours ago? She felt as if she'd aged years since this morning, when she'd awakened to find him staring at her.

Ignoring the butterflies in her stomach, Bethany crawled into his bed. The sheets were cold against her bare legs but the crisp percale smelled faintly of Brett. Smiling, she reached over to snap off the bedside lamp and found herself staring at a picture on the table. It was a portrait of a beautiful black-haired woman with warm brown eyes and honey-colored skin. Her arms were wrapped around the neck of a collie and she was smiling merrily into the camera. Her long hair was swept away from her face, her shoulders were bare and her brown eyes twinkled. In the corner of the portrait was a handwritten message:

Merry Christmas. All my love forever, Roberta.

Closing her eyes, Bethany ignored the stab of jealousy that cut into her heart and she snapped off the lamp.

Chapter Nine

Brett awoke stiff and sore. The couch was old and lumpy, and that, along with the past few nights of sleeping in cramped quarters, combined to make his entire body ache. He tossed and turned on the squeaky old pull-out bed, trying to get comfortable, but all he could think about was Bethany and the fact that she was only a few feet away, in the loft in his bed.

Feeling like a damned fool, he turned over and tried to relax. So what if she was the most intriguing woman he'd met since Roberta? So what if she was more than willing to make love to him? So what if he throbbed so badly for her he couldn't think straight? The fact of the matter was that she was Grant Mills's ex-wife, an official "suspect" in the investigation, definitely off-limits!

Groaning, he gave up on sleep, slid out of the

sleeping bag and swung his legs over the edge of the bed. The cold air made goose bumps rise on his bare chest, so, telling himself that he'd only gotten up to stoke the dying fire, he slipped into his jeans, tossed another couple of logs onto the grate and bent near the fireplace. He studied the coals as they glowed scarlet before catching on the pitchy wood.

Images of Bethany teased his mind. He remembered the feel of her skin against his, the way her body fitted tight to his, the scent of her perfume. Glancing over his shoulder, he looked up to the loft. For all practical purposes he held her hostage, trapped in this isolated mountain cabin without anyone knowing where she was.

Muttering under his breath, he stretched, felt the warmth of the fire at his back, then walked silently past the couch to the ladder of the loft. After only a second's hesitation, he began to climb.

Bethany's eyes flew open. The room was dark, the only light a soft glow coming from the fireplace below. She rubbed her eyes and recognized Brett as he stared down at her. His sleep-rumpled hair fell over his face and his naked torso, smooth dark skin stretched taut over corded muscles, flexed as he stood over her. Bethany's pulse jumped at the sight of him.

"What're you doing?" she asked, propping herself up on one elbow.

"Shh. I couldn't sleep. Thought I'd check on you," he whispered, sitting on the edge of the bed.

She yawned and pushed the hair out of her eyes, smiling as she looked up at him. "Is it morning yet?"

"Not quite."

"Then—"

"I told you, I just wanted to see that you were okay."

"I'm fine," she whispered, her heart beginning to pound as she looked up at his shadowed face. His eyes were dark, the angular planes of his face more distinct in the half-light.

"Good." He started pushing himself upright, but she placed her hand over his.

Swallowing hard, she asked the question uppermost on her mind. "Tell me about Roberta," she asked.

"Roberta was my wife," he said softly. "Why?"

Licking her lips, she stared straight into his eyes. "I just wondered. I saw the picture by the side of the bed and I thought maybe you were—"

"—involved with someone."

"Yes."

"I haven't been 'involved' with anyone since my wife died," he explained. "Until now."

"And now?" she asked, barely able to breathe.

He pushed his hair out of his eyes, stood and walked to the ladder. "That's a hard question." he admitted, his shoulder muscles bunching. "I keep telling myself that you're just part of a case; that you're the last person in the world I should be attracted to, that by all rights I should have my head examined for even thinking about you."

"And?"

She saw his coiled silhouette in the darkness. Bracing his hands on either side of the wall above the ladder, he let his head fall between his shoulders.

"And I just can't quite convince myself."

Sitting up and crossing her legs, she pulled the

comforter around her shoulders. "I'm having the same problem," she admitted. "I wish I could hate you. I try to believe that I don't care about you; that you're just stirring up trouble over a past I'd rather forget."

His head snapped up. Surveying her with cool blue eyes, he tried not to notice the wild tangles of her hair as it fell loose from her braid or the heavy eyelids that drooped seductively over her eyes. "So what's the problem?"

"You." She plucked at a thread on the bed. "This sounds crazy, I know. But there are times when I want to hate you and times…times when I wish that you'd just hold me and never go away."

Still gazing at her, Brett slowly returned to the bed. Once there he sat on the edge of the mattress and touched the rounded point of her chin. "You're a very beautiful woman, Bethany," he said, forcing her eyes to meet his. "Intriguing, exciting and beautiful. And if the circumstances were different, I know that I'd be trying my damnedest to seduce you right now."

"So what's stopping you?" she asked breathlessly.

"Our agreement, for one thing," he said, slowly running his fingers along her jaw.

"And the rest?" she asked, her eyes wide and bright. "Is it because you don't trust me? That you think somehow I still might be involved in Grant's embezzlement?"

"No." His hand slid along her neck to rest at her nape. Her sweatshirt slid to one side, exposing the soft white skin of her shoulders.

"Then what?" she challenged.

"Maybe it's because I don't trust myself. I can't

afford to get involved with anyone right now, Bethany, especially you.''

"Damn it, we are involved!" she whispered, surprised at her own reaction. "You forced yourself into my life, spent the night at my house, dragged me away from a party on Christmas Eve and pirated me up here, alone, where no one, not even my parents, can find me! If that isn't involved, what is?" she demanded.

His expression changed. "I meant romantically involved."

"I know what you meant," she retorted. "I'm just saying your excuses don't hold water."

"Oh no?" He took one of her hands, spread the fingers and pressed each fingertip to his lips. Heat curled deep within her. "Tell me, Bethany," he said, letting his tongue slide between her thumb and forefinger. "What do you want? A lover or a friend?"

Swallowing hard, she tried to concentrate. "I...just want you to be honest with me."

"Is that all?"

"Isn't it enough?" Dear God, his tongue was creating havoc with her senses. Her entire body began to quiver.

"I don't know." He pressed his lips against her hand and shifted so that more of his body was on the bed. "I'm getting mixed signals from you. Signals I don't know how to read. One minute you're pushing me away, the next you're coming on to me."

"I'm *not* coming on to you."

"I'm more than willing to take this relationship one step further," he said, "if you are."

"I thought you didn't want to get involved."

"I don't." He kissed her softly on the forehead. "But I can't seem to stop myself." His gaze lingered on her for a minute. She looked so innocent and vulnerable, warm and seductive. The ache in his loins pulsed and he couldn't think of anything but making love to her. "Bethany?"

"What?"

"Oh, God, I must be out of my mind," he whispered, as he swung his legs onto the bed and took her into his arms. Without another thought, he entwined his fingers in her hair and claimed her mouth.

Bethany moaned against him, feeling his tongue glide between her teeth to touch the insides of her mouth. Her arms wrapped around his neck, her fingers touched his bare skin, ruffling the dark hair at his nape.

Desire, hot and wild and wanton, raced through her blood, accelerating her heartbeat, making it impossible to breathe or think. She felt the sweet intensity of Brett's lips against her mouth, her cheeks, her eyes. Her head was swimming, her body aching for his touch.

Lowering himself, he nuzzled her neck, letting his lips and tongue whisper against her skin, sending wave after wave of passion surging through her. He lay over her and the rough denim of his jeans rubbed against her thighs. Indifferent to the sweet agony, she entangled her legs with his and moved slowly, rhythmically against him.

He whispered her name against her ear while his fingers entwined in her braid and tugged gently, letting her hair fall in wild waves of chestnut splendor around her face. "Bethany, dear sweet Bethany..."

His voice was a hoarse plea in the darkness and his hands cupped her face. "I want you so badly it hurts, but I've got to know that you want me, too."

"Can't...can't you tell?" she rasped.

"But it has to be more." He kissed her, then nipped the lobe of her ear with his teeth. "More than simple want."

"Oh, God," she said as his tongue touched the sensitive part of her ear, sending ripples of desire from deep within her.

Slowly he slid his hands under the hem of her sweatshirt and gently lifted it over her head.

Bethany didn't object. She couldn't. Lying on the bed she looked up at Brett. He straddled her hips and stared at her. All of her. Her body gleamed white against the dark coverlet, her dark-peaked breasts pointing gloriously up at him, her fiery hair a mass of curls surrounding her face.

Stripped of all clothing except her scant, lacy underwear, Bethany met his gaze, hardly daring to breathe. She felt his eyes rake over her face to rest on the proud points of her breasts.

Groaning, he slid his rough thumbs down her side, feeling each delicate rib of her ribcage, touching her sensitive skin and setting it on fire. Slowly, he moved one hand upward to explore the soft, yielding white mound that beckoned him.

She moaned when he rimmed one nipple with his fingers. "Please, Brett..."

Slowly, still straddling her, he lowered his head and touched his mouth to one nipple.

Bethany thought she would die with the delicious torment of his tongue licking and toying with her until she reached up for his head, anxious for the feel of his mouth against her as he suckled. Her fingers threaded through his hair, moving gently, slowly, as he took more of her breast into his mouth, salving it with the gentle ministrations of his tongue.

Melting inside, she whispered his name.

His hands were everywhere, touching, exploring, feeling the small of her back, the rounded muscles of her bottom, the gentle length of her thighs until Bethany was writhing beneath him, arching against him and moaning in surrender.

Somewhere in the back of his mind, Brett heard a screaming warning that he was about to make an irreversible mistake, but he was beyond caring. He slipped off her panties, stared down at Bethany's waiting, quivering body, then jerked off his jeans and covered her body with his own in one swift motion.

"Tell me you want me," he demanded, pressing her knees apart.

"I want you."

"Tell me there'll be no regrets."

"No regrets," she promised, lifting her hips.

"Oh, God, Bethany," he groaned, his mind blanking out his disquieting thoughts as he entered her and felt the heated, pulsing warmth of her body enveloping him. "Love me." He moved, gently at first and then, with her urging, at a faster tempo until the nagging voice was silenced and he was lost in the warm wonder of her.

Bethany clung to him, felt the exquisite heat building and building, hotter and hotter, spiraling her upward until she couldn't think, couldn't see anything beyond the feel of Brett. Her hands dug into his shoulders, feeling the corded flesh as he pushed her over the bounds of earth and she rocked with an explosion starting deep within her and splintering apart everything save the feel, touch and smell of him.

A moment later he stiffened, all of his muscles flexing and growing taut as he fell against her with a ragged groan. "Bethany," he whispered. "Bethany, God, what have I done?"

"It's what *we've* done," she said, holding his body close. "Shh. No regrets, remember?"

He opened his eyes and stared into hers before offering a tentative smile. "No regrets," he repeated, wrapping her in his arms and holding her so that her naked body pressed snugly against his. A minute later he was asleep.

Bethany woke up and shivered. For a few seconds she couldn't get her bearings. Then, looking around the small room, she remembered she'd spent the night in Brett's arms. But he was gone. Levering herself up on one elbow, she pushed her hair out of her eyes and stared through the soft gray light of early morning at the cluttered interior of the loft.

Winston stirred, then whined from the top of the ladder.

"Want to go out?" she asked, slipping on a pair of cords and her sweatshirt, and scooping the puppy into her arms. With one hand firmly around the pup and the other hand on the ladder, she slowly descended to the first floor.

Brett wasn't on the couch. His sleeping bag had been rolled up and tossed into a corner of the room, and the bed was folded back.

Bethany walked into the kitchen just as Brett opened the back door, letting in a blast of frigid air as he stepped inside. "Morning," he drawled.

Blushing slightly, she managed to meet his gaze. "Good morning." She let Winston outside and waited for a few minutes until the puppy was whining on the back porch. "Too cold for you?" she asked the dog as he shook the snow from his coat and settled down beside the warmth of the wood stove.

"Sleep well?" Brett mocked.

Smiling, she tossed back her hair. "Like a baby. You?"

"Well enough." He looked into her wide hazel eyes and felt the same twisting in his gut that he'd had since the first time he'd laid eyes on her. The need of her was burning deep inside him, a physical lust that he couldn't control.

"I didn't hear you get up."

His face softened. "You were sleeping so soundly, I didn't want to wake you." If only she knew how sexy she looked with her slumberous green-gold eyes, flushed cheeks and wild red-brown hair tumbling to her shoulders.

Heat radiated from the stove and a pot of coffee was already brewed, its warm, enticing scent filling the small rooms. Bethany rubbed her arms. "What were you doing outside?"

"Looking for tracks in the snow," he said.

"Tracks? From wild animals?"

He hesitated, then shook his head. "Human."

"You really think we were followed up here?" she asked, incredulous.

"I don't think so. But I like to be certain."

"So what did you see?"

"Nothing," he admitted, shifting uneasily and looking out the window to the stately firs. "It's quiet." He turned to the stove again and poured them each a steaming cup of coffee.

"So what's on the agenda today?" she asked, accepting a chipped enamel cup from Brett and warming her fingers around it.

"First breakfast and then we'd better go into town. We need a few supplies and I want to make a couple of calls."

"Me, too," she whispered, thinking of her parents before pushing the troubling thought aside. "So, tell me, how does someone get hold of you?"

"Who?"

Shrugging, she frowned. "Anyone. Say, the electric company, for example."

"I've got a post office box in town. Anyone who doesn't want to write can drive up here."

She laughed and looked out the window. "Sure. Why not? After all you're right in the middle of the metropolis—"

Brett grimaced and bent on one knee to stoke the fire. "If someone wants me badly enough, he can find me." He dusted his hands and stood looking at her with concerned blue eyes. "'Course the same holds true for you. It won't take whoever trashed your place long to figure out you're with me. And then, after a few days of tracking, they'll probably end up here."

"I thought we would be safe here."

"We will be. For a few days. But just until I figure out what our next step is."

"Don't you know?"

He took a long swallow of coffee. "I wish I did," he admitted. "But ever since I met you, I've had a feeling that things wouldn't go exactly according to plan."

"Which is?"

"Finding your ex-husband."

"Right, back to that again. Well, we certainly won't find him up here," she said, taking a chair at the small table.

"No, but it gives us a little time."

"For?"

"For planning our strategy." He eyed her tousled hair and wrinkled sweatshirt and grinned. "Now, we don't have a lot of time. Why don't you get changed while I fix breakfast? I'd like to get into town and back by midafternoon."

"Why?"

"I don't know," he admitted, looking through the window and eyeing the gray sky. "Just a feeling I've got. Like maybe there's a storm brewing...."

After taking a hot shower and eating a hearty breakfast of sausage and eggs, Bethany zipped up her ski jacket, pulled on her gloves and followed Brett out to the Jeep.

Nearly an hour later, Brett turned from the winding country road they'd traveled down the mountain, and onto the freeway. He drove for a few miles before exiting to a town Bethany had never heard of. "Bentwood?" she said, reading the weathered sign as the Jeep drove into the city limits.

"It's a little obscure."

"A lot obscure, I'd say," she replied, wiping the

condensation from the window and staring at the few rustic buildings lining the single street that ran through town.

"It was planned as a ski resort, but the developer went bankrupt and only a few people stayed on." He parked near the curb in front of a general store.

They climbed out of the Jeep and walked into the bleached wood building. Bells jangled as they entered and a short, red-haired woman with small brown eyes, tiny glasses and a crisp white apron looked up and grinned. "Well, hello, stranger," she said, beaming at Brett.

"Hello, Rosie."

"Jed! Look who's back!" Rosie called to the back of the store where an elderly man was busy stocking shelves.

"Brett," the old man said, ambling to the front of the store. "How the hell are ya?"

"The same as always."

"Good. Good."

"What can we do fer ya?"

"Just stopped in to pick up some supplies and make a couple of calls."

"No time for a game of checkers, I don't suppose," Jed said, his blue eyes twinkling when he looked at Bethany.

"Not this time," Brett said, clapping the old man on the back. "Next time 'round."

"I'll hold ya to it."

"Don't think he won't," Rosie agreed.

"Look, this is Bethany Mills. She's a friend of mine, and whatever she wants to buy, just put it on my bill."

"Will do," Rosie said, looking Bethany up and down and offering her a tentative smile.

"Good." Brett glanced uneasily toward a pay phone in the back corner, then turned to Bethany. "You want to phone your folks?"

"Not really, but I'd better. If my uncle called, they'll be out of their minds with worry."

She placed the long-distance call and waited while the phone rang. No one answered. "Come on," she whispered, praying that her parents were home.

A few seconds later she gave up and placed the receiver back in its cradle.

"No luck?" Brett asked.

"Nope." She pushed her hands deep into the pockets of her jacket. "Maybe they're outside, or visiting. I'll have to call later."

Brett offered her an encouraging grin. "We'll get hold of them. It'll just take time."

"I know. I know." But she didn't feel any better.

"Look, I've got to make a couple of calls myself. Why don't you pick up a few things, including something for the dog? This'll only take a minute."

"Okay."

Bethany watched as Brett slid into the old-fashioned phone booth and carefully closed the door behind him. She browsed through the short aisles of the store and glanced at the booth every now and then, but Brett's back was to her. She could see his turned-up sheepskin collar, the rust-colored suede stretched across his shoulders, his thick, black hair, but little else. No doubt he was calling his detective friend in Portland and maybe Jim Benson as well.

Feeling a little guilty, she walked over to the sacks

of dog food and lingered longer than necessary near the phone booth, hoping to hear snatches of Brett's conversation. But all she could hear was the muffled sound of his voice, the hum of refrigeration machinery and the tinkle of bells over the door when someone entered the small building.

"Damn it all anyway," she muttered, selecting a ten-pound bag of dog food and carrying it up to the counter.

Brett scowled and waited, his fingers drumming on the side of the phone while Jim Benson took his own sweet time about answering.

"Brett!" Benson finally said. "How're you?"

"As well as can be expected."

"Oh? Trouble?" Benson asked.

"Nothing I can't handle," Brett said evenly, his voice cold. "I just wanted to know if you've got anyone else working on the Grant Mills case."

"Of course not! Why would we do anything like that?"

"You tell me."

There was just a slight pause and Brett could imagine Jim loosening the silk tie at his throat. He hoped the old man was squirming, but good.

"Look, I'm a banker, son. I don't see any reason to pay two men when one should be able to handle the job."

"Let's keep it that way."

"What're you getting at?"

"Just that I don't like to be crowded. You know that."

"Can't blame you."

"So, tell me, has Karl Weathers surfaced?"

"I was hoping you'd tell me."

Brett's neck muscles tensed. "I haven't found him or Mills yet. But it's only a matter of time."

"You sound sure of yourself."

"I am," Brett said, thinking back to Bethany's vandalized house. The only explanation for the vandalism was that he was getting too close to someone, and whoever he was getting close to was nervous. Damned nervous. Whether she knew it or not, Bethany was a link to her ex-husband's crime. He looked over his shoulder and saw her lugging a bag of dog food to the cash register. Something about the way she held her head and walked made him smile.

"Brett?"

"Yeah?"

"I'm expecting a report from you soon."

"You'll get it." Brett rang off, and then made another call. This time to his friend in Portland. The man was efficient, when he was off the bottle, and he owed Brett at least half a dozen favors. This time, Brett was calling in all his markers. At the very least, someone was trying to frighten Bethany. And at the most— He couldn't think about that. Didn't want to consider the consequences.

Just then a groggy voice answered the phone.

"Greg?" Brett asked.

"Who the devil is this?"

"It's Hanson."

"Who?"

"Brett Hanson."

"Jeez, Hanson, give me a break. I've got one helluva hangover and it's not even eleven, for God's sake."

Brett felt himself stiffen. "I thought you were on the wagon."

"I was. Can't help fallin' off now and then."

"Well try to stay sober for a few days, okay? I need a favor."

He heard Greg groan. "Give me a minute, will ya?" There was a long, crackling pause in the conversation before Greg's voice, clearer now, came across the wire. "Okay. I just had breakfast. Two aspirins and a beer. Now, tell me, what can I do for you?"

"Will this be it?" Rosie asked Bethany. She began ringing up the few items Bethany had carried to the front of the store. Bread, milk, eggs, fresh fruit and vegetables were stacked by the cash register.

"I'm not sure. This is all for…my friend. He might want to add something." She heard Brett approach and when she turned to face him, noticed that his expression had grown watchful, his eyes hard. Whoever he'd spoken to hadn't given him the answers he wanted.

"She didn't quite buy out the store," Rosie observed. "You want to add anything to it?"

He eyed the counter and shook his head. "I don't think so. No, wait. There is something; in the back."

"Jed's there. He'll ring it up back there. Just bring me the slip."

As Rosie rang up the food items, Bethany watched Brett walk to the back of the store to a counter near the phone booth. He searched the display of hunting and fishing equipment. Jed smiled, nodded to Brett and then sold him five packages of rifle shells. Bethany's entire body went cold as Brett stuffed the packages into his pocket.

"Goin' huntin' or expectin' trouble?" Rosie teased when Brett returned. She had just about finished placing the food in large sacks.

Brett smiled. "What do you think?"

Rosie's eyes sparkled. "With you, it's hard to tell. There ya go. Ya need any help with these, Jed'd be glad to give ya a hand."

"I think we can handle it," Brett replied, grabbing two bags while Bethany handled the one remaining sack and jug of milk.

"Keep yer eye on the sky," Rosie called after them. "The weather service says there's a storm brewin'."

"Great," Brett muttered under his breath.

"And don't make yerself such a stranger," Jed yelled, holding up a hand and waving.

Once they'd packed the Jeep and were on the road again, Bethany leaned back in the seat and eyed Brett's hard profile. "Who did you call?"

"My friend in Portland. The detective."

"Is he going to help us?"

"He's gonna try."

"Who else?" Bethany asked, watching for any hint of a lie. Brett's fingers tightened over the steering wheel. "I called Jim Benson."

"And?"

"And he claims that I'm on this case alone."

"Do you believe him?"

"I'm not sure. But it beats the hell out of me why he would lie, or why he would hire someone else when he's already paying me."

"It doesn't make much sense," Bethany agreed, turning to look out the window at the snow covered woodland. "But then, nothing seems to make sense anymore."

The first few flakes of snow started to fall as they turned onto the lane leading to the cabin. Brett looked up at the sky and the grooves on either side of his mouth deepened. "Looks like Rosie was right," he said, shifting down. The Jeep shot up the remainder of the hill and slid to a stop near the woodshed.

"Better get inside," he said to Bethany. Shielding his eyes from the snow, he grimaced and stared at the surrounding hills.

Nodding, Bethany grabbed a sack of groceries and walked in through the back door. She brushed the snow off her jacket and jerked off her stocking cap as Winston barked and danced around her feet. "Miss me?" she asked with a smile. The fluff of fur wagged his tail and yelped. "You are adorable," she murmured, bending down to pet the puppy.

While Brett carried in the remaining groceries and stacked wood near the fireplace, Bethany started putting the food away. She was just fixing sandwiches when she heard the first shriek of wind scream through the surrounding hills.

"What was that?" she asked.

"Just the beginning," Brett said, coming into the kitchen.

"The beginning?"

"Ever been in a storm in the mountains?"

"Not really, I guess."

"Then you'd better prepare yourself. It won't exactly be a picnic."

As if to add emphasis to his words, the lights flickered. Frowning, Brett took the kerosene lantern Bethany had lit earlier and walked to the pantry. Once there, he filled another lamp and carried them both into the living room. "The lights will probably go out; they always do. And because we're so remote, it might take a week before the power comes on."

"But we're not going to be here a week," she said, studying him as she placed the top piece of bread over the sliced ham and cut the sandwich in half.

"I hope not," he replied, looking out the window and studying the gray sky.

"You hope not?" she repeated, worried. "You'd better be sure. I have to be back to school on the second of January."

He placed his hands on her waist. "Would it be so bad, snowbound here with me?"

She tried to stay angry, but couldn't help smiling. "It sounds wonderful," she said, ducking the kiss he tried to plant on her cheek. "But highly improbable."

"For once in your life, Bethany Mills, be impulsive."

"I was; when I let you talk me into coming up here."

He arched a brow. "I can't be held responsible for unpredictable weather."

"But you made a bargain with me. Two weeks, remember? The way I see it you've only got a little over a week left and then I'm out of this entire mess."

"What if I decide I can't let you go?" he asked, his blue eyes serious. "What if I fall in love with you?"

The room went deathly quiet and only the sounds

of the fire crackling and the storm raging outside disturbed the silence.

"Don't," she said, trying to quiet her racing heart. "Don't talk about love. Not yet."

"Why?"

"It's just too soon, that's all."

"Too soon since your divorce?"

"No. Too soon since I met you." She looked away. "I've made more mistakes than I want to count. I don't want to make any more."

He placed his hands on her shoulders and forced her to look into his eyes. "Do you think falling in love with me would be a mistake?"

Closing her eyes, she nodded. "Maybe the worst," she said.

He clenched his jaw and let her go. "So you think that after two weeks you'll be able to just turn and walk away?"

Shaking her head, she fought the stupid urge to cry. "No—but I think I should. Remember, we have a bargain."

"That's right," he said, turning to face her, his features hard. "And a deal's a deal. Right?"

"Right." She handed him the paper plate and sandwich and marched into the living room. Winston followed her and plopped down at her feet, watching as she began to eat.

Brett ignored the food and tried to focus on the situation at hand. He stared down the lane and wondered if the snow was a blessing or a curse. It would either provide them some protection or make them sitting ducks for whoever was out there.

Chapter Ten

As the storm increased, so did the tension in the
small cabin. Brett stared out the window, and Bethany
could read the restlessness in his eyes, see the strain
of his shoulders. His brow was furrowed and his lips
had thinned in frustration. He spent the day working
on the cabin, both inside and out, making sure it was
weather-tight against the strong winds that roared
through the mountain canyons.

The lights flickered and died just as night's shadows darkened the rooms. With a curse, Brett lit two
lanterns and handed one to Bethany. "I guess we'd
better go to bed and hope that the pipes don't freeze,"
he said. "I've kept the water running, but that may
not be enough."

"You really think it will be that bad?"

"I don't know," he admitted, seeing the worry in her eyes. "I just don't know."

"That's not exactly comforting, y'know."

He grinned crookedly and nodded, the lamplight reflecting in his winter-blue eyes. "We'll just have to make the best of it, won't we?"

"I guess."

"Okay. For starters, I think we'd better sleep down here. We'll move the desk and push the couch under the loft."

"Why?"

"Just in case some shingles blow off the roof."

"You think they will?" she said.

"I hope not," he said, squinting against the darkness. Then he began shifting furniture until the area under the loft had been transformed into a small bedroom, with the couch folded down and two sleeping bags zipped together. "Not bad, considering," Brett observed, eyeing his handiwork.

"Considering," she agreed. Outside, the wind whistled and buffeted the trees. Bethany shivered and rubbed her arms for warmth.

He climbed into the loft and carried some of his clothes and Bethany's suitcase downstairs. Once in the living room, he added fuel to the fire and then sat on the edge of the mattress and yanked off his boots and socks. Watching Bethany from the corner of his eye, he slowly unbuttoned his shirt.

She didn't move, but sat in an old rocker, her feet propped up on the mattress as she watched him slide his shirt off his shoulders. Light from the lantern played on the ripple of lean muscles under tanned skin. His nipples were barely visible in the thick mat of hair on his chest, and his abdomen was smooth and flat.

He tossed the shirt over the back of a chair and cocked his head in her direction. "Aren't you coming to bed?"

"In a minute."

"Something wrong?"

"No." She wrapped her arm around her knees. "I guess I just feel a little awkward."

"About sleeping with me?" he asked, his lips twisting into an amused smile.

Nodding, she met his eyes. "It's silly, I suppose, but I'm not used to spending the night with a man I've barely met. In fact, until last night..." She shrugged and looked away, her cheeks flushing with color.

"You'd never had an affair," he guessed.

"Right." She frowned at herself. "I hope this doesn't ruin your image of me. I'm not exactly the sophisticated, liberated woman of the eighties."

"And you don't need to pretend to be one." He placed his hands on his knees, stood and walked over to the rocker. Leaning down, he grabbed each of the chair's arms, locking her in and stopping her rocking motion. "You're perfect just the way you are," he whispered, blue eyes searching hers.

"Far from perfect," she muttered.

His gaze narrowing, he studied the pout on her features and touched her lips with his fingers. "Grant hurt you very much, didn't he?"

"A little."

He lifted his brows skeptically. "Maybe a lot?"

"Well, maybe. He nearly ruined my name as well as that of my family," she admitted.

Brett waved her explanation aside. "I'm not talking about that. I'm talking about his affair with Billie Henshaw. That really bothered you, didn't it?"

Her lips twitched at the unpleasant memory.

"He isn't worth it," Brett said, pushing a wayward lock of hair from her face.

"I know. But it was hard," she said with a sigh. "I...I was pregnant when I found out he was seeing other women. As I said, I was pretty naive. And the thought of him sleeping with other women...well, it was hard to accept. Until then, I'd thought he wanted children, a permanent home, all the things I wanted."

Brett's jaw tightened. "So what did you do?"

"There was nothing I could do. I told him about the baby."

"And?"

"And he pretended to be interested in it. Told me that it was over between him and his girlfriend and that all he wanted was for us to be a family." Feeling like a fool all over again, she looked up at the rafters.

Brett waited, his hatred for Grant Mills mounting with each second that Bethany couldn't meet his eyes.

"It was a lie, of course. He never wanted the baby. Later, he even tried to talk me into having an abortion; but it was too late, I was too far along, and even if I hadn't been I would never have let anything happen to the child!" Her fingers curled into a fist on the arm of the chair and tears filled her eyes. How much she had wanted that child! Even today, despite Grant's infidelity and crimes, she wished she'd had that baby.

"But the baby?"

A tear rolled down Bethany's cheek. "I lost it," she whispered. "About a year ago. We tried to get to the hospital, hoping that there was a chance to save the baby, but the roads were slick and Grant ended up in the ditch. It took another hour before the ambulance could get to me and return to the hospital. By then it was too late. The baby was gone."

"I'm sorry," he said, almost inaudibly.

"I am, too," she whispered, her throat thick. "I wanted my baby."

Before she could break down, he picked her up and held her close against him. She buried her face in his neck and he felt her warm tears against his skin. Silently, he carried her over to the bed. Carefully laying her on the sleeping bags he kissed the tears from her eyes and held her once more against the protective wall of his chest.

"There'll be more children," he said, not really understanding how he could promise something so far out of his control, but needing to reassure her. "You're a young, beautiful woman, and you can have as many babies as you want. The time just wasn't right for you."

She looked up at him, eyes wet and glistening. "Will it ever be?"

"Of course." He kissed the top of her head and gently rocked her. When she tipped her face up to his, he kissed her, gently at first, then harder, his fingers twisting in the fine strands of her auburn hair. He kissed her eyes, her lips, her cheeks, tasted the salty tracks of her tears.

Passion burned bright deep in her soul. She clung

to him fiercely, as if in loving him she could deny the pain of the past.

"I'll make it right," he promised, as he slowly slipped the sweater over her head, then kissed and moistened her breasts with his tongue. Moaning, she sucked in her stomach while his fingers worked with the button of her jeans before pulling them down. His hands were warm against her skin. No longer feeling cold, she shivered from the want of him and ached to have him fill her, make her forget.

His hands moved easily on her skin, down the firm muscles of her back to mold her buttocks and pull her tight against him. "Just trust me, sweet Bethany," he whispered against her hair. And then he lowered himself onto her, tasting again of the swollen mounds of her breasts before dipping lower, touching her abdomen and navel with his tongue, leaving a dewy path on her skin.

As he breathed against her she gasped and burned with a hot, desperate craving that centered deep inside her and radiated outward, aching to be filled.

"I love you, Bethany," he murmured, splaying his hands against her back as he buried his face in her soft skin. "And I'll never hurt you."

She wanted to believe him. When he parted her legs to settle against her, she welcomed him, cradling his head against her breasts, listening to his ragged breathing and the muffled sound of the rising wind. She closed her eyes and began to rub against him, feeling his hard muscles press against hers as he suckled and plucked with his teeth at her breasts.

White-hot desire shot through her body, as slowly,

excruciatingly slowly, he moved sensually against her yielding flesh as he began his rhythm of love.

For three days snow continued to fall. The wind howled through the rafters. Limbs from nearby trees thudded against the side of the cabin and split from the trunks, cracking from the weight of ice and snow and then thundering to the ground.

Inside the cabin, Brett was as nervous as a caged cougar. Alternately pacing the small rooms, sifting through the same information on Grant Mills that he'd studied before and stoking the fire, he was tense as a bowstring.

"We're not getting anywhere," he grumbled on the third day as he closed Bethany's high school annual with a thud and dropped it into a box of discarded papers and pictures on the floor near his desk.

"There's nothing in there," she said. She sat on the couch, rereading an old magazine. "If there had been, believe me, the FBI would have found it."

Ignoring her, he pulled some of her old jewelry out of his suitcase. He looked at a charm bracelet, dropped it into the box on the floor, then picked up a silver-colored ring.

"Why'd you bring that?" she asked.

"Because it was there. Who gave this to you?"

She looked at the ring and frowned. "Who do you think?"

"Grant?"

"Of course."

"So why do you keep it?"

Sighing, she shook her head. "I don't know. For

sentimental reasons, I guess. It's not worth anything. None of it is. It's all just costume stuff.''

''Including the ring?''

''Yes.''

''Where did he get it?''

''I don't know.'' Her brow puckered as she tried to remember.

''It's engraved,'' he muttered, trying to read the worn inscription. ''What does it say?'' He tossed the ring to her and she caught it.

Squinting a little, she read the inscription. ''Fullerton Rodeo,'' she whispered, remembering the hot July day, the smell of horses and dust, the gleam of anticipation in Grant's eyes as he watched the bareback riders. She set the ring on the table. ''He…he gave it to me the summer before my senior year. We'd gone to the rodeo together.''

''In Fullerton?''

''Yes. It's on the Idaho-Oregon border.''

''In Idaho?''

''No.'' She shook her head. ''Just across the river, in Oregon.''

Brett thought for a minute and then scooped up the ring. ''Was he a rodeo buff?''

She shrugged. ''A little, I guess. He liked horses.''

''Riding them?''

''Anything about them,'' she said, looking up at him. ''It doesn't really fit in with his banker image, does it?''

''No, but it does fit in with his outdoorsman, mountain climber, fisherman image.'' His fingers tightened around the cold ring as he walked to the window. Staring through the ice-covered panes to the swirling snow outside, he watched as the branches of the fir trees danced wildly in the wind and ominous gray clouds shrouded the mountains.

"It's bound to quit," Bethany said, forcing a smile. She picked up an old fishing magazine, flipped through the pages and tossed it back on the coffee table.

"I know."

"Any ideas when?"

"God only knows."

"Then I guess we'll just have to be patient."

Raking his fingers through his hair, he glanced at her. "That's a helluva piece of advice, coming from you."

She shrugged and lifted her palms. "There's just no use in arguing with Mother Nature," she said. "Or complaining, for that matter."

Stuffing the ring in his pocket, Brett walked across the room and eyed her speculatively. "Just where did you get so smart, lady?"

"I'm a schoolteacher, remember?" she quipped. "Patience is more than a virtue—it's a matter of survival."

"Is it?" He touched the fiery strands of her hair and sighed. Even bundled in faded jeans and one of his oversize flannel shirts with the sleeves rolled up, she was stunning.

"Absolutely." Tilting her head, she smiled and her hazel eyes twinkled.

Brett was captivated. He placed his arms around her neck and touched his forehead to hers. "There's something I think you should know."

"Oh?"

He undid the top button of her flannel shirt. "You look so damned sexy, you're driving me out of my mind."

She giggled and shook her head. "I think you've been cooped up too long, cowboy. You're beginning to lose it."

He slid another button through its hole.

Bethany's heart began to pound at the touch of his finger against the skin between her breasts.

"I can't think of another person in the world I'd rather be snowbound with."

"Give me a break," she said, but her voice was breathless. "Not even a glamorous movie star?"

"Nope." He slipped one arm under her knees and lifted her from the floor. Then slowly carrying her to the couch, he grinned almost wickedly and his blue eyes gleamed. "And right now, I'm going to show you."

"Show me what?"

His crooked grin widened and he looked down through the gaping front of her shirt to the rounded swells of her breasts. "Just how much I appreciate your company." Covering her mouth with his, he gently lowered her onto the sofa and lay down beside her.

"I can't wait."

The next morning Brett poured himself a cup of coffee and stared out the window. The storm had finished unleashing its fury in the night and had finally stopped, leaving over a foot of snow. A few scattered flakes continued to fall throughout the morning, but occasionally the rays of a pale sun managed to filter through the gray clouds.

Swallowing some of the lukewarm liquid, he turned and watched Bethany as she made up the couch. Her hair was pulled back into a ponytail, she was dressed in baggy jeans and a sweater, and she was still the sexiest woman he'd ever met.

Since Roberta. He frowned at the thought of his late wife. Only a few years before Roberta had given meaning to his shallow life. She had made this ratty old cabin seem like the Garden of Eden. Her presence had seemed to make the mountains come alive. In the years since her death he'd often thought that he'd never feel as hopeful as he had then. Her death had been the end of his world. Until now. Until Bethany.

He watched her bend over the bed. Her sweater gaped from her jeans, exposing a piece of soft white skin as she worked. And even after a night of love-making, he still wanted to throw Bethany back onto the couch, strip off her clothes and never stop making love to her. Just the thought of pulling her sweater over her head to bare her breasts made him uncomfortable. He had to shift positions, move around, to avoid the overt male reaction that looking at her always caused.

"Boy, you've got it bad," he admonished, draining his coffee and walking into the kitchen to pour himself another cup.

"Pardon me?" Bethany picked up a sleeping bag and turned to look over her shoulder at him. "What did you say?"

"Nothin' important. Want a cup?" He held up the enamel pot.

"I'll get some later." She stretched and rotated her head, loosening the kinks in her neck. "After breakfast." Coming up to him and wrapping her arms around his waist, she tilted her head up at him. "So, tell me. Just how bad is it?"

He looked down and saw the teasing glint in her hazel eyes.

"The snow, I mean."

"It's bad," he admitted, "but nothing we can't handle."

"We?" she asked, her heart pounding.

His off-center grin slashed across his face and he grabbed her waist. "We," he repeated, his gaze dark and slumberous. "Haven't you figured it out that we're a team?"

"Like Martin and Lewis," she said with a laugh.

"Nope. They broke up. I was thinking more like Nick and Nora Charles in the *Thin Man* series; you know, madcap, frivolous adventurers." He spun her off her feet until she was breathless.

"Nick and Nora? And what does that make Winston? Asta?"

"You're making fun of me."

"And you deserve it." She slipped out of his arms, picked up her coffee cup and took a long drink. "Nick and Nora Charles, for God's sake! Isn't that analogy a little lofty?"

"Well, maybe a little." His eyes crinkled at the corners. "I suppose when you get right down to it, we're more like Jennifer and Jonathan Hart."

She nearly choked on a swallow of coffee. "Same difference. Just more recent. Give me a break!" She looked around the rustic cabin with its beat-up furniture, wood stove and rough pine walls as she finished her coffee and set the empty cup on a scratched end table. "I think those two couples were a little out of our league socially."

"But they were in love and together, enjoying life no matter what," he pointed out, slipping his arms around her and pulling her close.

"And that's how you see us?" Laughing, her heart racing, she tried to pull away from him, but his strong arms held her tight.

"Don't you?"

"No!"

He cocked a dark brow. "So tell me, how do you see us?"

"You're serious?"

"Completely."

"Actually, I think you're Jeremiah Johnson, one rugged man in the wilderness and I'm...I'm...I don't know..." Her smile faded as she looked into the blue intensity of his eyes. Swallowing hard, she said, "I'm just a woman, a very scared woman, who doesn't want her past blown wide open; just a person who wants to live a nice, quiet life in Portland."

"Without me?"

Hardly daring to breathe, she shook her head. "Without the turmoil you've caused."

He lifted her chin with one finger. "Think beyond the turmoil; to the future. Will I be in it?" he asked, his voice low, his blue eyes reaching into hers.

"Will you want to be?"

He smiled sadly. "Of course. That's what I've been trying to tell you; that I'm falling in love with you and whether I like it or not, I want you to be a part of my life forever.''

Pulse thundering, she stood unmoving in his arms, mesmerized by the conviction in the hard planes of his face.

''I love you, Bethany,'' he whispered. ''And I want you to marry me.''

''But...we hardly know each other. It's barely been a week since we met.''

''Almost two. And in that time, we've been together almost every minute. We've lived with each other, seen each other at our worst. Hour for hour, we've been together longer than a lot of people who decide to get married.''

She bit her lower lip and struggled against the urge to smile, radiantly, stupidly. She was afraid to break the fragile, magic spell. ''I—I'm not as impulsive as I used to be,'' she said, thinking of her disaster of a marriage to Grant. ''Maybe we should give it some time.''

He frowned and rubbed his jaw, his gaze never leaving hers. ''Fair enough,'' he finally said. ''But when we get off this mountain and find Grant, I'll expect an answer.''

She nodded and he bent his head lower, brushing his lips against hers and holding her body tight against his, as if he expected her to flee.

She listened to the steady beat of his heart and slid her hands inside his shirt. How good it was to trust him; forget about Grant and the ever-present feeling that Brett wasn't being completely honest with her.

When his lips found hers, she gave herself to him

completely, without reservation, lost in her feelings of love for him.

"I think today's the day," Brett said with a satisfied smile as he opened the door and looked at the clear blue sky two days later.

The wind still whistled through the mountains, rustling the trees, but there wasn't a cloud in sight and the sunlight glistened on the new-fallen snow.

"This is the day for what?" she asked, walking to the door and feeling the cold air pierce her sweater.

"Our getaway."

"Thank God."

"Got a case of cabin fever?"

"And how!" Bethany stepped outside and watched as Winston jumped off the porch to land in a drift of snow well over his head. Only his black-tipped ears were visible above the drift.

"Idiot," Brett muttered, picking up the small dog and getting his face washed for his pains. "I think we'd better take off soon," he said, observing the sky. "This wind is bound to bring in more clouds and snow."

They packed quickly and Bethany, after throwing all her clothes in her suitcase, straightened the cabin. She looked around the rooms and felt a trace of sadness. Though the past few days had seemed unreal, part of a fantasy, she'd been happy hidden on the mountain with Brett, away from the real world and all her problems.

While Bethany cleared up inside, Brett loaded the Jeep. The morning was cold and clear, and though the snow was deeper than he would have liked, the Jeep could handle it. He tossed in his sleeping bag, then froze. There was the familiar sound of an engine whining uphill.

Listening intently, he racked his brain. Who could it be? No one knew they were there. The closest cabin was two miles south and the sound of the truck was much closer. Each of his muscles tightened with apprehension as he scanned the mountainside. The engine died and the mountains went deathly quiet.

Carrying her overnight bag, Bethany opened the door and walked onto the porch. She stopped in her tracks when she saw Brett's grim expression and when he waved her inside, she didn't hesitate, but backed through the open door, whispering to Winston to do the same.

She looked out the window and watched as Brett moved slowly around the Jeep. His gaze was fixed and hard, his jaw rigid with concentration.

Bethany's heart was pounding so loudly she didn't think she could hear anything. But she did. The blast from a rifle split the cold mountain air, echoing between the ridges.

Brett fell to the ground, then took cover behind the Jeep. The bullet ricocheted through the trees. Snow and ice fell from the branches.

Bethany peered through the window, but Brett waved her back away from the glass as he crouched behind the Jeep.

Sick inside, her throat dry with fear, Bethany huddled behind the couch and held Winston tight against her. *Who was outside and what did they want? Surely they weren't firing at Brett?*

But she felt her fear mounting just the same. She hugged Winston so tightly that he whined in protest.

"Shh!" she warned, her eyes glued to the windows.

The rifle cracked again and Bethany jumped. Winston slid away from her and began to growl and bark. "Shh! Come here!" she whispered.

Who was it? Was it Grant? No, Grant wouldn't be shooting at them. He'd never even owned a gun.

Cold sweat trickled down her back. *Dear God, what was happening?*

Again the rifle fired and Bethany, her mind racing, knew she had to do something. Brett was outside and unarmed. Terror gripping her heart, she slid on her belly to the kitchen and from there worked her way into the pantry.

A few days earlier, when she'd been looking for potatoes, she'd seen a rifle propped against the wall. If only it was still there.

The pantry was dark. She ran her hands over the dusty rough floorboards and splinters pierced her fingers. She searched quickly, managed to find the gun, and swallowing hard, took hold of the cold barrel. It had been years since she'd fired a gun, and then it had been a small .22 caliber back on the farm in Idaho. Her target had been rusty tin cans. She'd never killed anything, and had never pointed a gun at a man.

Until now, if she had to, if it meant saving Brett's life.

Summoning all of her courage, she checked the chamber. It was empty. Sweat began to collect on her forehead. She remembered Brett putting several boxes of shells in his coat, but he was wearing the suede jacket. "Think, Bethany!" she told herself, pushing her hair out of her eyes. She dug through the closet and when the rifle outside fired again it sounded closer. Much closer.

"Please, God, help us...."

Stomach twisting with fear, she rummaged through the pockets of old coats hung on nails in the pantry, wondering why Brett hadn't come back inside. Fear consumed her. Maybe he was hurt, wounded, bleeding in the snow. Or maybe he was already dead.

"Oh, God, no!"

She was shaking when her fingers found the box of shells in an old ski jacket. Still standing in the pantry, she loaded the Winchester with quaking fingers.

The rifle shots still blasted and she told herself to be grateful—the noise meant Brett was still alive. She stiffened each time she heard the report of the powerful gun and tried not to picture Brett lying face down in the snow, a spreading pool of blood staining the snow red beneath him.

"He's alive...he's got to be alive."

The front door burst open to bang against the wall. A young, hard-looking man with straggly blond hair, an unshaven face and a long-barrelled rifle rushed into the cabin.

Bethany stifled a scream. She'd just finished loading the gun and jerked it to her shoulder, taking aim. But he was quick. He rolled onto the floor, knocked her off her feet and grabbed the rifle. Breathing hard, he wrenched the gun away from her and was on his feet again as quickly as a cat.

Bethany backed away from him, toward the back door near the pantry.

"Don't move!" His face twitched nervously and he pointed the barrel of the gun at her face.

Bethany froze.

"That's better." He wiped his nose with the cuff of his sleeve and sniffed, all the while standing on the balls of his feet, his entire body shaking in jerky, nervous movements. His eyes were small, but dark and cold as midnight.

"Who are you?" she demanded.

He ignored the question and quickly scanned the room. Obviously deciding that she wasn't going anywhere, he backed to the front door, slammed it and shoved the dead bolt into place.

Bethany swallowed back her fear. "Who are you?" she repeated, her voice surprisingly steady. There was something about him that was familiar.

He stopped, glanced out the window and smiled a strange half grin that only affected one side of his face. "A friend."

"So that's why you're shooting at us."

"Yeah. That's it."

"What's your name?"

"Forget it, okay? I'll ask the questions around here."

"Where's Brett?" She pushed herself up by her hands, her back against the doorjamb of the pantry.

The rough-looking man grinned again and shrugged.

Nerves stretched to the breaking point, Bethany looked out the window but couldn't see anything other than the open tailgate of the Jeep. "Is he outside?"

"What d'ya think?" he said.

Oh, God, he'd been shot! "I don't know what to think," she snapped.

"Don't worry about him."

"You didn't shoot him!" she screamed.

"Maybe."

Without thinking of herself, she ran to the door.

"What the hell—" He was after her in a second, breathing heavily as his hands dug into her waist. He dragged her across the floor, away from the window and pushed her down on the hearth.

"He'll survive. Now forget about him."

"If he's out there, he'll freeze! We've got to get him inside." The temperature outside was below freezing and the shrieking wind brought the mercury down still farther. She stood and walked to the window.

"Too bad." The man laughed. Nervously he dug in his breast pocket. Bethany had visions of a long-bladed knife being withdrawn, but he pulled out a crumpled pack of cigarettes and a lighter. Shaking out a cigarette with his free hand, he lit up while he kept the barrel of the gun trained on her.

"Where's Brett?" She looked everywhere, but couldn't see any sign of him.

He blew out a stream of smoke letting the cigarette dangle from his lips. "Don't worry about him."

"But he's out there—"

"Bleeding to death?" he taunted. "Probably." Then his amused smile faded. He motioned to the hearth with the gun. "Sit down. I don't like you movin' round. Now tell me all you know 'bout where your husband is.''

Bethany wouldn't budge. Frantically, her eyes searched the nearby trees. *Where was he?*

"I asked you a question."

"I'm not married."

His unruly brows drew together. "But you was. Where's Mills? And don't play games. I'm not in the mood."

"I'm not telling you anything until I know that Brett is safe," she said, looking again through the panes and seeing nothing. Her insides were shredding with fear but she held her head high and tried not to show how scared she was.

"That's none too smart, little lady. And from what I hear you're a smart one. So quit worryin' 'bout Hanson; he'll be all right...if he don't bleed to death while I'm sittin' here waitin' for you to come clean. Now—" he settled onto the couch, leaned back and propped his scuffed boots on the table "—you just tell me everythin' you know about that louse of a husband of yours."

"I—I don't know anything about Grant. We've been divorced a long time—almost a year." Swallowing, she tried to plead with him. "But Brett's outside, we've got to help—"

"You haven't seen him since?"

"Grant? No!"

His eyes glinted as he looked Bethany up and down. "What if I was to say I don't believe you?"

"I'd say that's too bad. I don't have any idea where he is or what he's doing. I think he's dead."

"You do, do you?" He shook his head and his

dirty blond hair fell into his eyes. He pushed it out of his face and took a long drag on his cigarette before throwing the butt into the fireplace behind Bethany. "Well, unless somethin's happened to your old man in the last couple of weeks, he's alive all right. And a rich bastard to boot. I just want to find out where he is. He killed my brother, you know."

"He did what?"

"Jake. He killed Jake!"

"Your brother...Jake?"

"Come on, lady." He sized her up and calmed down a little. "Guess I forgot to introduce myself. I tend to do that when someone points a gun in my gut. The name is Weathers. Karl Weathers."

"Oh, dear God," she whispered, slumping against the wall. Though she'd never met him, she'd seen several grainy photographs of him.

One side of his mouth lifted. "I see you heard of me. Prob'ly from your old man."

"I told you I thought Grant was dead."

"Sure. And that's why Hanson is tracking him. Try again."

"Really, I don't know." Bethany's mind was racing. She darted a glance outside. If she could just chance it to the door, run out, the keys were probably already in the Jeep. And Brett. Dear God, Brett was out there somewhere. *But where? And was he still alive?*

"Don't even think about it," Karl said with a snarl. "You ain't gettin' nowhere." He reached into the pocket of his grimy jeans and extracted a key ring. Brett's keys. Bethany's heart sank. Karl curled his fingers around the keys and stuffed them back into his pocket. "If you want 'em, you just come on over here and get 'em yourself," he said, his grin turning sly as he flashed yellowed teeth in her direction and rubbed his pocket.

Bethany's stomach lurched.

"Yep. It's just you an' me." His eyes slid insolently up her body. "And we're gonna figure this thing out. Now, where's your old man?"

"I told you, I don't know."

He scowled and his fingers tightened over the rifle. "Cut the crap."

"Really!" Bethany pushed her hair out of her eyes, trying to think of a way, any way, to get out of the cabin without being shot. She had to find Brett and—what? Carry him down the mountain over her shoulder? She needed the keys. And they were in the pocket of Karl's grimy jeans. She looked at the bulge in his pocket and shuddered.

"You're lyin'," he accused, exasperated.

"I wish I was. Look, the last time I saw Grant was a couple of weeks before he got involved in this embezzling mess. I didn't know anything about it."

"What'd he say?"

"Nothing! We just talked about some financial matters because of the divorce!"

"I bet."

Her eyes flashed. "Look if you don't believe me, why are you still asking me questions! It doesn't matter what I say!" She stood abruptly and started for the door, hoping to call his bluff.

"Hold on a minute," he said, blocking her path with the glinting blue barrel of the gun. Just then a branch from a nearby tree began to bang against the side of the house. Karl jerked back. "What the hell is that?"

"The fir out back."

He didn't believe her. He glanced out the kitchen window, was apparently satisfied by what he saw, then motioned to the hearth. "You sit back down."

"Why?"

He strode to the front window and checked around. "Or else I'll take this here rifle and put it against the back of your boyfriend's head before I squeeze the trigger. You can watch if you like."

"You bastard!" she yelled. The knowledge that Brett was already hurt boiled inside her, and suddenly, like a woman possessed, she lunged for the door. Karl grabbed her arm and jerked her back to the fireplace on the other side of the room. He pushed her back onto the hearth and then sat down again on the couch. Placing the heels of his boots on the table, he watched her.

"I told you, he's probably bleedin' to death. Now, all you have to do is tell me where Mills is and we can bring Hanson in and warm him up. It's up to you."

"But I don't know anything!"

"Like hell!" Karl's boots dropped to the floor. "You and I both know that Grant's alive and that he was goin' to double-cross Jake and me all along! It was part of his plan. Billie, she told Jake about it. And then what happens? Boom! Their plane goes down. They're both killed. Convenient, wouldn't you say?"

"You think Grant was responsible," Bethany guessed.

"I'd stake my life on it. Matter of fact, I guess I already have, haven't I?" He leered at her and rubbed his stubbly chin.

"Well, you've come to the wrong person."

"That so? Then why's Hanson hangin' around, snoopin' into it all over again? If you don't know nothin', why the hell is Hanson stickin' to you like a flea on a dog?"

"I don't know."

"You don't know a hell of a lot, do you?"

"Just that Brett needs to be moved. We've got to—"

"Shut up! Maybe I'd better remind you. Hanson thinks you can help, don't he? And my guess is that he's right. Now, let's start at the beginning. Where's Mills?"

"If I knew, don't you think I'd tell you?"

"Nope. Not without some convincin'." He grinned again, and this time he ran the barrel of the gun up her leg.

Bethany shuddered and moved, but Karl kept the gun right alongside her body. The chill from the cold, hard steel permeated her sweater and jeans as the gun slid upward.

"Now, why don't you tell me about your old man?" he suggested, his eyes glinting.

"There's nothing to tell," she said.

"Fine, fine," he muttered. "Have it your way. You won't talk here, so you and me, we'll just go for a drive. Maybe you'll remember more when we get away from here."

"I'm not going anywhere," she said staunchly, her insides wrenching with fear.

"Don't think you've got much say in it." He yanked her to her feet, prodded her with the gun, heard an unfamiliar creak and looked quickly around the room. Nothing was out of place. He motioned toward the door. "Come on, let's go."

"I'm not leaving," she repeated, her chin high.

The muscles in his face worked convulsively. "You know what your problem is? You don't have any idea of who you're dealing with! I won't think twice about snuffin' Hanson. But you don't believe me. I guess I'll just have to prove it. We'll start with your dog." Swinging the rifle away from Bethany, he took aim at Winston, who was lying under the kitchen table.

The little dog sensed the attention and wagged his tail.

"No!" Horrified, Bethany grabbed for Karl. She scratched his arm and nearly knocked him off balance.

"Get outta my way!" he ordered, cuffing her aside.

Bethany fell away from the furious man and then she saw Brett from the corner of her eye. He was standing in the loft, by the ladder, ready to spring. A deep red stain was seeping through his jacket and he swayed for a minute. The moment Karl swung the rifle away from Bethany, Brett jumped on the scraggly-haired blond man. They fell to the floor. The rifle blasted and sprayed glass through the living-room window. Brett grabbed at the gun and it spun crazily across the floor.

Bethany lunged for it.

The two men rolled on the floor, one atop the other. Bethany pointed the rifle at them. But neither took notice as they wrestled on the hard planks that were beginning to be smeared with Brett's blood.

"Stop it!" Bethany yelled.

Grunting and cursing, they pounded at each other. It was over in seconds. Brett had Karl pinned down and was pulling the younger man's arm behind his back, threatening to force the shoulder out of its socket.

"Had enough?" Brett demanded.

The other man didn't respond.

Brett jerked on his hand and Karl swore hard and violently.

"Careful," Brett said, his lips twisted into a grim smile. "There's a lady present."

"Go to hell!"

Brett yanked on Karl's arm and the younger man screamed.

Bethany leaned against the fireplace and watched as Brett forced Karl to his feet. "You're a miserable son of a bitch," Brett said. "Now sit down. It's time for you to answer some questions."

"No way, man."

"I don't see that you have much choice in the matter." Brett waved the gun Bethany passed to him. "Talk. Tell me about Grant Mills and your brother." Blood was trickling from the corner of his mouth. He wiped his lip with the cuff of his sleeve.

Bethany went into the bathroom, grabbed some bandages and returned. "I think I should look at your shoulder."

"Not just yet. Go into the pantry. Grab some of that rope on the third shelf and bring it back here."

Bethany left the room and returned a moment later.

In the few seconds she was gone, something had changed. Karl's stiff body had slumped and the snarl had left his face. He'd paled considerably and didn't protest when Brett, with Bethany pointing the gun steadily at Karl, tied his hands behind his back and bound his feet.

"We've got to get out of here," Brett explained, once Karl was properly restrained. "Just in case there's another storm or Karl here has some friend tucked away in the woods."

"Not until we take care of you." She heated some water and then ripped off Brett's bloodstained shirt. The hard muscles of his left shoulder were bruised and she could see the spot where the bullet had grazed his skin, searing his flesh as it passed. He winced as she washed and bandaged the wound. "You have to go to a hospital, you know. I'm no doctor."

Brett struggled into a clean shirt. "I'll be okay for now. I'm just sorry that he—" he cocked his head at Karl "—got in here. I must have blacked out when my head hit an edge on the Jeep. I remember being hit and falling backward, reaching for the Jeep, then nothing."

"Don't worry about it," she said. "I'm just glad you're all in one piece—well, almost."

The younger man glowered at his captor. "I just wish I'd a killed ya."

"Maybe next time."

"Count on it!"

Brett looked at him coldly. "Where you're going you won't have a chance. And when you get out, I'll be waiting."

Disgusted, Karl spat on the floor.

Brett didn't move. "Okay, pal, let's talk. Did you trash Bethany's house?"

Karl's jaw jutted forward and he didn't speak.

"I told you what your options were," Brett reminded him, his eyes becoming slits. "Your choice."

Some of Karl's bravado slipped and he glanced, full of hatred, at Bethany. "Yeah, I was there."

"Looking for what?"

"Same as you. A lead to Mills. I figured since you were interested in her she must know somethin'."

Brett grabbed a kitchen chair, swung it around and stared at Karl. Huddled in the corner of the couch he looked dirty and beaten. "Now that you've got our attention, why don't you tell me everything?"

Realizing there was no escape, Karl accepted his fate. He talked slowly at first, but the more he said, the more he had to say, and eventually his story gushed out like water spilling over a dam.

Karl had been looking for Grant because Mills had double-crossed everyone when he'd jumped off the plane nearly a year before. No one had expected it. Jake and Billie had been as surprised as Karl when Grant had strapped on a parachute and jumped into the wintry night. In Karl's opinion, Grant had taken a bad risk by parachuting out in the United States.

"We were supposed to go to this remote fishing village in British Columbia," he recalled. "But Grant got greedy and parachuted out while we were still somewhere over northern Idaho or Washington. Maybe he was smart, because when we landed in Canada the FBI was waiting for us. They'd already worked the whole thing out with the Canadian officials.

"When we came back to the States, the police were all over us. But there wasn't any evidence to link us to the crime. Oh, sure, there were a few pieces of circumstantial evidence, but not enough for the D.A. to press charges. Maybe Howie did us all a favor, huh?"

"Howie?" Brett repeated, his eyes bright. "What're you talking about?"

Karl shook his head and grimaced. "Nothin'."

"Did Grant go by the name of Howard Sparks?" Brett asked slowly.

Bethany gripped the edge of her chair.

"Sometimes. No big deal."

"Maybe you just did us a favor, friend," Brett said, his lips lifting at the corners.

Bethany felt cold inside.

"How about a cigarette?" Karl asked.

"Forget it."

"Come on, man, give me a break."

"Bad for your health. Besides, you got more to say."

Frowning, Karl let out a weary sigh. "Okay, okay. Anyway, Jake, he calls me up one day and says he's located Mills and forced his share of the bonds out of him. The first thing I do is ask where he is so I can hit him up for my cut, too. Billie, she had the same idea. Jake had been taking Billie to see Grant when their plane went down. Seems pretty coincidental to me. My guess is that Grant paid someone to tamper with the plane and it went down."

"No!" Bethany stood and walked to the window. "I'll believe a lot of things about Grant, but I can't believe that he's a murderer!"

Brett's eyes held Karl's. "So where's Mills now?"

"I don't know."

"You bastard!" Brett pushed his chair aside and leaned over the couch, over Karl's anxious face.

"If I knew where he was, would I have bothered following you up here?"

Brett eased back a little. The fear in Karl's expression convinced him that he was telling the truth. "Where *was* he?"

"In California. North of San Francisco. In a little town near Redding on Lake Shasta. Jake said that Grant had originally gone to Vancouver to let some of the heat die down, cashed in quite a few of the bonds and then made tracks south, through Washington, Oregon and California."

"And now he's just vanished into thin air." Brett was skeptical.

"Look, man, I don't know where he is! Why else would I have started following his old lady?"

"You?" Bethany said. "You were following me?" She thought back to all those weeks of fear, looking over her shoulder, feeling unknown eyes boring into her back. It had been Karl Weathers!

"Sure. And I knew I was on the right track when Hanson showed up. Him being a private investigator for First Security and all. I knew that Jim Benson wouldn't rest until he'd tracked down Grant, and I figured he'd decide to use his stepson to do it. Looks like I was right."

"Stepson?" she repeated, her head snapping up, her gaze fixing on Brett's as she paled.

Karl glanced from Bethany's stricken face to Brett's hard expression, and for the first time in two hours, he smiled. "Sure. Everyone in Boise knew that before his wife died, Hanson here was the best P.I. in the business. Worked for his stepfather all the time."

Bethany didn't move. "You?" she repeated, not daring to breathe. "You're related to Jim Benson?"

A muscle worked in the side of Brett's face. "My mother married him when I was young."

"He's your *father?*"

"Stepfather."

"Oh, God," she whispered, wanting to sink through the floor. More lies! "So why didn't you tell me?"

Karl tried to get up, but couldn't, and Brett's hard glare forced him back to the couch.

"It's nothing I'm particularly proud of."

"And all the talk about owing him money. That was a lie?"

"No! I do owe him. For this place. He inherited it from my mother. It's the only thing I've got of my family—my real family."

"And so you'd do anything, including worming your way into my life to get it," she said, feeling dead inside. All the time they'd spent together had been nothing more than lies, one on top of the other, just like the snowflakes that had buried them in this small mountain cabin. She leaned against the wall for support and barely heard Karl admit that he'd been the man in the red car who'd nearly run her down by accident. He'd been scouting out her house, and had been afraid she'd recognize him, so he'd raced down the hill.

Unable to feel relief even at getting that mystery solved, Bethany numbly stood aside as Brett boarded up the broken window, then escorted Karl to the back of the Jeep. They then drove into the nearest town and located the police station.

Bethany didn't say a word during the long ride. She glanced at Brett, his jaw tight, his eyes steady on the road ahead, and wondered how she'd ever believed him.

Because I love him, she realized, letting her head rest against the window of the passenger side of the Jeep. The cold glass couldn't cool the hot feeling of betrayal in her heart.

Once again, she'd fallen for the wrong man.

Chapter Eleven

The sheriff's office was a small concrete building that was part of the county jail. Nearly empty except for a couple of drunks and one deputy, it smelled of stale cigarette smoke, sweat and day-old coffee.

While Bethany had watched in silence, Brett had explained his business and talked to the deputy on duty. The deputy in turn had called the sheriff, the state police and finally the FBI.

Now the small building was crowded with officers and agents, sitting on hard, wooden chairs, leaning against the concrete slab walls, their sleeves rolled up, their eyes squinted against the thickening smoke as they took turns questioning Karl, Bethany and Brett.

Bethany cradled a cup of cold coffee in her hands and watched as Brett's shoulder wound was cleaned and bandaged by a paramedic. He told Brett to check into a local hospital and have his shoulder examined by a doctor, but Brett waved away the young man's concern.

When the paramedic was finally finished with him, Brett took a seat by Bethany. She met his gaze for a minute and then stared into her coffee cup. When he tried to touch her, she moved away from him and prayed that the interrogation would soon be over.

It took hours before the questions stopped.

Bethany's eyes burned and her mouth felt cotton dry. Throughout the lengthy ordeal she couldn't forget that Brett had lied to her. Every minute he'd been with her, he'd lied to her. The fact that he was Jim Benson's stepson, part of the bank that had hounded her parents as well as herself, was more than she could bear.

She was shaken and pale when Brett finally helped her into the Jeep.

He climbed inside and started the engine. "I think we should get a few supplies and go back to the cabin."

"Why?" she asked, incredulous that he'd suggest returning to the mountains.

"It would be safe there."

"Are you out of your mind?"

"With all the publicity surrounding Karl's capture, Grant is bound to steer clear of here."

"I want to go home," she said, her eyes blazing. "To Portland."

"It's still not safe. Mills may be there. He'll be looking for you."

"I don't care." The thought of spending more time

alone with Brett was frightening because she couldn't trust herself or her wayward emotions.

"Bethany, think about it—"

"I have! You lied to me, Brett," she said, shaking. "All this time, you pretended to be against the bank and Jim Benson."

"I am."

"You're part of his family!"

"Not by choice."

"But you work for him!" She braced herself as they rounded a sharp curve in the road. Slush and snow sprayed from the wheels of the Jeep.

"This was the last time. Besides, I was working on the side of the law."

"Barely," she mumbled.

He grimaced in frustration as he maneuvered the Jeep toward the freeway entrance. "Does it even matter to you that Karl Weathers might have killed you?"

"You mean if you hadn't saved my life?" she taunted, her temper snapping. "I wouldn't have even been up there in that cabin if you hadn't dragged me there!"

"But he'd already found you in Portland."

"Because you were looking for me!"

"He almost ran you down *before* I was involved."

She huddled in the corner of the Jeep, patted Winston on the head and stared out the window. "I don't want to talk about it, okay? I've talked enough about Grant, the embezzlement, and everything to do with it to last me for the rest of my life."

He glanced at her and set his jaw. "Just one more thing, Bethany."

"What?"

"I do love you."

Her heart began to pound and she had to avoid looking at his hard, proud profile.

"Whether you want to hear it or not, I do." He didn't even glance in her direction. Instead, he stomped on the accelerator and concentrated on the traffic.

A thick lump clogged her throat and she turned her attention back to the window and the dark night beyond. She didn't want to think about the love they'd shared so fleetingly; a love that was based on lies. All her trust for him had crumbled around her feet and she couldn't help but wonder if all the time she'd spent with him had just been part of his charade to get to know her better. "If you love me," she whispered, "then please take me home."

"Later. When it's safe."

Balling her fists, she stared silently out the window all the way back to the cabin. Dawn was just beginning to lighten the sky as they arrived. "I thought you were afraid of another storm," she taunted him.

"I am." He hoisted her bag out of the back of the Jeep and walked to the front door. Winston barked excitedly and jumped to the ground. "But I'm also dead tired. I called the weather service. There might be a small storm, but the forecast is clear for the rest of the week." His gaze softened when he saw the fury in her eyes. "Maybe we can go back to Portland then. In the meantime you've got a day or two to decide what you really want out of life. Believe me, I won't force myself on you."

She still hadn't gotten out of the Jeep, but sat in the passenger seat, eyes turned on him suspiciously.

"Come on, Bethany," he said, his voice weary. "Give it a rest." As he picked up his bag, he winced.

Bethany jumped out of the Jeep and marched to the cabin, her conscience stinging all the way. Brett was tired and wounded. The least she could do was co-operate with him for a few more hours. Besides, despite it all, she still loved him.

Telling herself she was a fool of the highest order, she walked through the small rooms, lit a fire in the kitchen stove and scrounged around in the pantry for something to cook.

Brett built a fire in the living room and then, content to watch Bethany busy herself in the kitchen, he stretched out on the couch. His eyelids drooped as he stared at her with lazy, bemused eyes.

She knew she should be angry with him for keeping her captive on the mountain, but she couldn't. He looked so tired and weary, his dark hair rumpled against the worn arm of the couch, his mouth bracketed with lines of worry.

By the time she'd finished making a kettle of soup, he was fast asleep, snoring loudly on the couch. She walked over to him, smiled to herself and pulled up the blanket around his neck. "You're impossible, but I love you," she whispered.

"Do you?" His eyes opened and he grabbed her wrist, pulling her on top of him. For a minute she stared into his gray-blue eyes and thought about living the rest of her life without him. Alone, the future seemed as cold and bleak as the long winter nights.

Swallowing hard, she looked away. "It would just be so much easier if I hated you."

He smiled crookedly. "But not nearly as much

fun.'' He tugged on her wrist, pulling her gently forward so that her hair fell around his face and his lips
touched hers. ''Make love to me, Bethany,'' he suggested.

''And forget that you lied to me?''

''I didn't lie.'' He kissed her soundly and her
breath caught in her throat.

''Just omitted the facts,'' she whispered. ''Same
difference.''

''Not at all.'' His eyes held hers and then he moved
downward, tasting the sweet-scented skin of her
throat and sending erotic tingles down the back of her
neck. His fingers twined in her hair and he closed his
eyes, savoring the feel of her warm body lying over
his. ''Maybe we should stay here forever.''

''I don't think so.''

''No?'' He kissed the pulse that was fluttering at
her throat.

''No.'' But she wavered. Spending the rest of her
life with Brett was all she could ever want. She felt
his hands slide beneath the hem of her sweater to
reach upward and surround the swell of her breasts.
''Brett, please...''

But he wasn't listening. He'd positioned himself
beneath her and, while holding her and lifting her
sweater, he drew her forward so that the tip of her
breast fell into his open mouth. He began to tug and
suckle, and Bethany felt a familiar ache deep within
her, an ache only he could fill.

''Brett,'' she whispered, but didn't protest when he
lifted the sweater over her head.

The next morning Bethany was fit to be tied. Brett
was still wounded; the gauze dressing covering his

shoulder was stained dark red, but he wouldn't budge.

"Tomorrow I have to be at school," she said, for what seemed to be the thousandth time.

"Forget it. We're not going back. Not yet. It's too dangerous. The papers are probably filled with the story of Karl Weathers's capture." He slipped his arms through the sleeves of his flannel shirt and winced a little as his shoulder muscles rebelled.

"So it would be safer up here, where he was caught?" she retorted. "Give me a break! I need to get back to work and you need a doctor."

"I'm fine," he growled.

"Yeah. Right. Superman and Dick Tracy all rolled into one!" she said sarcastically. "Well, we had a deal, remember? Two weeks. Time's up."

His eyes narrowed as he glanced out the window and then back at her. "We can't leave."

"We don't have a choice, Brett," she snapped, her eyes blazing. "I'd like to stay up here and play house and pretend that the rest of the world doesn't exist, but I can't. I have a home, which is probably a total wreck by now, and responsibilities back in Portland, one of which is a job, a good job, a job that I love."

"So what about Grant?"

"I can't spend the rest of my life hiding, can I?" she asked, her hazel eyes delving into his. "The past is just that, and for the last year I've been hiding from what used to be my life. I've let you and Grant and Jim Benson run my life—hiding like a mouse in a hole in Portland, afraid to let my boss know that I used to be Grant Mills's wife. Well, no more. It's time I lived up to the fact that my ex-husband was a con man and a thief, but it doesn't affect me or the person I am now." She lifted her chin and tossed her hair out of her face. "I want to go home, Brett."

He rubbed his chin and pursed his lips. "And after that?"

"I don't know."

"What about us?"

She felt her jaw begin to quiver, but managed to meet his gaze. "That's something I don't know either. You're committed to hunting down my ex-husband, and you'd do anything to put him behind bars. I understand that. What I don't understand, can't begin to fathom, is why you thought you'd have to deceive me to do it."

He leaned against the wall. "Seemed necessary at the time."

"So I would trust you?"

"Yes."

"Well, it worked, didn't it?" she said, gathering up her things and flinging them into her bag. "I trusted you with my life."

"And now?"

"And now I don't know what to think. Except that I have a life waiting for me in Portland, and I want, I need to go home!"

By way of response, he pushed himself to a standing position and reached for his jacket. "All right, Bethany. You win. You want to go back to Portland and I'm tired of arguing. I'll pack my things and be ready to go in fifteen minutes. Good enough for you?"

"Yes," she said, looking around the cabin one last

time and wondering why she felt as though she'd just closed and locked the door to her happiness.

As Brett pulled into the driveway following Bethany, who had picked up her car, he scowled. Thick drops of rain ran down the windshield of the Jeep, blurring the few colored Christmas lights that winked from neighboring houses.

Bethany's house looked different without a mantle of snow surrounding it. The leafless maple trees and tall firs stood tall and stark against a hazy, gray skyline. Clumps of snow and slush, covered with mud and soggy leaves, were piled at the side of the drive.

"Home, sweet home," Bethany whispered once Brett had cut the engine. She climbed out of her Toyota, walked to the Jeep and opened the door. Winston bounded to the ground.

"You don't have to stay here, you know." Brett grabbed their bags and followed Bethany inside.

"Yes, I do." She unlocked the garage and then walked into the kitchen. The house was pretty much the way she'd left it, and her heart twisted at the sight of the mess. She took one look at the flour spilled on the floor and shuddered. What had she gotten herself into?

Refusing to become discouraged, she picked her way between the overturned chairs and picked up the phone. It was answered on the third ring.

"Hello?"

"Dad!"

"Bethie!" he exclaimed before his voice became muffled. "Eleanor, it's Bethany. Get on the extension, for God's sake!"

"Bethany?" her mother asked.

"Hi, Mom."

"Where have you been? Skiing?"

"Not exactly," Bethany hedged. "I did spend a little time in the mountains, though, and I did try to call you once."

"We were worried sick. We heard that your place had been broken into—"

"It's all right, really," she said.

"And you?"

"I'm fine. Just fine." She looked at Brett and smiled.

"Good, good," her mother said with a sigh. "I was really worried, but Father, well, he thought maybe you'd gone skiing."

"It...it wasn't quite like that," Bethany said.

"Oh?" Her father cleared his throat. "I don't suppose it had anything to do with Karl Weathers being caught by the FBI up in Washington, now, did it? We read something about it in the local papers, but the details were pretty sketchy."

Bethany decided there was no time like the present. "I had a little trouble here. The place was vandalized and I went to the mountains with a—" she looked guardedly at Brett, who had righted a chair and, sitting on it with his legs propped on another one, was eavesdropping on her conversation "—with a friend."

"Just what the devil's going on out there?" Myron demanded.

Carefully Bethany told her parents most of the story, including her part in the capture of Karl Weathers. She downplayed the danger, her involvement with Brett and the fact that she felt her life had been turned inside out. Her parents listened in stony silence.

"That does it!" her father exclaimed. "You're coming home right this instant and the minute you do I'm going to give that bastard Benson a piece of my mind!"

Bethany closed her eyes and rubbed her forehead. "No, Dad. I'm staying here. I've got a mess to clean up and school in the morning. I can't just run back to Idaho every time something goes wrong."

"This isn't exactly a normal, run-of-the-mill problem," her father reminded her.

"I know, but—"

"Every time I think of Grant and what he's put you through I see red! If I ever lay eyes on that son of a bitch again, I'll kill him."

Bethany's head began to throb. "Dad, please. I just called to let you know what's been going on and that I'm all right."

"Are you, Bethany?" her mother asked, unable to hide the worry in her voice.

Bethany smiled and looked at the toppled furniture, the stained carpet, the footprints of flour all over the house. "Of course I am, Mom," she lied. "Now listen, I'll come visit you on spring break, come hell or high water."

"Promise?"

"Promise!"

"Okay."

"Goodbye," Bethany said, smiling despite the lump in her throat.

"You talk a good story," Brett said, once she'd hung up.

"It's not a story." Bethany rolled up her sleeves and began righting the furniture. Then, while she swept and vacuumed the floor, Brett installed dead bolts, took out the garbage and put together her bed.

"What do you want me to do with this?" he asked, pointing to the bedraggled Christmas tree. Brown needles and broken branches littered the floor.

"I'll take off the ornaments, then you can put it outside," she said, shaking her head at the dilapidated little fir. "Doesn't exactly put you in the Christmas spirit, does it?"

"Nope. But Christmas is over."

Sighing, she nodded. "That's right and we're into a new year. Let's just hope it's better than the last."

"I don't know," Brett said. "Seems to me there were a few good things about last year." Offering his most ingratiating smile, he walked up to her and placed his arms around her waist. Once in front of her, he leaned over and kissed her, his lips warm and tender against hers.

"What are you trying to do?" she whispered.

"Shh..." He rimmed her lips with his tongue and splayed his open hands against her back.

With a moan she fell against him and forced herself to forget that all too soon he'd be gone, back on Grant's trail.

He held her tenderly at first, and then his arms tightened and he pulled her hard against him. His lips were urgent and hungry, his hands anxious as he molded her to him. He kissed her so passionately she could barely breathe; the air seemed trapped in her lungs.

Instinctively, she wrapped her arms around his neck and didn't protest when he lifted her off her feet and carried her to the bedroom. Though he'd lied to her and used her, she didn't care. This one last night, she meant to love him body and soul.

He placed her on the down coverlet and slowly took off her clothes. Once she was naked, her skin creamy white on the dark-blue comforter, he lay down beside her on the brass bed. "What am I going to do with you?" he whispered, as he tenderly pushed a lock of auburn hair off her cheeks.

Shivering at his touch, she looked deep into his eyes. "I was wondering the same thing."

His hand moved down her shoulder, then slowly past her ribcage coming to rest at the curve of her waist. "I never expected to feel like this again."

"Again?"

"Maybe that was the wrong word." He gazed into the shadowed depths of her green-gold eyes. "After Roberta—"

"Oh." Sadness stole into her heart. "Your wife."

"Yep." His gaze grew distant for a minute. "After she was killed, I told myself I'd never let myself become so emotionally involved with another woman; that I'd never open myself up to that kind of pain." His expression became sad and distant at the painful memory. Closing his eyes, he shook his head. "And the damned thing was that there was nothing I could do. She was alone when it happened. I was out on a case." His eyes grew dark. "I thought I'd track down that bastard and nail him to the wall."

"But you didn't?"

"No. There just wasn't even evidence to find out who was behind it."

"But you think it was an accident, don't you?"

"I hope so. I hope it wasn't some guy I'd sent to prison who'd been set free and decided to take out his revenge." He flung himself back against the pillow and stared at the ceiling. "But there just wasn't a clue."

Bethany touched him gently on the cheek. "And you've felt guilty about it ever since, haven't you?"

He shrugged. "I don't know. Maybe. Anyway, I swore when she died that I'd never let a woman get that close to me again." He shifted his gaze and looked deep into her worried eyes. "And I have with you." Sighing at his own foolishness, he brushed his fingers across her cheek. "I didn't plan to fall in love with you, Bethany, but I just couldn't help myself."

"Is that supposed to make me feel better?" she asked, feeling the emptiness of the future steal into her heart.

"It's just the truth." He turned back to her and wrapped his arms around her. "I just wish everything else in my life were as simple as loving you." His lips claimed hers with renewed passion and Bethany's heart began to race.

She clung to him in desperation. Though she didn't doubt for a minute that Brett loved her, or thought he did, she knew that as long as Grant, alive or dead, wasn't found, he would always stand between them.

Brett listened to the regular rhythm of Bethany's breathing and smiled in the dark room. Clasping her shoulders more firmly, he felt her move and snuggle against his chest. Just the slightest movement of her hair against his bare skin caused a sexual response and he had to shift his legs away from hers in order to cool his blood.

Now that he was back in Portland, he had to pick up Grant's trail again. Unfortunately, he didn't have much to go on. There was Karl Weathers's explanation of Mills's whereabouts, of course, but it was a long shot at best. And, most likely, an out-and-out lie. Then he had the alias, Howard Sparks, to work with and the knowledge that Grant was an outdoorsman, a mountain climber and a rodeo buff...nothing that tied together. He closed his eyes and tried to think calmly. Maybe with what he'd learned plus what Greg Connelly, the detective who'd promised to look into the case, had dug up, they'd have something. Then again, maybe not.

He glanced at the clock and grimaced. Ten after six. A few cars had begun to drive down the hill; the noise of their engines disturbed the silence. Bethany stirred, groaned and then sighed against him before drifting off to sleep again. Brett kissed her crown and relaxed. Just a few more minutes in bed with her and then he'd get up and tackle the day.

"I'm going to school and that's that!" Bethany said, a glint in her eye. She checked her watch, realized she was going to be late and, sighing, tugged on her boots. Then she grabbed her coat and slipped her arms through the sleeves. "Twenty-two students, one principal and countless parents expect me to show up!"

Brett straddled a kitchen chair and watched her as he sipped the one cup of coffee that was breakfast. "What if it's not safe?"

"I'm going to Johnson Elementary, not the battle of Little Big Horn," she pointed out as she twisted her hair into a stocking cap. "Look, some of us have to work for a living. Now, if you would kindly move your Jeep so that I can get my car out of the garage…"

"I don't like this," he muttered.

She smiled and placed her hand on his shoulder. "I know. But it's been over two weeks. Our deal's off and I'm tired of hiding. Remember? Besides, Christmas vacation ended yesterday."

He grimaced again, set his empty cup on the table, scraped back his chair and stood. "Okay. Have it your way. But you be careful today."

"And what're you going to do?"

His mouth twisted cynically. "I still have a job to finish."

Her heart missed a beat. "Uh, will you still be here when I get home?"

He stared at her a minute and rubbed his jaw. "That depends."

"On?"

"On what I learn." He grabbed his jacket and shrugged into it. "I have a couple of people I need to talk to."

"Jim Benson?" she asked.

"For one," he admitted.

She felt the sting of disappointment. "I don't suppose you'll try to beg off the case."

"Can't."

"Or won't?"

His eyes narrowed and his cheekbones suddenly appeared more prominent. "Is that what you want me to do—drop the case and leave Grant alone?"

"I don't know, Brett," she admitted, tired of the whole damned mess. "I just don't know." Opening the door, she stepped into the garage.

Brett followed and locked the door behind him. As she was getting into her car, he grabbed her arm. "You be careful, okay?"

"Okay."

He lowered his head and brushed his lips against hers, then he left. She watched in her rearview mirror as he started the Jeep and backed out of the drive.

"He'll be back," she told herself. "You'll come home tonight and he'll be here waiting." But her hands shook as she placed the key in the ignition and started the car.

A half hour later, Bethany stepped into the kindergarten room, took one look at the Christmas decorations on the walls and decided to get to work. Now that she was in Portland, she had to get back into the familiar patterns of her life, including the routine of teaching the children.

The less she thought about Christmas and the time she'd spent alone with Brett, the better. Her time with him almost seemed a fantasy, as if their shared moments in the snow-covered wilderness had happened to someone else.

And here she was—back at Johnson Elementary. What Brett decided to do was his business. Though she loved him with all of her heart, she knew that their time together was nearly over. As soon as he found Grant, if Grant really was alive, Brett would be gone, back to his hermitlike existence in the northern Cascades.

She yanked off her stocking cap and hung her coat in the closet. Then, kicking off her boots, she climbed onto one of the tables and started pulling out staples from the wall. She put the Christmas decorations in boxes, holly wreaths in one, reindeer in another.

Looking up, she saw Marianne, carrying two cups of coffee, walk into the room.

"So you made it back after all," Marianne said, grinning from ear to ear. "Hey don't let Chris see you standing on the table! He'd have a fit. He's on a big campaign to lower the insurance rates for the school."

"That's his job."

"So don't let him see you dancing up there," Marianne teased.

"I won't. And I'm not dancing. It's just that I didn't have time to get the ladder." Bethany jumped off the table and took the cup of coffee that Marianne held out to her. "Thanks. I could use this."

"Thought so." Marianne leaned against the corner of Bethany's desk and her rounded abdomen strained against her wool jumper. "So tell me, what did you do on vacation?"

"You wouldn't believe it."

"Try me," Marianne insisted.

Taking a long swallow of coffee, Bethany glanced up at her friend and grinned. "Okay. How about this? Would you believe that I was kidnapped, taken to a remote mountain cabin and held captive during a snowstorm by a handsome, mysterious stranger?"

"Yep." Marianne's dark eyes lost their teasing glint.

"You would?"

"I guess I'd better come clean," Marianne said, nervously twisting her cup in her hands. "After you left our party, I got worried. After all, you didn't seem to be too pleased that Brent or whatever his name is—"

"Brett."

"Right. For him to show up. At the time, Jack told me I was being ridiculous, but I couldn't help worrying. I tried to call you for a couple of days and you didn't answer. So, being naturally nosy and worried, mind you, I went to your house. I was greeted by a couple of very intense policemen who very politely but firmly told me to go away. When I asked where you were, they wouldn't say anything, other than that you were all right. Then I ran into this little girl... Janey or something?"

"Jenny," Bethany corrected her, still stunned. She hadn't thought about the policemen or the neighbors or what little Jenny had thought of her vandalized home and hasty disappearance.

"Jenny, that was it. And she was worried sick about you and some puppy named—" Marianne waved her hands frustratedly in the air "—oh, I forget."

"Winston." Bethany squeezed herself into one of the small chairs and sipped her coffee. "I should have talked to Jenny before I left."

Marianne nodded. "Anyway, I got to talk to the child's mother and she and I compared notes."

"And?"

"And what we both discovered is that we didn't have a clue as to where you were. I thought about calling your folks, because I could have come to the school, dug in your personnel records and found their number, but I didn't phone them because I thought I might get them all worried and upset."

"You would have," Bethany agreed, thinking about the complicated mess her life had become. She'd been a fool to think she could just come home and act as if nothing had changed. Her entire life had been turned inside out, and it was Brett's fault. Well, Brett's, Jim Benson's, First Security's and Grant's. Forcing herself to get up, she started changing the calendar from December to January. Within twenty minutes the quiet room would be teeming with wound-up five-and six-year-olds.

"I didn't mean to be the bearer of bad news," Marianne said, "but I was really concerned."

"I know you were. I should have called, but I wasn't near a phone. It's a long, complicated story, but I'm back and safe and when I have the time, I'd like to tell you all about it."

"Anytime," Marianne said, starting for the door.

"Come back after classes, okay?"

"Will do. Oh, and Bethany?"

"Yes?"

Marianne hesitated, shifted from one foot to the other and then muttered, "Oh, damn it all anyway!" She opened her purse, pulled out a wrinkled newspaper clipping and handed it to Bethany. "You know Jack," she explained, "he reads every page of the paper. He saw this and thought it might be connected to you and your disappearance." Almost disgusted with herself, Marianne sat on a corner of one of the small tables.

Bethany stared down at the scrap of newsprint in her hand. It was an article about the capture of Karl Weathers and the people involved. The clipping reported that Brett Hanson, a private investigator and alleged embezzler Grant Mills's wife were both involved in bringing Karl Weathers to the police.

"Great," Bethany murmured, paling. She crumpled the article in her hand and met Marianne's worried eyes. "I suppose it's a safe guess that the principal and superintendent have seen this."

"I suppose. But Chris hasn't said anything to me about it."

"Wonderful," Bethany muttered just as the first group of students, voices high and excited, rushed into the room.

Greg Connelly's life had obviously gone downhill. Brett knocked on a dingy door in an old hotel and noticed that the only illumination of the outer hallway was a single, dim bulb dangling from an exposed wire. The paint on the walls was peeling and cracked.

He knocked again, a little more insistently.

"Hold your horses, I'm coming, I'm coming!"

A few seconds later the door was opened by a man Brett barely recognized as Greg. His eyes were bloodshot, his thick gray-peppered hair shaggy and uncombed. Once one of the finest detectives in Portland, Greg had managed to pour his life into a bottle after blaming himself for the death of his wife and child several years earlier.

"Mornin'," Brett drawled as Greg stepped out of

his way and in a sweeping gesture motioned him inside.

"Is it?"

The apartment was just one step up from a flophouse: three rooms of dingy green walls, cracked linoleum floors and sparse overstuffed furniture that was shiny and stained from wear.

"Hell, you rise with the blue jays," Greg said as he poured coffee into two chipped mugs. Wearing faded jeans, a wrinkled T-shirt and scuffed loafers without socks, he set the tin pot back on the stove and then pushed his graying hair out of his eyes.

"I like to get an early start."

"Hmph. Don't you know that the day doesn't start before eleven," Greg muttered. "How d'ya like your coffee?"

"Black."

"Good. Out of sugar and the milk's gone sour." Greg grinned cynically, but the effort cost him and he had to steady himself. He placed Brett's cup on the scarred table and hoisted himself up onto the counter as Brett took a seat in the single chair. "I s'pose you're here to learn what I managed to dig up on Grant Mills."

Brett leaned back in his chair and took a swallow of the bitter coffee. "Right. So what have you got?"

"Not much. I learned from the police that Karl Weathers vandalized Mills's wife's place."

"Ex-wife," Brett cut in.

Greg shrugged. "Whatever. Anyway, the police found a set of his prints somewhere in the house. So I started trying to find old Karl."

"And you found out that he was already in custody."

"Right. So you beat me to the punch." Greg grinned. "Again."

"What else?"

"I checked out Karl's story. Seems as if he's telling the truth. Mills was seen in Vancouver, B.C., where he managed to sell some bonds before heading south. Next, he was spotted in Seattle and then again near Lake Shasta in California. The old boy seems to get around."

Brett met Greg's gaze. "So tell me something I don't already know."

"The last place Grant Mills was spotted was in Redding, California."

"When?"

"Last week, before the news broke about Karl."

"You're sure?"

"As sure as I can be. I have a...'friend' with the FBI."

"Letting out that kind of information could cost him his job," Brett thought aloud as he scrutinized his friend.

"That's the way the game's played. You know it as well as I do. You scratch my back and I'll scratch yours." Greg slid off the counter and rubbed his aching muscles. "We have a working arrangement. I help him and when I need it, he helps me."

"You're an informer?"

Greg snorted. "A paid information gatherer. Unofficially, of course."

"Of course," Brett muttered. "Convenient."

"It can be."

"So why haven't the FBI got Mills in custody?"

"He's a slippery devil."

"Does he go by an alias?"

"Beats me."

"What about the name Howard Sparks? Mean anything?"

Greg shook his head. "Should it?"

Brett rubbed the back of his neck. "I don't know," he said, wearily. "But maybe…just maybe." The wheels began to turn in his mind.

Greg poured himself another cup and then pulled a bottle of bourbon from one of the cabinets over the greasy stove. He waved the bottle in Brett's direction. "Want some?" he asked, as he poured a stiff shot into his coffee cup.

"Too early."

"Never."

"Maybe next time." Brett stood, rubbed his neck and turned to leave. "Thanks for your help."

"Don't thank me. Just remember that we're even."

"If I end up finding Mills because of this, I'll owe you," Brett said, reaching for the door.

A lopsided grin spread across Greg's face. "That's what I like to hear. Maybe you'd be interested in a partnership."

"With you?"

"Why not?"

Brett glanced at the bottle. "Not right now. I'm out of the business."

"Sure ya are. That's why you needed to know about Mills," Greg scoffed, but he smiled at his friend. "Go on, get outta here."

"See ya around."

"Yeah."

"And Greg?"

"What?"

"Take care of yourself."

"Always do," Greg replied, lifting the cup in salute.

Brett walked down the stairs and stepped outside. Rain was pounding the streets of Portland and running in the gutters. Turning up his collar against the wind and rain, he grimaced and thought about Greg Connelly. Losing a wife and kid would be tough. Brett had nearly given up on his own life when Roberta died, but fortunately he'd been able to pick up the pieces. But Greg hadn't been so lucky.

He crossed the street against the light, jumped into his Jeep and decided to drive straight to the airport. The sooner he found Mills and settled his debt with First Security, the sooner he could return to Bethany without anything separating them. He stopped at the nearest phone booth, called the school and left a message with the secretary for Bethany, since she was still teaching.

Cursing his luck, he climbed back into the Jeep and drove to Portland International. He hoped to catch a flight to Northern California that afternoon. He glanced into the back seat, frowned at the sight of his bag and then turned his attention to the road ahead.

By the time that Bethany got home, she was bone tired. The first day of school was always difficult and on top of a hectic day of teaching, she'd had to explain herself to the principal of the school, Chris Bingham, and then tell all of her story to Marianne.

Fortunately the principal had been understanding and didn't hold Grant's crime against her.

But Marianne had been horrified. "So Brett is working with the bank that's been harassing your folks?" she'd asked.

"'Fraid so."

"And you still trust him?"

"I don't know," Bethany had replied.

"But you're in love with him, aren't you?" Marianne had prodded, her brown eyes filled with sadness.

"Yes," Bethany had admitted ruefully.

"Just take care of yourself, okay?"

"I will," Bethany had promised, leaving her friend to worry and shake her short dark curls.

Now, as she parked the car in the garage, Bethany felt empty inside. She walked into the house, looked around for a note from Brett and knew before she searched that she'd find none. He was gone, far away, tracking down the ghost of her ex-husband.

Unable to eat, she made herself a hot cup of tea, fed Winston and then walked down to Jenny's house. The little girl was outside riding her tricycle. When she looked up and saw Bethany and Winston, a huge grin split her small face. "Bethany, where have you been?" she demanded, just as Winston ran up and washed her face.

Bethany didn't have time to answer. Jenny giggled and tried to grab the slippery pup. He barked and ran in crazy circles around the wet asphalt, splashing through puddles and yipping excitedly each time Jenny just about caught up with him. Despite her worries, Bethany had to laugh.

"What's going on?" Linda Porter asked when she opened the door. "Oh, Bethany! Thank God you're all right! Where have you been?"

"Out of town."

"So I gathered."

Jenny stopped chasing the dog and looked at Bethany curiously. "I seen policemen."

"You saw," her mother corrected.

"Yeah, I know," Bethany said with a wink for her small friend. "I had a little trouble before I left. Someone got in and vandalized the place."

Linda clucked her tongue and sighed. "Want to come in and talk about it?" she asked. "Joey won't be home from basketball practice for another half hour. I've got some Russian tea heating. How about a cup?"

"I'd love it," Bethany admitted.

While Jenny played with Winston, Bethany sat at a cluttered kitchen table, sipped the hot tea and told Linda about her ex-husband, the embezzlement and that Brett, as a private investigator for First Security, was trying to find Grant. Once her story was finished, she stared into the dregs of her tea.

Linda let out a long, low whistle. "So you were married to *the* Grant Mills."

"Yes."

"I never tied the two of you together."

"When I moved to Portland from Boise, I tried to sever all connections with my past—except, of course, for my folks. Didn't really work, did it?"

"Guess not."

Bethany leaned back and placed her empty cup on

the table. "It doesn't really matter. Not any more. I've decided to quit hiding from my past."

"Good for you!" Linda exclaimed.

"But now I'd better get home," Bethany said, just as Joey, drenched with sweat from head to foot, burst through the front door and started chattering at his mother before he tugged open the refrigerator door and grabbed an apple.

"I'm starved, Mom," he complained as Bethany let herself out of the house and wondered where Brett was.

Brett slammed down the receiver and, grabbing his bag, ran down the concourse to his waiting flight. He'd called all afternoon and hadn't been able to connect with Bethany. Glancing at his watch, he slowed to a walk and let the flight attendant check his ticket and boarding pass before he made his way to his assigned seat.

As the plane gathered speed and the terminal building of Portland International flashed by, he stared straight ahead to the seat in front of him and the back of a stranger's bald head. The grooves around his mouth deepened when he thought that it could be days, possibly weeks, until he'd see Bethany again.

Chapter Twelve

Bethany didn't hear from Brett for several days. Though Marianne had told her that a man had called the school several times on the day after vacation, he hadn't bothered to leave his name. She could only guess that the caller had been Brett.

Worried about him, and telling herself that she was just being what her father would call a "damned fool woman," she threw herself into her work, trying to find the old satisfaction she felt in teaching eager young children. But even during the school day her thoughts would turn to Brett.

After one particularly rigorous day, she watched the last student board the bus and leaned against the wall just as Marianne walked into the room. "Rumor has it that you're knocking yourself out," she said, eyeing the dark smudges under Bethany's eyes.

Bethany sighed and shook her head. "No. Just having a little trouble getting back into the routine."

"But not pining away for Brett?"

"Not a chance," she retorted, and then blew a loose strand of hair out of her face before meeting her friend's concerned gaze. "Okay. So I'm pining. Who am I trying to kid, anyway?"

"Not me."

Bethany managed a small smile. "I couldn't even if I tried."

"Oh, I don't know, I'm usually a pushover. At least that's what Jack says."

Sitting down on the edge of a table and staring at the goldfish in the aquarium, Bethany sighed. "So am I—a pushover, that is. But always for the wrong man."

"Everyone's entitled to a mistake, y'know."

"But two?"

"Hey, don't get so down on yourself. And you don't know that Brett is all that bad."

"I thought you'd condemned him."

"Not me. Remember, I'm the one who told you what a hunk he was."

"But then you came in with the newspaper clipping."

"I know. But I was wrong. I've thought about it and I remember the way he stared at you at the Christmas party."

"Oh, and what did he look like?"

"Like he'd tear any man limb from limb for looking at you twice."

"I don't know."

Marianne touched Bethany's sleeve. "Look, I

know that you think he was using you, but there's a good chance he wasn't.''

"That's the problem, isn't it?" Bethany asked, her lips pursing at her own stupidity. "I don't know anything about him, except for what he told me." She lifted her chin and squared her shoulders. "And for all I know, he could have been peddling me a pack of lies, just to get me to help him."

"You don't believe that."

"I don't *want* to believe it."

"Then don't. Give the guy the benefit of the doubt."

Bethany smiled. "Is that your advice?"

"You bet it is. But, er, don't ask for Jack's."

"Why?"

"'Cause he'd tell you to get rid of the bum."

"I don't have to worry about that," Bethany said as she reached into the closet for her coat. "He's already gone."

"Maybe he's just busy."

Bethany wrapped her scarf around her neck and lifted a shoulder. "Right. Or maybe he's had second thoughts. Or maybe, God forbid, he's found Grant."

"Do you really think he's alive?"

"Karl Weathers thinks so," Bethany whispered, shuddering.

"Then Brett will find him," Marianne predicted.

"Maybe. But I don't know how. The FBI has been looking for him and so have half a dozen police departments. I don't know how Brett thinks he can do any better."

Marianne linked her arm through Bethany's. "Just

don't worry. Things will turn out all right. They always do.''

Bethany smiled sadly and walked out of the room. *If things were so right, then where was Brett?*

Brett looked through the windshield of the helicopter. Far below, partially covered with snow and the fallen limbs of nearby trees, was what was left of Jake Weathers's plane. Pieces of the fuselage were scattered between the towering pines. Charred, twisted metal protruded upward and glinted against the rays of a bright winter sun.

''So that's all of it?'' Brett asked above the whir of the chopper's blades.

''Yep. What's left of it,'' Rich Leland, the pilot for hire, replied.

''Can we get any closer?''

''Maybe.'' The pilot maneuvered the controls and the helicopter dipped over the trees before hovering a hundred feet above the ground. ''Too dangerous to go any lower,'' Rich explained. ''There's not much to see down there, anyway. The police took the bodies and all the personal belongings; anything they thought would help them identify the poor bastards. Turned out to be Weathers and that Henshaw woman. But you know that, don't you?''

''I heard. Any way to get down there?''

The pilot shook his head. ''Not this time of year, unless you want to rent a dogsled—not many of them available in this part of California,'' he added, smiling.

''I suppose not.''

''You could climb up in the spring, but right now

the weather's too unpredictable.'' He swung the copter around for another pass over the desolate cliffs and ravines. "Want to see anything else?''

"Nope. That should do it,'' Brett said, staring down at the crash site. The picture of the snow-covered wreckage turned his stomach and he felt the same dread sweep over him that he'd felt several times since leaving Bethany—that he'd made a big mistake in leaving her; that some harm was about to come her way.

Settling back into his seat, he waited as Rich turned the helicopter back toward the airport.

Since coming to California, Brett had followed nothing but dead-end leads. If Grant had been in Lake Shasta, he'd left with the tourists. So Brett was back to square one.

As the pilot landed the craft, Brett handed him a hundred-dollar bill and then made his way back to the rental car. Lost in thought, he drove directly to his small motel room. After tossing off his jacket and kicking off his shoes, he settled back on the bed and reached for the phone.

Bethany was in the shower when she heard the phone ring. Still dripping, she grabbed a towel, wrapped it around her torso and walked into the bedroom. She was shivering when she picked up the receiver.

"Bethany?''

"Brett! Where are you?'' she asked, warm again. Unwanted tears gathered in her eyes and her heart beat a quick double time.

"Lake Shasta.''

"And?"

"No luck. No sign of Grant."

"Maybe Karl was mistaken," she said, curling her legs beneath her and drawing the down comforter up to her chin.

"I tried to call earlier," he said. "But the secretary at the school wouldn't interrupt your class."

Bethany leaned back on the pillows and smiled. "I don't blame her. It's my job, you know."

"I've called since then; whenever I could get to a phone. Is everything all right up there?"

"Great," she lied.

"You're sure?"

She wanted to tell him just how much she'd missed him, how empty the house seemed, but she couldn't. Pride held her tongue. "What could be wrong?" she quipped, managing to sound lighthearted. "Just because you left without so much as a note?"

"You're mad."

"Not really." Hurt maybe. Angry? Well, a little. Nonetheless, she was relieved to hear from him.

"Good. Look, I'm going to Idaho to report to Benson and then I'll be back in Portland."

"When?" she asked, hoping to sound nonchalant and hearing the breathless tone of her voice.

"A couple of days, a week at the outside. Are you sure you're okay?"

"Of course I am. I've lived here alone for almost a year. I think I'll survive a few more days."

"I'll see you then."

"Good."

She heard him disconnect and her soaring spirits crashed to the ground. She'd acted like a ninny—a complete fool. He was coming back to Portland and she was feeling like a schoolgirl anticipating her first date. "You're an idiot," she admonished, throwing back the covers and marching into the bathroom. While she towel-dried her hair, she told herself just how much of a fool she was. "You deserve to fall for the wrong men," she scolded her reflection. "You let them walk all over you. Oh, Bethany, I hope someday you'll learn!" But she couldn't wipe the smile off her face or hide the blush in her cheeks. Brett was coming back!

Brett waited for the elevator in the reception area of First Security Bank. The lobby was crowded, filled with the noise of chattering voices, typewriters clacking, computers humming and footsteps clattering on the polished brick floor.

When the elevator doors opened, he stepped inside and pushed the button for the suite of executive offices that was located on the sixth floor. Though Jim Benson wasn't expecting him, he didn't care. After nearly two weeks of running down dead-end leads, he wanted out. By now, Grant Mills could well be out of the country, and the damned thing about it was that Brett really didn't care. All he wanted was to get back to Portland and Bethany. Her life and happiness were more important than anything—including his mother's land.

The elevator hummed to a stop and the doors opened. Brett stepped onto the thick carpet of the reception area. He stated his business with Jim's secretary and waited while she called her boss on the intercom.

Brett leaned against a mahogany bookcase. A door down the hall opened and Harry, his suit as impeccable as ever, bustled toward Jim's office. He stopped dead in his tracks at the sight of his stepbrother. "Brett?" he asked, casting a disparaging glance at Brett's jeans, sweater and ski vest. "What the devil are you doing here? I thought you were out looking for Mills."

"I was."

"Then you found him?" Harry looked relieved. His thin moustache stopped twitching.

Brett's lips curved into a friendly smile. "Nope. Just thought I'd drop by to buy you a beer."

"You what?" For a second Harry's facade fell and he grinned, before he realized where he was. "Wait a minute! Why are you here? Don't give me any cock-and-bull about buying—"

"Brett!" Jim Benson strode out of his office, walked up to Brett and clasped his hand grandly.

As if the prodigal son had come back to the fold, Brett thought sourly.

"What a surprise! Come into the office—er, you, too, Harry." Then he turned to his secretary. "Gloria, bring us in some coffee, will you?"

"Sure."

"Now, come in, come in," he urged, smiling broadly and leading the two younger men into his office. Two of the walls in the expansive room were of glass. The corner suite offered a commanding, panoramic view of the city of Boise. Treetops and tall buildings, church steeples and apartment houses were visible against a backdrop of steel-gray clouds.

"Have a seat," Jim urged.

Brett slipped into a leather and chrome chair near the desk.

After tapping softly on the door, Gloria came in with a tray of coffee, added the appropriate amounts of sugar and cream to Jim's mug and then offered them each a cup.

Once she'd left the room, Jim took off his glasses and leaned back in his chair. Sipping coffee, he leveled cold but interested eyes at his stepson. "Now, I suppose you're here to tell me that you've found Mills."

Brett shook his head. "I think he's left the country."

Jim paled slightly, but quickly recovered. "Then follow him."

"I can't; he disappeared."

"But—"

"I talked to Karl Weathers again but didn't learn much new. Then I followed Mills north to Vancouver, British Columbia, back down through Oregon and Washington along the coast, then to Lake Shasta and finally Redding."

"And what did you find?"

"Nothing more than the FBI or the police did. A trail of cashed bonds and nothing else. I talked with a few people who'd seen him or thought they'd seen him, and all the reports were the same. He's tired and haggard-looking, drinks too much beer and is constantly looking over his shoulder."

"He should be!" Jim muttered, his color rising. "So what do you plan to do?"

"Nothing."

"What in God's name—"

Brett placed a manila envelope on Jim's desk. "Here's a full report along with copies of all the leads and clues I found. Unfortunately, it doesn't add up to a hill of beans."

"Nothing!" Harry repeated, nearly spilling his coffee on his crisp white shirt. "You had the nerve to come back here with empty hands?"

"I suppose you think he's paid for his crime," Jim said.

"Of course not. But I've run out of places to look."

"What you're saying is that you've failed."

Brett's jaw tightened. "Maybe."

"Then I can't consider your debt with the bank paid." Jim's face had flushed slightly and a pulse was beginning to throb under his collar. He jerked at the knot of his tie.

"I understand that."

"And I'll be forced to sell off that piece of land in the mountains," Jim warned.

"I figured as much. But the note isn't up for another couple of months."

"You think you can come up with the money by then?" Jim paused to pick up his pipe and light it.

"I don't know."

Harry looked at his father, glanced at Brett and then let his eyes rest on his father's agitated face. "Maybe we should forget about Mills. The police and the FBI are still looking for him."

"Forget about him?" Jim repeated, staring incredulously at his son. "Forget about him, for God's sake? When he made this bank the laughingstock of the state? When he gave every opportunist in this community the idea to stick it to First Security? Are you out of your mind?'' His cold eyes narrowed and he thumped the desk with his fist. ''I want Grant Mills behind bars!''

''Because of what he did, or because of that feud you've had with Bethany Mills's father, Myron Wagner?'' Harry asked.

''What's that got to do with this?''

''I don't know, but the way you send me traipsing out there, I wonder,'' Harry snapped.

''Are you questioning my authority?'' Jim demanded.

Harry tugged at his tie. ''No.''

''Then butt the hell out!''

Harry sat farther back in his chair and Brett scowled. It was a damned shame that Harry was scared of his father. ''Well, I'm out of it,'' Brett said, putting his coffee cup on the corner of the desk and standing.

''I don't suppose this has anything to do with Mills's wife?'' Jim said slowly as he fingered Brett's report.

Every muscle in Brett's body tensed. ''Why?''

''Rumor has it that you've got it bad for her; that she's twisted you around her little finger so that you won't find Grant. She still loves him, you know. He divorced her, not the other way around.''

''Rumor has it?'' Brett repeated, knowing he was being baited, but furious just the same. His teeth were clenched so tightly that they ached.

''Sure.'' Jim settled back in his chair. ''Boise's not that big of a town. Her father and mother still live here, and there's still a lot of talk about Bethany Mills and her ex-husband, the man who ran off with a million dollars of First Security's money.''

"You got paid. The insurance finally came through.''

"And it cost. Big. Bonding employees costs more than ever, and that doesn't begin to count the cost of stopping all those other attempts to rip off the bank.''

"So it's Bethany's fault, or whoever else is close enough to point a finger at, especially her father,'' Brett said, glancing at Harry before drilling Jim with hard blue eyes. "Even if I decide to continue to look for Mills, it's not because you've got some goddamned rope tied around my neck.''

"It's your mother's property.''

"Yeah, but it has too many strings attached.''

"You put them there, son.''

Brett glared at him. "You're a miserable son of a bitch, you know that, don't you?''

Harry gasped, but Brett turned on his heel and stormed out of the plush office. He strode past the secretary, past the elevator and took the stairs. He thought he heard Harry running after him and calling his name, but he didn't care. He was ready to jump onto the next plane back to Portland. All that mattered was getting back to Bethany and convincing her to marry him. Even his mother's land didn't really mean much any more. For the first time in years, Brett Hanson had a reason to live. And it was all because of a beautiful, auburn-haired woman with intelligent hazel eyes!

But before long he had calmed down enough to think things through. Climbing into his car, he headed west, away from the airport, deciding to drive back to Portland through Fullerton. If Grant Mills had been in that town once before, there was a chance, albeit a slim one, that he'd been back. Knowing he might just be wasting his time, he nonetheless decided to follow up his hunch and leave no stone unturned. That he was out of it with Benson didn't matter; he had to be free of Grant Mills before he could marry Bethany.

Bethany stared at the telephone. It had been nearly a week since Brett had called and she hadn't heard a word from him. She had almost given up and decided that she'd imagined that he'd called and said he'd be back. "Don't do this to yourself," she chided as she wiped a final dish and put it away. "He said he might be gone a week, so give him time."

She tried to watch television, but couldn't find a show that held her interest, so she picked up a book Marianne had recommended, but soon tossed it aside. With Winston curled on her lap, she spent the evening watching the fire die. At last, sometime after ten, she got off the couch and stretched.

"Tomorrow's a school day," she told the puppy, who wagged his tail. "Yeah, a lot you care." Then she snapped off the lights, made sure the doors were locked and got ready for bed. She tossed and turned and listened to the rain beat against the windows, then fell into a restless sleep.

Sometime after midnight, she awoke at the sound of relentless pounding. Thinking a tree was being blown against the side of the house, she turned over— then realized that someone was knocking frantically on the front door.

Brett!

She leaped out of bed, grabbed her robe and raced
down the hall. Still tying the belt at her waist, she
flung open the door, looked into Brett's tired eyes,
and threw her arms around his neck.

Chapter Thirteen

"It's over," he whispered, clinging to her so tightly that she had trouble breathing. But she didn't care. Tears ran down her face as she cradled his head in her hands.

"Over? What?"

"Grant's in custody."

Her knees went weak. "But how?"

"It's a long story," he said as she stepped aside and closed the door behind him. Slowly he took off his jacket and hung it over the hall tree.

"But where? How…?"

He offered a tired smile. "If you make me a cup of coffee I'll explain everything."

Dashing aside her tears, she hurried into the kitchen, made a pot of coffee and felt Brett's eyes on her back as she worked.

"It's good to be back," he whispered, as she offered him a cup.

"It's good to have you back." Her eyes met his.

"Even if I'm responsible for finding Grant."

"I don't care," she said, linking her arm through his and walking into the living room.

Brett kicked off his boots and started a fire before settling back on the couch and holding Bethany tight. "I've been everywhere imaginable in the Pacific Northwest," he said, leaning his head back against the cushions of the couch and feeling warm for the first time in over a week. "I'd just about given up. Even told Jim Benson I was off the case."

"I bet he liked that."

Brett grinned at the memory. "Not much."

"So…"

"I planned to jump the next plane back here, but decided to check out one last clue: Fullerton."

"The rodeo?"

"Nope. Wrong season. But the town's small. I flashed Grant's picture a few times, gave several people the name of Howard Sparks and then hung around. Eventually I ran into a guy who'd known Grant, aka Howie. They'd been rafting a couple of times. He had an old address."

"And Grant was there?"

Brett shook his head. "It would've been easier if he had been. But there was a woman there who'd known him as Howie. I explained who Grant really was and then I called the local police. They got in touch with the FBI, ran some checks on Howard Sparks and eventually found Grant a couple of counties away, working as a horse trainer."

"But why, with all that money?"

"Bonds. He couldn't cash them without drawing too much attention to himself, I guess. He planned to go to Mexico eventually, I think, and cash them in."

"Why didn't he earlier? It's been nearly a year."

"Because of Jake and Billie."

Bethany closed her eyes. "Don't tell me he was responsible for their deaths," she whispered.

Brett touched her chin and looked deep into her eyes. "I don't know. But he's screaming his innocence."

"I just hope he is," Bethany said. "The embezzlement was bad enough."

"But it's over. Well, almost."

"What do you mean?"

He pushed his fingers through his dark hair. "The press will get wind of this, and soon."

"I see," she said, her jaw jutting.

"I'm afraid they're going to find out about you."

Bethany let out a long sigh, but set her shoulders. "Well, I guess I'll cross that bridge when I come to it. I was a fool to think that I could hide out here in Portland." Lifting her head high, she forced a shaky smile. "Maybe it's about time I owned up to who I really am."

"You don't have anything to be ashamed of," he reminded her.

"I know, but it's not going to be easy."

Brett set down his cup of coffee and took her into his arms. "At least we have tonight," he said, breathing in the fresh scent of her hair.

"And then?"

"And then we face the future. Together."

* * *

The news hit the papers the next morning. The first phone call didn't bother her; the second was irritating, and she hung up on the third.

"I told you it wouldn't be easy," Brett said, his face grim.

"I'm not going to let it get me down," she promised as she gathered laundry together. "It's just not worth it."

Just then the doorbell rang.

Bracing herself, Bethany walked to the front door and threw it open. On the doorstep were three reporters. "Mrs. Mills?"

"Yes?" she said, cautiously. She heard Brett come up behind her. He placed an arm protectively around her waist.

The young freckle-faced reporter wasn't deterred. His dark gaze never left Bethany. "Is it true that you were married to Grant Mills?"

"Yes; a long time ago."

"Did you harbor him in your house?"

"No!"

"Did you have any idea that he'd be accused of stealing those bonds—that he supposedly jumped out of a plane in northern Idaho?"

"Of course not," she snapped, lifting her chin and meeting the young man's interested stare. "I had no idea what he was doing."

"What do you think, Mrs. Mills, of your husband's bizarre stunt? Were you relieved to find out that he was alive?"

"That's enough," Brett cut in, sheltering her from the reporters. "Mrs. Mills isn't interested in answering any more questions." With a glare, he slammed the door shut. Then, turning to her, he said, "It's not going to get any better, you know. At least not for a while."

"I know. I can handle it," she said staunchly, determination blazing in her eyes.

"You sure?"

"Yes!"

"Vultures," he muttered, glancing out the window as the doorbell rang again. "Don't get it."

"It's just their job," she said, as the first of another of a round of phone calls came through. After the third telephone conversation with a newsman from Denver, Bethany took the phone off the hook.

"You can't go to school on Monday," Brett said as he made a pot of coffee. "For the next couple of days you're big news, lady."

"Wonderful."

"So you'd better forget about going to work."

"I can't!"

"You want your students subjected to that?" He hooked his thumb toward the window and Bethany looked outside to see cars and camera crews parked in front of her house.

"They wouldn't follow me to school, would they?"

"What happened last time—when Grant first took the money and ran, er, jumped out of the plane?"

It had been hell. The reporters hadn't given her a minute's rest. "I see what you mean." Bracing herself by finishing her coffee, she set the empty cup in the sink and then walked over to the phone. The conversation with her principal was difficult, but both she and Chris thought it would be in the best interest of

the school to let some of the notoriety and interest in
the Grant Mills story die down. Chris agreed that she
should take at least a week off.

He called back a few minutes later to tell her he'd
found a substitute for the following week.

"Okay," she said, once she'd hung up. "What's
next?"

"Pack your bags."

"My bags?"

"That's right. I've been thinking, and I've decided
it's about time you visited those folks you missed so
badly at Christmas time."

"I don't know if that would be such a good idea,"
she said, frowning. "They've already had a lot of bad
publicity because of me. If I go back home now, some
of the reporters will follow."

Brett's blue eyes twinkled. "Didn't you say your
father owned a rifle?"

When she nodded, he took her hand and stared into
her eyes. "I think that should keep the reporters at
bay, don't you?"

She couldn't help but chuckle. Though bone tired
and wrung out, she felt good knowing that Brett was
back with her. "I suppose."

"Besides, I think it's about time I met your folks."

"You do?"

"Uh-huh. Just to check them out."

"For what?"

"To see if they'd make suitable in-laws," he said,
his arms surrounding her.

"What!"

"That's right, Bethany. I've spent the last couple
of weeks miserable without you. So..." He pulled a

small black case out of his pocket and handed it to her. "Consider this a belated Christmas present."

She opened the velvet box and felt tears sting the back of her eyes. A bright diamond ring rested on the satin-lined velvet.

"Marry me, Bethany," he whispered, slipping the ring on her finger.

"I...I don't know what to say," she stammered.

"Just say yes."

"Yes," she said, swallowing the huge lump that was forming in her throat. "Yes, yes, yes!" His arms drew her tight against him and his lips captured hers in a kiss that was a promise of the future.

"I can't believe this is happening," she murmured.

"Believe it. Now, go on, get packing. And wear your sunglasses, just so no one will recognize you."

"What?" Then she saw that he was teasing.

"I'll call the airport and make reservations on the next flight to Boise and we'll surprise your folks."

"Will we ever," she said, glancing down on her ring.

"Go on, get going," he insisted. "The sooner we're out of here, the better."

A few hours later, Bethany was nearly home. Her palms were sweating and she bit her lip nervously. What if the reporters had already gone to the farm? How would her folks feel about Brett?—after all, he was Jim Benson's stepson.

"So this is where you called home," Brett said. He turned the steering wheel and the rental car slid on a patch of ice as the car started down the long lane leading to her parents' house.

"This is it," she whispered, her throat dry as she

stared at the farm that had been in her family for generations.

The two-storied farmhouse was as white as the snow surrounding it. Topped with a red roof and faced with green shutters, the old house stood proudly against the gray sky. Black-barked walnut trees guarded the wide front porch and a rusted swing hung limply from the lowest limb of the leafless maple tree in the side yard.

Brett parked the car near the barn and Bethany jumped out. Without bothering with her bags, she raced up the front steps and smiled when two old collies bounded around the side of the house, barking and growling and wagging their tails. As she bent down to pet the excited dogs, she thought about Winston. Linda and Jenny had promised to take care of the puppy while she was gone.

The front door creaked open and Bethany looked up just in time to see her mother gasp. "Bethany! Is it you?" She flung open the screen and hugged her daughter fiercely. "Myron! Myron!" she yelled over her shoulder. "It's Bethie! She's home!" Laughing and crying at the same time, Eleanor looked over her daughter's shoulder to see Brett. He was leaning against one of the front porch posts and watching Bethany's every move.

"What the devil is all the screechin' about?" Myron grumbled as he came to the front door. Then his eyes landed on his daughter and his face split in a wide grin. "Well, look who's finally got some sense in her head and come home!" he exclaimed, his eyes bright as Bethany let go of her mother and hugged her dad. "You're lookin' good, gal," he said.

"Bethany...?" her mother reproached her.

"Oh, right." Clearing her throat, Bethany walked over to Brett. "Mom and Dad, I'd like you to meet Brett Hanson." She grinned, showing all the happiness deep in her heart.

"Nice ta meet ya." Myron stuck out his hand and pumped Brett's.

"Same here," her mother chimed in. "Now come on in before we all freeze our tails off out here."

The house was filled with the familiar scents of cinnamon and tobacco, roasting chicken, bacon grease and strong coffee. Eleanor wiped her hands on her apron and bustled them all to the kitchen before placing a platter of peanut butter cookies and cups of hot black coffee on the oilcloth-covered table. "Sit down, sit down. You just rest a minute, both of you. You've had a tiresome trip." She took a long, hard look at Brett, and managed a smile for the handsome, rugged-looking man her daughter had brought home.

Before Bethany could say anything, her mother was scurrying around the kitchen. "I bet you're both so hungry you could eat a horse," she said, obviously pleased. "But you're in luck; I've got two chickens in the oven."

"Great."

"But no dessert."

"Really, Mom, don't worry about—"

"If you'll help me pare the apples, I'll fix us the best deep-dish apple pie in the state."

"Mom don't believe in being humble," Myron explained to Brett.

"Oh, you just hush and bring in that bucket of Jonathans on the back porch," Eleanor ordered, though she couldn't help but cast her husband of thirty-five years the same girlish smile he'd fallen in love with so long ago.

"Henpecked, that's what I am," Myron grumbled, pushing his chair aside and running the errand none-theless.

"And you wouldn't have it any other way," Eleanor muttered.

Once he'd returned with the bucket, Bethany started peeling the apples at the sink and her mother began cutting shortening into flour and salt for the pie crust. Myron and Brett sat at the table, sizing each other up.

"So you're the fella that finally caught up with Grant," Myron said, his lower lip protruding a bit.

"With Bethany's help." Brett took a long swallow of his coffee and met Myron's scrutinizing gaze.

"Let's just hope it's all behind us now," Eleanor whispered, as she spread the dough on a large cutting board.

"I never did like that guy."

"Oh, Dad…"

"And I was proved right, wasn't I?"

"Yes, Dad, you were right."

"I just didn't like Jim Benson rubbing my nose in it," her father grumbled.

"Benson's been here?"

"Not lately. Before Grant was locked up, he'd sent that snot-nosed kid of his around to bother us."

"Harry?" Brett had to smile.

"Yeah, that's the one. Stupid bastard."

"Dad!"

"Harry's okay," Brett said. "His old man's just got him all screwed up. He'll turn out all right."

"That so?"

"I hope it is."

"How'd you know so much about it?"

Brett grimaced and glanced out the window. "Benson's my stepfather," he said.

Myron glanced at Bethany. "Your *what?*" he demanded, bristling.

"My mother was married to him until she died. But, that's as far as it goes. I worked for First Security to find Mills and pay off a loan against my mother's land. Other than that, I have no use for Jim."

"But Harry's another story?" Myron asked.

"He's misguided, that's all."

"Hmph."

Brett looked at Bethany. "There's something else you should know," he said to the room in general.

"What's that?"

"I've asked Bethany to marry me."

Myron set his coffee on the table. "And?"

"And she agreed. We wanted you to know before we told anyone else."

"Kind of ya," Myron said, his eyes narrowing as he twisted in his chair and looked at his daughter.

"Bethie? You sure about this?"

Bethany turned from the sink, and her eyes shimmered with the love she felt for Brett. "Very."

"I just don't want you to make another mistake."

"I won't."

"Oh, hush, Myron. Bethany's all grown-up. She can make up her own mind. And as for me, Mr. Hanson—"

"Brett."

"Brett." Eleanor walked over to the table and extended her hand. "Welcome to the family."

"Thank you."

Myron stood and walked over to the refrigerator. "Don't suppose we have any champagne left from Christmastime."

Eleanor's blue eyes twinkled. "There's one bottle out in the cooler."

"Well, I guess this is as good a time as any to open it. Seems as if we're going to have ourselves a celebration!"

Bethany threw her arms around both of her parents and tears of joy tumbled over her cheeks. "Thank you both."

"Don't thank us. We're happy for you," her mother said. "Now, when's the wedding?"

"How about this weekend? Here?" Bethany asked. "Perfect!"

While Myron went out to find the champagne, Brett came over to Bethany and slipped his arms around her waist. "Perfect," he repeated, chuckling. His breath ruffled her hair and she smiled.

"Here we go," her father said as he walked back into the kitchen, grabbed a towel and forced the cork out of the bottle. It exploded with a loud pop and frothy champagne spilled onto the old linoleum floor. After pouring four glasses, Myron held his in the air. "To the bride and groom." His eyes rested fondly on his daughter and his voice grew rough. "May you find the true happiness your mother and I discovered a long time ago."

"Thanks, Dad," Bethany said, her throat thick as

she took a swallow of her drink. Never had she been so blissfully in love.

Jim Benson, his hands clasped behind his back, paced in front of his office window. His son, Harry, was sitting on the corner of his desk.

"He came through," Harry repeated, watching his father's anxious movements. "Now you've got to come up with your end of the bargain."

"I know, I know," Jim snapped, glaring at his son. Ever since Brett had collared Grant Mills, Harry's attitude had changed, for the worse. "Have Gloria draw up the deed."

"I already have."

Jim turned on his heel and stared at his son. "Without my okay?"

"I decided that it was an executive decision even a vice-president could make." Harry tugged at his tie and grinned at his father.

"Is that so?"

"Yep. And I also figured that you wouldn't mind if I took off a few weeks to go skiing."

"Now?" Jim rubbed the back of his neck furiously. His entire ordered world was crumbling. "Why the hell now?"

"Why not? Mills is behind bars, he was indicted this morning and Brett is through with us. Everything's just fine. Right?"

"Mills hasn't been tried yet."

"Just a matter of time. Since Karl Weathers is turning state's evidence, Grant is as good as convicted."

"So you think it's a good time to go skiing?"

"Exactly."

There was a sharp knock on the door. "Come in," Jim barked and Brett entered.

"Hey, good to see ya," Harry said, jumping off the desk and clapping Brett on the back. Then he sorted through a stack of papers, found the original note Brett had signed and returned it to him. Across the front of the document was the bank's stamp, which stated that the loan had been paid in full. "Dad?"

Jim scowled at Brett before looking at his son.

"Just need your signature on the dotted line," Harry said, pulling off the cap of his pen with his teeth and handing the pen to his father.

Biting his lower lip, Jim Benson signed the deed over to Brett. "I guess I should thank you."

"No need," Brett said, folding the deed and slipping it into the inside pocket of his jacket. "Just part of the job."

"But you did it," Harry said, gloating a little when his father's face reddened.

"I was lucky."

"Doesn't matter; a deal's a deal. Right, Dad?"

"I thought you wanted out of it," Jim said.

"I did. But then I had some inspiration."

"And Mills is behind bars," Harry said.

"Whose side are you on?" Jim asked.

Harry spread his hands. "The right side, of course. You made the deal, and even though Brett wanted to walk out of it, he didn't."

"Right," Jim muttered.

"Good. Come on, Brett, tell me all about it over lunch," Harry suggested, grabbing his coat and slinging it over one shoulder. "You don't mind, do ya, Dad?"

"As a matter of fact—"

"Good. See ya later." Grinning, Harry led Brett out of the office.

"What was that all about?" Brett asked, as they walked down the stairs.

"Freedom." Harry winked at his stepbrother. "Come on, I'll buy you a beer. I've been thinking about what you said for a long time, and you were right. I'm too young to end up a stuffed shirt like Dad."

"What convinced you?"

Harry pushed open the doors of the building and weak sunlight reflected on the snow piled at the sides of the streets. "A lot of things. Health, for one—I found out I was getting an ulcer. The doctor talked about stress, exercise and eating right. Then there were all those damned arguments you've been peddling me for years. I think it's time I got out and lived a little."

"Good idea."

"And you?"

"Me?" Brett shook his head. "It's time for me to settle down."

"Don't tell me—with Bethany Mills."

Brett laughed and his breath fogged in the cold morning air. "You have been keeping your eyes open, haven't you?"

Shoving his hands into the pockets of his slacks, Harry grinned. "You always were a great teacher. You know, once summer hits, I might just come up your way and go fishin'. What do you say?"

"Just name the time." Brett slapped Harry on the back as they walked into the dark interior of a local tavern. "But, I think you'd better forget the beer today. Barkeep—a milk for my friend," he said.

"Not today," Harry said with a laugh. "Ulcer or no, we're going to have that beer!"

Bethany was leaning over the top rail of the fence, watching the distant herd of cattle try to graze in the snow-covered fields, when she heard the sound of a car's engine. Lifting her head, she saw Brett return. Smiling, she waved as he parked the rental car and walked toward her.

"How'd it go?" she asked.

"Surprisingly well, thank you," he said, his eyes gleaming. Extracting the deed from his jacket pocket, he held it up for her to see. "Jim was as good as his word, though I think Harry had a lot to do with it."

"Harry? You're kidding."

"No. We even had a couple of beers together; just like old times."

Bethany grinned. "I can tell."

Placing one boot on the bottom rail, Brett squinted against the sun and stared at the faded red buildings of the farm, the bare trees, the solid old farmhouse and dusky-blue mountains in the distance. "It's beautiful here."

"I know. Sometimes I think I had the best childhood any kid could ever want."

"But you still left?"

"I had to."

"Would you want to move back?"

"Maybe someday," she admitted. "But right now

I've got commitments in Portland. You know that, don't you? That if we get married—''

''*When* we get married,'' he corrected, placing his arm over her shoulders and kissing her lips lightly.

''Okay, when we get married, I'll have to return to Portland, at least until the end of the school year.''

''That's fine with me. I like the idea of being a 'kept man.'''

''Give me a break!'' She laughed and the light-hearted sound whispered across the snow-dusted fields. ''Now, really, what will you do?''

Brett sobered as he thought about Greg Connelly. ''Maybe help an old friend get back on his feet.''

''Can't argue with that.''

''But in the summer, we go back to the cabin.''

''Agreed,'' she said, tossing back her head and laughing.

His fingers slid around her waist, drawing her close. ''And then we'll make love all summer long.''

''All summer long?'' she teased.

''Night and day.''

''This is beginning to sound more interesting all the time.''

''But I haven't told you the best part.''

''Which is?''

''The reason we'll be making love.''

''Not just because we want to?'' Her eyes glistened merrily as she looked into his rugged features.

''That, too. But I think it might be time for me to become a father,'' he said. ''Unless…you can't handle the thought of a baby.''

Bethany smiled slyly. ''It may be too late already,'' she said. ''You see, I have a confession to make. That baby you're talking about could already be on the way.''

Brett was startled. "Really?"

"Really."

"Then what're we waitin' for? We'd better call the preacher."

"He's coming Saturday evening. Remember? That should be soon enough."

"Okay, okay," Brett said, the thought of their child overwhelming him. He glanced at her flat abdomen and felt his chest swell with pride. "But I don't know if I can wait that long."

"Try to control yourself." Bethany linked her arm in his and they walked back to the house.

"I now pronounce you man and wife," the Reverend Barnes said. "You may kiss the bride."

Brett lifted Bethany's veil and looked deep into her eyes before he wrapped his arms around her small waist and pressed his lips to hers. She was wearing a simple ivory-colored dress, but Brett thought her the most elegant bride in the world.

Bethany felt tears of happiness dampen her eyes. When her new husband released her, she smiled at the small crowd of people gathered in the living room of the old farmhouse. One by one her relatives greeted them and wished them happiness.

Brett didn't take his eyes off her, and when the cake had been eaten, the champagne bottles emptied, he tugged on her hand.

"What're you doing?" she whispered.

"Trying to lose the crowd."

He'd already yanked off his tie and had one final

bottle of champagne tucked under his arm when he pulled her outside, through the brisk night air to the barn.

"Brett?"

"Shh. Come on." He led her inside and then helped her up the ladder to the hayloft, where a patchwork quilt had already been spread.

"You're incorrigible!"

"Nope. Just in love." With that he pulled her to him and kissed her with the pent-up passion he'd kept at bay for nearly a week. His hands moved to the back of her dress and deftly opened the zipper. Cold air rushed at her skin as his weight slowly toppled them both onto the old quilt.

"You had this planned," she accused, her skin warming at his touch.

"Guilty as charged." He slipped the dress off her shoulders and kissed the creamy skin.

"I'm glad."

"So am I."

She shuddered when his tongue pressed against her skin. "I love you, Brett."

"Good, because I expect to hear just those words for the rest of my life."

"You will," she promised, as she twined her fingers in his dark hair and returned the fever of his kiss. "From this day forward."

* * * * *

If you enjoyed what you just read,
then we've got an offer you can't resist!

Take 2 bestselling love stories FREE!

Plus get a FREE surprise gift!

EXTRA! EXTRA!

The book all your favorite authors are raving about is finally here!

The 1999 Harlequin and Silhouette coupon book.

Each page is alive with savings that can't be beat!

Getting this incredible coupon book is as easy as 1, 2, 3.

1. During the months of November and December 1999 buy any 2 Harlequin or Silhouette books.

2. Send us your name, address and 2 proofs of purchase (cash receipt) to the address below.

3. Harlequin will send you a coupon book worth $10.00 off future purchases of Harlequin or Silhouette books in 2000.

Send us 3 cash register receipts as proofs of purchase and we will send you 2 coupon books worth a total saving of $20.00 (limit of 2 coupon books per customer).

Saving money has never been this easy.

Please allow 4-6 weeks for delivery. Offer expires December 31, 1999.

I accept your offer! Please send me (a) coupon booklet(s):

Name: _____

Address: _____ City: _____

State/Prov.: _____ Zip/Postal Code: _____

Send your name and address, along with your cash register receipts as proofs of purchase, to:

In the U.S.: Harlequin Books, P.O. Box 9057, Buffalo, N.Y. 14269
In Canada: Harlequin Books, P.O. Box 622, Fort Erie, Ontario L2A 5X3

Order your books and accept this coupon offer through our web site
http://www.romance.net
Valid in U.S. and Canada only.   PHQ4994R

Celebrate Silhouette's 20th Anniversary

With beloved authors, exciting new miniseries and special keepsake collections, **plus** the chance to enter our 20th anniversary contest, in which one lucky reader wins the trip of a lifetime!

Take a look at who's celebrating with us:

DIANA PALMER

April 2000: SOLDIERS OF FORTUNE
May 2000 in Silhouette Romance: *Mercenary's Woman*

NORA ROBERTS

May 2000: IRISH HEARTS, the 2-in-1 keepsake collection
June 2000 in Special Edition: *Irish Rebel*

LINDA HOWARD

July 2000: MACKENZIE'S MISSION
August 2000 in Intimate Moments: *A Game of Chance*

ANNETTE BROADRICK

October 2000: a special keepsake collection,
plus a brand-new title in
November 2000 in Desire

Available at your favorite retail outlet.

Where love comes alive™